Believe ?

By

Alison Turner

Best Wishes

Alison Turner

Paperback edition published 2023

Paperback ISBN: 978-1-7392921-0-2
eBook ISBN: 978-1-7392921-1-9

Book designed by Sam Wheeler

Cover image: ulza-stock.adobe.com

Acknowledgements

To Jenny
For her patience and support.

~~~

My pseudonym is for my mother. She chose my name 'Alison', but when registering my birth, Dad however, used names of two aunts instead. For you Mum, and may my wonderful father be finally forgiven. Bless you both.
~~~

Introduction

After a narrow-squeak or an amazing piece of luck, we may say someone or our guardian-angel is looking after us. Then usually just put it down to coincidence, but what if? . . . .

So,

meet the Chapman family. Drawn back together to solve their mother's financial predicament, . . . and does he exist?

A light hearted story of love, humour, deceit, and with a mythical twist!

Contents

~ 1 ~

It was no good avoiding the situation any longer. Wide awake at dawn, Ellen had risen rather than toss and turn with troubled thoughts.
She opened the back door and stood leaning against it, breathing in fresh morning air and absorbing the quietness. With fingers clasped around a hot mug of tea for warmth, she gazed down her beloved garden. A cold breeze lifted wisps of hair across her face, making her shudder. She rewrapped her dressing gown to cover the gap around her neck. How could she bare to leave this place with all its memories.
Back inside, she sat at the kitchen table and reopened the letter. The figures on the bank statement made her position obvious. In front of her lay the information she'd been dreading. Squirrels Chase would have to be sold.
Wallowing in memories wasn't helping. "Needs must," she said aloud, trying to be positive while washing up her breakfast things, and considered phoning her daughter Suzy for advice.

In her positive mode Ellen decided to make a start on tidying the front garden. Carrying her kneeling mat, tools and a bucket for weeds, she walked to the edge of the drive. Working along the borders in the sunshine, briefly forgetting her troubles. She didn't hold with so-called gardening experts' nonsense designs of 'oasis of green leaf structures, cool shades and quiet hues'. For Ellen, summer meant colour! Her borders bedazzled, including jewels that wafted a variety of heavenly perfumes.

Squirrels Chase sat back from a bend in Beeches Road. It's semi-circular gravel drive swept up in front of the house and garage, round a low stone walled flowerbed and lead back to re-join the road. Shade from three mature chestnut trees kept the area cool from hot summer sun.

After a brief stop for lunch, Ellen returned to her gardening. Feeling happy with her progress, she knelt back down onto her mat. Bent over the low wall of the circular flowerbed, she was totally engrossed in snatching out weeds.

"Watch out!" a voice snapped crossly.

"Sorry," she replied instinctively, but looking round couldn't see anyone. She shuffled along, picking up her trowel to continue. Lowering her gaze to where she was about to dig, her eyes met with another pair of eyes . . . real eyes on a very small real face. Ellen froze, her eyes widened as she stared at the figure of an old man. She hated garden gnomes, whether they were of stone or hideously painted plastic. They all gave her the creeps, but this small creature sitting in front of her on one of the large Cotswold stone rocks was made of flesh. She recoiled in shock and couldn't move. He continued to stare back at her.

Trembling, she struggled to stand, and made her way back to the kitchen. Shaking like a leaf, she could hardly fill the kettle to make herself a cup of tea. Feeling the colour drain from her face, she sat down and began to worry. What did this mean? Had she been seeing things? Was she going mad?

It brought back an uncomfortable memory of a visit years ago to her late elderly mother, who'd been chatting away to an imaginary policeman supposedly sat beside her. The policeman was as 'real' to her mother, as he was 'invisible' to her. Mortified, Ellen called out the doctor, who admitted her mother to hospital for a check-up and rest. Assuring her it was probably just dehydration which can cause hallucinations. Thankfully this had been the case.

Ellen knew she wasn't dehydrated or physically ill. Had some joker slipped one of those weird hallucinating drugs into something she'd eaten? She remembered watching a detective drama on the TV using that storyline, but doubted if anyone would target her or the boring shopping items loaded regularly into her shopping basket, . . . or was she really going doolally?

One hour, two cups of tea and four chocolate biscuits later, she'd summoned the courage to return, if only to retrieve her tools and put them away. She rose from her chair, straightening her aching back, feeling her joints and muscles stiffen. She'd tackled the gardening like a bull at a gate. Digging and weeding like a woman possessed, a much younger woman at that.

She went back to the front garden, deliberately averting her eyes from the place of her imaginings. With tired arms, raked up the scattered weeds that lay wilting on the ground, loading them into her large plastic bucket. Picked up the tools and carried it all through to the back garden.

A mixture of curiosity and fear made her return to the spot. She looked down, hoping with all her heart to see only flowers. The little figure sat as before, looking straight at her. Her stomach lurched causing her to inhale deeply. He lifted his head slightly waiting for her to speak. Ellen's legs returned to jelly and her heart beat so fast she could hardly breathe. "Are you . . . real?" she struggled to ask.

The irritated expression on his small face told her she had asked a stupid question. "Am I going mad?" her voice faded to a whisper, suppressing tears she could feel forming.

"I am here," he answered in a matter-of-fact manner, looking up, anticipating her reaction.

Still unable to believe her eyes, Ellen wasn't sure whether to be relieved or not. Briefly she studied his appearance, wanting to recall him in detail from head to toe. She walked back, closing the side gate behind her, knowing now how it must feel to witness a UFO or see a ghost, unable to tell anyone because no sane person would believe you.

She phoned Suzy in the evening, hoping eight o'clock would be the best time to least inconvenience her daughter. The phone rang out for some minutes before Suzy's answer machine clicked into action. Ellen had thought carefully of what she wanted to say, but not expecting to speak to a machine, it threw her. "Can you phone me . . . er, when you're not busy?" she said in flustered haste.

-

Ellen felt sure there was a logical explanation, but it was unusual for Suzy not to return her call.
Two days later she phoned but again received no reply. Most Fridays they'd phone each other, catching up with family news and putting the world to right. With no reply by Friday evening she decided to phone Suzy's mobile. Just as the instruction to leave a recorded message began, the phone signal cut off.

- -

Switching off her car engine, Suzy gave a big sigh of relief, 'thank goodness for that,' glad to be home safe and sound. The long drive back from London had made her back ache and her bottom numb. She hoped Richard had noticed her arrive so he could help with her heavy case. Gathering her bits and pieces she waited a few minutes for him to appear. Then, blessing her husband for not helping, unloaded the car by herself. I bet he's asleep in front of the telly, she thought unlocking the front door. Leaving her baggage in the hall, she kicked off her shoes and walked wearily into the lounge. Flopped down into a chair and put her feet up onto the wooden coffee table in front of her. She closed her eyes relaxing for a moment, enjoying the peace and quiet of the empty house and wondered where Richard could be.

Waiting for the kettle to boil, she wandered around peering into every room. Everywhere was neat and tidy, in fact just as she had left it. Upstairs in their bedroom she slipped tired feet into comfortable slippers, exclaiming "good heavens!" when she saw their bed. Richard had never made a bed in his life, so this had to be a first. Back in the kitchen she checked the phone for recorded messages, . . strangely, there were none. Sipping her tea, she checked her mobile, turned it on and recognised her mother's number listed under missed calls.

The ringing phone woke Ellen up. The newspaper she'd been reading slid off her lap as she reached across the table nearby to answer it.
"Hi, Mum are you OK, is anything wrong?" Suzy asked concerned, knowing her mother wouldn't usually phone her mobile.
Not fully awake, Ellen spoke too soon. "I need to sell the house Suzy." She hadn't meant to blurt it out straight away before explaining her reason.
"Mum, are you sure?" Suzy was shocked.
There was an emotional pause, while Ellen tried to regain her composure, struggling to add "needs must."
Feeling her mother's anguish, Suzy promised to visit, assuring her they'd find a way to sort things out and not to worry.
"I don't want to put you out Suzy. Anyway, where have you been? I've been trying to reach you all week."

Suzy apologised for not warning her mother about attending the conference in London. It had been a last minute decision to replace a colleague suddenly struck down by flu. Then she remembered switching off her phone before driving home so it wouldn't distract her, and explained the mix-up. Suzy chatted about her business trip, describing the hotel hosting the event, and accompanying 'Carol from Planning' who'd given their Company's presentation.

Listening to Suzy's news and intended visit cheered up Ellen immensely.

Suzy had just replaced the receiver when Richard walked in. He threw his keys and newspaper onto the coffee table. Sat himself down on the settee and switched on the TV, flicking through channels looking for a football match which had already started.

"Hi," Suzy called from the kitchen. "Tea? I'm making a sandwich, do you want one or have you eaten?"

"No thanks," he answered. "I called in at Mum's, didn't think you'd be back yet, . . how was the traffic?"

She opened the fridge and was surprised to find it full, just as she'd loaded it before leaving for the conference. 'Lazy-whatsit' she thought, I bet he's been eating at his mother's rather than feeding himself. She sat down alongside and handed Richard his mug of tea.

"Is your mum OK?" she asked, before taking a large bite from her sandwich.

He nodded, his concentration fixed on the football.

"I've just phoned my mum, she's thinking of selling her house."

"About time," Richard said, without taking his eyes off the screen. "Thought she'd do that when you lot left home.

What does she want with a big place like that on her own? Must be worth a bob or two."
Suzy winced, why do men always have to relate everything to money?
"Anyway, now she's getting on a bit, probably glad to get rid of it." he added for good measure.

Suzy put her empty plate and mug into the kitchen sink, she would deal with them in the morning. "I'm going up to unpack, have a bath, then bed. That drive's worn me out, will you be long?"
Richard didn't answer, he was too engrossed in football.

-

On Monday morning in her office, Ms Helen Carter-Jones thanked Suzy and Carol personally for their work at the conference. She'd read through their reports, appreciating Suzy's observations and figures from what Ms Carter-Jones considered rival branches. "Well done ladies," she trilled in her Welsh lilt. "Keeps us ahead in the corporate loop," indicating to their reports on her desk.
"Phew," Carol whispered as they left their Head of Department's office, "it's not often she gives out praise."

Walking back to her own office, Suzy spotted her manager Karen. Catching her now would be a good opportunity to ask for some time off. Explaining about her mother's stressful state during their recent phone call. Thankfully, Karen understood.
"Three days starting Wednesday would be ideal, that'll give me the weekend too," Suzy appealed.
"Not being a dire emergency, how about next week?" Karen questioned, checking her computer screen.
Suzy agreed gratefully. Now she could phone her mother and start to look forward to spending the time together.

Rushing home from work, she planned to cook Richard's favourite meal. It would be good to have an evening together, lately they hardly seemed to spend any time with each other at all.
They'd both increased their working hours when Kate mentioned going to university. Both felt they couldn't deny their only child that option. If it was what she truly wanted, such had become their financial commitment.

It had taken months getting used to Kate moving out. The house felt empty without her and her friends. Suzy missed their noisy chatter and the general chaos of having them around. Phone calls and home visits became less frequent as Kate settled into 'Uni' life, spending more time away with her new friends.

Richard began to work Saturdays and stayed late at least three evenings a week, grumbling 'only he could organise the driver's schedules efficiently'. Based mostly in the office, he no longer drove the long-haul big lorries. Transits and two smaller vans had been added to the fleet for local deliveries. Occasionally he'd test-drive a new long-haul delivery route using one of the small vans, and if necessary stayed away overnight.

Feeling alone at home gave Suzy the incentive to spend more time working in the company of her colleagues. A small promotion increased her workload, but she enjoyed the challenges her new position presented. She wondered how they'd let their jobs evolve into priorities, gradually consuming their lives.

After the meal, Richard relaxed in front of the TV with a beer while Suzy cleared the table. Taking advantage of

his good mood, she mentioned her intention to visit her mother. Surprisingly, he didn't seem bothered at all.
"Don't know why you don't stay all week," he urged. "You know you won't settle till you know what's going on."
"I'll be back Sunday morning at the latest," she assured him. "I don't want to push my luck at work, they're chasing new contracts."
"Up to you," he said putting his feet up and closing his eyes

- -

Wednesday couldn't come quick enough for Ellen. Happy butterflies fluttered in her stomach and relief replaced anxiousness. She couldn't remember when Suzy had last stayed overnight, or when they'd spent any length of time together.

Staying on motorways and major roads, Suzy made good progress. At this rate she would arrive an hour earlier than expected.
Turning into her mother's drive, she felt the sentimental feeling of coming home. She didn't understand the pull Squirrels Chase still had on her emotions. It was more than a safe haven, and she wasn't comfortable thinking of it being sold. She took out her small weekend case, flowers and a box of cakes.

Ellen heard Suzy's car arrive on the gravel drive and rushed out to greet her. Mother and daughter held each other tightly in a long overdue emotional hug. "Can I carry anything?" she offered.
"You can take these," handing her mother the most colourful bouquet of flowers she could find in the supermarket.

In the kitchen, Suzy filled the kettle to make tea while her mother arranged her flowers.
"Lovely," Ellen smiled, stepping back to admire the result. "I'll put them on the dining table."
Tea and fresh cream doughnuts was the perfect start to their few days together.
"Is there anything you'd like to do while you're here?" Ellen asked, aware her daughter had taken the time off especially.

Suzy suggested a walk around Kirston and lunch at The Black Rabbit. She'd forgotten how picturesque the old part of the town had been. Wandering around, she could see changes since her last visit.

Her mother had made no mention of 'selling'. Suzy didn't want to be the one raising the subject, but if she was there to help it had to be done.
When they were sitting together in the evening, She seized the chance. "So, how can I help?"
Ellen handed over her bank statement for Suzy to read. Feeling her mother's eyes watching, she cordially hid her true thoughts knowing she was waiting for a positive response. "I need to talk to the boys," referring to her brothers.
"I'll not take charity!" Ellen defended with pride.
"I'll only be asking for their advice. Matt and Phil deal with complicated finance every day, and you know how clever they are. It won't hurt to ask," hoping she'd put her mother's fears to rest and praying her brothers would provide a solution.

-

When Suzy woke up in the morning, she was surprised how long she'd slept. She could hear her mother bustling about downstairs in the kitchen. She'd stayed in her old bedroom, and closing her eyes could picture exactly how it used to look throughout her childhood, wallowing briefly under the cosy blanket of nostalgia.

In the kitchen, Suzy leant against the sink, looking out of the window. She watched a blackbird bob in and out of view in the lush grass. "Mum, when's your gardener due?, that grass could do with cutting."
"Brian retired two years ago, he sent someone else round but he was far too expensive" Ellen replied.
Suzy felt her conscience prickle. She'd been too busy to notice any changes in her mother's life, totally missing any warning signs.
"I've managed," Ellen said shrugging her shoulders.
Suzy decided cutting the grass would be her first task of the day. How hard can that be? she mused.

Expecting to find a lawnmower in the garage, she stepped inside with trepidation, convinced the place was full of spiders. As her eyes adjusted to the dim light she looked around, catching sight of a large beast of a lawnmower. The old green painted ATCO lurked in a corner. Seeing its heavy roller, gears and petrol tank wondered how on earth she could use it, never mind getting it to start.
"I use this one," her mother announced, standing behind her, making Suzy jump. Hidden by the open door, the modern electric mower hung from a wide hook on the wall, it's reeled extension lead underneath. "It's not man enough really but it does the job."
"Thank heavens for that," Suzy sighed with relief. She sent her mother to fetch a rake from the garden shed,

giving herself a few moments alone to inspect her mother's car, also housed in the garage. Covered in a thick layer of dust, it hadn't been taxed for two years - clearly another sign of economy.

It took Suzy the rest of morning to mow the grass back and front. Her mother was right about the lawnmower not being powerful enough, although it managed to fling random stones at high speed dangerously across the garden. "How do you do it Mum?" she asked, exhausted and boiling hot.

Ellen confessed, usually she mowed in stages and on consecutive days.

"What's next?" Suzy asked, trying to be useful.

Ellen wanted to mention tackling the hedge at the bottom of the garden but changed her mind, insisting Suzy had done enough already.

If Suzy had known she'd be doing all this gardening, she would of roped Richard in to help. Not expecting all this when she'd booked these days off, he'd laugh when she told him.

After lunch and while Ellen dosed in her chair, Suzy crept quietly out of the room to phone Richard. According to her watch, he should be in his office. She let it ring out for ages, but he didn't answer. Disappointed, she assumed he was out driving.

While her mother slept, she took a look at the hedge. It towered above her, straggly and possibly unclipped for a year. Intending to have a go, she gathered a stepladder and tools. Shears were soon abandoned in preference of a saw.

An hour later and almost hidden behind a pile of lopped branches, Ellen found Suzy at the bottom of the garden. Rosy cheeked, sweating and with random leaves attached to her hair. "Goodness! you've almost done it."
"Nearly," Suzy puffed, feeling muscles seizing, but determined to finish before her aching body gave in.

While her mother cooked their dinner, Suzy took a bath. Blissfully soaking sore limbs and doubted whether she'd be able to move at all the next day.
After they'd eaten, she laid on the settee, snuggled up in one of her mother's dressing gowns. Once again she tried to get hold of Richard, but without success.

When her mother went upstairs for her evening bath, Suzy dialled Matt's number. "Hello Matt, long time no speak." she giggled, not having spoken to her elder brother since Christmas.
"Suze?" he answered, astonished. "Everything OK? Where are you?"
"Staying at Mum's."
"Is she alright?" now he was worried.
"Mum's well, but there's a problem. I need to talk to you A S A P, any chance we could meet?"
"Suze, Saturday night I fly to Ireland on business for two weeks."
"Matt, it's serious!"
He thought for a moment, then made a suggestion. "If you're at Squirrels Chase and I'm heading for the airport Saturday, we could meet up halfway, around lunchtime."
"Thanks Matt, let me know where and not a 'dickybird' to Mum until we've spoken. See you Saturday," she said, thankful she'd caught him in time.

-

On Friday morning during breakfast Suzy announced "definitely no chores today. How about a day in Westdale?"
While Ellen went off to get ready, Suzy tried to phone Richard. She would be back home tomorrow and wanted to remind him. Again there was no answer, where on Earth was he?
Although Westdale was a good hour's drive, it had a large variety of shops and chain stores, all housed in a new shopping Mall.

Suzy didn't mention speaking to Matt or their impending meeting the next day. She felt uncomfortable discussing her mother's private affairs behind her back. Although for her benefit, it still felt like a betrayal of trust. Regardless, it would be great to see Matt again, they hadn't seen each other for more than a year. Perhaps she'd find something new to wear in Westdale for the occasion.

On arrival, she found a parking space just inside the Mall's multi-storey.
By luck, a hairdressing salon could accommodate them both, their afternoon appointments allowing plenty of time to peruse the shops beforehand.
Suzy bought herself a dress, being exactly what she'd had in mind.
She sent her mother into changing cubicles with armfuls of clothes to try on, insisting they wouldn't leave Westdale until she'd chosen something.
Ellen picked a pale green summer dress and a printed floral cardigan before they headed off for lunch.

In the salon, Suzy could see her mother's reflection in the mirror ahead. She watched her chatting to the hairdresser while she worked, convinced her mother's worry-lines were melting away. They emerged later, both pleased with their new styles.

Suzy thought of Richard and looked forward to arriving home in her new dress. He wasn't the greatest romantic but felt sure he would appreciate her new look. She'd bought a box of his favourite mints, the ones he liked to keep on his desk at work. A little something to say she'd missed him.

Arriving back at Squirrels Chase, Ellen got out to open the front door while Suzy unloaded their shopping. Spending the day together at Westdale had been wonderful, bringing them closer if that were possible.

Pleased with their purchases, they tried on their new outfits, repeating that timeless pleasure most girls enjoy. Suzy saw a definite twinkle in her mother's eyes as she paraded across the room in her new clothes. The colours definitely suiting and both treasured finds.

After consuming the treats they'd bought for dinner, Ellen began to tire and was ready to relax in front of the TV for the rest of the evening.

Suzy went upstairs to pack. She phoned Richard, but again there was no answer. Presuming the signal could be poor for mobiles, went downstairs to use the house phone. She'd so much to tell him, especially that she'd be leaving in the morning. Despite leaving the phone ringing, it remained unanswered. Was he in the bath, under the shower? There was no point worrying, besides she'd be back home tomorrow anyway.

-

In the morning Suzy was sorry to leave, having enjoyed every minute spent with her mother. Even the tough gardening work if she was honest, but she'd done all she could for now. Trying to sound convincing, she told her mother not to worry, it was all in hand. With her car loaded and ready to go, Suzy kissed her mother goodbye, promising to return soon.

Ellen stood in the drive waving until Suzy drove from view. Already missing her daughter's company, tears formed as she turned to walk back indoors. Just before she reached the front door, something rustling about in one of the borders caught her attention. Had a neighbour's cat caught something? She walked over to investigate.

It wasn't a cat. The little 'man' creature was bent over, out of sight until he stood up. He turned to face her, his reappearance causing alarm.

"You're back," she said, feeling deep unease. "Why?"

"Please go away" she urged, tension reducing her voice once more. Before her eyes, his image faded to nothing, yet eerily she knew he was still there. She returned indoors troubled.

Ellen couldn't settle at anything, the little creature kept coming to mind. She sat down at her kitchen table and drew a picture of it on her writing pad. Underneath her sketch, she described every detail of its manifestations. Turning the situation repeatedly over in her mind, trying to make some sense of it. Suddenly it occurred to her, if he could appear or disappear at will, he'd wanted her to see him! So what did this strange creature want with her, and why now? She slid her sketch under some papers in a drawer of the bureau that stood in the hall.

Suzy drove for an hour heading homeward, before turning east towards the airport route Matt would be using. She had to concentrate, not wanting to miss the junction to Roxtem. The volume of traffic subsided once she got off the main roads. Following Matt's clear instructions without a hitch, just as he predicted the country pub came into view. With only a few cars in the carpark, she assumed he was still on his way and parked close to the pub's main entrance.

Before going inside she gave Richard a quick call at work, hoping to catch him at his desk. One of the drivers answered, telling her Richard was outside in the yard and offered to give him a message. The driver took a big piece of white card from the wastepaper bin. In large letters he wrote 'Your wife Suzy will be home today' and left it on top of Richard's desk.

In the pub Suzy made herself comfortable, ordered a coffee and sat close to a window that looked out over the carpark to see Matt arrive. Feeling peckish she began reading through the pub's menu. Engrossed in choosing food, missed his arrival.

"Hungry Suze?" Matt stood beside his sister.

Surprised, she beamed and quickly rose to give him a hug. It was so good to see him. They made their way towards a table at the back, choosing a quiet corner.

A young waitress came over to take their order, and returned with drinks.

"You're looking well," Matt flattered.

Waiting for their food became an ideal opportunity to catch up, chatting about their jobs and lives in general.

"How's Kate?" Matt asked. He'd always been fond of his niece and hearing about her progress.

Suzy spoke about the last time she and Richard had gone up to Leeds to see her. They'd travelled up because Kate had said she wasn't coming home during the university's summer break. This year Kate wanted to stay in Leeds and work during the holiday period, she was already applying for jobs.

Suzy had sensed a glow of happiness within Kate and suspected a special friendship, although it was unusual for their home-bird daughter not wanting to return.

"Talking of special friendships, is there anyone?" Suzy quizzed her brother. Matt smiled, but kept his silence.

She held her gaze.

"There might be," he admitted finally, looking down at his meal which had just been served.

She gave him a little smile as they began to eat.

Promptly changing the subject, Matt asked about the urgency for their meeting, wanting to know why she was so worried about their mother.

Suzy relayed details of the three days she'd just spent with her. Retrieved their mother's bank statement from her handbag and gave it to Matt to read.

She heard the intake of air through his lips as he read, and watched his eyebrows rise as information registered. He sat staring at the page, quietly digesting the figures and their mother's situation. "How long have you known about this?" he asked gravely.

"About a week, Mum phoned, asked if I could help her to sell Squirrels Chase!" Suzy explained. "I went up there as soon as I could. Matt, I had no idea before, it was completely out of the blue." As she spoke her emotions took hold, hot tears rolled down her cheeks and she wanted to cry. She fought to stay in control, not wanting to cause attention.

Matt handed her his clean white paper napkin to catch her tears. He hadn't meant to make her cry, this wasn't his sister's fault. He was battling his own feelings of guilt. It had been easy for him to send his mother flowers, gifts and make the odd phone call, oblivious to her true plight.
"Sorry," Suzy sniffed, regaining her composure.

Matt reached across the table, took her hand and gave it a reassuring squeeze. He copied details from the statement into a small black notebook, which he slipped back inside a top jacket pocket. "Don't worry, I'll sort it," he said handing back Ellen's bank statement.
"Tread carefully Matt, Mum won't accept charity, you know what she's like," suspecting his intentions.
"It's not charity, Suze, I'm buying her time. I owe her that. I haven't made the effort to go back home for years, I've been thoughtless."
This time Suzy reached out to console him. He looked down trying to hide his discomfort.
"Matt, is there anything we can we do?"
"Whatever it takes," he said positively.
"We have to tell Phil," Suzy insisted.
"Leave that to me." As he spoke, she knew he was already making contingency plans. Matt was a born organiser, his adept skill of resolving financial problems had served him well, having risen high in the world of corporate business.

He spotted a waitress carrying two large portions of apple pie with cream to a table nearby, bringing his thoughts firmly back to food. "Shall we?" he grinned.
"I shall fall asleep at the wheel and your plane won't be able to take off due to excess weight," Suzy cautioned.
"Oh go on then," she smiled.

The puddings lightened the mood, returning their meeting to a pleasurable one. The waitress reappeared with coffee. Matt took a sip and checked the time on his watch. "I have to go Suze. I'll phone you when I get back in a couple of weeks," he said, rising to leave. "Don't get up, finish your coffee," patting her shoulder as he turned to go.

She watched him swiftly make his way to the bar to settle the bill. Completed, he gave her a quick wave before going through the door that led out to the carpark. She sat for a short while mulling over their conversation.

Back on the road she reminded herself to stop and pick up some milk, Richard couldn't be relied upon to remember such things. Now feeling slightly more relaxed about her mother's situation, she was happy to be going home. She'd so much to tell Richard about her days away, and wondered what he'd been doing during her absence.

Richard had been in the yard trying to sort out a delivery with one of the drivers when Sally caught up with him. She was waving an invoice looking fraught. "Here comes trouble," the driver announced in a loud voice to tease her.

Like Richard, Sally had also worked at Penns Haulage for years. Dealing with the firm's clerical work, she understood as much about running the business as he did. "Wilson Graphics want their stock before Monday," she said, indicating a date underlined in red on the invoice. "And?" Richard queried.

She pointed to the truck which had just come in, "it's on that lorry. Only two boxes," opening her arms wide

displaying their size. "It's a new contract and Mr Wilson's waiting for them now . . . . at his shop!"
Richard took the invoice, glanced through its details and cursed when he saw the address. "I haven't even had a cup of tea yet," he grumbled. Mr Wilson's shop was in Woodgate Green, forty miles away.
"Please," Sally begged, "pretty please."

When Richard reluctantly walked off to organise moving the consignment from the truck to one of the small vans, Sally dashed into the office to make his tea. She knew there wasn't a spare driver, so it would be down to Richard to cover the delivery. She put a mug of hot steaming tea onto a tray, and trying to make amends added a large slice of her homemade fruitcake. She placed the tray on top of everything on Richard's desk.
After his break, the newly loaded van was ready to go. "Don't know how long I'll be, may be late bringing the van back," Richard called out as he collected the van's keys. Sally offered to lock up if he wasn't back in time, repaying the favour was the least she could do.

Almost home, Suzy pulled in for fuel. Picking up milk and a bunch of flowers for her mother-in-law in the garage's shop. She wanted to thank Rita for feeding Richard while she'd been away at the conference, and no doubt he'd been popping in while she had been visiting her mother. It would only take a slight deter to deliver them on her way home.

Roadworks were causing chaos, workmen had dug a long deep trench along Green Lane where Rita lived. Unable to stop, Suzy followed diversion signs that led her further out of her way. Proceeding down roads of old terraced houses, and squeezing between cars parked both sides of the narrow roads was a nightmare. Soon she'd no idea of her whereabouts in relation to Rita's house and stopped to ask directions. She managed to pull into a gap along the curb to park.

The overcast sky darkened as clouds began to gather. Getting out of her car, she wondered if it would rain. Standing on the pavement looking around for someone to ask, she spotted one of Penn's small green vans parked further along the road. The bright blue arrows of their logo stood out, and surmised one of the drivers must live near.

A smartly dressed woman wearing a dark suit and heeled shoes came out of the house Suzy had parked outside. Heading for the car parked in front, she smiled "are you lost?"

"I think I am, could you direct me back to the main road?" Suzy asked.

The woman stared at her. "Suzy Martin! I don't believe it!", the woman exclaimed, clearly recognising her.

Suzy looked blank. Mystified and without a clue, trying desperately to think who this person could be?

The woman took a deep breath and puffed out her cheeks, positioning her arms either side to imitate a very large rotund built lady.

Suzy looked closer and wondered, "Rachel, . . . Rachel Collins?"

Rachel laughed, "thank goodness for that, I was about to burst." The two friends hadn't seen each other for many years.

"Oh my goodness," Suzy exclaimed, sorry she hadn't recognised her.

"I'm a tad smaller these days," her friend laughed.

"What are you doing here?" they both asked in unison.

Large drops of rain began to fall. Rachel reached into her pocket for a business card to give Suzy. "It's a long story, phone me Suzy, we have to catch up," she said dashing to her car to escape the rain.

Suzy shouted "how do I get out of here?"

"Left at the end of this road, then left again." Rachel shouted back as she got into her car.

The heavens opened and down came torrential rain. Suzy got back into her car soaking wet. Rita would get her flowers another day, she was going home.

Any hopes of surprising Richard in her new dress and trendy hair style had been dashed by the weather. His car wasn't in their drive, but she knew he was due home any minute. By the time she'd unloaded her car in the pouring rain, she was totally bedraggled. She headed straight upstairs for a shower.

The hot water warmed and soothed her body. Perhaps it had been fortuitous having this time alone to get ready, now she could greet Richard dry and refreshed. Drying her hair, she thought about the many things she wanted to tell him. The serendipitous meeting of her long lost friend Rachel and having lunch with Matt had made this Saturday extra special despite getting soaked. She'd always been a 'glass half full' type of person. Sadly Richard didn't appreciate her optimism, it was one of her traits which irritated him.

She checked the time, he should have been home by now so phoned his mobile and waited. It was difficult to hear when he answered due to background noise. "Where are you?" she asked.

Richard's phone displayed Suzy was phoning from home.

"You said, you were coming home tomorrow," he answered, sounding agitated.
"No, silly," she chortled, "I said tomorrow at the latest. Anyway, I phoned your office this morning to remind you. Didn't you get my message?"
"I'm leaving now, be about twenty minutes," he groaned.

She was in the kitchen assembling a few bits and pieces for supper when she heard him come in. "Only sandwiches and crisps, it's a bit late to start cooking," greeting him with a smile.
"I've just eaten at the pub. I didn't get any message, who did you speak to?" Richard moaned, mentioning the delivery he'd done earlier and returning late back to the yard.
She was convinced he worked too many hours, and no wonder he'd been grumpy if she'd disturbed his meal at the pub.
Watching his eyes close while she spoke, knew he wasn't listening. Only when she mentioned taking flowers to Rita, he suddenly perked up, insisting he'd deliver the flowers first thing when he fetched the Sunday papers.

-

Richard had already left when Suzy woke up. Various thoughts came and went as she lay leisurely appreciating not having to get up. Knowing Kate wasn't coming home meant they could go away on holiday any time during the summer. She couldn't remember the last time just the two of them had been away. Smiling to herself, she decided to treat themselves to something special. Maybe Richard would fancy somewhere abroad or a short cruise? At work tomorrow, she'd enquire about available dates to book the time off. Gradually niggling thoughts of unpacking and laundry seeped into her mind. Regrettably, she would have to get up and make a start.

-

It didn't take long to slip back into their routine of work. Kate phoned one evening, describing her latest job offer for the summer. Working in a garden nursery had appealed. They'd giggled when Suzy hinted about how many plants could die, knowing Kate's lack of knowledge of growing anything green.

Suzy wondered about visiting Phil while Matt was away. It might be best to explain their mother's situation before Matt contacted him. There'd been slight sibling rivalry between her brothers as they grew up at home. Although it had evaporated instantly when their father had his fatal car accident. Never-the-less she didn't want any male feathers ruffled, their mother's financial circumstances needed the help of them all.

Suzy had phoned the number from Rachel's card, but so far hadn't been able to catch her and had left a message. It would be great getting together after all these years, they'd so much to catch up on.

- -

Ellen rose feeling tetchy from another night of broken sleep and decided the only way to deal with this situation was head on. It was time for a confrontation. Midmorning and still irritated, she strode outside into her front garden and positioned herself in front of the rock where the little creature had first appeared. Now unafraid, she was on a warpath!

"I know you're there, so you'd just as well appear!" she addressed the stone. Despite no evidence of the creature, she continued "you appeared to me, so clearly you wanted to be seen.. Now I want to know why?" Determined, she

stood her ground and waited. "Are you some kind of Leprechaun? Pixie?" Still, there was no sign. Without wavering she persisted, "are you something bad or evil?"
The creature appeared, his expression of anger unmistakeable. "Arrogant humans!" he blustered. "Think they save this world when it's them destroys it!" He glared at her, blatant.
Shocked, Ellen wasn't expecting that, nor could she disagree. "We're not all bad," lowering her eyes, feeling chastised.
He'd vanished and probably in a huff too.
Aware of the ridiculous situation of talking to a large stone, Ellen swallowed her pride and continued. "With respect, how long have you been here?"
"Respect?" Ellen heard him grunt crossly.
Had she been communicating with an intelligent being, or could she be going mad after all? She needed to digest her thoughts. One thing for certain, her number of questions had only increased.

Turning round to walk back to her front door, a small van pulled up alongside her.
"Mrs. Chapman?" the driver inquired as he wound down his window.
Ellen recognised the local florist's van, "yes."
She watched him get out, walk round to open one of the van's back doors.
"Then these must be for you," the driver announced smiling, handing her a huge bouquet of roses.
"Oh my goodness," she said amazed.
Closing her door, she laid the coloured rainbow of flowers on the hall table to admire their beauty. Lilac bows and curled ribbons adorned the bouquet. A small envelope stapled at the top revealed the sender.

To the best Mum in the world,
love always, Matt xx.

Her low mood had suddenly evaporated, uplifted she went off to arrange her flowers.

- -

There was a message on the notepad by the phone when Suzy got home. 'Ring Rachel tonight' Richard had scrawled.
"Who's Rachel?" he asked while they ate dinner.
Suzy reminded him of the friend whom she'd recently bumped into, knowing full well that he hadn't been listening before. "We're going out one evening for a meal and a good old fashioned girlie catch up. I haven't seen Rachel since?" Suzy thought, . . . "our Kate was at school."

Rachel answered her phone, but admitted she couldn't chat as she was still working. She suggested they met at the Bricknell Lodge, Wednesday evening at seven.
"The Bricknell?" Suzy questioned.
"Is that awkward Suzy?"
Suzy wanted to say she wasn't expecting to go anywhere posh and expensive, which Bricknell Lodge certainly was.
"My treat, see you there."
"Wait!" Suzy protested "I can't let you pay Rachel."
"Suzy, I work there, so my treat, see you Wednesday."
She realised Rachel must have been setting off to work when they met, explaining her smart appearance.

-

On Tuesday, Suzy had finished all of her assignments by lunchtime. She phoned through to her manager to ask if she'd any more work for her.

Surprisingly Karen said no, explaining Suzy's department had got ahead of itself workwise. "It's just a glitch, you'll probably be on overload next week," she laughed. "Just a thought Suzy, if you'd like a couple of days off to visit your mother, this could be a good time," Karen suggested, remembering Suzy's earlier request.
"Thanks Karen, I'll let you know." Replacing the receiver, Suzy's mind went into overdrive. She hadn't wanted to visit her mother without answers or void of solutions, but this was such a good opportunity and it might appear rude not to make the most of her manager's offer. Then she had a brain-wave! She could visit Phil, and began looking in her personal diary for his phone number. Two landline numbers were written alongside his name, but no mobile. There was no reply to the first, which she vaguely remembered to be a home number. Not wanting to leave a message, decided to try it again later.

A polite officious secretary answered the second phone number.
"May I speak to Mr Phillip Chapman please?" Suzy requested.
"I'm afraid he's in a meeting, may I take a message?"
By the woman's crisp tone, Suzy had the feeling she was being fobbed off.
"It's important I speak to him, I'm his sister." Suzy assumed this explanation would get her through.
"May I take your name?" the secretary asked in her curt manner.
Clearly Suzy wasn't going to get passed this person without known identity. She gave her name and asked for a personal appointment with Phillip on Thursday.
"Mr Chapman will not be free before three o'clock, and I can't guarantee he won't be running late."

"That will be fine and if necessary I shall wait," Suzy replied equally concise. Hmmm, she thought, I can't wait to meet this madam.

Suzy made herself a coffee and spent the next few hours catching up with filing and tidying her office. With Karen approving her extra two days holiday at the end of the week, a stress free happy Suzy drove home.

She wondered what Richard would make of her taking more days off, but he showed more concern about her evening with Rachel at the Bricknell.

"Don't worry, Rachel is insisting on paying," Suzy assured him.

"Make sure she does," he griped.

Suzy pursed her lips tightly together, there'd be no point in verbal retaliation, it would only make his bad mood worse. "I think you're working far too hard Richard and it's making you miserable. Every night you come home stressed, over tired and grumpy. Why don't we treat ourselves to a holiday?" she suggested with hope. "We both could do with a break, and now our Kate isn't coming back during the summer months we can go anytime."

He didn't answer. Suzy took his hand and gave it a loving squeeze, she could feel his tension, clearly something was worrying him. "Well, have a think about it," she said softly.

On Wednesday, Suzy became the general 'dog's body' for her manager. Delivering papers and documents to various departments throughout the day and making everyone's coffee. It gave her a good insight to who worked where, within the other offices and departments.

Karen began to gather her notes in readiness for the board meeting at four o'clock. After thanking Suzy for her help, mentioned she wouldn't be returning to her office after the meeting. "Let's hope Mr Saggers doesn't attend or we'll be there forever," Karen said, raising her eyebrows. "We've finished here for today, so you just as well get off home. See you Monday," she called, heading towards the door.
When Karen had gone Suzy looked at her watch and smiled, it was almost four o'clock. Now she'd have plenty of time at home to sort out something for Richard's tea, and to get ready for her evening out. As she left Karen's office, Mr Saggers rushed past carrying a pile of folders. Suzy smiled to herself, it looked like they'd be having a long meeting after all.

The evening with Rachel gave Suzy another opportunity to wear her new dress, and hopefully for Richard to see it .. if he came home in time. She turned around checking her reflection in the long mirror in the hall. "That'll do," she said to herself, pleased with her appearance and wondered if she could coax a compliment out of Richard before she left.
Once again he was late. Disappointed, Suzy reluctantly placed a large glass lid over the meal she'd cooked and left it on a tray by the oven. Adding a note alongside about a fresh cream cake in the fridge for his dessert.

The Bricknell Lodge had been a large substantial house in beautiful landscaped parkland, part of the estate originally owned by the Hyde family. Over time it's many acres of land had been sold, and now Bricknell Lodge was the flag ship of the Powell Hotel Group.

Suzy arrived on time, from her parked car she could see its impressive façade. She wondered how many changes and events this resplendent house had witnessed throughout the years.
Inside the main entrance she could see Rachel standing by the reception desk.
"It's so good to see you again," they both said together. Suzy followed her into the dining lounge to a reserved table discreetly positioned in a corner. Seated, she looked around taking in the grandeur. Slightly overwhelmed by the menu and knowing Rachel was paying, tactfully asked her to order for them both.

"So what brought you to Leake Road?" Rachel asked.
"Trying to deliver flowers to my mother-in-law on my way home, until I got lost. Rita lives in Green Lane," Suzy explained.
"I can't believe we haven't met before, our in-laws only live a few roads apart and I frequently pop in to see Elsie," Rachel puzzled.
Suzy confessed she wasn't exactly close to Rita. Richard usually visited his mother on his own, hence she wasn't often in the area.

"So, what's your Ross doing now?" Suzy asked cheerfully, swiftly changing the subject.
Rachel leaned back in her chair, a loving smile enveloped her face as she spoke about her eldest son. "Ross is a brilliant mathematician. He sailed through two and a half years at Bristol University, achieving the highest results with distinctions. His tutors predicted a successful future in banking or with the Stock Exchange. Bored at home during his last Uni summer break, on a whim, took himself off to work on a farm in the Midlands. Suzy, he'd never owned a pet, or even asked to look after the school

hamster at weekends. I guessed he'd probably last about a week before he came home, but he fell in love. Besotted with his girls, told me he couldn't possibly leave now they all were pregnant!"
Suzy sat riveted as Rachel continued.
"Ross hasn't been back home since. Basically, he's as happy as a pig in muck, his beloved girls are prize sows!" She smiled with a hint of exasperation. Rachel scrolled through photos on her phone, trying to find recent ones Ross had sent of the farm. She passed her phone over for Suzy to see.
Suzy had to agree, he did look blissfully happy. "I bet he's made a few local girl's hearts skip a beat," she grinned, handing back the phone. With his tousled blonde hair and big sky blue eyes, there was no denying Ross was the image of how Suzy remembered his father.

"And Michael," Rachel continued "has recently started working for Coombs Laboratories. God knows what he's checking, Plague? Black Death?" Rachel joked, questioning her other son's choice of employment. "He says it's a job and so long as he can play his guitar with his mates in pubs at weekends – he's happy. Who'd be a mother?" Rachel laughed. "That's enough about us, now tell me all about Kate," adding "lucky you, having a daughter."

"My favourite subject," Suzy expressed with a smile. Bringing Rachel up to date and showing photos reminded her how much she missed Kate. "We used to be so close, until this last year," she said sadly.
"Maybe she's met someone?"
"Quite possibly," yet deep down Suzy sensed a niggle. Summer job or not, it wasn't like Kate not to come home.

She relayed their move to Ashton for Richard's job at Penns Haulage, and glossed briefly over her own work.
"Where's Adam working now?" Suzy asked in innocence.
Rachel's smile instantly faded. "He runs a bar in Spain, took off years ago with his secretary, the bastard!" Rachel looking away, waiting for the hurtful moment to pass.
"I'm so sorry Rachel, I feel awful now," Suzy said softly, and hurriedly changed to more mundane subjects.

"Rachel, look at the time, these poor people want to close." Suzy thanked her for the wonderful evening, apologising once more as they walked back to their cars.
"We must do this again," Rachel insisted, still having plenty to catch up on.
"My treat next time," Suzy promised "how about a tearoom?"
"I'll look forward to it," Rachel called back.

Driving home, Suzy reflected on the evening. It had all been going well, until she'd asked that unfortunate question. Trust her to put her verbal big foot in it, and felt guilty about hurting Rachel's feelings. It had been a shock, remembering how happy Rachel and Adam always appeared to be.
Adam had been the most handsome man Suzy had ever met. On the odd occasion he met Ross from school, she knew hearts fluttered among the women at the school gate, Adam was charismatic. Although his smile caused many a swoon, he only seemed to have eyes for Rachel.

Suzy pulled in and parked her car next to Richard's. She wasn't surprised to see the house in darkness. It was very late and he'd probably gone to bed hours ago. As she walked passed Richard's car two bright green eyes

stared at her, making her flinch. Next door's black cat was sitting on the bonnet of his car. "Shoo," Suzy hissed, taking a swipe at the cat. The cat stayed, forcing her to lean across to push it off. The bonnet of Richard's car was warm, no wonder the cat had sat there.
When Suzy got into bed, Richard gave the impression of being sound asleep. She was too tired to ask, it could wait until morning.

Up early as usual, Suzy was busy making Richard's sandwiches, depicting her evening while he sat finishing his breakfast.
He couldn't remember Adam or Rachel, despite her descriptions. "Ah," he said, finally remembering. "Was she that tubby girl with long hair, always dressed like a Hippy?"
Suzy informed him "that buxom pretty girl with waist length hair, is now elegantly slim and a very attractive lady."
"What does she do at the Bricknell?"
Suzy confessed she hadn't thought to ask.
Richard took his last gulp of tea and stood up getting ready to leave for work. "Are you coming back tonight or going on to stay with your mother?" he asked, putting on his coat.
"Depends on what Phil has to say."
"Just as well stay with her for the weekend as you're up that way," he encouraged. "I'll be at the yard all Saturday anyway, got drivers to interview now Jim's thinking of retiring this year."
"If you really don't mind, I'll come back Sunday morning." Suzy walked with him towards their front door intending to wave goodbye. "Oh heavens!" she gasped,

suddenly remembering she hadn't phoned Phil and scampered back to phone him.
Richard closed the door and went off to work.

Suzy called the number she'd guessed to be their home. Julia, her sister-in-law answered. After the usual pleasantries, Suzy explained she'd hoped to catch Phil before he'd left for work. Alas, she'd just missed him. Hearing about her appointment, Julia insisted Suzy called in before for coffee. "Phil's office was only minutes from their home," she said, intrigued by her sudden visit.

It was a good job Suzy had spoken to Julia, she needed a reminder of Phil's office address and where to find it. Although Julia was pleasant enough, Suzy had never warmed to her, finding her far too materialistic. Unintentionally the years had slipped by without visits, no specific reason, just everyone getting on with their own busy lives.
Suzy went off to get ready, now she'd have to rush.

The house was bigger than she remembered. A white builder's van was parked behind a brand new 4x4 in Julia's drive.
Julia seemed genuinely pleased to see her and welcomed her inside. Suzy followed her through, taking a seat in their vast bespoke kitchen. Julia apologised, dashing away for a quick word with the builder before he left. While she waited, Suzy looked about. The kitchen was impressive, in fact from what she could see, the whole house interior could easily feature in any glossy 'Home' magazine. Through the window she watched them walking around outside. The builder kept pointing to the house and referring to a catalogue.

Back inside, Julia took out a tray of sausage rolls from her huge inbuilt oven, - a hot snack to enjoy with their coffee.
"What are you thinking of having done?," Suzy asked, acknowledging the pile of brochures.
"Extending and upgrading the conservatory." Julia showed her a couple of designs, "aren't these fabulous?"
Indeed they certainly were. Julia had always been a spender and clearly she hadn't changed a bit.

Armed with directions to Phil's office, Suzy thanked Julia for her hospitality and continued on her way.
She managed to squeeze her car into the last space in the car park and followed Julia's directions inside. Suzy presented herself at a desk where a woman, 'possibly in her early sixties' sat typing.
With total focus to her screen, she didn't acknowledge Suzy until she'd finished her task. "Please take a seat," she said crisply and continued to type.
From her seat Suzy observed Phil's name plaque on the door ahead. According to the large faced clock on the wall, she'd arrived twenty minutes early. Suzy sat for ten full minutes in silence, her hackles rising at being totally ignored. Fuming at the woman's rudeness, she approached the desk again.
"Please take a seat," the secretary repeated and made a point of visibly checking her watch. "I'll let Mr Chapman know you are here," yet made no attempt to phone through until three o'clock.

"Mrs Martin to see you sir," the woman announced as she opened the door for Suzy to enter.
"Sir?" Suzy questioned as she walked in.

Phil's face lit up with surprise. "Suzy!" walking forward to give her a hug. "I had no idea, why didn't you let me know?"
"I did, I'm your next appointment," she said, flashing stern eyes at the secretary.
"Mrs Finnis let me introduce you to my sister," Phil invited.
Suzy stiffened, "we have already met."
"A pleasure to make your acquaintance Mrs Martin," Mrs Finnis replied curtly and closed the door.
"Sorry Suzy, I didn't connect with your name. Gosh it's good to see you, but why did you want to see me here?" Phil queried.
"That woman's a harridan!" Suzy hissed with anger.
"I know, isn't she marvellous?" Phil praised.
Suzy was speechless.
"Do you remember going to the doctors when we were kids?" he continued. You couldn't see our doctor unless you got passed Miss Byrne, Dad called her the Scary Dragon guarding her knights."
Suzy smiled, remembering their dad's wicked sense of humour. He always saw the funny side of things, growing up was fun with him around.
Phil lowered his voice, whispering with a grin "she's my dragon."
Suzy remained miffed. "With her rudeness, I'm surprised you have any clients."

Mrs Finnis knocked on the door, before entering with a large heavy tray of refreshments. Phil got up to relieve her of the burden.
"We don't like those new-fangled vending machines along the corridor do we Mrs Finnis?" Phil winked at Suzy.

"Most unpalatable," Mrs Finnis remarked as she served them tea from a china tea service before leaving the room.
"She's right about that," Phil said with a smile, placing a plate of biscuits between them. "Right, now Sis, what's brought you here?"

Suzy explained why she'd taken the short break, and was utilising this day to see him. He listened intently as she brought him up to date with their mother's financial predicament. "There must be a way to keep Squirrels Chase for Mum," Suzy pleaded. "Can you remember seeing anything useful amongst Mum's documents when Dad died?"

"There were no financial or legal mistakes made during the time I oversaw Mum's affairs following dad's death Suzy," Phil assured her in his professional tone of voice.
"Oh Phil, I'm so sorry, I never meant any such implications. I was thinking along the lines of maybe a 'provision for the future', sort of 'rainy day' fund? . . I'm clutching at straws aren't I?" she said wistfully.
Phil thought for a moment, turning her words over in his mind. "It's worth a try, I could read through the papers and documents again," giving Suzy a glimmer of hope.
"I have to confess Suzy, I allowed Mr Bennington the firm's senior partner to deal with most of it. I'd just qualified when dad died and was newly appointed. Mr Bennington, aware of my grief gallantly offered to personally guide me through the documents and necessary procedures. Thinking about it now, I don't remember any specific details at all."
"Phil, I'm sure the best decisions were made at the time, given the circumstances," she reassured.

Suzy began to think about leaving. "I should go Phil, I can see you're busy. It's been good to see you, and it will be such a help if you can read through those documents of Mum's as soon as possible. She really could do with a bit of optimism to cheer her up."
"I didn't keep them Suzy, they're somewhere up in Mum's loft in a black case," Phil stated. "Try to locate them for me while you're there."
"Oh goodness," Suzy gulped, as it dawned on her "Mum doesn't know I'm coming, I must phone her."
"I'll let her know you're on your way," Phil smiled.
"Thanks Phil, she'll love that."
Suzy placed her bag on the corner of his desk, before standing up to put her coat on. Her bag dislodged a small pile of brochures which dropped to the floor. "Sorry Phil, I'm so clumsy," she said picking them up. The glossy brochures featured sports cars.
Phil retrieved a Porsche brochure that had landed by his feet. "Look at these 'beauties'," he said with a gleam in his eye. "I've been saving for one of these for years," pointing to a black car. "I reckon by the end of this year," kissing the picture.
"You men and your cars!" she laughed, shaking her head totally unimpressed.
Walking towards the door, she turned to ask "does Julia know about your savings? . . only that's the second pile of brochures I've seen today."
"What brochures?" he asked, having an uncomfortable feeling where this was leading.
"Large luxuriously designed conservatories," she answered with a knowing smile and said "Good bye," leaving his office.

Mrs Finnis gave Suzy a pleasant smile and wished her a safe journey. Suzy wasn't convinced Phil's dragon had metamorphosed into a nice person.

Ellen never expected her boys to phone, not with their busy professional lives. So she was very surprised to hear Phil's voice when he called mid-afternoon, knowing he'd be working. He told her about Suzy's visit to his office earlier and said she was on her way. While referring to the documents, he suggested a change of scenery and invited her to stay with him and Julia for a few days. She thanked him for his kind offer and promised to think about it.

Suzy was glad to see her mother's drive appear in the distance. She was getting tired and it felt as though she'd been driving forever. Caught up in rush hour traffic for the past hour, she could feel the beginning of a head ache. Opening the door, Ellen beamed. "What a wonderful surprise," giving Suzy a hug. She could see her daughter looked tired and began to fuss around her.

Once inside, Suzy could smell the aroma of cooking wafting through the hall. Throwing her coat over a chair, she slipped off her shoes and following her mother's instructions went into the lounge to sit down.

Ellen headed back to her kitchen. She re-appeared with a hot meal and mug of tea on a tray. "This should make you feel better," she said handing it over. Ellen switched on the TV for the News and went back to collect her own food.

Suzy looked down at her mother's signature dish of chicken casserole with crusty bread, savouring the feeling of being home and spoilt. She entertained her mother with the delights of Phil's battle-axe of a secretary, and the joy of meeting up again with her friend Rachel.

Suzy took a hot drink up to bed, she was tired and didn't want a late night. Also she wanted to phone Richard. He usually retired after the 10 o'clock news, unless there was a football match on the TV. He'd asked her to let him know when she'd arrived safely at her mother's, which had slipped her mind earlier. He didn't answer. Too tired now to fuss, she left him a message.

In the morning Suzy planned to catch him at his office. If she could speak to him early before he started work they could both get on with their day.
"Penns Haulage, can I help you?" Sally chirped brightly at the end of the line.
"Hi Sally, can I speak to Richard?" Suzy asked.
"Richard?" Sally sounded puzzled, "I didn't think he was in today. I'm probably wrong, I usually am," Sally chuckled. "I haven't seen him yet, but when I do I'll get him to call you," adding "he could be out in the yard."
"Thanks Sally," Suzy replied.

During their breakfast Suzy suggested a shopping trip to Kirston "but, only if you fancy it Mum."
"Yes please," Ellen accepted gratefully, knowing it would be easier to load Suzy's car than struggle on the bus later in the week. She slipped her list into her purse and gathered her shopping bags. "Shall I take an umbrella?" she asked before shutting her front door, observing the grey cloudy sky.
"There's one in the car," Suzy answered, wanting to get going, although wasn't quite sure where. She liked to

browse and meander around the little individual shops in Kirston. The supermarket was small but quite adequate for their needs.

With their shopping loaded into Suzy's car, they headed for Polly's Cafe. A trip to Kirston wasn't complete without a visit to the little tea shop. Where tables were laid with white linen tablecloths and tea was served in floral patterned china cups with saucers, . . but most importantly, their home made cakes were to die for.
Ellen found a table by the window while Suzy queued at the counter. Enjoying hot sausage rolls as they watched busy shoppers passing by outside in the street. The tasty snack reminded Suzy of the ones she shared with Julia in her fabulous kitchen. Speaking about it, prompted Ellen's memory and she mentioned Phil's kind offer to stay.
"Will you go?" Suzy asked.
"I may do, they might be offended if I refuse" Ellen reasoned.
"I think you should, it could do you good to get away from the house for a while."
The next big decision involved cake, unable to pick just one each, they chose a variety to take home in a box.

Back home at Squirrels Chase Suzy carried the shopping through to the kitchen. She put the kettle on while her mother unpacked the bags.
"I think I'll have a glance through the newspapers before I go up and tackle finding that case in the loft," Suzy announced making their drinks.
"Good idea," Ellen agreed, feeling ready for a sit down.
"Marmalade!" she remembered crossly, "I forgot to get marmalade."

"I'll pop up to that corner shop we passed on the way home." Suzy offered, picking up her car keys. "I shan't be long."

The shop was further away than she'd thought. As she drew up outside, a small green van parked outside caught her eye. It's funny illustration depicted a hot red-in-the-face man pushing a lawnmower. The lawn-mowing service advertisement made her smile. It reminded her how she'd felt mowing her mother's grass on her last visit. This was an opportunity too good to miss and waited to see if the van owner would appear.

A chap wearing grubby overalls and carrying a pack of sandwiches came out of the shop. He seemed the likely candidate and sure enough he walked towards the van. Suzy shot out of her car and rushed up to him, not wanting him to escape.

'George the mower man' as he introduced himself was happy to oblige, arranging to call round to see them tomorrow morning to view the size of the job and give a quote. If her mum was happy, he could start next week.

Suzy entered the shop euphoric, with luck she may never have to tackle her mother's grass again. Her smugness soon faded when she realised she'd forgotten what she'd come in to buy. With her mind still blank she picked up three women's magazines and headed towards the counter, only remembering the marmalade while she queued for the till. Outside the dark clouds finally began to fulfil their promise, sending her scampering to escape the rain.

Carrying the old stepladder upstairs, Suzy wasn't looking forward to getting up into her mother's loft. She placed it underneath the hatch and gingerly climbed the rickety steps to the top. Her mother stood on the bottom rung, attempting to keep it steady. The hatch door hadn't been opened for many years and took a lot of pushing to free. Once opened, Suzy pulled down the built-in loft ladder. Clouds of thick dust rained down catching them by surprise. "Ugh!" they spluttered, shaking their heads.

With the loft ladder firmly down, she braced herself ready to climb it, "wish me luck."

"There's a light switch on the inside of the hatch, . . to your left, can you feel it Suzy?" Ellen called, trying to help.

She found it and flicked it down. To her amazement and relief two lightbulbs hanging from the rafters came on. "I'll be OK now," Suzy called, scrambling up inside. The cooler temperature made her shiver, but at least it wasn't dark. Once her eyes had adapted to the subdued light she began to look around not knowing where to start. Not surprising, there were piles of dust covered boxes and general clutter everywhere. It was tempting to peek inside every box just out of curiosity, but unless she intended to be up there for hours she needed to remain focussed. "Suitcases, where's the suitcases?" she said aloud.

Ellen came upstairs and stood at the bottom of the ladder. She looked up trying to catch sight of Suzy. Unable to see her, shouted upwards "Suzy your phone's been ringing."

Suzy wasn't sure how long she'd been up there. She'd moved piles of books, furniture and rummaged through two large boxes in pursuit of the illusive black case. She felt cold, answering her phone would be a good reason to finish for the day.

"I'll come down," she called. "I'll have another look up here tomorrow."
Ellen was pleased to see her safely down and offered to make a hot drink to warm her up.

Suzy assumed it was Richard who'd called, perhaps he'd just remembered the message from Sally. She looked at her hands covered in black dust. Brushing herself off as best she could, went downstairs into the lounge to use the house phone to call him back. "Hi Richard, I'm sorry I didn't phone yesterday." Explaining her reasons, telling him how he'd laugh if he could see her now, covered head to foot in dust, and casually asked when Sally had passed on her message.
"Sally?" Richard's attitude appeared to change.
Suzy repeated Sally's words.
"Daft bitch," he snapped. "I was in the yard!"
Suzy was shocked, she'd never heard Richard refer to Sally in that way. They'd worked alongside each other for years, and usually Richard had the greatest regard for her.
"Are you OK Richard?" she asked with concern. "Would you like me to come home earlier?"
"No, I'm fine, really I'm fine," he insisted. "You just caught me off guard. Anyway, while you're away I can get a lot of stuff sorted here at the yard."
"Don't overdo it Richard, go home if you get tired," she instructed, accepting his reasons. "I'll be back Sunday morning, but only if you're sure, . . love you," she added tenderly.

Suzy joined her mother in the kitchen for her tea.
"Oh my goodness! look at you Suzy, you're covered," Ellen said handing Suzy a steaming mug of tea. There was no denying the state of her.

"Do you think I need a bath?" Suzy laughed, holding out her grimy hands to show her mother.
"And how's Richard?" Ellen asked, having unintentionally overheard his name mentioned while Suzy was on the phone.
"He's OK, but I think he's spending far too many hours at work. I wish he would delegate some of the workload. I don't know why he insists on doing it all. Right," she said finishing her tea, "I'm off to have that bath."

Submerged under hot soapy bubbles and relaxing in the bath, Suzy began to ponder over the last few days, ticking off the issues she'd dealt with and debating what to do to solve the rest.
She'd yet to tell her mother about George the 'mower man' who would be appearing in the morning, surely her mother would be pleased? She planned to share his regular fee between herself and her brothers, something else she would need to organise.
She thought about Richard. The way he'd spoken about Sally was totally out of character, clearly he was stressed. As soon as she returned to work on Monday she'd book two weeks off for a holiday, he definitely needed a break.

When Suzy made their last hot drink of the evening, she carefully slipped into the conversation her meeting with George. Casually mentioning she'd asked him to call on them in the morning and was thankful her mother made no contention.

-

George arrived at ten o'clock in clean navy blue overalls. Ellen was impressed by his manners and compliments on her beautiful garden as she showed him around.

"I usually mow weekly during the summer, less frequent during other months or according to my customer's request." He thanked them both for their time, presented a copy of references, cost and details of his service should Ellen decide to accept. Finally bidding them 'Good day', and got into his van to depart.

Despite the fact he was adept in flattering senior aged ladies, Suzy thought George seemed nice. The meeting had gone well and as far as she could tell, her mother appeared at ease with his company.

"What do you think Mum? should we give him a try?"

Ellen thought for a moment "he seems pleasant, and he's got an honest face."

"Well so long as the rest of him is honest too, we shouldn't have any trouble."

Ellen chuckled, Suzy had her father's sense of humour and agreed to give George a month's trial.

"After a coffee and one of Polly's cakes, I'm going back up into the loft," Suzy announced. Assuring her mother she didn't need any help, now she'd fathomed how to get the loft-ladder down and found the lights. "I'll take my phone with me, so if I get stuck, I can call the Fire Brigade," she joked.

"What are you actually looking for?" Ellen asked.

Suzy reminded her, she was hunting a black suitcase containing papers to give Phil.

"I don't ever remember seeing a black suitcase up there," her mother replied, "and Dad and I never owned one."

With those discouraging words Suzy re-entered the loft. Carefully moving piles of dusty boxes to peer behind, lifted material draped over chairs but found nothing

resembling a suitcase. Each failure sank her spirits and decreased her enthusiasm.
She'd searched through most of the clutter in the loft's space. There were no suitcases to be found, black or any other colour. At the far end she could see several full plastic carrier bags lined up along the floor, and moved closer to investigate. The first bag she grabbed split, scattering its contents. "Blast!" she cursed. The flexibility of the plastic had changed over time into brittleness. Suzy surveyed the items - a variety of typed official letters inside old brown envelopes, adverts, brochures and general postal bumf had been stuffed into the bag. A quick glimpse into the other bags seemed to suggest they contained the same.

She picked another bag at random to check, this time carefully supporting it before tipping out. A collection of bereavement cards held together with a blue ribbon fell out, followed once again by general junk mail. She couldn't resist untying the ribbon to look through the cards her family received on losing her father. Their loving sympathetic uplifting words brought tears. This discovery hadn't helped present matters so she scooped it all back into the bag. About to return it back to the others when she spotted a very dusty black briefcase. Whether someone had piled the bags on top, or perhaps somehow they'd slid across and covered it. Of course, Phil had meant a briefcase, not a suitcase! Eureka, she'd found it.! The case was unlocked. Although tempted to look inside decided against, owing to the state of her dirty hands. In triumph, Suzy carried the case down from the loft to show her mother.
Leaving her to wipe away years of dust while she took a shower.

Ellen waited, wanting them to open the case together. In the shower, Suzy hoped and prayed they'd find something inside to solve her mother's financial plight.

Dressed in clean clothes and with almost dry hair, she sat down at the kitchen table ready to investigate the contents of the case. Ellen was as excited as Suzy was anxious. Suzy extracted various papers and documents, copies of her father's death certificate and letters. It did seem to be the case Phil had spoken about, now he could take it back to examine. "Hopefully Mum, we've hit the jackpot. You can phone him tonight and tell him we've found it," relieved her task had been accomplished.
Ellen put the case on top of the bureau ready for Phil to collect.

After dinner Ellen phoned Phil. He was pleased to hear the case had been found. "I'll come up to collect it one evening next week." Hesitating before asking if she would go back with him for a short stay. "You know we'd love to have you here. I'll take a few days off and take you out, . . how does that sound?"
"That's very kind," Ellen answered, and surprised Suzy by accepting.
"No pressure?" Suzy grinned.
"Precisely," her mum replied warily.

They sat together enjoying the evening, chatting about the day and drinking their last hot drink before retiring. Suzy thought about the loft, it could do with a good sort out and suggested making a start on it next time. She might find some treasure up there, who knows? If Richard came too, he could give her a hand, . . or was she being too optimistic?

On Sunday morning Suzy sat dipping biscuits into her coffee, happy with her achievements and how her short visit had gone. She'd loaded her car earlier and sneakily slipped an envelope containing George's payment under the black case in the hall. It was almost time for her to go.
Ellen finished her drink and awkwardly began to fidget.
"Have you got everything?" she asked, making conversation, knowing the house would feel empty the minute Suzy had gone.
"I'll phone when I get back to let you know when I'm home safe," Suzy promised as she gave her mother a good bye hug before getting into her car. Ellen waved until Suzy's car left her drive and disappeared into the distance.

Richard was mowing the front lawn when Suzy arrived.
"You've been busy," she said getting out of her car. Carrying her overnight bag, she walked over to give him a peck on the cheek. "Shall I put the kettle on?"
"Good idea," he agreed.
"It's good to be home," she smiled, sitting together on the garden seat outside the back door drinking their tea. She started to tell him about her weekend.
"You'll have to tell me later, I need to get this finished. It's supposed to rain tomorrow," he said, getting up and walking back to the mower.
Reluctantly Suzy got up and went indoors, remembering to phone her mother as promised and mention George's money.

-

The minute she had a moment of free time, Suzy scurried off to her manager's office.

A stranger sat at Karen's desk. "Hello, I'm Jackie," she said, introducing herself. "I'm standing in for Karen this week, can I help?"
Suzy presented her holiday dates.
"Hmm, I'm not sure I can agree these days," checking her screen. "Look," and showed Suzy the chart displayed.
"Everyone books their two-week summer holiday slots early, especially if they have children."
Suzy sighed, she'd forgotten about that.
"There are the last three days of August, and the first weeks of September?" Jackie pointed out, trying to be helpful.
"I'll note down your name for any cancellations. Karen's back next week if you'd like to discuss it with her."
Crestfallen, Suzy pre-booked two weeks of the dates offered.
"There are some Fridays and Mondays free if you want to tie them up for a long weekend," Jackie suggested.
Suzy booked the first long weekend available. Although in three weeks, it would have to do. On a brighter note she thought, walking back to her office, it would give her more time to study holiday brochures.

- -

Ellen phoned Suzy on Wednesday evening, wanting to tell her all about George cutting the grass.
"What did you think of him Mum?"
"He knocked the door to ask if it was OK for him to proceed, and then just got on with it. He was very thorough, did all the edges with a pair of those thingymabobs, . . you know, shears with long handles."
Suzy laughed.
"And he swept loose grass off the paths."

She could tell her mother was impressed, and it sounded like George was a 'keeper'. "Have you heard from Phil?"
"He's picking me up tomorrow, when he's finished work, says I can stay till Sunday if I'd like to."
"Will you?" Suzy asked, picking up a nervous tone in her mother's voice.
"I'll see how I get on, . . maybe."
"I'll come up to see you the following weekend, then you can tell me all about it," wishing her 'a good time' before ending the call. Although confident Phil and Julia would spoil her, Suzy couldn't help feeling apprehensive, her mother hadn't been away from her home for a very long time.

On Thursday evening Suzy managed to track Rachel down.
"Sorry I've been illusive, it's been absolutely manic here," Rachel apologised, lowering her voice as she was still working."
Suzy could hear people talking in the background.
"Are you free this weekend Suzy?"
"I could do Saturday while Richard's at work."
"That's great, where shall we meet?" Rachel asked.
Suzy confessed, she hadn't thought that far ahead.
"Have you been to Pearson's Arboretum? It's just this side of Billerton, easy to find, along the main road and first left. I take Elsie there for a wander if it's warm enough, then we pop into their cafe."
"Sounds perfect," Suzy agreed, arranging to meet Rachel at ten and making a mental note to fish out a warm coat in case the weather turned inclement.

-

The sun had already made its appearance when Suzy got up on Saturday morning, and according to the radio station's weather girl they were in for a dry day.
"Someone's happy," Richard remarked as he began to get himself ready for work. He was right, with only herself to please and the sun shining, all was well in Suzy's world. She'd told him about meeting Rachel but the only information he retained was that she was going out. "What time will you finish today?" she asked, unloading the washing machine.
"Depends on deliveries," shrugging his shoulders to indicate anytime.
When she came in from hanging out her washing, he'd gone.

Rachel was already standing by her car, when Suzy drove into the car park. "What shall we do first, coffee or walk?" Rachel asked.
"Definitely the café, 'tea and a wee', then I'll be OK for hours," Suzy declared with a grin. "And this is my treat, don't forget."
She carefully carried the tray, following Rachel who'd chosen to sit at a table outside. "I can see why Elsie loves it here, the view over that lake is stunning."
"And their teacakes," Rachel confirmed "Elsie always has one of their teacakes toasted."
It was easy to sit there relaxed, drinking and chatting about their lives.

Rachel spoke about her previous weekend. She'd taken Elsie away for her birthday, staying in the same village where Ross worked on the farm. "I thought after we had seen him, she'd like to visit a cathedral or a big house with gardens. Oh no, not Elsie, she wanted to spend the day on the farm with Ross." Rachel showed Suzy pictures on her phone of Elsie wearing wellingtons and feeding piglets. "Would you believe Ross took his Nan for a ride around the farm sitting beside him on a quad bike!" shaking her head with astonishment, . . "and Elsie loved it."

"She sounds quite a woman," Suzy remarked.

"She's amazing," Rachel said with admiration, getting up. Strolling along the pathways, they continued to chat, occasionally stopping to admire a view or to study a flowering shrub. Laughing at Suzy's encounter with Phil's dragon of a secretary, Rachel confessed to meeting a few 'ratbags' herself.

"I'm ready for a perch" Suzy admitted, seeing a wooden bench come into view. She rummaged in her pockets for sweets. "Humbugs?" offering the bag. "So when did you and Adam split?" hoping her question wasn't too intrusive.

"We didn't part, he left," Rachel revealed sadly. "We moved to Brandsby for Adam's new job. He'd rented a house, telling me it gave us time to look around for a place to buy. Michael was only five months old so it seemed sensible at the time. Two months later Adam had gone. He left me a letter, it said he was leaving, he'd sold our previous house and divided the proceeds, enclosing a cheque for what he considered fair. I never saw him again."

"No!" Suzy gasped, her eyes widened, utterly shocked. "Rachel, what on earth did you do?"

"I cried for a month, waiting for him to come home. We'd been so happy, I had no idea what he'd been planning. When he didn't come back, I wondered if he'd gone back to his parents. I wrote to Elsie begging her to ask him to return, or at least let me know where he was. When Elsie read my letter, she assumed we'd just had a row. It was only when Adam sent them his new address, she realised he'd gone. Elsie and Pop came to find me, maybe they wanted to see for themselves what was going on." Rachel gave a hint of a smile, remembering their kindness. "It took them a whole day to reach us in their old Morris Minor, Pop driving while Elsie read the map."

"When they arrived I was a mess, unable to cope, I could only cuddle my children and weep," Rachel took a breath to recompose.

"Elsie, 'always metaphorically ready to roll up her sleeves and deal with whatever drama came along in her life', took one look at me and with compassion undertook our plight. A week later she'd arranged for us to move back here and live with them. Squeezed into their little terraced house, they helped me to get back on my feet. I can't imagine what would of become of us if she hadn't stepped in, I owe them so much."

"That's dreadful," Suzy whispered appalled.

"I haven't spoken about it for years, . . to anyone," Rachel confessed.

"No wonder," Suzy sympathised.

It was the first time Rachel had been able to talk about it without shedding tears, perhaps telling Suzy had been therapy.

"Come on, if we're quick, we'll get a good seat in the café for lunch," Rachel proposed, moving the conversation away from her past.

After they'd eaten Rachel checked the time, "I'd better think about going, I've got so much to do at home."

"Me too," Suzy replied, standing up ready to leave. They walked back to their cars, "call me when you get back from your Mum's, . . I'm so glad we met up again."
"Me too." Suzy agreed with a smile.

Back home, before starting her chores Suzy phoned Kate.
"Are you alright Mum?" Kate asked, sounding anxious.
"I'm fine, why?"
"No reason," Kate answered. They hadn't spoken for a while, so had plenty to catch up on. Laughing at the antics in her Nan's mucky loft, and her mother's description of her Uncle's secretary. "Where's Dad?"
"At work Kate, always at work," Suzy grumbled.

Suzy wasn't surprised when Richard arrived home late. He was only supposed to work mornings on Saturdays, but often returned late afternoon. She didn't bother to ask why, he looked tired and would only moan.
It made a nice change to serve their meal on trays, eating informally in front of the TV, even if it was only watching football. She never understood the fascination of the game and waited tactfully for the match to end before telling Richard about her day and Kate's call.
"Shall we go out tomorrow, treat ourselves to a Sunday roast at a nice country pub?" she suggested, offering to drive if he wanted a drink.

On Sunday Richard drove Suzy's car, arranging she would drive back. They headed for The Plough just outside Ashton, but it was obvious by the full car park they wouldn't get in.

"There's bound to be another pub further along," Suzy petitioned, looking forward to their meal out. "Look, I can see a sign, The White Heart," she pointed, pleased they'd found one so quick.
Richard seemed reluctant to pull into the car park.
"Come on Richard, I'm hungry," she coaxed, directing him to an empty parking space. By the time he'd fiddled about locking the car, she'd already made her way inside to book a table.
The barmen turned around to serve them. "Hello Richard, bought the wife out for a treat?" he smirked.
"I'm just popping to the 'ladies'," leaving Richard at the bar.
When she came out, Richard was waiting for her. "Come on, we're going," and ushered her outside.
"Why?" she protested, but he'd started to walk back to the car.
"Didn't you like that barman?" She'd registered the look on Richard's face.
"He used to work for us," he bristled. Driving away, changing direction and suggested they tried at The Mill. Owned by one of the big brewery chains, the modern pub was comfortable inside but characterless.
Starving, Suzy had given up caring about surroundings, and the carvery provided a 'roast' never-the-less.

She drove home happy, The Mill's food had been surprisingly tasty. Whether by sheer luck or judgement, Richard's idea had saved the day.

-

Suzy dropped several hints throughout the week of needing help to bring items down from her mother's loft at the weekend, but nothing registered. Finally she asked Richard direct.

"I can't suddenly not turn up for work on Saturday," he protested. "I do need proper warning."
She realized he did have a valid point. "Well make sure you're free in two weeks' time," she instructed, thinking of the long weekend she'd booked off.

Driving up to Squirrels Chase, she wondered how her mother had got on staying with Phil, and if he'd managed to find anything of financial use in the old briefcase. She'd packed a roll of strong garden refuse sacks to use when sorting out the paraphernalia and clutter in the loft.

Ellen couldn't wait for Suzy to arrive, having so much to tell her. Soon they were sitting together in the kitchen drinking tea talking about her time away.
Phil and Julia had made a big fuss of her, taking her out and about to lots of places.
"They've invited me back in a couple of weeks' time, Julia's trying to get theatre tickets at the Hetherton."
"What are you going to see?"
"I've forgotten," her mother confessed smiling.
Suzy laughed, it was good to see her mother happy and looking forward once more.

"I'm going to look for big clear plastic storage boxes while we are out shopping today. We can fill them with whatever you wish to keep from the loft, then you can see at a glance what's inside."
Ellen agreed with Suzy's clever idea.

There were none of the boxes to be found in Kirston. It didn't matter, she could pick some up from the big DIY shop at home. With their shopping done and loaded into her car, Suzy suggested 'Polly's'.
"Yes please," Ellen smiled.

Back at Squirrels Chase Suzy left her mother putting away her shopping. "Onwards and upwards," she said pointing to the ceiling, there was plenty to do in the loft.

Despite the dirty conditions, she enjoyed peering into each Pandora's box, curious to see what was inside. Finding old jigsaw puzzles, balls of knitting wool, jam jars, and faded pairs of curtains all packed away in boxes a long time ago. She moved them to the hatch door ready to bring down, then set off exploring again.

Inside a heavy trunk, she found keepsakes her mother had saved from their schooldays. Loading the nostalgic contents into the stronger bags to look through later.

Next, she turned her attention to an old wooden chest of drawers. The deep heavy drawers had seized on their runners and proved a challenge to open. Each drawer was stuffed to capacity with papers, photos, and old celebratory cards. By the time she'd emptied every drawer and filled more bags, the fun of discovering had gone.

Deciding she'd had enough for the day, Suzy began to drop the bags down through the hatch, watching them land below with a heavy thud. She slid the loft-ladder and hatch door back into place before lobbing the bags to the bottom of the staircase. After she'd dragged the bags into the kitchen, her mother helped to stack them in a corner.

"You've certainly earned this," Ellen smiled, handing Suzy a hot mug of tea."

Suzy felt grubby and could taste the dust. "I'll take my tea with me," she said stretching to straighten her back, and heading towards the bathroom.

While Suzy was soaking in the bath Ellen couldn't resist peering inside the bags, inquisitive to know what they contained. She spent a happy hour delving, re-reading the cards before discarding them. She'd kept some photos and cards from Alex, seeing his handwriting had tugged heartstrings. Eventually, when Suzy emerged clean and refreshed, Ellen had gone through most of the bags.

By the time Suzy came down for breakfast, Ellen had sorted through the last of the bags. "To be honest, I've enjoyed going through them. A few memories, but this de cluttering is very satisfying," she said, full of achievement and ready for the next lot.

After her breakfast, Suzy dragged them to the front door in readiness to take to the nearest tip. She was just about to open the door, when the bell rang. George stood on the front step. "Hello George," Suzy smiled "what can I do for you?"

"Is the boss in?"

Suzy called her mother to the door.

"Been busy?" he asked, seeing the bags at the door.

"We're attempting to clear the loft, I'm heading to the tip with this lot later."

"Don't throw anything away," he advised. "You know what they say, 'one man's rubbish is another man's treasure'."

"I don't think there's any treasure here," Suzy laughed.

He insisted on helping, grabbing two bags at a time in each hand. "In the boot?" he called getting near to her car.

Suzy followed in pursuit, carrying a lighter one. "Yes please," she said breathless.

"You open the boot Misses and I'll carry them." It only took him a couple of trips and he finished in minutes.

Ellen stood watching "thank you, that was a great help."

"Anything else you ladies want lifting while I'm here?" George offered.

Ellen and Suzy both answered in unison, but not with the same answer. Suzy had said 'no', not wanting to bother

him any longer. Ellen said 'yes', she was thinking of the boxes Suzy said she'd put by the hatch door ready to bring down. Suzy flashed her mother a glare.
"Come on then," he laughed "where is it?"

Before Suzy could decline further, her mother had him following inside while she explained. Obeying orders, Suzy climbed the ladder and got back into the loft. Handing down each box to George who carried it down, placing it onto the floor. Once again the whole job didn't take long.
"Many hands make light work," Ellen chirped, delighted.
"Thanks again George, sorry you got roped into that," Suzy apologised, giving her mother another scornful look.

"Have you time for one of these?" Ellen asked, offering him first choice from the box of cakes from Polly's tea room. "I can put a couple into a bag if you can't stop." George weakened when he saw the cakes and joined them for a cup of tea in the kitchen. He was too polite to mention he'd only come round to ask if he could change her grass-mowing day. "I could ask my mate to look at your stuff, he'd tell you if you had anything worth selling," George offered, choosing another Eccles cake. "Might be worth thinking about."
He excused himself and got ready to go. "See you every Tuesday, instead of Wednesday if that's alright with you." Ellen saw him to the door, thanked him again and handed over a bag containing the last two pastries. "For your tea," she winked and closed the door behind him.
"I saw that, you floozy," Suzy said, giving her mother a devious smile.

While the ladder was still down, Suzy went back up to do another half hour of sorting. She moved more boxes towards the loft hatch, and wistfully hoped Richard would come with her next week. It was all very well coming up most weekends to sort out her mother's problems, but she missed his company and reminded herself to find somewhere nice for their long weekend together.

-

Intending to call into the DIY place at Datton's Retail Park after work, Suzy forewarned Richard about coming home late. She loved walking around the huge store. Their Homeware department always gave her fresh ideas and inspiration. She was wandering along the decorating section looking at wallpapers when a familiar voice called her name.

"Hello, what are you doing here?" Rachel asked, surprised to bump into her friend.

"I'm supposed to be buying plastic storage boxes but I can't resist having a look round," Suzy replied "and you?"

"I came in to buy a toaster," admitting she loved looking around the place too. "Michael got a hot-cross bun wedged and filled the kitchen with smoke. It's a wonder he didn't burn the house down!" she grumbled.

"Did it wreck the toaster?" Suzy asked.

"It's not white anymore, sort of scorch brown."

"I'm going to pop into that fast-food place next door after this, do you fancy joining me for a burger?" Rachel offered.

"I can't believe you said that, 'Queen Bee' of posh catering eating a burger in there?" Suzy teased.

"I've been in my office all day and somehow missed lunch, I'm so hungry. Anyway I'm not a food snob, cheeky madam," Rachel jessed back. "Go and grab your boxes and we'll meet at the tills."

Being reminded of food made Suzy feel hungry. She loaded the storage boxes into her car and joined Rachel inside queuing for food. "So what completely consumed

your attention at work to override hunger?" she was intrigued to know.
Trying to hide her excitement, Rachel explained she'd been working on a new catering programme, designing it herself. A niche in the hotel market she knew they could fill. When she was happy with it, she'd present the complete package to the corporate bosses.
"Wow Rachel, that's seriously impressive."
"Early days yet and it could be rejected," she said, being realistic and grounding herself.
"Can't really toast your brilliant idea with cans of Coke can we?" Suzy thought for a moment, "oh why not, 'May your idea fly with wings! Cheers!" clinking their cans.
"I know I was starving but this burger's really good," Rachel sounded almost surprised.
"They have lots of practice Rachel, they cook them all day." Suzy chuckled. "Talking of tasty food, Richard and I ate out last Sunday. We'd set off to The White Heart, but ended up eating at The Mill instead," without elaborating the reason. "The Mill's carvery was very good."
Rachel sat thinking for a moment, "somebody spoke about eating at The White Heart recently, now who was it?" she asked herself. "Err, it's gone, forgive me, I have the memory of a goldfish some days."

They both got up to leave. "Ah, wait a minute!" Rachel said, as a thought crossed her mind. "Something I meant to ask, do you fancy a Spa weekend starting twenty fifth of this month? I'm viewing Rowben Court for a wedding, you can come with me if you like, free of charge. I haven't been up there since it's refurbishment. A fabulous place, it has everything."
"Sorry Rachel, that's our long weekend." Suzy replied.

"Never mind, we'll catch up when we both get back," Rachel said leaving.

-

In what seemed like a blink of an eye, the weekend was once again imminent. Suzy was happy, she'd managed to pre-book three days in a small coastal hotel at Shelton-on-sea for their long week end. "Don't forget to book next Friday and Saturday off work, including Monday, it's very important," she'd nagged Richard throughout the week.
"I don't suppose you could help me at 'Mum's' this weekend? Some of the stuff in the loft is too heavy for me to get down," she asked, trying to appeal to his better nature.
"Well leave it up there, you have two brothers who could help, . . if they could be bothered to put themselves out," he mumbled crossly.
Suzy heard every word. "Being horrid doesn't help," she snapped.
"Just saying," he said, making his point, before closing the door, leaving for work.
She wouldn't ask him again.

When Suzy arrived at Squirrels Chase, she could tell by the mischievous expression on her mother's face she was hiding something. "You've been up to something, what is it?" she quizzed playfully.
"Nothing," Ellen answered, looking pleased with herself. "You'll see later," and promptly changed the subject.

It wasn't until Suzy opened the hatch door, she realised why her mother was being coy. All the boxes and bags she'd previously left by the hatch door the week before

had gone. Ellen stood at the foot of the ladder waiting for Suzy's reaction.
"Ah," Suzy said discerning, "and where did that lot go?" she called down.
"It's all in the garage and I've sorted it all out." Her mother shouted back proudly.
"I hope you didn't pester poor George,"
"He offered," Ellen confessed, raising her voice "we thought you'd be pleased."
"I am," Suzy admitted, now there was space to restack. She spent a couple of hours peering into more boxes and moving them towards the hatch. There were piles of books, including the reference ones Matt and Phil had used during their university days.

Suzy came down for a drink and a short rest. She didn't have to move many boxes before being able to taste the dust.
"Did you find any treasure?" her mother asked with optimism.
"Dozens of books, abandoned craft projects, bric-a-brac, and some tarnished metal items," Suzy listed.

There was a knock at the back door. Ellen invited George inside. Suzy gave her mother a questionable look.
"I thought you ladies might need a hand today," he offered kindly. "I've taken the liberty of asking my friend Jack if he'd look at your stuff in the garage. Be a good opportunity tomorrow morning while you're here with your mum," he addressed Suzy, reassuring he wouldn't bring Jack round without her present.
Once again George helped to bring the next load down from the loft and carry it into the garage.

It made sense to let Jack peruse the objects in hope of him finding something of value, helping them to defy the fate of what remained - charity shops or the tip.

Later, Suzy phoned Matt, she needed to ask about his old reference books. He'd been working in Belgium for the past month and only arrived back that morning. After a chat Suzy handed the phone to her mother, watching her smile throughout their long conversation.

-

The two men arrived mid-morning. For some unexplainable reason, Suzy had expected Jack to be a scruffy, cunning wheeler dealer sort of guy. Perhaps she'd watched too many such characters on TV. She was surprised to see a well-dressed man step out of George's van and even more so, by his clear middle class accent when he spoke.

George escorted Jack into the garage, with Ellen and Suzy following behind.

Jack took his time examining the contents of every box. "The commercial law and accountancy reference books are popular with foreign students and craft items always sell," he told Ellen. He was about to dismiss the rest when he spotted the old ATCO lawnmower in the far corner of the garage.

George watched his friend's eyes light up, as only an engineer with a hobby of restoring old machinery would. Jack suddenly lost interest in Ellen's boxes and walked over to the mower.

"How much would you take for this?" he asked, already infatuated.

"That all depends on how much you give this good lady for her clobber, and she'd want a fair price for her antique mower," George said giving Ellen a sly wink. Jack left with more boxes of Ellen's junk than he wanted, but was elated with his purchase of the mower.

"Gosh, that was unexpected," Suzy remarked as they watched the two men drive away in George's loaded van. "That old mower was in the garage when we bought the house, it never got used. God bless George," Ellen praised.

"Did you know about that old mower in there?" Jack asked, as George drove back.

"I might of," he answered.

"You old fox," Jack laughed.

- -

The first thing Suzy planned to do when she got home from work on Monday, was to fetch down the big suitcase from on top of the wardrobe in their bedroom. Once she'd organised dinner, she was free to start packing. In her mind she'd been planning what to take for days. Laying her things inside the case, being careful not to hog too much space. She picked out some clothes from Richard's wardrobe and put them in a neat pile beside the case, knowing he'd choose for himself what to pack.

While she was busy back in the kitchen, items to add to her things-to-take and must-do lists kept popping into her head. She wanted every minute away to be just for them, no work worries for Richard and no problems at Squirrels Chase for her to solve. Tiredness and work had robbed them of close tender moments for far too long, perhaps this weekend they'd start to claim some back.

Richard was aware of Suzy's increasing excitement as the days passed. He'd noted his best clothes alongside the open case, but his mind was consumed by other matters. On Wednesday evening Suzy reminded him about packing, hinting their destination was coastal if it would help.

Early Thursday morning he decided it was time to take the bull-by-the-horns. He felt wretched, his insides had been churning around for days and he felt sick. He sat Suzy down at the kitchen table, holding her hands firmly to keep her still. His serious expression told her bad news would follow.

"I'm sorry Suzy." Taking a deep breath, he started again, "I can't go away this weekend. On Saturday I have to accompany Mr Hyatt the owner of Penns to a meeting in London. I don't expect you to understand, but I really can't go."

Suzy sat in shock for a few moments absorbing his information. "Why didn't you say anything before? You knew I'd booked it? No, Richard, I don't understand!" Suzy's voice got louder as she answered, ending in floods of tears.

Awkwardly he tried to comfort her, but she pushed him away.

"Get your friend to go with you," he added.

"It was for us! Just for us, how could you put Penns first?" she sobbed.

"Until I know what's going on, I can't talk about it, I'm very sorry Suzy," he closed the door and left the house.

Suzy cried until there were no tears left. This was not how she'd envisaged her last day at work before their precious weekend. The realisation of how extremely late she was going to be dawned on her. She wiped her tears away and tried to think of a plausible excuse to give her manager. Blew her nose, took a deep breath and with no

idea of what she was going to say, began to press the numbers. Waiting for the connection, trying hard to assert herself.
"Suzy? Thank god, I was worried," Karen answered not giving her time to speak. "You're never late, is it your Mother?"
Suzy's unwelcome tears returned. She gave a big sniff and tried to control herself "I'm sorry Karen," but before she had a chance to explain, her manager interrupted.
"Don't worry Suzy, do what you need to do. You're off till Tuesday anyway, we'll see you then. Hope it all goes well," and hung up.
Suzy felt empty, she hadn't meant to mislead her manager.

There was no point sitting about any longer, she'd have to get on with the day whether she liked it or not. It was heart wrenching cancelling the hotel, the hotel which she'd taken ages to find. She didn't want to go on her own, what was the point? A wave of self-pity swept over her, . . why was life so difficult?

Upstairs she starred at the case. She didn't want to stay at home or go to her mother's, God knows she'd spent more than enough time there lately. Rachel's Spa offer crossed her mind. The situation was awkward, could she summon up the courage to ask? It was pointless pretending all was well if it wasn't, . . Suzy phoned Rachel.
"Hi Suzy, what's up?" Rachel asked, knowing she wouldn't usually call during working hours.
"I don't suppose your Spa weekend is still on offer?"
"I thought . . " Rachel started to say.
"Please don't ask," Suzy butted in, her lips beginning to tremble.

"Yes it is, give me an hour and I'll phone you back with details," Rachel replied wondering what had gone wrong. Suzy emptied the big case and put it away. She packed her things into the smaller one she used for weekends.

Rachel called back two hours later, apologising for being caught up in a meeting. "Rowben Court is in Netherton, thirty miles from Kirston if you know it," she said. "I can't get away tomorrow until about three-ish, and I have to leave Sunday morning. So would you like to come with me?" Rachel re offered.
Suzy instantly recognised the name of Kirston. "Can I follow you in my car Rachel, then I can call in to see my mother on the way back."
Rachel needed to pop into Elsie's before she left, so they agreed to meet and set off from there.

Suzy was in bed when Richard came home, he barely spoke before crawling into bed. She could smell beer on his breath but didn't comment.

She got up early to make breakfast as usual, they'd always managed to grab a cup of tea together before he left for work. He sat at the kitchen table slowly picking at a slice of toast. She wasn't sure if his silence was due to the drink the night before or something else, but whatever the cause, his face bore all the worries of the world.
Her emotions were still mixed, however Richard's countenance caused her benevolence. "I'll be back Monday," she said quietly, placing his morning mug of hot tea in front of him. She left him to his thoughts and went upstairs to get dressed, if he'd answered she didn't hear.

At three o'clock Suzy arrived outside Elsie's terraced house, surprising herself how easily she'd found it again. Rachel's car was already parked outside, should she wait outside in her car or knock on the door? Unsure if her car was visible from the house Suzy chose to knock.

Rachel invited her in to meet Elsie, who was sat in an armchair just inside the door of a small sitting room. Elsie was exactly as Suzy had pictured, petite in stature with a head of short white curls, a warm friendly motherly smile, sparkly blue eyes, and wearing a floral pinafore apron over her dress.

"This is my friend Suzy," Rachel introduced, "we knew each other when our children were small."

"Pleased to meet you," Elsie said from her chair. "Sit yourself down 'Duck', and have a cup o' tea. Rachel 'Duck', get your friend a cup," Elsie called out.

Rachel handed Suzy a cup of tea complete with saucer, having already anticipated the request.

"And this is Gwen," Elsie said, introducing the woman who was sitting opposite. "Gwen lives a few doors away."

Gwen smiled, she was blonde, pretty and similar in age to Suzy. Gwen finished her tea "I'd better be going. Elsie I'll pop in again Saturday," and stood up ready to go. She turned to face Suzy "Lovely to meet you," she said smiling before leaving the room "I'll see myself out."

"Bye 'Ducks'," Elsie called out, hearing the front door close. "She's an angel, gets me a bit o' shopping when Rachel's away, heart o' gold, do anything for anyone."

Rachel finished washing up the tea things in the kitchen. "We're off now, don't get up, I'll phone you tomorrow," she promised, giving Elsie a goodbye kiss.

"Lovely to meet you and thank you for the tea." Suzy smiled.
"Bye 'Ducks', you girls drive careful now," Elsie called out as they slammed the front door.
Rachel handed Suzy the address, "in case we get parted."

They arrived at Rowben Court before five o'clock, their good timing due to Rachel's knowledge of shortcuts. The hotel was impressive, a former manor house with spectacular grounds. No wonder it was chosen for weddings.
Wheeling her case, she followed Rachel into Reception, standing back while Rachel discussed the booking with the girl manning the desk. Rachel spoke with authority, clearly she held a respected position. A young porter approached to take their luggage.
"Let's have a drink in the lounge," Rachel suggested. The lounge was vast, soft comfortable chairs were dotted in groups around low glass topped tables, heavy lined chintz curtains draped from huge floor to ceiling windows.

Suzy flopped down into an armchair near a window. A waitress appeared to take their order "what time may I book your table for dinner Mrs Collins?" she addressed Rachel.
Suzy closed her eyes for a few moments, sinking into the large soft chair. She wanted to kick off her shoes and tuck her legs up underneath her body, probably not unacceptable behaviour here.
Rachel offered to give Suzy a guided tour before dinner. Their luxurious two bedroomed suite was on the second floor, with a comfortable seating area and windows overlooking the grounds. She warned Suzy she'd be tied up with clients and staff most of Saturday. "Will you be

Ok?" she asked concerned, knowing something must have gone terribly wrong for Suzy to cancel her weekend. "You can use the new Spa, sauna, indoor pool, and there's a state of the art gymnasium should you wish to physically punish your body," she smiled.

When Suzy woke up, Rachel had already gone. She'd left a note on the table suggesting Suzy should have breakfast brought up to their room rather than eating alone downstairs. Suzy had never stayed in such a fabulous place or been so spoilt, but deep down her heart ached. She wondered what Richard was doing now. The little hotel by the sea she'd booked wouldn't of been anything like this place, but she would swap it all in a heartbeat for their planned time together.

"Very fetching!" Rachel smiled, pleased she'd found her. Suzy, wearing the provided white towelling robe and slippers, was sitting in the Spa's refreshment lounge reading a menu card.
"I've ordered two 'orange and grapefruit' teas, I think they're just about drinkable," Rachel whispered. "So, what Spa treats have you endured?" confessing to not being a Spa fan. "All that mauling you about, . . I'm not keen."
"The massage was fine, incense and relaxing music, but I did feel daft lying naked with hot stones on my back," Suzy admitted.
Rachel stifled a laugh "and what's next?"
"Maybe I'll sit somewhere with a magazine."
Rachel drained her cup, "I'd better get back, The Orangery is a good place to sit and relax. If we don't catch up before, I'll meet you in there about three o'clock," she said, getting up to leave.

When Rachel had gone, Suzy changed and went back to their room. Laying on her bed she watched television, waiting for the tea and sandwiches she'd ordered to arrive.
Loud knocking on the door woke her up. The waitress carried in a laden tray and placed it on the small table. Suzy surveyed a crisp folded linen serviette, pot of tea for one, fancy garnished sandwiches accompanied by a variety of savoury crisp snacks served in refined china bowls. She wished Richard could see it, feeling alone and beginning to miss him even more. She phoned, first at his office and then home. She'd no idea what to say, she just wanted to hear his voice and know he was OK. There was no reply from either, and then remembered he said he'd be in London.

The Orangery, once a Victorian conservatory, now the modern glass equivalent, ran the length of the south side, housing huge ferns and spectacular colourful orchids. Suzy sat down on one of the upholstered loungers that were dotted about, lifted her legs onto the long chair, closed her eyes and relaxed, absorbing the warmth the sun beamed through.

Rachel arrived carrying two cocktails in tall glasses. She'd changed out of her dark suit into a fine jersey dress and sat down on the lounger next to Suzy. "Ahh," she wearily sighed, sipping her drink, "this feels better."
"All done?" Suzy asked.
"All done, "Rachel replied.
"Thank you for inviting me, this place is amazing. I think I've died and gone to heaven."

"Have you had a good time?" Although Suzy had replied 'fabulous,' Rachel saw a sadness in her friend's eyes. Remaining quiet and not her normal bubbly chatty self.

After a glorious hour of relaxing and flicking through magazines, Rachel said she needed to load her car. She'd so much paraphernalia to take back, and didn't want to have to carry it all in the morning.

"I'll come and give you a hand," Suzy offered. "I've been sat here far too long, I need to get up and walk around or I'll seize up."

Rachel got the young porter to help them carry the heavy boxes to her car. He carried the biggest box, Suzy carried a box of files and Rachel carried books.

"I hope it's not that black Porsche," the porter joked, hinting they wouldn't get everything in the boot.

"Mine's the blue car next to it."

"Phew!" he laughed, staggering under the box's weight.

Suzy stood at the side of Rachel's car while they finished loading.

"Good afternoon," a man in a tailored leather jacket addressed Suzy. She smiled and returned the greeting, wondering why he remained standing behind her, what was he waiting for? Then she noticed car keys in his hand. Feeling foolish, she apologised and moved aside so he could open his car door. He smiled back, got into the Porsche and drove away.

In order to be packed and ready to leave in the morning they decided to dine early. While Rachel was getting herself ready, Suzy phoned Richard, but once again there was no answer from home or his mobile. Was he there, or ignoring her?

She offered to pay for dinner but Rachel refused. "You're my guest," besides it had made a nice change to stay and appreciate it, normally she'd leave as soon as her assignments were complete.
Suzy had always been good company, but this weekend she'd lost her sparkle and the humour that usually had Rachel in fits of laughter.
The wine began to loosen Suzy's tongue. "Richard went to London with his boss this weekend, said it was for an important meeting and he's not answering his phone to me," Suzy revealed, staring down at her food.
Rachel knew she'd need to choose her words with care. "God knows how many occasions I've missed because of meetings. A person who works endless hours running the business usually knows more about the actual company than the boss himself. That's the person he needs at meetings, . . . and Richard probably doesn't know what to say if he's seriously upset you," Rachel soothed.
Everything Rachel said appeared to ring true, accepting her words, she began to feel better.

Suzy recognised the man sitting two tables away from them. "That's the owner of the black Porsche," she whispered, pointing him out to Rachel. Rachel hadn't seen him earlier, she'd been moving boxes around in the boot of her car.
"The one sat with his mother?" Rachel asked.
"She might not be his mother," Suzy cautioned.
"I hope she isn't his wife," Rachel whispered back, having a better view of the elderly lady.
Suzy stifled a wine fuelled giggle. "Talking of 'mothers', why don't you come and meet mine tomorrow? It's not that far out of your way."

Rachel said she'd love to, but couldn't stay long owing to the workload she was taking back with her.

Suzy thought again about the Porsche. "My brother Phil wants a Porsche, have you ever fancied owning an elite sports car Rachel?"

"Not really, I carry too much stuff around for work, sometimes I could do with a van. Isn't car infatuation usually just a 'man thing'?" Rachel queried.

"Probably," Suzy agreed. "My father adored his cars, and Richard spends hours polishing and preening his. So long as it's reliable, I'm happy." Then she corrected herself "although I don't fancy a bright yellow one. I like the colour of Richard's car, it's sort of purplish blue, reminds me of Cadburys chocolate," she described with a smile.

Rachel suddenly felt an intuitive stab. "I'm ready for my bed and we've got driving to do tomorrow," she reminded Suzy.

-

The girls arrived at Squirrels Chase at almost eleven. Before they got out of their cars, Ellen was standing with her front door open ready to invite them inside, the crunch of the gravel having announced their arrival. She loved having visitors. "Come in and make yourselves comfortable, I'll put the kettle on," she welcomed.

Rachel handed Ellen a box of cakes "compliments from Rowben Court."

"I hope you didn't steal them?" Suzy jested.

Rachel gave a sly grin, "I know the head patisserie chef rather well,"

Suzy left her chatting to her mother in the lounge and took over making the tea.

“Thank you both for popping to see me, such a nice surprise,” Ellen said beaming. “Especially as I thought Suzy was away this weekend.”
“I think that’s next weekend,” Rachel lied, hoping to spare Suzy some awkward questions.

Rachel stayed for an hour. Then said her farewells to Ellen, insisting she didn’t come outside in the chilly breeze to see her off. Suzy walked Rachel to her car, thanking her again for their weekend.
Before opening her car door Rachel paused and took her last look around, “this house is lovely,” feeling it’s safe aura. “I’ll phone you towards the end of the week, and re-book that weekend,” she instructed, getting into her car and driving off.

Suzy wouldn’t stay much longer. Unable to catch Richard this morning, she’d left a message on his phone saying she’d be home in the afternoon.
“I’ll go and make some sandwiches for lunch,” Ellen offered, heading to the kitchen.
“I’ll bring the tray,” Suzy said, gathering up the used cups in the lounge.
The phone rang, it was Phil. “Hello?” he said, surprised to hear his sister’s voice.
“Mum’s in the kitchen. Before I call her I need to confess, I gave your old accountancy books to Jack to sell.”
Phil laughed, he’d forgotten about them years ago, and he knew all about Jack and him buying the old ATCO. “How are you getting on clearing the loft, found any treasure?”
“Sadly not and it’s almost clear now. Did you find anything useful in that black case?”

"There's an old bond in Mum's name I'm searching into, but it will only raise a couple of grand at most. If we can't find anything soon Suzy, Squirrels Chase will have to be sold."

Ellen was just about to enter the lounge. In one hand she held a large plate stacked with sandwiches and carried tea plates in the other. She stopped, nudging the door open with her foot . . . and overheard Phil's last sentence

~ 2 ~

Ellen collapsed with a large thump onto the floor, the plates smashed, pieces of china and food lay scattered around her.
"Mum!" Suzy screamed and ran to her aid. Ellen lay unconscious on the floor, blood oozing from a gash on her head. Suzy grabbed a cushion to put under her mother's bleeding head. "Mum! Mum! Mum!" Suzy tried to coax her awake, shaking her gently and frantically rubbing her hands. She ran to the kitchen, soaked a towel in cold water to lay across her mother's forehead. Ellen lay lifeless on the floor.
"Suzy! Suzy!" Phil kept shouting from the handset lying on the floor. Suzy had dropped it when she'd raced to her mother, he'd heard it all happen.
She rushed back and picked up the phone, shouting "Phil, Mum's fallen, she's unconscious, I'm going to call an ambulance, I'll call you back!"

Ellen's head pounded, she could hear strange sounds and voices, she felt sick and sluggish. Slowly she began to open her eyes and struggled to recognise where she was. She knew Suzy was beside her holding her hand and rubbing it gently.
"Hello Mrs Chapman, I'm Dr Pearce," the blurred vision of a person in white announced. Ellen couldn't make sense of it, she didn't know where she was or how she'd got there.

"You're in hospital, you've had a fall, do you remember?" The doctor spoke, peering through an instrument shining light into her eyes. "I'm sending you down for a C T scan."

Ellen closed her eyes, her head throbbed, she just wanted to sleep. Black congealed blood glued hair to her pale skin.

Suzy watched nurses wheel her bed out of the ward. "Go and have a cup of tea," one of them kindly urged. Suzy phoned Phil from the waiting room, passing on all the relevant information. She would stay at the hospital and promised to let him know of any developments and offered to phone Matt.

Feeling shaky, it occurred to her that she hadn't eaten since breakfast and made her way to the hospital's cafeteria on the next floor level. Forcing down tea and a sandwich without tasting either. All she could think about was her mother lying on the floor deathly white, unconscious and bleeding. Suzy's eyes shimmered with unshed tears.

Her phone rang, it was Matt, Phil must have called him. She told him all she could.

"And how are you Suze?" Matt asked.

"Numb, . . it's probably just shock, I'll be ok," she said unconvincing.

"I'm back in Belgium Suze, they called me back yesterday. I'll fly back tomorrow if you need me." He sounded as concerned for her as he did their mother.

"I'm OK Matt, I'll stay with Mum and let you know what happens."

She couldn't say anymore, his phone signal faded away. She went back upstairs to the Waiting Area.

An hour later Suzy was led into a side room which Dr Pearce was using for an office. He was trying to find the cause of Ellen's collapse. "Did she trip? Did she have a shock? Had she been feeling unwell?"
Suzy thought back to just before it happened, when she'd been talking to Phil. Had her mother overheard Phil say the house would need to be sold?
Dr Pearce was sympathetic, whatever the cause Ellen had no memory of it. Her wound had been dressed and nothing more serious had been found. She'd been unconscious too long to be sent home, so as a precaution would be kept in hospital overnight for observation. "Your mother is sleeping now, come back for her tomorrow," the doctor instructed.
Suzy thanked him, she would be glad to get back to Squirrels Chase, already it had been a very long eventful day.

She swept up the mess where her mother had fallen, wiping it over with a wet cloth. The house felt very quiet and empty. She went into her mother's bedroom to find her some clean clothes to wear home, adding night wear and a dressing gown in case she didn't feel like getting dressed.
The house phone rang. It was Phil, he'd phoned the hospital for an update on their mother and been told she was sleeping, and just wanted to let Suzy know. "Would you like me to come over Suzy? I could be there in an hour," he offered, "are you OK on your own?"
Suzy assured him she was alright, she'd phone him tomorrow after she had bought their mother back home.

Suzy sipped her tea, late afternoon had slipped into early evening. She needed to phone Richard, he would be worrying where she was. All weekend she'd been thinking about him, wondering if he was ok, yet he hadn't returned her calls. She felt tired and cynical, would he bother to phone if she never came back? Now she was being silly, of course he'd worry. She phoned him at home, but again there was no answer. It wasn't late, he could be anywhere, visiting his mother or eating at the pub. She left a brief message 'Mum's in hospital, I'm staying here to help, Suzy.'

A large bouquet of roses arrived from Matt while Suzy was eating breakfast.
"Dr. Pearce doesn't start his morning rounds before ten o'clock," the nurse warned Suzy, when she phoned.
Surmising it would be at least another hour on top, before her Mother would be discharged, it gave her time to clean through and pick up some shopping beforehand.

Suzy's second phone call was to her boss Karen. Jackie answered, she was standing in for Karen again. Suzy gave her reason for absence, she'd keep them informed and promised to be back as soon as possible. Today Suzy's priority wasn't her job.

A young Irish nurse took the bag from Suzy. "I'll help Mrs Chapman get ready while you speak to Dr Lynsey. Directing Suzy to a dashing young man who looked about eighteen, perched on a desk reading papers clipped to a board which he kept flipping over.
Dr Lynsey introduced himself and held out his hand to shake. Suzy obliged.
"Mrs Chapman – your mother?"

Suzy nodded."
"Head wound and slight concussion," he read aloud from his list. "Does she live alone?"
"I will be staying with her," Suzy confirmed.
"OK, Paracetamol when necessary, keep the head wound dry for as long as possible. The bruising and any swelling will fade with rest, if you're worried take her to see her own GP, . . any questions?"
Suzy shook her head.

Ellen arrived dressed and being pushed along in a wheelchair by the Irish nurse. Dr Lynsey squatted down to Ellen's seated level. "Mrs Chapman, when you get home I want you to put your feet up and take it easy for a few days." He smiled, shook her hand gently and said goodbye. The nurse handed Suzy their bag, "Would you like to fetch your car, we'll wait for you at door by the Main Entrance."
Ellen was very quiet on the way home. To break the ice Suzy mentioned Matt had sent flowers.

Ellen spent her convalescent days in the lounge with her feet up, pillows to support her back and a soft snuggly blanket to keep her legs warm. She dosed on and off throughout the day, but slept in her own bed at night. Matt and Phil phoned often to check on her progress. Suzy noticed the change in her mother's demeanour and doubted if her fall was the only cause. The chatty happy character with a wicked sense of humour had gone. She felt certain her mother heard Phil say the house would be sold.

Caring for her mother had kept Suzy busy, gobbling up her hours and now days. Lurking at the back of her mind Richard's lack of communication niggled. Not once had he attempted to call her or answer his phone. Worry and irritation began to gnaw. On Wednesday afternoon Suzy phoned Richard's office.

"Good afternoon, Penn's Haulage," Sally answered.

"Can I speak to Richard please," Suzy requested.

"He's not in today, Suzy is that you?" Sally had recognised her voice.

Suzy explained about her mother's fall and not being able to get hold of Richard.

"Ahh, I don't suppose you know, he's off sick." Sally continued "when he accompanied Mr Hyatt to London they must of eaten something dodgy or caught a 'bug'. I've heard they've both been very sick." Lowering her voice to almost a whisper "and the other end, poor things. We've told him not to come in till he's completely better, none of us here want to catch it. I'm so sorry to hear about your mother's fall Suzy," Sally commiserated.

A great surge of relief swept over Suzy as she replaced the handset. Illness! She'd thought of every possible scenario but not that one. No wonder Richard hadn't replied, he was the worst pathetic patient ever when he was ill.

Ellen was feeling better. "Why don't you pop into Kirston tomorrow Suzy, do a bit of shopping," she suggested. "You must be going bonkers being stuck here all this time with me."

"Are you sure you'll be alright?" Suzy asked. Admittedly she was beginning to feel hemmed in.

Her mother had never been one to make the most of illness. Ellen insisted she was fine, she'd been walking around the house to stretch her legs in preference to watching the day time 'tripe' on the TV. Suzy could tell her mother was getting stronger, and in her opinions too.

After supper they settled down together to watch a film on the TV.

Suzy had seen it before. "It's quite good, a bit farfetched and has some clever special effects," trying to interest her mother. "It's about four people with special powers, a bit like Super Man, and Wonder Woman all working together saving our world."

Ellen closed her eyes, dozing and missed most of it. "You watch the end Suzy while I make a drink."

Suzy sprang up "I'll make the tea," she said, not wanting another déjà vu fall episode.

Ellen watched the end of the film, she was intrigued by the character with the gift of foresight and invisibility. The 'film foursome' kept their powers secret in fear of being seized and exploited by dangerous warlords. Ellen thought about the little man creature in the garden, was he being secretive for security? She hadn't decided how she felt about him, all her powers of reason still told her he couldn't exist.

By ten o'clock in the morning, Suzy was ready to leave for Kirston. "Are you sure you'll be OK?," she asked, checking once again.

"Suzy, I'll be fine," Ellen insisted "now go and enjoy some fresh air and freedom."

Having arrived at her mother's place for what Suzy thought would only be a mere hour or two, had turned into almost a week. Already she'd borrowed one of her mother's cardigans, hence a shopping list of her own.

Ellen began to tidy the lounge. She folded the blanket and noticed something colourful tucked behind a cushion and pulled out a scarf. She assumed it was Suzy's and draped it over the banister at the bottom of the stairs. She hadn't been outside since her journey home from hospital, now she was looking forward to a gentle stroll around her garden. Keeping to pathways, she wandered around, breathing in the fresh air and looking at the flowers. In the front garden, sun shone through the canopy of the tall mature trees creating light and shady patterns below on the gravel drive. Ellen sat on the low stone wall absorbing the warmth from the sun, closing her eyes for a few moments enjoying the tranquillity. She began to feel the presence of someone watching her. "Isn't this heaven?" she said aloud. "I know you're there, I can feel your eyes watching me."

Slowly the little man creature manifested into view. He sat a few feet away on one of the bigger rocks at a higher level.

Ellen turned slightly to face him. His skin was gnarled and weathered, his blue grey eyes were piercingly sharp.

"How long have you been here?" she asked. "Years? Decades? Lifetimes?" She had no energy left to be scared or emotional.

He looked straight at her "many lifetimes, eons."

"Then I'll call you Merlin." Thinking about the film she'd watched prompted more questions. "Do you have powers? . . what do you use them for?"

He didn't answer, his face bore a look of disappointment at Ellen's questioning.

"You don't have to speak to me, I'll be gone soon," she said, finally admitting to herself that Squirrels Chase would be sold. The hot tears accumulating in her eyes began to

overspill down her cheeks. She searched for a tissue in the cuff of her sleeve, but couldn't find one so got up to go back inside.
"You'll stay here," the little figure emitted.
"I can't, there's no money," she said sniffing.
"You will stay here." he repeated.
Ellen began to walk back to the house, she stopped and glanced behind her. She wanted to ask him how he knew, but not surprisingly he'd gone.

Sat at her kitchen table with a mug of tea for company, she began to mull things over, trying to make sense. Most of her reasoning accepted he was there, yet at the back of her mind she had the tiniest doubt. Philosophising reasons of belief, she hadn't yet met a vicar who could honestly admit to talking physically to angels, yes they all proclaimed to feel a sense within, that nobody doubted, but how did they know if they were truly there? . . and so called 'Mediums' . . once pooh hooed, but now were gaining respect. She'd read somewhere of some helping police. When did these people realise they could see and talk to spirits, when nobody else could?
Her thoughts only raised more questions, who would believe her phenomenon when she needed more proof for herself.

The fresh air and walk around her garden had cheered her up, she began to feel more like her old self. Also she'd received the first positive news about Squirrels Chase, even if it was from a dodgy mythical source. Ellen went to the bureau in the hall. She took out her sketch of the little man creature and wrote above it 'Merlin' and replaced it back in the drawer.

Suzy was enjoying her morning in Kirston. She'd successfully purchased everything on the list, including some new garments for herself. She'd been in Polly's for a coffee and bought some of their cakes. Next, she'd call Phil. Preparing herself for a verbal confrontation with his battle-axe secretary, she phoned his office.

"Good morning Mrs Martin," Mrs Finnis addressed in her prim officious voice. "I'll let Mr Chapman know you are on the line," and put her straight through!

"Suzy what's up?" Phil answered.

"What's up with your secretary, she was pleasant to me," Suzy replied with sarcasm.

"You're on her be-nice-to list," he chuckled.

Suzy relayed her suspicion about their mother overhearing. Phil had more or less surmised the same. "She must realise we're all doing our best for her." He was waiting for a cheque from the bond he'd found in the case, it would only help for a while. He remained hopeful something would be found at the house, had Suzy looked in the old bureau?

"I haven't quite finished emptying the loft, fingers crossed," she said. Phil suggested their mother stayed with them for a while, wanting to give Suzy a rest.

"That would be marvellous," mentioning Richard being unwell and not wanting to overstretch the patience of her manager by being off work for much longer.

Phil promised to phone their mother later.

"Thanks Phil, I would really appreciate that." They said their goodbyes.

It was time to head back, she hadn't intended to be away so long.

Suzy was in the kitchen unpacking the shopping when the phone rang. Ellen went to answer it.
Suzy expected it to be Phil, remembering their discussion earlier.
Ellen called out "Suzy, it's for you, it's Richard."
Suzy dashed to the phone, she hadn't spoken to him since their fallout.
"How's your mother?" he asked. They had a long conversation, finishing with how soon before she could come back.
"I expect he's missing you Suzy, perhaps it's time you went home." Ellen said she felt much better and today she'd had a walk around the garden.
"Let's see how you are this evening Mum," Suzy reasoned, although feeling homesick since Richard's call.
"I found your scarf today, I've hung it over the banister, did you see it?"
Suzy was puzzled, she hadn't lost one, but as soon as she saw it, knew it belonged to Rachel. "I'll take it back for her."
She was preparing dinner in the kitchen when Phil phoned and could faintly hear them talking.
"Phil's invited me to stay with him and Julia for a few days."
"Would you like to go?" Suzy enquired.
Ellen had agreed to stay. Phil arranged to pick her up as before, after he'd finished work the next day.
They both knew she'd only accepted so Suzy could return home without worrying.

Suzy packed her things after their evening meal, she was looking forward to going home to Richard and sleeping in her own bed.

She took a tray of tea into the lounge where her mother was watching TV, and sat down with her to watch the News.

Ellen decided to tell Suzy about Merlin. "I want to tell you about a little creature I've seen in the garden. It will sound ridiculous, but I assure you I'm quite sane."

Suzy was expecting her mother to describe a weird bug or some sort of vermin. Having one eye on the TV, she was only half listening to what her mother was saying. By the time Ellen had described Merlin, she had Suzy's full attention.

Seeing the expression of shock and disbelief on Suzy's face, Ellen stopped speaking.

Suzy swallowed hard, her forehead wrinkled into a frown and her mind raced. Had all this anxiety affected her mother's mental state? Whatever her mother thought she saw definitely wasn't plausible. Suzy gave a false smile and said she would look out for him.

Ellen knew she hadn't believed a word and probably thought her mother was deranged, . . and who could blame her? What on earth had possessed her to mention it in the first place? Her only option was never to speak about Merlin again.

The next morning Suzy phoned Richard early, hoping to catch him before he left for work, but there was no answer. Maybe he was in the bathroom with the water running and couldn't hear, so left a message on his phone to say she was coming home later that day. She needed to satisfy herself that her mother was OK, what had she been talking about last night? Had the film her mother dosed through inspired hallucinations? Deciding to keep an eye on her during the morning and leave at lunchtime.

Her mother appeared fine, rational and bright as a button, whatever 'that' was, had passed.
Ellen insisted Suzy should drive home after breakfast, reminding her Phil would be picking her up late afternoon anyway.
It seemed pointless to disagree, her mother was right and she really did want to go home. Having said their goodbyes, each promised to phone during the week.

Making good time driving back, Suzy planned to return Rachel's scarf on route. Elsie's house wasn't far from Suzy's road home and knowing Rachel popped in most days, seemed the most logical way to do it.
She pulled up outside Elsie's house, folded the scarf and got out of her car. Turning round to shut Elsie's gate, Suzy thought she saw a car the same colour as Richard's parked further ahead.
"Come in Ducks," Elsie persuaded, recognising Suzy at her door.
Suzy stepped inside, declining the offer of tea saying she needed to get home. She explained about her mother finding Rachel's scarf.
"Oh my lord, the poor lady, is she alright?" Elsie sympathised. "Come ere Ducks," Elsie pulled Suzy towards her, giving her a hug "must have given you such a fright."
Suzy handed over the scarf.
"She's gone up to town, gone to show her boss this idea she's had, bless her. I'll see she gets this. Bye Ducks," Elsie said, waving the scarf and closing the door.
When Suzy turned to walk back to her car, the purpleyblue car drove off. It looked like Richard's but of course it couldn't be, he was at work. Now who was imagining things? Suzy smiled to herself.

Back at home, she phoned her workplace to say she would be in tomorrow morning. Her manager Karen answered, and expressed how extremely pleased she'd be to have her back. Suzy wondered what must be happening at work.

-

First thing in the morning, Suzy called into her manager's office. Two new, very attractive young girls were standing by Karen's desk. Karen introduced Suzy to Miss Lucy Besselton and Miss Carol Dobson, explaining they would be spending time learning about the work in each department."

Suzy smiled and said "hello."

Before she could say anything more, Karen handed the girls some papers and dispatched them swiftly away to work with other colleagues, closing the door firmly behind them. "As if I haven't got enough to do!" she said irritated. "Mr Walters, the new 'Head of Management' clearly wants to make a name for himself. He keeps proposing new ideas, and this is his latest brainchild," Karen huffed. "His scheme, which he announced during our last committee meeting, is to have two candidates trained adequately enough in all departments to cover absence, maternity leave etc. Says it would ease pressure and stop short term employment."

Suzy thought this was a brilliant idea if it was given half a chance, but hearing Karen's attitude didn't want to say so. The atmosphere in her office was definitely frosty. "Of course it won't work" she snapped "not with those airheads, they haven't got a clue between them!"

Karen calmed down, apologised for her outburst and remembering being told about a fall, asked after Suzy's mother.

If Suzy wanted to make any significant progress through the workload which had been piling up during her absence, she would need to work through her lunch hour. It wouldn't be the first time she'd eaten her sandwiches at her desk. She slipped out to pay a quick visit to the coffee machine in the corridor.

One of the new girls stood at the machine with three older male colleagues offering to help her. Lucy, the prettiest one with long blonde hair almost down to her waist, and long legs up to her armpits, appeared to be helpless, while the men fell over themselves to assist. Suzy smiled to herself, this blatant male adoration possibly had some significance with Karen's unfriendly attitude towards the girls.

Lucy's long scarlet nails unmissable, as she carried the tray of coffees. Two of the men rushed to open the door for her to pass through.

The next time Suzy caught sight of the girls, they were standing by the photocopier talking. She went over to ask how they were getting on. Carol answered tactfully about the work they'd been doing. Suzy deduced it wasn't the training Mr Walters had intended the girls to receive. Sadly it had only taken two pretty young girls to ruffle staid office feathers. She knew Lucy and Carol would just have to stick it out and prove their worth.

-

"Where's your friend today?" Suzy asked Carol, when she passed her on the stairs Thursday morning.

"Mrs West has sent her to work in Planning," Carol replied. "She's been there since Wednesday."

When Suzy delivered some folders to Karen's office, she met Jackie. She was holding the fort while Karen was

at a meeting. "What do you think of our new young ladies?" Jackie asked.
Lowering her voice, Suzy asked why had Karen taken against them.
"I'm not sure, but according to the office grapevine, last Tuesday Karen walked into Mr Harward's office and found the blonde one eating her lunch with him. Seems our manager took a dim view of the situation, and when she saw the girl pass a written message to him, well? I think that's when she banished her upstairs to 'Planning'," Jackie explained.
"I wonder why Mr Harward would invite the girl into his office? Very strange, that's not like him is it?" Suzy queried.
"No," Jackie agreed. "He's very quiet and usually keeps himself to himself."
Suzy walked back to her desk puzzled. Mr Harward had always been kind, helpful and a total gentleman. She refused to believe anything untoward against him.

Carol came into Suzy's office, struggling to carry a heavy box of files. "Hello Mrs Martin, where would you like me to put these?"
Suzy took it from her and plonked it down with a thud on her desk. "Carol would you like a coffee?" she offered on impulse.
Carol smiled "Yes please, I haven't had my break yet," glancing nervously at the clock.
Suzy fetched her a chair, "I'll only be a moment," she said, scooting off quickly to the coffee machine. She returned with their drinks and cleared a space to put them down. "I've got some biscuits in here somewhere," peering in a drawer. She found the biscuits and put them on top

of the desk. “Help yourself Carol,” Suzy offered kindly “and relax, Mrs West is in a meeting for at least another hour.”

After a few minutes of general chat, Suzy picked her moment. “So how did Lucy end up in Mr Harward’s office last Tuesday?”

Carol began to explain “it was only our second day here, and nobody had told us where we could eat our packed lunches. It was raining outside, so we asked the gentleman standing behind us at the vending machine where we could go. He noticed Lucy’s name on her badge, . . well I suppose Besselton is unusual. Turns out he was at university with Lucy’s uncle. He kindly said we could use his office.”

“So you were there too?” Suzy asked.

“Yes, but not when Mrs West came in. While Lucy was talking about her uncle, I slipped out to make a phone call. Mr. Harward had lost touch with his friend years ago, so he was pleased to have bumped into Lucy.”

“And Lucy gave him her uncle’s address and phone details?” Suzy said, realising what had actually happened.

“Yes, she wrote it down for him,” Carol replied.

Suzy liked Carol, she was bright, intelligent and appeared to be totally unflappable. “Did you volunteer for this job?”

“Not exactly, when the memo was read out, nobody in my department wanted to do it. I was the youngest and last to join the team, so they put my name forward. I didn’t mind really, I thought it could be an interesting challenge.”

“And Lucy?” Suzy asked.

“You would have to ask her,” Carol answered with tact. She thanked Suzy for her coffee. “I’d better get back before I’m missed.”

Suzy phoned Karen's office to ask if she was back from her meeting. She'd just that minute returned and answered the phone.
Suzy took a deep breath for courage, knowing what was needed to be said. "Can I speak to you about Lucy?"
"Man's best friend?," Karen replied, unable to keep the spite from her voice.
"Mr Harward was at university with Lucy's uncle." Suzy continued bravely. "He recognised the surname on her badge. After discovering the connection, Mr Harwood asked Lucy for his old friend's address and phone number. I just thought you might like to know." Suzy didn't wait for Karen's reply and hung up.

- -

Mr Hunt was extremely pleased with the level of work Lucy was achieving in the short time she'd been in his department. He could see her potential and asked Mr Walters if she became free, he'd like her transferred to Planning on a permanent basis.
Karen was surprised to hear his opinion, perhaps she'd misjudged the girl after all, such was the pressure of her job, and put the matter behind her.

Suzy was looking forward to the weekend, although Richard remained distant. It had been their first big disagreement for years, so she wasn't surprised it was taking him a while to get over it, . . or was he just milking it? Whatever, she was glad to be home and no doubt he'd come round eventually. Gingerly she asked if he had anything planned.
He warned her about another meeting in London coming up. He wasn't sure if it was this weekend or the next, regardless, he'd need to go over the paperwork in

readiness. Giving her a strong hint, she probably wouldn't see much of him during the weekend.
There was no point in her making a fuss, it hadn't helped the last time. Disappointed, but being realistic she could do some serious catching up with jobs indoors, and indulge herself with a very long phone call to Kate, really she'd no reason to mope.

- -

Phil phoned Wednesday evening, he wanted to reassure Suzy their mother was OK. Julia had managed to get tickets for a musical their mother wanted to see. "The local Amateur Dramatics are putting on a show at The Hetherton."
"Are you going?" Suzy asked.
"Not likely," he laughed. "Anyway, as they're going to the Saturday matinee, I thought we'd take Mum back Sunday afternoon, stopping off for lunch on the way. It'll give you another free weekend. Thought I'd let you know early in case you and Richard want to plan something."
Suzy thanked him for stepping in, hoping Julia hadn't minded having their mother all this time.
"To be honest they're both getting on like a house on fire," Phil admitted.
"Give Mum my love," Suzy said before hanging up.
Re-joining Richard in the lounge, she told him about Phil's call, but knew by his expression that work would take precedence. There'd be no point in discussing his over-commitment this side of the London trip, but once he'd returned, Suzy intended to have her say. She couldn't understand why Penns Haulage had such a command on his life, already she could see it was affecting his health.

On Thursday, after what had seemed like an endless day at her desk, Suzy drove home. Her mind wasn't on her driving, in fact it was a miracle she got the car and herself home in one piece.

As she opened the front door, she heard their phone ringing. Dropping her bags on the floor and kicking the door shut behind her, she rushed to answer it.

"Hi Suze, where is she?" Matt asked, referring to their mother.

"Mum's staying with Phil and Julia for a little break." Admitting, she never envisaged their mother would stay away from home this long. "Having a whale-of-a-time by all accounts."

While he had some time off, Matt planned to visit and now typically she wasn't home. "And how are you Suze?" he asked with genuine interest.

They'd always felt close, even if they hadn't seen or spoken to each other for months. It was good to have someone to talk to, Suzy began to unburden her worries.

"If Richard goes away next weekend, why don't you come and stay with me? You can bring me up to date about Mum."

"Oh Matt, I'd love to, but by the time I've driven up to you Saturday, I'd only have a few hours before I'd be planning to drive back again. I don't think I could face another weekend whizzing up and down in my car, sorry."

Matt rescheduled his offer, "I could pick you up when you finish Friday at your workplace and drive you back home Sunday."

"If Richard goes to London, I'll be standing outside, case in hand at five." she promised. With a hint of gilt Suzy

changed her tune, now she hoped Richard would attend the London meeting.
Matt had to go, "see you next Friday Suze."
She said goodbye and hung up, now with her spirits uplifted, went off to find something for dinner.

-

All day Friday Suzy couldn't help clockwatching and was convinced the clock in her office had stopped. She hadn't been able to let Matt know for definite until that morning. Richard had put off telling her, probably knowing she would moan.

Dead on five o'clock she walked out of the building. Before she had time to look around for Matt, a brand new dark blue BMW convertible glided up to her side. She heard the passenger door unlock with a click.
"Hop in then," Matt said smiling. He got out of the car to put her overnight bag in the boot.
"And you wanted me to drive all that way up to your place in my poor little old car, . . and you have this!" rolling her eyes in a pretend huff.
"I'm sorry Suze, I wasn't thinking. Pub or take away?" Matt asked as he drove off.
"Whatever, I'll leave it up to you," she said, slipping off her shoes, appreciating not having to drive home through the busy rush hour traffic.
Matt drove to The Feathers, an old coaching inn ten minutes' drive away from his flat. Not a big place but knew from experience they served good home cooked food. After they'd eaten Matt drove on to his flat.
Suzy hadn't been there before and was looking forward to seeing inside.

It certainly had the Wow factor, which wasn't surprising knowing of his high powered job and no doubt matching

salary. Everything appeared brand new and looked newly decorated.
"The builders only left a month ago, I had the whole place gutted. Look," he said, closing the blinds in the lounge with a remote.
"You have electric blinds?"
"Why not?" he grinned.
Suzy put her things in the guest bedroom before going on a tour of discovery around the spacious apartment.

Matt opened a bottle of wine and poured the rich red liquid into two large wine glasses. They sat on Matt's bespoke grey soft corduroy covered settee, it's wide shape following along a curved wall in the lounge area.
"You have a very beautiful home," she told him.
He'd enjoyed watching her reactions as she peeked into every room and cupboard, but now his smile faded.
"It's not a home Suze, there's something missing."
"Missing?" she queried drinking her wine, she certainly couldn't see anything missing.
"Me," he said "I'm never here."
She didn't understand, or know what to say.
"I bought this place ten years ago, since then I've worked nonstop. The day Phil phoned to say you were at a hospital with Mum because she'd had a fall, I looked around me and wondered what was I was doing? In a meeting with powerful men dealing in millions, suddenly none of it made sense. I just wanted to get on a plane home."
"Bless you Matt, it was probably just the shock. Mum's fine," Suzy soothed, although she hadn't forgotten the bit of nonsense of Merlin.
Matt took another gulp of wine. "I've had enough."
"Retire?" she challenged surprised.

"Not quite, not yet," his smile returned. "I've decided to buy a place down in the West country, somewhere I can settle and stay put."

Wine always made Suzy talkative or giggly, sometimes both. She pictured Matt in designer wellingtons covered in muck and straw getting into his posh car. "Farmer Matt," she giggled.

They chatted into the night about their mother's situation. "We're all trying to do our best for her," Suzy reassured him. She said good night and felt herself almost float to her room to sleep very soundly.

Not surprisingly, Saturday started with a late brunch. Matt took Suzy for a stroll along the river, stopping at a riverside pub to eat.

"Won't you be lonely in the depths of the countryside?" she quizzed.

He smiled, knowing his sister could read him like a book. "Stop fishing," he grinned.

"You're a good catch for those country maidens," she persisted.

"Stop it," he mused, knowing she wouldn't give in unless he told her about Gina.

In the evening he ordered a Chinese take-away. They ate, sprawled out on his long comfortable settee, watching the huge TV set into the lounge wall. He fetched another bottle of wine.

"Definitely not," she protested "I'll have a fruit juice, your wine floored me yesterday."

He returned with a beer for himself and her drink.

"So who is she?" Suzy probed.

"I've known Gina for a few years, we kept bumping into each other at the same venues during conferences. We've spent a couple of holidays together. Last year, she mentioned leaving the business circuit, . . and before you ask, she has her own money."
"Children?" Suzy cross-examined.
Matt shook his head in disbelief at her cheek. "Anyway, we'll see how it goes, so no telling Mum or Phil."

Matt's phone rang, he read the screen and shot off to his bedroom to answer it.
Suzy had a pretty good idea who he was talking to.
"Sorry about that." he said returning.
She held up the palms of her hands towards his face "just feeling the warmth from your inner glow of happiness," she teased.
"Idiot!" he laughed.
He put two wineglasses down on the coffee table "just as well finish this," he said holding a bottle they'd started the night before.
Once again their discussions drifted back to their mother's health. Suzy mentioned the odd conversation she'd had with her recently. "Matt she was quite serious," she said concerned.
"In her defence, I've never known our mother to be wrong," Matt affirmed.
Suzy began to laugh, then collapse hopelessly in giggles.
"What have I said?" he asked, beginning to chuckle, her giggles being infectious.
Tears from laughter ran down her face as she tried to catch her breath to speak. "Are you, Matt the business wonder of the world, telling me you believe in pixies?" Wiping her eyes, trying to suppress her giggles.

Matt started to see the silliness of the situation and topped up her glass chuckling.
"I think I've had more than enough," she laughed "I'm off to my bed.

In the morning Matt packed a case to take with him. "After I've taken you home, I'm going on to spend a few days in Cornwall."
"Looking at properties?" she quizzed.
"Might be," he grinned.
They set off after breakfast, stopping half way for coffee.
Suzy was glad to be home before Richard returned. Matt didn't want to stay once he'd dropped her home, he'd many miles to cover to the West country. He carried Suzy's case to her door. "Thanks for coming Suze."
"Thank you for a wonderful weekend," giving him a peck on the cheek and a hug. "Now go and find that new life. Safe journeys," she called, waving to him as he sped away. She felt privileged he'd shared his private life with her. Of course she wouldn't speak of it, or mention his beautiful car to Richard, . . . no probably best not.

Suzy had been home a couple of hours before she heard Richard's car pull into the drive. She could see him through the lounge window, sitting outside in his car gathering up and sorting paperwork. She watched him put it into a leather document case and lock it in the boot of his car.
She met him at the front door with a hug. "Good journey?"
He nodded, leaving his things in a heap on the hall floor and headed wearily towards the lounge.

When she took him a mug of tea, he was fast asleep in the armchair.
He slept for an hour. She watched him rouse and got up to make him a fresh drink.
"Did you go to your brother's place?" he asked.
"Yes, I had a nice time," she answered simply. Choosing not to mention Matt's fabulous upmarket flat which overlooked the park with the view of the river from her guest bedroom window.
"And your mum?" Richard enquired.
Suzy reminded him she'd been staying with Phil and Julia.
He sat for a moment taking in her news. "I think I'll get in the bath and have an early night," hauling himself slowly out of the chair.
"Look at you," she said worried. "Richard, you can't keep on working like this, you're killing yourself."
"I'm just tired, it was a bit of a drive that's all. I'm not going in till the afternoon tomorrow," he verified, leaving the room.

- -

Ellen was glad to be back home. Phil and Julia had been perfect hosts, taking her out and refusing to let her lift a finger to help. Although there wasn't much she could do in their house, it seemed Julia had a machine for everything.
She'd missed her daily constitutional walk around her garden. Being the beginning of summer, her garden became more colourful each day and George had worked wonders with the lawns, they had never looked so good.

- -

When Suzy walked into her manager's office, Karen was in a flap. "This should have been posted yesterday!"

she cursed, waving a large brown A4 envelope mid-air. The packet bore a red URGENT label on the front.
"I can do it now," Suzy offered. "It's almost my lunch hour. I'll go straight to the Post Office and use their Next-Day service. I'm sure it will be fine," she assured, taking the envelope from Karen's hand.
"You're a star," Karen replied, looking relieved and calming down.
"Call them, tell them it's on its way," Suzy advised, leaving the office.

She had to rush, remembering it was Wednesday and early closing. Just in the nick of time, she squeezed past a cashier about to close the Post Office door and joined a long queue inside. Phew!
The assistant shut the door behind her, turning over the door sign to 'Closed' before returning to help her colleague serve the waiting customers.
"Enjoy the rest of your day," the cashier smiled cheerfully, bolting the door behind Suzy as she left.
Suzy walked over to the Travel Agents opposite to ask for brochures. Without any firm idea of where, or exactly how, the assistant filled a large carrier bag for her to peruse at home.

She couldn't wait to browse through them in the evening and hoped Richard would take an interest, . . well there was always hope! She hadn't realised an important football match, 'important to Richard' was being screened live at his local pub that evening.
"I could be late," he warned, "and I'll eat there, save you cooking."

Suzy took herself happily off to bed with a hot drink in one hand and the heavy bag full of brochures in the other.

-

On Friday morning, before leaving for work, she spread the brochures across the dining room table. She hoped Richard would take the hint and flick through them while she stayed at her mother's during the weekend. Surely there would be something there he'd like. If he didn't want to fly, the cruises covered the world, or the escorted travel destinations catered for their every need or so they claimed

Straight after work, Suzy drove on to Squirrels Chase. She wanted to hear all about the time her mother had spent away and to resume clearing the loft. She needed to find something of significant value up there, it wasn't fair relying on Matt to bankroll their mother's expenses, although he'd never complain.
Her mother looked refreshed and well, clearly staying with Phil and Julia had been a good convalescence.

With her mother describing her cupboards as 'Old Mother Hubbard's' and Suzy wanting to get stuck into loft-sorting, it prompted an early start on Saturday to Kirston. A sandwich board strategically placed near the entrance to the car park announced a new coffee shop had opened. Although early, many shoppers were already wandering about in the morning sunshine. Suzy spotted the new shop ahead at the end of the street. Clearly visible by their big red umbrellas over tables outside and pointed them out to her mother.
"Used to be an Estate Agents," Ellen remembered.

"Let's give it a try, if they're busy we'll sit at one of the tables outside," Suzy suggested.
The new coffee shop was bustling with plenty of curious people like themselves who'd come in to investigate. Large black and white floor tiles gleamed in contrast to the red and black décor inside. A large black and shiny chrome percolating machine hissed and spluttered behind the new glass counter. Muffins and cookies individually wrapped in cellophane were stacked on stainless steel trays underneath.
"Looks very modern," Ellen remarked, looking uncertain.
Suzy laughed "Ultra-modern I'd say, I think Kirston is waking up."
"She's awfully young," Ellen whispered, watching a teenager on the cusp of adolescence wiping tables, smiling as she dispensed trays of coffee to customers. "We used to call these fairy cakes," Ellen criticized, reading the wrapper on her blueberry muffin that accompanied her latte'.
They sat outside, chatting, checking their shopping lists and watching the people go by. "So what's your opinion of Kirston's new coffee shop Mum?"
Ellen considered "Hmm, OK, but they can't compete with Polly's homemade cakes."

Back home and after lunch, Suzy headed for the loft. Ellen had bought a tray of bedding plants in the market which she intended to plant out while Suzy was busy. Suzy was on the first rung of the ladder when her phone rang. She stepped down, prizing the phone out of her jean's pocket. It was Rachel, she was buzzing with excitement.

"Suzy I've got it! I've got it!" she kept repeating in jubilation.
"Got what?" Suzy had to ask.
"Permission to set up my courses at The Bricknell. Mr Kavanagh the head corporate boss loved my idea, he's given me the go-ahead. We have to celebrate," she squealed, all of a tizzy, elated. "Where are you?"
"I'm at Squirrels Chase."
"Oh Suzy, I'm so sorry, how is she?" Rachel began to repose.
"Much better, thank you. Mum's gardening, putting in plants as we speak. We'll have to catch up when I get back, then you can tell me all about it. Well done," congratulating Rachel on her achievement before having to say good bye.
Rachel's fantastic news had been uplifting, now she'd start her search through the dusty cobwebbed attic in a brighter mood. There were only a couple of boxes left, sadly these didn't hold any treasure, just more old magazines and a tatty lampshade.
The last of filled carrier bags were stacked at the far end. She carried most of them to the hatch door. Finding a length of rope and a large canvas bag with stout handles gave her the idea of an easier way to get them down. If the system worked, filling and lowering the bag down to her mother to unload should prove quicker. Ready to try out her idea, she got down from the loft and went to find her mother.

Ellen had finished in the garden and was washing her hands.
"If we do it now, the job could be virtually finished this weekend," Suzy encouraged.

It didn't take long, Suzy filled and lowered the canvas bag, while Ellen emptied it, piling the bags around the floor. The few carrier bags that remained could be brought down another time, Suzy had done enough up there for the day. "We can go through them tomorrow," she said, stacking the bags against a wall in the kitchen. Pleased with their achievement and that her idea had worked.

In the evening they sat together in the lounge resting and watching TV. Suzy mentioned she'd been up to see Matt.

"I'd like to see him settled and stop all that gallivanting abroad," Ellen remarked. "I expect he'll tire of it one day."

Suzy smiled, if only her mother knew how close she was to Matt's future plans. "So how did you get on at Phil and Julia's?" Suzy had wondered if she'd feel comfortable in their modern showcase home.

Julia was known for her regular improvements, frequently changing everything on a whim, . . . something which hadn't gone unnoticed by Ellen.

"Well I told him, all this chopping and changing for no reason, that girl needs a little one to love," her mother said in matter-of-fact manner.

"Did you say you told Phil, his wife needed a baby?" Suzy was aghast!

"Well, not quite in those words, but it's obvious," Ellen defended her opinion.

Suzy was speechless. Poor Julia! Julia and Phil were childless, perhaps not by choice. Suzy scowled at her mother in disbelief. Where was the loving, kind, sensitive woman who'd brought them up insisting 'if you can't say anything nice, better to say nothing at all.' When did she

become the outspoken thoughtless mother-in-law from Hell? "What did Phil say?" Suzy was almost frightened to ask.
"I think he agreed," her mother answered.
This had to be the end of their conversation or she might say something to her mother she'd later regret.

During breakfast Suzy mentioned Rachel's phone call. Relaying the fantastic news of getting her company's backing to set up her courses, a massive achievement in itself. Suzy wasn't sure of the curriculum, but Rachel had personally designed the enterprise. It would take an enormous effort to set up and run, but Suzy knew she'd do it.
Although Ellen had only met Rachel once, she'd taken to her straight away. "I'd like to send her a Congratulations card."
"That's a good idea," Suzy agreed "I'll pop out and get a couple."

While Suzy drove to the corner shop for the cards, Ellen began to sort through the bags from the loft. She tipped out the first one onto the kitchen table. Faded circulars and leaflets, old letters, some unopened slid out. In front of her lay some of the post she'd received during her first year of widowhood. Her stomach lurched, recognising the contents, triggering memories to those terrible days of raw heartache. At that time amid her despair, she'd scooped letters into bags. Her 'out of sight, out of mind' solution for dealing with anything overwhelming helped her get through those painful months. Always intending to relocate them later, when she'd regained her strength. However, having more than enough to cope with raising her family, she'd totally forgotten about putting them up in the loft. Now here in front of her, like bad pennies they'd come back to haunt. Ellen reprimanded herself for being silly, all she needed to do was pick out anything that appeared important, although after all these years doubted she'd find anything. She sifted through ancient bills, receipts and insignificant correspondence. There was nothing worth keeping, and refilled the bag ready to dispose.

By the second bag, she could recognise building societies, banks and insurance company's distinctive logos on their envelopes. Their contents all seemed to be advertisements and promotions, a load of rubbish to her. She became quite blasé, and saw no point in opening the old envelopes of whom she'd no account with. They would just contain more flippin adverts she grumbled. She was sorting through the last bag when she heard the phone ring.

It was Phil, he said they'd be visiting friends of Julia's later that day for lunch. Julia's friends lived in Kirston, so being near they would pop in to see her before they drove home.

Usually she'd feel sad for a while when Suzy went home. After a weekend of her company the house would feel empty, but now she had their visit to look forward to.

Suzy returned with two cards. The first shop didn't have any, so she'd driven on to the next one.

Tactfully she gave her mother first choice, happy to give the other from herself. Ellen made a point of reading through the words, being very particular about their message.

"Phil rang while you were out." Her mother said, repeating the details of his call.

Normally, Suzy would of loved to see them, but after hearing about her mother's insensitive conversation didn't want to stay for what could of been an awkward meeting. She could see her mother had been busy. The last bag remained half sorted on the kitchen table. "Did you find anything interesting?" Suzy asked.
Her mother began to fill the kettle, needing a drink to wash away the taste of dust. Suzy took over the sorting, reading through the old bills etc., again not finding anything useful. She restacked the bags by the backdoor, intending to put them in the dustbin outside before she left.

Hearing her mother mention Phil and Julia going out for Sunday lunch gave her an idea. "Shall we go out for lunch?" She'd passed the Forrester Pub on the way back from the shop and seen hardly any cars in the car park.

Getting there early paid off, but while they waited for their food to be served the pub started to fill.
Their roast dinners had been hot, delicious and plentiful. Ellen puffed, saying she was so full, she couldn't eat another morsel. The noise level rose as the pub became full of happy diners. They left, preferring to enjoy a cup of tea at home in quieter surroundings.

Back home in her lounge, Ellen sat on the settee with her feet up and could feel her eyes closing.
Suzy brought her tea and the Sunday papers. While her mother relaxed, she gathered her things together, getting ready to go. "Don't get up, stay and have a rest before Phil and Julia arrive," she insisted, giving her mother a kiss goodbye. "Give them my love, I'll phone you later in the week," Suzy promised closing the door.

Ellen woke with a start, goodness knows how long she'd slept. She sat up, squinting to read the time on her watch. Now she'd have to scamper to make herself presentable for her immanent guests. She was just adding a splash of rosewater when she heard their car come into the drive.

Greeting them both at the door with a hug, they followed her inside. Phil carried flowers he'd picked up earlier in the garage shop when he'd stopped for fuel.
"Go and talk to Mum while I make the tea," he told Julia, and escaped to the kitchen. He'd had enough of listening to women chatter, having been doing it for the last three hours. Whilst waiting for the kettle to boil, he noticed the bags by the door.
Julia told Ellen about her friend's beautiful garden which backed onto a river. They had been feeding a family of ducks who'd nested at the bottom of her friend's garden.
Phil walked into the lounge carrying the tray of tea. "Been busy then?" he said, referring to the bags.
Ellen made them laugh as she described how she and Suzy used an old shopping bag on a rope to get them down from the loft. Dismissing their contents as rubbish, and asked if he'd mind putting them in the dustbin before they left.

All too soon the afternoon slipped by and they had to think about leaving. Julia took the tea things back to the kitchen to wash.
Phil found a thick garden sack in a drawer to use for transporting the old fragile bags. Filling them carefully, trying to avoid the puff of dust that rose in the air each time he dropped one inside. Panting for breath, he struggled to carry the heavy sack to the dustbin. No

wonder his mother had asked. The bags disintegrated, spewing out their contents as Phil emptied it. He saw unopened envelopes among the rubbish, what was going on? How could he be expected to find anything positive if Suzy hadn't bothered to open letters? Was this how she'd been searching? Furious, he stirred the rubbish around with his hand and took out several of the unopened envelopes, not a pleasant task in the un fragrant odorous bin. Holding his breath, trying not to breathe, he reached down again and managed to get four more. Without saying a word, threw them into the boot of his car. He would be phoning Suzy later!

Ellen waved goodbye from her front door, it had been lovely to see Phil and Julia again.

- -

Halfway home, Suzy remembered the bags in her mother's kitchen. In her haste to leave, she'd forgotten to put them into the dustbin. She cursed her dreadful memory and wondered if Phil would notice them. The crumbling bags were rather disgusting, perhaps her mother would ask George to do it instead.

A few miles further along, another thought came to mind, she didn't actually know Rachel's home address. With only a vague idea, she'd have to pop in to ask Elsie on her way home.

Suzy was able to park right outside Elsie's little terraced house. She'd hoped to see Rachel's car, but there was no sign of it.

In the distance, parked at the end of Elsie's road, Suzy spotted the car like Richard's. She wondered if he'd come across it when he'd been out driving, and decided to

check the number plate to see if it was a similar year to his when she drove past.
Finding no one at home, Suzy assumed Rachel had taken Elsie out. She posted both cards through the letterbox and returned to her car, with luck she could be home in thirty minutes.
Two lads in a white van suddenly appeared behind her, driving too close to her bumper for comfort. Their music blaring out through the van's open windows. She could see them in her mirror. The one driving hung his arm out of the window to catch the breeze, his mate sat next to him moving to the beat of the loud music. They were just having fun on a hot day, but Suzy wished their vehicle wasn't so perilously close. Thankfully when she turned left, the noisy van carried straight on, it's loud music still thumping away. She calmed down, for a few anxious minutes her heart had been beating like a drum. With the drama of the van, she'd forgotten to check the car.

When she got home the house was empty, so where was Richard this time? She couldn't complain, being the one who'd been away the most recently. No doubt he'd come back when he'd finished what he was doing. Before unpacking she walked into the dining room to see if he'd looked through any of the brochures. Alas they were exactly as she'd left them.

Richard came home an hour later. She greeted him with a kiss, noting no smell of alcohol on his breath so he hadn't been at his local pub.
"Been busy?" she enquired.
He knew she was fishing, "went to see a colleague."
"On a Sunday?" she continued.

He didn't reply, resenting her obvious attempt to check up on him. Suzy sensed him tensing, if she wanted to discuss their holiday, she would have to back off.

- -

Julia noticed Phil was quiet driving back home. She hoped it was only tiredness, although he'd been tetchy of late. This business of saving her mother-in-law's house was beginning to take its toll. She'd enough concerns of her own without Ellen's possible house sale.

At home, Phil threw the unopened letters onto the desk in his study. He felt under pressure, the family were expecting him to solve their mother's financial problems, but as the weeks were passing he was running out of options. He couldn't believe Suzy had been throwing away bank and building society correspondence without bothering to open them. What if one of them held the solution and she'd missed it? His stress levels began to rise. In anger he thumped his fist down hard on his desk and began to dial her number.

Julia walked in, she could tell by his expression something was wrong. "Come on soldier," she said, taking the phone from his hand. "The battle can wait until tomorrow," and gave him the glass of whisky she held for him in her hand.

He knew she wouldn't budge by the defiant look in her eyes. She was right, he followed, closing the door behind him.

- -

In the morning Suzy was up extra early, she wanted to catch Richard before he left for work. "Did you get a chance to look through the brochures?" she asked handing him his breakfast tea.

"No," he answered, concentrating on eating his toast, avoiding eye contact.
"We can't leave it too long Richard, they'll all be booked up."
He stayed quiet.
"Don't you want to go away? Richard, it's you who needs the break and we both deserve a holiday. Anywhere you like," she submitted, running out of words.
He looked at the kitchen clock, grabbed his coat and packed lunch. "I'll see you tonight," he said leaving.
She couldn't fathom what was wrong with him. Why didn't he want to go away? They'd always regarded holidays as a treat in the past.

- -

Rachel phoned, she'd been waiting patiently for Suzy to get home. "Can we meet up for dinner one evening?" She begged.
Suzy knew she was bursting to tell her about her new business venture.
"Wednesday?" Rachel suggested.
"I'd have to OK it with Richard first," Suzy answered.
"Assume yes, unless you hear different." They agreed to meet at seven in the carpark of the White heart, where they could chat in one of the pub's little nooks.
Suzy was just about to hang up, when Rachel spoke again. "Elsie would love to see you. If you've time, why not pop in first and we'll both leave together from there."
Suzy thought for a moment, by the time she'd got something ready for Richard's dinner it could be tight.
"If it's too much of a rush, don't worry, I'll see you at the White Heart's carpark," Rachel added.

- -

"I'm going to have a sit and let my dinner go down," Richard announced heading for the lounge.

"Tea or coffee?" Suzy called out while she finished tidying the kitchen. She couldn't pussyfoot around the subject any longer, if he seemed to be in a good mood, she'd ask. She put their mugs of tea on the coffee table and sat down alongside him. "Holidays," she said with conviction.

Richard didn't respond.

She was just about to repeat the word when the phone rang and got up to answer it. "Hi Phil," taking the phone with her as she walked into the kitchen for privacy.

Richard switched on TV.

"Mum asked me to chuck away those bags from the loft into the dustbin."

"Thanks Phil," Suzy apologised, telling him she'd forgot.

"Suzy, there were unopened letters in them, what's going on? I thought you were checking the stuff!" he said with angst. "Why were they up there anyway?" he fumed.

Suzy remained calm, she didn't want to add to his frustration. In her unruffled manner she began to answer his questions, hoping to pacify. "Mum sorted through those bags while I was out on an errand. I only sorted through half of the last bag. Like Mum, I didn't find anything important, . . . and I opened all the old sealed letters I came across."

Before he could butt in, she continued. "Mum spoke about them while we were having lunch. After Dad died, when she got overwhelmed and swamped by all the correspondence and post, she'd tuck it all in a bag to deal with later. She'd forgotten about putting them up in the loft. Poor Mum, those bags were a sad reminder of that awful time."

"Why didn't she open them before casting them aside to be thrown away?" Phil persisted.
"Mum said, she didn't have accounts with those companies, and their letters she'd opened before were just adverts. I'm sorry Phil, I will personally check the rest thoroughly."
"There's more?" Phil queered.
"Just a few, Mum and I were too tired to do anymore last Sunday."
Phil felt humbled, he'd jumped in with his big verbal feet. Suzy's explanation had brought him from up-in-the-air with temper, back to Earth with a shameful thump. Now he understood the situation and apologised, reasoning he'd had a lot on his mind of late."
Remembering what their mother had said, Suzy sympathized, her forgiveness assured.

By the time Suzy returned to the lounge, Richard was half asleep dozing in his chair. There would be no point in trying to talk to him about holidays now, she'd missed the moment, . . . and besides Phil's call had quite taken the wind out of her sails.

- -

On Tuesday afternoon, two of Phil's clients cancelled their appointments at the last minute. Mrs Finnis adjusted her records and prepared to bill them for unscheduled cancelations. 'Owing to lack of data, still waiting for documents to arrive by post', she informed him, giving their reasons for cancelling.
"It happens," he said philosophically, leaning back in his chair. "No charge, Mrs Finnis."
"If you're quite sure Mr Chapman," pursing her lips tightly together as if the loss would painfully affect her own finances.

Phil decided to finish for the day, instructing Mrs Finnis to call him at home should any emergencies arise.

At home Phil made himself a coffee and took it into his study. He wanted to look through the letters he'd rescued from his mother's bin. Julia was out, so he could analyse them in peace. He sat looking down at the eleven envelopes on his desk.

He didn't want to admit his mother and Suzy were right, but the contents didn't appear to have any importance whatsoever, . . . yet he had a gut feeling the answer was staring at him. He read them over and over again. The dates did correspond with his mother's early years of widowhood, now he wished he'd read them before firing both barrels at Suzy.

Although all advertising bumf, three of the letters were from Chambers and West building society. He wondered if that amount was significant. His mother had said she'd no account with them, so was it just coincidence?

He was sitting staring at them blankly when Julia arrived home. She popped her head around his study door, "Home early?" she queried.

"Obviously," he said, without taking his eyes off the letters.

"Oooh, has Mrs Finnis sent you home for being miserable?" she joked, trying to lighten his mood. Julia could see whatever was causing his anguish lay before him. "OK Mr Grimnasty, what's all this then?" casting her eyes over the papers on his desk.

"You wouldn't understand," he said looking fed up.

"Probably not, unless you explain," utilizing her stubborn streak.

Phil put her in the picture, including his unfortunate thorny phone call to Suzy. He decided to fetch the rest of the bags from mother's loft. If he'd no personal appointments with clients tomorrow, he would go then.

-

Mrs Finnis checked the diary. His only appointment was at three and he promised to be back in time.
Phil phoned his mother to let her know he was on his way, forewarning her of the reason.

The florist shop situated on the corner was his first port of call. Acting on Julia's advice he sent Suzy a bouquet, accepting the florist's choice of flowers for suitability. He wrote on the accompanying card -

'Sometimes I'm right, sometimes I'm wrong,
this time I'm very sorry.'
Phil xx

Still following his wife's advice, asked the florist to make a large bouquet for his mother incorporating plenty of colour. He looked around for the blue flowers he knew Julia loved, his pitiful knowledge of flowers didn't stretch to knowing their names. "A bunch of those," he requested, pointing to the Irises. Carrying the flowers back to his car, knew he'd have to get a move on.

Ellen was thrilled with her flowers. He didn't reveal his true reasons for buying them, or why he'd made a special trip. It could still turn out to be a wild goose chase.
George was sitting in Ellen's kitchen drinking tea when Phil arrived. She'd asked him to help, not fancying getting covered in dust and bits that always seem to float down from the open hatchway.

Under Ellen's instruction, the two men soon had the situation under control. George offered to go up inside the loft to locate the bags, leaving Phil to receive them from above.

George's help had been a Godsend and insisting he was glad to help refused payment. He stood outside brushing off the dust and cobwebs from his clothes while Ellen said goodbye to Phil.

"Sorry it's been short n' sweet, but if I'm late back Mrs Finnis will kill me," he laughed giving her a goodbye hug. George helped to carry the bags to Phil's car, knotting them inside strong refuse-sacks before loading them into the boot.

"Thanks George. Couldn't have done it in time without your help, really appreciated it," Phil praised and tucked two folded twenty pound notes into George's top pocket. Before George could object, Phil got into his car, started the engine and was gone.

It was fiddly trying to retrieve the cash from his small top pocket, the opening being tight for man size fingers.

"Well that's a turn up for the books," he said pleasantly surprised, poking the notes back.

"Another cupper?" Ellen offered.

"Don't mind if I do, that dust gets right down your throat," following her back inside to the kitchen.

Phil made it back to his office with only minutes to spare.

Mrs Finnis handed him the client's files with a clothes brush on top.

"What's that for?" he asked.

"Cobwebs," she said, leaving the room.

Phil made a dash to the cloakroom. Sure enough, grey webs stretched across the back of his hair and jacket. The thought of spiders made him shudder and took off his jacket to shake thoroughly before returning to his desk.

- -

For all intents and purposes, Richard was happy with Suzy going out with Rachel after work. "Don't worry about food for me, I'll get fish and chips on my way home," he offered.
She suspected he was grateful of another evening he could get out of discussing holidays.

Now able to be earlier, Suzy could call in to see Elsie as Rachel had suggested. A few houses from Elsie's, Suzy could see a gap along the pavement big enough to park. Rachel's car was already parked outside. Suzy manoeuvred into the space, switched off the engine and got ready to get out. Her handbag had fallen into the front passenger foot well. She reached over to retrieve it, catching the handle on the gearstick. It sprang open, emptying half of the contents onto the floor. "What on earth am I doing?" she chuckled, seeing the funny side of the situation as she wriggled and stretched almost prostrate across the passenger seat trying to retrieve her things. Her cheeks flushed red with effort and she realised it would have been far easier to get out and recover them via opening the front passenger door. She sat up and glanced into the mirror on the driver's sunshade, rectifying the hair flopped across her face with her hand. Checking for traffic before getting out, she paused, suddenly recognising the figure ahead. He walked to his car, got in and drove away. It was Richard! A shudder of unease ran through her body. When he hadn't arrived home before she'd left, she assumed he was still working. Now she was perilously close to admitting he'd been here. . . and not for the first time. Unsettled Suzy started her engine and headed for the White Heart's car park.

Rachel entered the carpark just after her. They found a table in a corner, perfect to eat and chat amongst themselves undisturbed. Rachel did all the talking, describing every aspect of her new venture. If it became a huge success, it could be a major step up in her career. Although Suzy had listened intently to every word and hopefully reacted appropriately, she retained very little of the conversation. Her mind kept wandering, what was Richard doing in Leake Road?

- -

When Phil got home he carried the two heavy bags to his study, anticipating making a start on them after he and Julia had eaten. He was in her 'good books'. Not only was she delighted with her flowers, she'd been impressed he'd remembered her love of blue Irises. He assumed she'd be quite happy watching TV all evening, leaving him free to delve into the bags. There were four bags altogether, inside the tied refuse-sacks. Phil emptied the first one onto his desk. The thought of failure was daunting, but at the same time if he was going to find anything, it could be among this lot.

Two hours later Julia went to see how he was getting on. She found him face in hands, leant on elbows, looking lost and starring at the piles of letters in front of him.
"Penny for them?" she offered.
"I'm not sure I know what I'm looking for anymore," he replied despondent.

"What you need my Darling is a pair of 'new eyes'," drawing another chair up beside him.
"What I need is a miracle," he sighed.
"Ah, they take a little bit longer. Now, how far have you got?" she said taking over.
He'd removed the trash and segregated the 'plausible' into piles.
"Observations? Anything jumped out at you? Anything unusual?" she questioned.
Phil looked reluctant, he'd had a long day and was about to give in.
"Come on," she insisted with determination.
Phil explained his sorting. The biggest pile spanning a few years later than the rest, mostly dating March and June. "Oh Lord, Dad's birthday and he died in June." Reflecting for a moment in silence, understanding the times his mother hadn't coped.

Julia picked up the pile nearest to her, casting shrewd eyes over the pages. Working her way through, ending with the 'later' pile. "Now why would Chambers and West repeatedly send to your mother?" she thought aloud, rereading the pages. "Ooh, because she's a customer!" Julia announced triumphantly. "This looks like her account number." Admittedly it was only to be found printed on one page, but he'd missed it.

"Mum was certain she didn't have any accounts with these people, in fact she insisted." he said baffled.
"She probably didn't recognise the name, perhaps they amalgamated or were taken over," offering an explanation. There was no guarantee of any money languishing in an old account, but now he had something positive to chase. Liberated from gloom, he kissed his clever wife. "I'm

shattered, I'll sleep tonight," he said rubbing his eyes and following Julia out of his study.

- -

"I'll make dinner early tonight so we can sit down and go through those brochures," Suzy suggested, sitting next to Richard at breakfast. Once again he appeared to ignore her.

"Did you hear?" she asked, trying not to annoy, he was never at his best first thing. "I said . . "

Before she could say another word, he raised his eyes to meet hers. "Suzy, I don't want to go away, not abroad, not anywhere . . and I don't want to talk about it either!, . . I . . ." He picked up his coat and stormed out, slamming the door behind him.

She was stunned by his outburst. His raised voice sounded more in desperation than temper. She managed to hold back tears, but her head swam with questions. What was going on? Why wouldn't he talk to her anymore? . . What was he hiding? In her heart of hearts she had a sinking feeling she wasn't going to like it. She looked at the kitchen clock, it was time to leave for work. She'd have to talk to him tonight, they couldn't go on like this.

- -

Phil's day at the office usually began with Mrs Finnis bringing him his morning coffee. She would give him a few minutes to read through and absorb the day's schedule and the appointment timetable she'd prepared. Any necessary alterations were discussed when she returned to collect his cup.

Today, her first assignment was different.

"I've got just the job for you," Phil said smiling. "It's a bit of detective work, the investigation of Chambers and

West building society. If you could trace their past forty years of business, take overs, amalgamations etcetera."
"Are we to locate a lost, or dormant account Mr Chapman?" she asked.
"A financial light at the end of the tunnel would be most appreciative, Mrs Finnis." She was the most shrewd woman he knew, nothing got past her natural intuition.
"Could there be a reward?" she enquired with a suspicious glint in her eye.
Phil knew she'd sussed immediately, the job was personally for him.
"The photocopier has been playing up for weeks, I'm sure it needs replacing," she said utilizing the opportunity to her advantage.
"Mrs Finnis," Phil feigned pain "you know how sensitive an accountant is about spending his own money!"
"It's probably not worth mending," she continued stubbornly.
He drew in a deep breath "my wallet feels quite bilious," pretending to wipe his brow.
Mrs Finnis tolerated his humour with her normal lack of diplomacy, shook her head and tutted, walking back to her desk, closing his door.

- -

The bleak misty drizzle Suzy drove through on her way to work matched her mood. Ploughing through assignments with her lack of enthusiasm meant it was going to be a long day. Stuck on a paragraph she'd read through twice and still didn't understand caused her to think of coffee. She left her office and walked down the corridor towards the vending machine, and noticed Carol and Lucy together through an office window. She hadn't

seen or spoken to them for ages and it would be rude to ignore them and not say hello.
Suzy started to open the door. The girls were deep in conversation, talking very quietly and judging by their body language, the subject looked secretive. She didn't want to intrude on their personal confab, so hovered for a moment.
The girls were oblivious to her company and continued in all but a whisper. "Richard Martin?" Lucy gasped, covering her mouth with her hand to muffle her voice. "No, it can't be!" replying to Carol's information.
Suzy stood rooted to the spot, her insides clenched. Were they talking about her, and what did they know about Richard?
The door opened further with a creak, the girls looked round. Now aware of Suzy's presence, both fell silent and looked at each other, concerned to how much she'd overheard.
"I just popped in to say hello," Suzy said, wearing a nervous smile as she approached them. "What were you talking about?"
"We can't tell you," Lucy replied, looking sheepish and feeling very awkward.
"I heard my husband's name," Suzy struggled to say.
"She'll find out soon enough," Lucy pleaded.
"Find out what?" Suzy's voice trembled, her facial colour began to pale.
Lucy shut the door and lingered nearby to stand guard.
Suzy leant against a desk, grateful for its support, her legs had turned to jelly.
Carol spoke in a hushed tone "Penns may close."
Suzy gasped "how do you know?"

"My uncle works for Windslow Haulage down in Whitton, he's heard the rumour they're taking over Penns. His brother-in-law drives for Penns, so he warned him last night. Nothing's been officially said or made public, it could fall through but that's unlikely."

Suzy was shocked to the core.

"You didn't know?" Carol was surprised.

"No," Suzy answered, still shaken. Why hadn't Richard said anything, all these months he'd kept it to himself, why?

Carol read her mind, "Mr Martin couldn't tell you, it's obvious."

It wasn't obvious to Suzy.

"There's several people here who's family work at Penns. One way or another, if they knew you had a connection or information, your job here would become intolerable.

"What about Richard?" She wanted to know why his name was mentioned.

"He's spoken to some of the older men. I think he's trying to secure jobs, sort out redundancies if it happens," Carol answered. "Mrs Martin, it's seriously important you don't say a word."

"Of course I won't, I promise , . . . thank you." Suzy fell silent, still phased by the information.

Lucy handed Suzy the tea she held, "have this Mrs Martin, I haven't touched it. We'll leave you to have a moment to yourself."

The girls slipped out of the empty office. Suzy stayed there for a minute and sipped the tea, struggling to untangle her thoughts. Poor Richard had been carrying that knowledge and worry all this time. His past inconsistencies and bad moods fell into place.

She wanted to hug him, tell him she knew, but of course she couldn't for the reasons the girls had given. Also because he didn't want her to know. Whether she liked it or not, she'd have to wait for him to tell her himself. He'd certainly kept his cards close to his chest.

She left the office and continued on her way to the vending machine. Lucy's kindness had been touching, but the machine's version of tea was an acquired taste. The coffee wasn't much better, but now Suzy needed reviving. Her doleful mood began to lift, the thought of Richard wanting to protect her was accompanied by an immense surge of relief, . . she was cherished after all.

- -

"Any developments on Chambers and West?" Julia asked during dinner.

"I've got the best man on the job," Phil replied.

"Mrs Finnis?" Julia asked knowingly.

"Mrs Finnis." He smiled, aware she'd uncover every detail in her pedantic way, and probably have it itemized and ready for him by morning.

"She spoils you," Julia teased.

"Not without cost."

"Really?" Julia was curious.

"She wants a new photocopier for the office! I've warned her not to use those words in front of me, she knows they make me come over all unnecessary." He started to mop his brow with his handkerchief feigning heat.

"What words?" she asked.

"Spending money!"

Julia started to laugh "and let her order a decent one," supporting Mrs Finnis.

"Don't you start," he mocked. "I can feel the cash already sliding from my wallet!"

As Phil predicted, first thing in the morning Mrs Finnis stood before him ready to present the entire history of the Chambers and West building society. "The details of that building society you requested Mr Chapman," handing it to him. "Sir James Robert Pashley started the bank for merchants in 1822, it's rather interesting," she said watching Phil flip through the first few pages, before returning to her desk to resume her usual work.
Phil flicked through, noting down the changes of the company as it progressed over recent years. Amalgamation and two take-overs had resulted in complete name changes during their past thirty years.
He planned to return to Squirrels Chase at the weekend, somewhere in that house documents lay waiting to be discovered.

- -

Julia already had previous plans, joining two friends for a Spa weekend. A timely opportunity for Phil to spend the weekend searching. It would be strange staying on his own at Squirrels Chase with his mother, something he hadn't done since his student days.

Ellen fussed and fluttered about preparing the spare bedroom. It had been so long since she had either of her sons back home to stay.

Phil arrived laden, Julia had packed a large box brimming full with food. She didn't want Ellen tiring herself out waiting on him, as she guessed she might.
He took his overnight bag upstairs into the spare room, the same room Suzy usually used. The decor and furniture had changed over time, but like his sister he could shut his eyes and feel the nostalgic memories flood back. He walked into the adjacent bedroom that had once been his

own. The posters and dartboard had left the walls many years ago, but the same view from the window remained. Standing, looking down the garden took him back.
"Phil!" Ellen shouted up the stairs "I've made tea."
Her voice broke his reminiscing, drawing him instantly back. "On my way," he called.

During their refreshments, he told her about finding details of a building society account. "I recon it's here somewhere Mum, any ideas?"
Ellen shook her head, to be honest she wasn't sure what he was looking for.
"Mum, would you mind if I searched through Dad's old bureaux?"
Ellen nodded agreement and followed him out to the hall. They both stood looking at the old dark wooden writing cabinet.
"Where did Dad get it from?"
"I'm not sure, it's possible it came with the house," she couldn't honestly remember.
Phil knew nothing about antiques, but assumed it's age made it valuable. Perhaps they should get it valued in case the financial need should arise.
The key to the bureaux was always left in the top lock of the closed sloped lid. Four deep drawers underneath, each bore two swagged brass handles and a central brass keyhole.
He could remember his father sitting at the desk writing letters and sorting out orders. His father didn't have an office, just the big old bureaux stood in a corner of the lounge. Phil couldn't recall when it was moved into the hall. It must of been quite a job as this solid lump of furniture weighed a ton.

As a young boy he'd been fascinated by the small drawers and cubbyholes that were revealed when the lid was opened down. Finding only paper clips, stamps and elastic bands inside most of them, his early interest soon waned.

"Some bureaux's have secret drawers, did Dad ever find one?"

"He never really spoke about it, just used it to work on," Ellen said, hunching her shoulders.

Phil's curiosity increased, that was something else he could look out for.

To make sure nothing had slipped down inside, he would remove the large main drawers. Beginning at the top, he took out the first one and placed it on the hall table nearby.

Ellen only used the top drawer. "I keep receipts in here," she said taking out an envelope folder, not mentioning the particulars she'd written about Merlin within.

He scrabbled among the rest of its contents. An address book, Ellen's current diary where she listed appointments and bill payments. Finding nothing of interest, he moved on to the next drawer down.

This one contained an old family photo album, a handful of school reports and the family's old medical cards. Once again nothing special.

Ellen sat, reading out snippets from the old school reports to Phil while he continued his search. "Has no interest in figures, would rather play football, . . could do better."

"Who wrote that?" he asked.

"Mr Doyle, your maths teacher," she laughed.

"He never liked me and I never understood half of what he was talking about."

"That's good coming from an accountant," Ellen said with a grin.
Phil replaced the top two drawers. The next two down were locked.

He unlocked the sloped lid at the front and took out the key. Open, it revealed the bank of small drawers inside. at the back of the desk. One by one Phil took them out for inspection, hoping to find a secret opening somewhere. "I guess you have to know where to look."
The idea of a secret compartment aroused Ellen's curiosity and she joined in the hunt.
Under the middle cubby hole at the back, was a small raised wooden block with horizontal grooves carved out for pens, and housing a china inkwell at either end. "Filling those inkwells would of been awkward, do you think they come out?" she asked intrigued.
Grasping it's small central ivory ball shaped knob, Phil was able to lift out the entire block. He peered down into the gap. "I think we've found a hidden space." Sure enough, the gap underneath was much deeper.
"Any treasure?" Ellen asked with excitement.
Phil felt around inside with his fingers. He took out three old rusty pen nibs and a tarnished silver charm, handing it to Ellen.
"I think it's a cat," she said looking at the black object. "It may be lucky, we must each have a wish before putting it back."
"OK, one wish," he smiled, returning it and closing the lid. He thought they were being silly, but there again they really did need some luck.

He unlocked the third big drawer down. Inside lay two faded wedding card telegrams with his parent's marriage certificate tucked inside one.
Phil's optimism was beginning to wane as he unlocked the last drawer. Opening it slowly, praying it wouldn't be empty. To his relief, he could see some old dog-eared A4 size envelope folders inside.
Ellen couldn't bare the anguish and went off to busy herself.
He knelt down and carefully lifted out the bottom drawer, tipping it out onto the floor. Checking the space behind for anything that may of slipped down. Full of trepidation he began to peer into the folders. The first contained old documents and garage bills from cars his father had owned.
Another held the paperwork from his father's accident. He stuffed it back inside with haste, not wanting his mother to see.
Two off white folders remained. Phil paused for a moment, summoning the courage to continue. Selecting the thickest first. Two brown envelopes addressed to Mrs. E Chapman slid out. One contained a total compilation of her finances upon widowhood, written and signed by Mr Bennington. Phil replaced the contents to study later. Inside the next brown envelope was a culmination of financial settlements. Mr Bennington had enclosed a personal letter with suggestions of a small investment for the future. Again Phil replaced the contents to read later.

He remembered his first boss, the late Mr Bennington with fondness. These two envelopes revealed the work he'd kindly done. Phil sent up a heartfelt 'thank you' heavenwards.

Ellen appeared with tea and biscuits on a small tray. "Are you winning?" she asked, handing it to him.
He was still knelt down beside the folders. "Maybe," putting the tray down alongside him on the floor.
"I'll leave you to it then," and returned to her kitchen.

Phil picked up the last large folder. Pins and needles painfully prickled as he tried to stand on numb legs. He staggered towards the wooden chair nearby, sat down heavily and rubbed his calve muscles.
He pulled out a dark green envelope, it's front embellished by the Watson and Wallace coat of arms. Inside, a glossy brochure advertised their bonds and other investments. An old proposal form fell out, half complete and unsigned. Phil's heart sank. He pushed it back inside, adding it to the other items to read later.
He filled and replaced the drawers, leaving the two big envelope folders on top of the bureaux. Deflated and weary, he'd scrutinize them later on.

After their dinner, Phil dosed on and off in the armchair for most of the evening while Ellen watched her programs. She nudged his arm, waking him with a hot drink before she retired.
"I'll take mine upstairs to bed with me," he said yawning "see you in the morning." On the way he collected the folders, tucked them under his arm and headed upstairs. In bed he skimmed through the pages, but was too tired to properly concentrate and gave up.

Unable to sleep, he tossed and turned. There was something about the green envelope that kept bugging him. It was no use, he switched the light back on, sat up and pulled out the contents, intent on reading every word. An hour later, bleary-eyed, he'd found what he'd been looking for. Two bonds had been taken out, one lump sum of money had been invested for five years, the other for ten. Phil had no recollection of these arrangements, yet he and his mother must have known and agreed the terms at the time. This had to be the result of the guidance given by Mr Bennington. "God bless you Sir," Phil said aloud in gratitude before turning over and going to asleep.

Phil slept soundly, probably the first good night's sleep he'd had in weeks. He reached out for his watch. The bedside cabinet was unfamiliar, and for a split second he wasn't sure where he was. Grasping reality he looked at his watch, surely that couldn't be the time? Slowly he remembered his find. He wouldn't mention anything until he was sure of the outcome, 'counting chickens' and all that. He heard his mother moving about downstairs, it was high time he got himself up and ready.

"Morning, tea or coffee?" Ellen asked when he finally made an appearance. "What would you like for breakfast?" He settled for tea and a slice of toast. He apologised for his bad company, having slept most of the evening and now it felt like half the day had gone.
It didn't matter, she could see he'd been tired. "Did you manage to find what you were looking for?"
He suppressed a smile, not wanting to say anything at this early stage.
"Thank goodness for that," Ellen said looking relieved.
"I haven't said anything," he protested.

"Yes you have, I can tell by your face," looking deep into his eyes. "You have your Dad's eyes Phillip Chapman, and I can read them like a book," she said tenderly.
Her words swamped him for a moment. "Mum, is there anywhere you'd like to go today?" changing the subject and trying to regain his composure.
"You don't have to take me out, I'm just happy to have your company," and gave his arm a gentle squeeze. "I know how hard you all are working to help me at the moment, and how lucky I am to have . . ." Ellen couldn't finish her sentence, her emotions got the better of her.
"Come on, get your coat, or we'll both be sobbing. We'll go out into the countryside, and if I can find them, we'll feed some ducks." He took a few slices of brown bread from her breadbin and put them into a bag.

He drove through villages and along winding country lanes. Ellen was in her glory, seeing farm animals in their fields and taking in the beautiful scenery.
"If I'm not mistaken, the pond's up here," Phil said recognising the area.
The Dog and Duck pub faced the village pond.
"We'd better eat first, this place gets busy at weekends," he advised.
"Have you been here before?"
"It's one of Julia's favourites, a bit of a trek from our place but a nice drive on a sunny day."
Half way through their meal Phil remembered Mr Bennington. "I'd like to propose a toast to Mr Bennington."
"Is he a friend of yours?" Ellen asked.
"He's been a very good friend to us both. "To Mr Bennington!" they toasted, chinking their glasses together.

Before driving back, Phil walked his mother over to the pond.
"I haven't fed ducks for years," she smiled, throwing her bread to a family of swans who'd pushed their way in front.

Back at Squirrels Chase, Phil gathered his things. He wanted to get back and read through the documents. "I'll phone you later to let you know how I get on."
Ellen gave Phil a good bye hug, telling him she'd had a wonderful day and sent her love to Julia, thanking her for the things she'd kindly sent. Standing at her front door Ellen waved until Phil's car sped out of view.

~ 3 ~

The next morning Ellen stood on her gravel drive in front of the raised circular garden. With no questionable regard as to Merlin's existence, she was confident he would appear, . . well, he could read her thoughts, or so it seemed.
She didn't have to wait long, spotting him sitting on the low stone wall. "Phil has found some bonds, so I may be able to stay here." About to turn round to walk back inside, when it dawned on her, . . "but I suppose you knew that."
The little creature sat, patiently waiting for her to finish speaking and her mood to change. Knowing a very different thought would occur to her sooner or later.
"If you know the future, my future," she said getting cross "why didn't you tell me about the bonds instead of letting me, and my family worry all this time? That wasn't very kind or helpful!"
She was about to flounce off in annoyance when another thought surfaced. Realisation painfully hit her square between the eyes and her expression changed. "When Alex left home before his accident, did you know he wouldn't be coming back?"
Merlin looked down without answering.
Ellen stared into Merlin's face through eyes that grew increasingly blurred with tears. "How could you not tell me? . . I could have stopped him, I loved him so much."
Merlin didn't meet her gaze. "To want the impossible is to want for nothing. It gives no comfort to be told the

future, I am not here to change it," he said, in his quiet gravel voice.
"I beg to differ," Ellen said softly, wiping away her falling tears, turning to go back indoors.

- -

Armed with Mrs Finnis's extensive documentation, Phil was able to contact Chambers and West for the redemption of his mother's bonds. He spoke to three people before finally getting through to the correct department. The next person he spoke to introduced herself as Maxine, she listened patiently while he relayed the relevant information to trace the bonds. She listed documents of which they'd require copies. "Plus, a signed letter for his authorisation from Mrs Chapman. We occasionally do random phone calls to check identities," she said, "so please warn your mother of this possibility. Once everything has been successfully processed, Mrs Chapman will receive a statement bearing the final sum. She can advise us of her chosen form of payment." Maxine gave him the name and departmental address to forward his mother's paperwork. Phil thanked her for her help.

He phoned his mother as promised, updating and asking for a letter of authority. "I'll need to enclose it with the documents," and offered to collect it the next day after work."
"I'm not sure what to write, I don't want to put the wrong thing," Ellen expressed concerned.
"Don't worry Mum, I'll help, see you tomorrow," he reassured.

When Mrs Finnis came in with his afternoon tea, Phil handed over his mother's documents and papers to photocopy.

"I'll do my best, but you know that thing isn't working properly," her eyebrows rising up her forehead as she spoke.
"I'm sure you can coax it into action," giving her a wicked grin. He knew he would end up buying a new machine but he'd string her along a little bit longer.

- -

A week later Ellen received confirmation of her bonds being located, plus the final sum she could expect to receive. Forty-nine thousand, give or take a few pounds, reading the letter over and over again in joyful disbelief. She would have been delighted to receive anything. From having nothing, this amount seemed to be a fortune.

Using his accountancy skill Phil had surmised a similar figure, analysing each bond's terms and interest. The original amounts invested weren't large, and the recent poor interest rates had not helped, but it would keep his mother comfortably at Squirrels Chase for some years. She could tell Suzy and Matt herself, he wouldn't want to steal her thunder. All he could do now was wait for their mother to receive her money.

Three weeks later Phil phoned Chambers and West trying to chase them up. Everyone he spoke to was very pleasant, promising to resolve the issue but he was just going round in circles.

By the fourth week he was getting tetchy, his patience worn thin by no apparent reason for them not to dispense the cash.

Mrs Finnis brought in his morning coffee as usual and noticed his countenance consumed with exasperation.
"No luck?" she enquired.

"I'm getting nowhere and no sense from anyone," he growled, grateful for the coffee intermission.
"Would you like me to try?" she offered.
"Feel free," he said, handing her the file. As far as he was concerned, she was welcome.

Phil looked at his watch, surely Mrs Finnis should be bringing in his twelve o'clock cup of tea? She was never late, you could set clocks by her routine. Today his tea was late! He got up to see where she was.
Mrs Finnis was busy speaking on the phone.

"Sorry about that," she said, finally bringing in his tea. "I was talking to my sister, business of course!" she reiterated crisply. "Kitty used to work for one of those big conglomerate building societies. I asked her how Mrs Chapman's cheque could of got stuck in their system."
"And?" Phil asked.
"Informative," she replied "very informative," leaving his office with a determined look on her face.

The afternoon seemed to be dragging, Phil looked up at the clock on the wall. It was time to make an executive decision, 'refreshments!' to boost his flagging spirit. Normally he'd summon Mrs Finnis, but he needed to stretch his legs and walk around.
He opened his office door, Mrs Finnis was at her desk on the phone in full waspish flow. Whoever she was addressing was receiving her professional opinion on their dire capability of serving clients.
"I shall personally contact Mr Sawyer to enlighten him of his company's unacceptable unprofessional mishandling regarding Mrs Chapman's account. If this matter isn't resolved to a satisfactory conclusion within seven working

days, I will forward a detailed written complaint to the county ombudsman! Good day Mr Colman! That should do it," she said aloud to herself, replacing the phone.
"Tea? Mrs Finnis . . and a biscuit?" Phil requested.

He wasn't surprised to receive a phone call five minutes later from Mr Colman.
"Mr Chapman, I have just had a disturbing phone call with one of your staff," he blustered. "Are you aware of a Mrs Finnis?"
"Mr Colman, Sir, we are a small accountancy business who employ efficient staff. Should any member of your team need a kick into action, I have just the woman to do it," Phil said with calm professionalism.
"Quite!" Mr Colman replied, and hung up.

Julia was sitting up in bed reading her book. Phil was lying beside her, awake and waiting for her to turn off the light.
"Did you know Mrs Finnis has a sister?" he said.
Julia heard but continued to read.
"If I had both of them working for me, I could conquer the whole accountancy world," Phil said whimsical.
"Why would you want to do that?" Julia asked, not paying full attention.
"Just saying," he said, twiddling his thumbs.
"Anyway she might be a pussycat, not necessarily like her sister," Julia implied.
Phil suppressed a laugh.
"What have I said now?" Julia asked, watching him grinning.
"Her name's Kitty." He started to laugh.

"You've made that up," Julia protested, playfully hitting him with her book.
"It is Kitty," he said laughing, fending off the blows.

- -

As soon as the mail arrived on Thursday morning Ellen phoned Phil at his office. She was thrilled to bits with the cheque she'd just received. "I thought you'd like to know, and read out the amount to him. Thank you so much Phil for getting that for me. Oh, and could you thank Mr Colman for sending it, his name's on the letter that came with the cheque." Ellen was unaware of the shenanigans Phil had dealt with to get her money.
"Glad you're happy Mum, take care," he said hanging up. Phil relaxed back in his chair, relieved that saga was over. The cheque had arrived three days after Mrs Finnis's curt phone call.

"Mrs Finnis, my mother's received her cheque," he announced when she came in with his coffee.
"Oh that is good news," she affirmed.
"She thinks we ought to thank Mr Colman for sending it," Phil said knowingly winding her up.
Mrs Finnis pursed her lips tightly together "that man doesn't know his arm from his elbow!" she snapped tersely.
Phil grinned, he'd never heard that saying so politely expressed before. "Perhaps you would like to peruse some offers on photocopiers? . . if you have time," Phil suggested with a twinkle in his eye.
Mrs Finnis's irritated expression began to soften "I will Mr Chapman, . . if I get time."

Mid-afternoon Mrs Finnis put through a call from Julia.

"Mrs Finnis, I'm going home early, I'm needed urgently elsewhere."
"Oh dear, nothing serious Mr Chapman?" she said concerned.
"No, and I'll probably be late in tomorrow morning, so no appointments before the afternoon please," Phil instructed, leaving the building in haste.

Ten minutes later Mrs Finnis took delivery of a very large heavy box carried in by two burly men.
"You can put it beside that unit," she instructed and refused to sign any documentation until the men had unpacked and checked it's condition.
"Would you like us to take away the packing?" the younger chap offered.
"Of course," she said firmly, expecting no less of their service. While he gathered up the packaging and debris, the elder man handed her the invoice to sign. They turned to go.
"Aren't you going to set it up and check to see if it works?" she said vexed.
"No? Lady, we're just the delivery guys. Everything you'll need is in here, cables, manual and set-up guide." He handed her a plastic bag. "If you get stuck, give 'em' a call," and pointed to the helpline printed on the bag.
"Well this is most inconvenient and not the service I expected!" she snapped with obvious displeasure.
The two men left the office, glad to escape. "Christ! What flew up her nose?" the elder one said to his mate.

Mrs Finnis tipped out the polythene bag onto her desk, picked up the set-up guide and began to read. How hard can this be, she wondered.

Concluding straightforward, she followed the instructions word by word, ticking off each step completed. Only as a precaution, she phoned the Helpline.
Mohammed, the young man at the end of the line, went right through the whole process before she could stop him. "Well done Madam!" he praised in his strong Indian accent, and ran through all the photocopying machine's functions and options.
She stood in front of her 'all-singing, whistles and bells' new office toy. It's illuminated buttons displaying readiness to work. "You'll do nicely," she said patting the top gently, stepping back once more to admire her work, and slipped the manual into her bag to read at home.

- -

In the evening Ellen phoned Suzy, "I have some good news to share with you and Matt about the bonds Phil found. Would you like to come up for a celebration tea on Sunday so I can tell you all about it? . . and Richard if he'd like to come."
"That's wonderful Mum, I'll see you at the weekend."
Thank goodness and what a relief Suzy sighed, then realised just as one worrying situation in her life had been resolved another had replaced it.

Ellen phoned Matt, repeating the same news and invitation. He wasn't sure he could make it, but he said he'd try.

- -

On Friday morning Suzy needed to return the files she'd borrowed back to 'planning.' Usually she'd hand them to Maureen who worked in the department, but today Maureen was busy talking on her phone.
Suzy waved the files to show Maureen what she'd come in for. "I'll do it," Suzy called, walking across the office to

the cabinet. While carefully replacing the files orderly in the drawers, she couldn't help overhearing Maureen's conversation.

"I know Mum," Maureen said, "Jeff thinks they'll keep the van part of the business at the yard and sell off the lorry park. They'll have to let the men know soon," Maureen disclosed.

Suzy gave Maureen a quick wave as she left the office, recognising her conversation had involved Penns.

- -

Early Friday afternoon on route to his office, Phil passed the new photocopier. "That's an impressive piece of kit."

"I told them it was urgent," Mrs Finnis explained abruptly.

"Tea would be nice," he hinted, before closing his door.

Mrs Finnis entered with his tea. She couldn't wait to blind him with the advanced technology of the new machine. "It prints, scans, copy's and fax, uses network and wireless, air print, auto double sided printing, oh and it can take A3 size paper," she established with pride. Omitting to tell him she'd ordered it a month ago.

"So long as your happy Mrs Finnis, I'm happy." Despite listening, he'd not taken in a word of the machine's many functions. "Whoa, chocolate biscuits! You're spoiling me," Phil commented with humour.

Mrs Finnis left his office, convinced he was in one of his daft moods.

- -

On her way home Suzy popped into the supermarket to pick up a few bits of shopping. Pricking up her ears, when she overheard two women ahead in the checkout queue discussing Penns.

“I’ve heard a developer has bought it for housing, or was it the council?” one said to her friend. “Mind you, we could do with houses.”
“I wondered if one of the big supermarkets would put in an offer, think of the jobs that would bring,” her friend chipped in. The two women casually moved on to a different subject.
Suzy realised already people were talking openly about Penns, yet Richard still had said nothing to her.

In the evening she told Richard about her mother’s invitation. She wasn’t surprised when he gave a glib excuse not to go.
“You go,” he insisted.
There was little point staying home for Richard, who appeared to be working day and night at present. She phoned her mother to let her know she’d arrive tomorrow and stay over. “Then I can help you with the tea,” she volunteered.

-

On Saturday morning Suzy got up early to have breakfast with Richard and spend some time with him before she left. “I don’t know why you can’t come with me,” she grumbled.
“It’s difficult,” he said, not wanting to discuss it further.
His silence wasn’t just provoking, but infuriating. “Richard, I know what’s going on,” she said riled.
He looked mortified, “you do?”
“I know all about Penns, half the town is talking about it.” She wrapped her arms around him. “Don’t worry, we’ll get through it.”
He looked relieved.
The phone rang and Suzy rushed off to answer it.

It was Phil "Mum says you're staying with her this weekend."
"That's right, I was just about to leave."
"We've got somebody here we'd like you to meet," he said, full of intrigue.
"But what about Mum?"
"She'll be here when you arrive, Julia's gone to fetch her."
"What?" Suzy asked, but Phil wouldn't elaborate further.
"See you shortly," he said and hung up.
She wondered what Phil's strange and unexpected call was about. With no option, she'd just have to drive to their place to find out.
She looked for Richard, but he'd already gone without giving her the chance to say goodbye.

When she arrived, Phil was already at the door ready to welcome her inside. "Mum's in the lounge with Julia," he said smiling, "come and meet Alice."
Walking through, Suzy could hear them talking. Julia had her back to her when she entered the room, but she could see Julia was cradling something small in her arms, gently swaying as she spoke to her mother.
Julia turned round to face Suzy, "would you like to hold her?"
Suzy beamed as Julia gently handed over her precious bundle. Two sleepy eyes opened briefly, little snuffles and squeaks emitting.
"Hello little Alice, . . oh Julia, I'm in love," Suzy said softly with her heart melting. With a motherly smile, Julia tenderly stroked the tiny head.
"How old is she?" Suzy whispered.
"Twelve weeks," Julia cooed.

"She's almost edible," Suzy nuzzled into the pup's soft fur. Ellen watched the blissful scene.
Suzy looked up at her mother "and I thought you meant . . !" Suzy stopped herself just in time.
Ellen realised what Suzy was about to say, and what she'd thought earlier. This time it was Ellen who was aghast, her furrowed brow full of indignation. "Suzy! how could you think I'd say such a thing!" she mouthed crossly, so as not to frighten the sleepy pup.
Phil bought in a tray laden with hot toasted tea cakes and coffee. Suzy had never seen him behave so tenderly towards Julia and the tiny new life that had entered their world. No two-ways about it, these two would have made wonderful parents.

After their snack, Ellen announced she needed to get back. She'd things to do and collect for her tea party tomorrow.
Suzy didn't want to hand back the soft little bundle of fur she'd cuddled since her arrival. "Here you are, back to your Mum," gently kissing the golden silky head of the sleeping pup, before reluctantly giving her back to Julia.

Stopping in Kirston to pick up Ellen's order from Polly's on their way back to Squirrels Chase, gave Suzy time for a quick wander around. She could happily loose herself browsing here.
Back home, Ellen began to assemble her things in readiness for the party. A freshly laundered white tablecloth and napkins, the best china and her favourite crystal vase were put aside.

In the evening they sat together watching the TV and catching up with family news.

“How’s Richard?” Ellen enquired “still putting in long hours at that job of his?” Sensing a problem when Suzy didn’t reply straight away. Ellen could recognise a half-truth even when it was said in earnest. “Suzy is anything wrong?”
“There’s speculation of Penns closing, well it’s more than speculation actually.”
“Oh goodness! What is Richard going to do?” her mother gasped.
“He doesn’t want to talk about it,” Suzy answered, grateful to be able to discuss it.
Ellen commiserated “that must have come as a terrible shock, he’s worked for them for years. Perhaps he’s struggling with the uncertainty of change.”
“We can’t make any decisions until we know officially what Penns intend to do, but once we get our heads together, we’ll be fine,” Suzy reasoned. It sounded good, but deep down she wasn’t so sure.

On Sunday morning Ellen was gaily preparing things for her tea party. She’d filled the vase with garden roses and now was arranging the table.
Suzy watched her mother, without the stress and worry she had renewed energy and her confidence back. She looked years younger wearing the green dress they’d bought in Westdale, it gently caressed her figure giving a perfect fit. Ellen was still an attractive woman, if only their father could see her now.

Phil and Julia arrived early, she carried in a large bouquet for Ellen. Phil carried a wriggling lively Alice, wide awake and eager to explore. “She’s got teeth like needles, little minx!" Phil said putting her down onto the kitchen floor.

"Watch her," Julia reminded, handing him a kitchen roll and wipes.

Alice was wearing a new pink collar and looked more cute than ever, if that were possible.

"Shall we sit outside in the garden, it's warm enough?" Phil suggested knowing he was on puddle duty. "I'll fetch the chairs from the garage." Alice bounced along behind him on unsteady legs.

Armed with a wet cloth in case any of the chairs needed wiping, Suzy went along to help. "Mum showed me her cheque, well done Phil," She praised, inspecting the chair seats.

They spilled out into the garden, making the most of the sunshine.

"Please help yourselves to food," Ellen called out.

Suzy offered to make tea, and walked indoors to put the kettle on. She heard the crunch of gravel, and looking out of the window saw Matt arrive. She watched him lift a big plant out of his car and staggered up to the front door with it. No one truly thought he would come. Surprised and excited to see him, she opened the front door and threw her arms around him. "You made it! Mum will be thrilled."

"That bloody thing is full of prickles," he said, brushing off leaves and pink petals. Suzy heard a quiet stifled laugh.

Matt pivoted round "may I introduce you to Gina."

A small framed lady with short cropped dark hair stood behind. "Hello," she said, "I'm pleased to meet you, it's Suzy isn't it?"

"And it's lovely to meet you too," Suzy beamed, giving Gina a warm welcome. "Come in, they're all in the garden, go on through."
Matt took Gina's hand and led her through the house. They all were thrilled to see him if not amazed, and delighted to meet Gina.
"You did a great job Mate, well done," Matt said giving Phil a brotherly pat on the shoulder.

While Gina was fussing Alice and talking to Ellen, Matt slipped back into the house to give Suzy a hand with the refreshments. "So what do you think of her?" he asked eager for her opinion.
"I haven't had a chance to speak to her, but I'm sure she's lovely."
"Did you expect a tall, leggy blonde half my age? I meet plenty of those, all hanging onto their boss's every word with a fixed false smile," Matt said cynically. "Gina's different."
"Have you managed to find a new place yet?" Suzy asked.
"We've seen a few, but apparently not the right one."
"So, what are you looking for?"
"I've liked them all, but Gina says they haven't felt right. I think this 'feeling' must be a womanly thing," he said, not quite understanding. "We're going to start looking again when she gets back from America next week."
"Gina's absolutely right," Suzy agreed "now grab that tray and carry it outside for me."

Ellen was enjoying her party, happy to see all the family laughing and chatting together. Alice stole the show, amusing everyone with her antics as she romped playfully around the garden.

Gina remembered the bottle of champagne they'd brought with them for the occasion, but had left in the car so went back to fetch it.

Receiving all the glory for finding the bonds hadn't sat comfortably with Phil. Appreciating the rare event of having all the family together, he stood up to make an impromptu speech. The family's chatter faded as they waited to hear what he wanted to say.

"I'd like to thank the five people who helped to make this day possible," Phil began. "Suzy, for making Matt and I aware, for giving up many of her weekends to sort out Mum's spidery, dusty loft, and for being here to look after our mother."

"Julia, who spotted Mum's account number, I'd been staring at those blessed papers for hours and missed it."

"Matt, who's support was very gratefully appreciated."

"The late Mr Bennington, my old boss who looked after our mother during that extremely sad time when I, to use a phrase recently spoken by my secretary 'didn't know my arm from my elbow.' Under his guidance, Mum set up the bonds."

"And my tenacious secretary Mrs Finnis. I'd chased that blasted building society for a month without success, yet three days after her blunt phone call Mum received her cheque!"

"I sincerely thank you all, and of course our wonderful mother for inviting us all here today," Phil concluded and received a hearty round of applause.

Ellen tried to add her words of gratitude, but overwhelmed by emotion just managed "thank you."

Gina arrived carrying the bottle of Champagne. "Have I missed something?" she said hearing the applause.

Suzy rushed inside to fetch glasses. “To Mum,” they all toasted.

At four o‘clock Matt and Gina were ready to leave, explaining she had a plane to catch in the morning. Matt gave his mother a big hug and promised to phone. Gina thanked Ellen for a lovely afternoon and said her goodbyes to the rest of the family. Suzy and Phil walked back with them to Matt’s car, wanting to see them off personally.
“Great wheels,” Phil said, admiring Matt’s car.
“Hopefully I’ll be swopping it for a Land Rover soon. Good speech Phil, . . and what’s your secretary’s phone number?” Matt asked.
“Do you want to thank her?” Suzy queried.
“No, I’m going to offer her a job,” Matt teased.
“Get out of here, you rascal!” Phil laughed, slapping his hand on the roof of Matt’s car as he drove off.
“We should send flowers to Mrs Finnis,” Suzy suggested “to thank her.”
“Already taken care of, she received them yesterday.” Phil said, walking back with her to re-join the others. “Why a Land Rover?”
“Tell you later,” Suzy smiled.

Driving away from Squirrels Chase, Matt turned to Gina “so what did you think of my family?”
“They’re great, your mother’s lovely and they all made me feel really welcome,” Gina answered. “I like your brother, he’s funny.”
“My sister’s the funny one, she’s a giggler, especially after a few glasses of wine,” Matt chuckled.

“We’d better think about making a move soon,” Phil announced. “This little one’s had a busy day,” he looked down at the pup who’d fallen asleep, her head resting on Julia’s feet. He returned the garden chairs to the garage while Suzy helped her mum tidy up.
“Thanks for the tea,” kissing his mother goodbye.
“That went well didn’t it?” he said to Suzy. “We should all get together more often.”
She agreed, “just one more kiss before you go.”
“Oh go on then,” he said puckering up.
“Not for you, for Alice,” Suzy giggled, pushing his face away.
With his girls loaded Phil drove off, giving a short beep as he left the drive.

Ellen and Suzy went back indoors. “I’ll just stay for a quick cup of tea, then I must go too,” Suzy forewarned her mother.
“That was a turn up for the books, wasn’t it? Matt showing up with a lady friend,” Ellen said. “Did you know he was courting?”
“I had an idea,” Suzy answered, unable to lie. “Did you enjoy your party Mum?”
Ellen smiled “I couldn’t have asked for anything more, and the sun shone down for us.”
“I can’t remember the last time we were all together, or when my brothers looked so happy. Did you speak to Gina?” Suzy asked.
“Lovely girl, very clever by all accounts. I can see why she caught Matt’s eye.”
Suzy could see her mother was getting tired and suggested she should put her feet up. By the time she’d

washed their cups her mother was sleeping. She wrote a message, propped it up against the kettle and crept out.

- -

Although he'd taken the day off, Matt woke up early. He intended to collect Gina from the airport later, knowing she wouldn't feel like driving after such a long flight. He lay there thinking things over, with her away he'd plenty of time to evaluate his life. He'd had enough of international commerce. For years he'd thrived on tenacious adrenalin fuelled challenges, executing tough deals using his adept skill and proficient strategies. His single status enabled freedom to work continuously and to accumulate the financial rewards.

His Mother's fall and love for Gina had been a wakeup call. It was time to step aside to new 'ambitious blood'. he'd seen too many buckle under continual stress, better to leave at the top than burn himself out.

He began to plan the day, he'd drive down to see his mother and take her out to lunch. Now she'd met Gina, he wanted to tell her about their plans of buying a place and moving in together.

He truly missed Gina and longed for their time together, settled in a new home, . . should they ever get time to find one.

Suzy didn't seem to be her usual bubbly self at the party. If she had a problem their mother would know, another good reason for the visit. He could go on to the airport from Squirrels Chase. Happy with his schedule, got up to get himself ready.

Ellen was surprised to hear Matt's voice when he phoned, and thrilled to learn he was coming to see her. Two visits in a week? Before her party, she hadn't seen him for more than a year. Her sharp motherly instinct told her he must have something important to tell her, surmising Gina could be linked to the cause.

It was almost midday by the time Matt arrived. He'd made a couple of phone calls and lost track of time. He suggested The Forrester for lunch, having passed it on route.

Ellen wasn't exactly startled by Matt's news, she'd noticed how smitten they appeared to be during her party. Seeing him settled down with someone he truly loved would give her immense pleasure. She was pleased to hear they planned to settle somewhere in the West country. With all his globetrotting, she'd feared he might want to live abroad.

"I've had enough of commerce and the endless travelling," he told her. "I'll keep my hand in for a while, but I intend to slide out."

Ellen was relieved, she'd never liked his constant gallivanting around the world.

He didn't beat about the bush and came straight out with it, "so what's up with Suzy?"

Ellen knew there had always been a special bond between them. Although not twins, Suzy and Matt instinctively knew when each other were in trouble.

"She's worried about Richard, he could lose his job, Penns is being taken over. Suzy doesn't know what's going on because he won't discuss it with her. I think he's done the job for so many years, he can't handle change," Ellen reasoned.

Matt thought for a moment, "hasn't he been running that yard successfully for years?"

Ellen nodded agreement.

"With his skill and local business knowledge Richard would probably be the only one they wouldn't want to lose. New companies usually like to keep the cream of the workforce. Richard could be offered a significant rise, . . or he could be hanging out for a better redundancy offer, who knows?"
"Let's hope your right," she said, feeling a tad more optimistic.

When they got back from lunch, Ellen showed Matt the secret hiding space in the bureau. She took out the little charm for him to see. "Take it with you when you look at houses, it will help you find the right place. Its work is done here," she said placing the little cat charm into his hand. Matt didn't want to offend her, so slipped it into his top pocket. "Thanks Mum," he said, indulging her magical fantasies.
"Can you stay for a cup of tea? I know how busy you are, always having to dash off somewhere."
His mother was right, he was always rushing away. "I'm going to stay with you all afternoon," he declared.

By five o'clock when Matt left to drive to the airport, Ellen felt she knew Gina by everything he'd told her. He'd sat describing many of the marvellous places he'd travelled to, and amused her with some funny business anecdotes.
Before he left, she hugged him tight "Matt, I'm so glad you came today."
"So am I," he said kissing her goodbye.
When he'd gone Ellen went back to her armchair. Before switching on her TV for the evening, she sat mulling over the last few weeks. She thought about her

party with all her family, the special time she'd spent individually with each of her children and the relief of being able to stay in her home. Her life couldn't get any better, before going to sleep tonight she would send up a heartfelt prayer of thanks.

~ 4 ~

George tried to start his van for the second time. Each time the engine coughed, spluttered and died. “Come on old girl,” he coaxed, “we’ve only got Mrs Chapman’s grass to do today.” The engine limped into life. It had been playing up for days, George knew he would have to take it into Derek’s garage for attention. Half way to Squirrels Chase the engine stopped again. “OK you win, I’ll take you to the garage now,” George grumbled, addressing his van. The engine restarted straight away as if it knew it had got its way. George drove into the garage forecourt. Derek came out to greet his old friend, he’d heard the van come spluttering in.

“It’s not right,” George said.

“I can hear that,” Derek answered, wiping the grease from his hands with a rag, “lift the bonnet.”

While George attempted to keep the engine running, Derek fiddled and poked, murmuring a series of ‘hmms and ahhs.’ “You’d best leave it here.”

“What’s wrong with it?” George asked.

“Neglect!” Derek stated. George had been bringing Derek his vehicles for longer than they both could remember.

“I’ve only got Mrs Chapman’s grass to do, five minutes away, you can have it after that. I’ll be about an hour.”

Derek shook his head, chuckling “give us a call if you get stranded.”

“Aye Aye Sir!” George replied, playfully giving Derek a sergeant major’s salute.

Ellen wondered where George could be, he wasn't normally this late. She remembered his van had sounded ropey last week and wondered if it had broken down. She heard a large vehicle stop outside and went to investigate. A big lorry had parked, almost blocking her drive. Living on a bend, she knew George would have trouble seeing around it and decided to politely ask the driver to move further along. The driver was using his phone. Just as she got near, he ended his conversation and drove off.
She turned to walk back to the house, and saw Merlin sitting on the stonewall in almost the exact spot where she first saw him. He was looking down, concentrating on something he was holding in his tiny hands. She hadn't seen him since she'd spoken to him about Alex's last day. "I haven't forgiven you," she said, walking by.
"I know," he said quietly.
"If you sit there much longer George will see you."
The little figure smiled, "bye Ellen," he said.
"Bye Merlin," she called back.
Ellen went back to her kitchen to make herself a drink. She took out the mug she kept for George, no doubt he would be along soon. She carried her drink to the seat halfway down the garden. The rose bush behind it was covered in deep red blooms, wafting it's perfume into the air. Alex had planted the rose for her, complaining bitterly about its thorns. She liked to sit there quietly listening to the birds singing. It was her favourite place in the garden.

George appeared "here you are," he said as he approached, "all on your own."
"No," Ellen smiled "I never feel alone sitting here."
"Sorry I'm late Misses, trouble with the van."
Ellen got up to make his drink, "tea?"
"Yes please," he answered and started the mowing.

"It's on the table," Ellen shouted, putting his drink on the small round garden table outside the backdoor.
He gave her a 'thumbs up' sign and carried on mowing. She closed the door, his lawnmower was a noisy machine. Sitting at the kitchen table to finish her tea, she thought about Merlin. She'd been surprised to see him and she'd never known him to smile before, or say her name, . . or come-to-that, say goodbye. He must be in a good mood. She closed her eyes to rest for a few moments.

George finished his mowing. He loaded his mower, and sacks of grass mowing's into his van. Usually he would leave his empty mug on the table outside, but thought he should knock the door to warn her his van was going into the garage. If Derek had to order new parts, he might have to alter her next mowing day.
He couldn't make her hear, looking through the kitchen window he could see she was having a nap. He knocked again, opening the door and calling her name as he stepped inside. She was in a deep sleep. Not wanting to startle her, he gently touched her hand.
Ellen remained asleep. "God bless you Mrs Chapman," he said gently. There was a list of phone numbers above the phone in the kitchen. He saw his own written underneath family members. George phoned the doctor's number first.

Suzy was at her desk, she couldn't find the page she needed. She'd had it in her hand a minute ago, but now it was gone. She sat infuriated, trying to remember where she had it last.
Karen came into her office and approached her desk.
"Hi," Suzy said, looking down, going through her top desk drawer.

"You're needed downstairs Suzy," Karen said quietly. "You're husband needs to speak to you."
Suzy was puzzled, but looking at Karen's serious face told her something was very wrong. She grabbed her bag and dashed downstairs. Claire the receptionist kept her eyes fixed down on the book in front of her.
"Richard, what's wrong? Is it Kate?" Suzy flustered.
"Your Mum has been taken to hospital," he said, gently ushering her out of the door. Suzy began to walk towards her car.
"This way," he said "I'm taking you home." He put his arm over her shoulder, steering her towards his car.
"How do you know?" she asked, her heart thumping frantically and her mind beginning to race.
"The gardener found her," Richard said. It wasn't until she was inside his car that he said "Suzy, she's gone."

At home he helped her out of his car, she clung onto him sobbing, her tears soaking his shirt. Indoors, he handed her a handful of tissues as he pulled away to make her a cup of sweet tea.
"Who told you?" she asked between sobs.
"The gardener phoned here looking for you."

-

For days Suzy was inconsolable, at night despite being desperately tired, sleep evaded her.
Richard stayed with her, patiently and kindly supporting her when she needed it most. Occasionally he went out, but only for an hour or two.
A close friend had given him a booklet "it's an old one, but the list of necessary procedures are the same," she'd said. Richard was grateful, feeling the time for those procedures drawing near.

Matt had switched off all forms of communication, he was unreachable.
When Richard spoke to Julia, she said Phil was 'in bits' and not able to make decisions at that time.
"Suzy," Richard asked tenderly, "there's certificates and things you need to organise for your Mum when you're ready to face them."

The next morning Suzy made herself presentable. Her womanly survival instinct had kicked in. She would cope, probably just as her own mother had done before. At least she had Richard for comfort and support.
He drove her to the hospital to pick up Ellen's belongings and to collect the death certificate. A young nurse wanted Suzy to check the bag before signing for them. Seeing the look of panic in Suzy's eyes, quickly said she'd already made sure everything was enclosed, and pointed where Suzy needed to Sign. Richard snatched the bag and guided Suzy out, he could see her fragility returning.
He drove on to the Registrar's office in Westdale. The elder lady registrar was kindly spoken, passing on advice as she went through forms. Suzy was relieved to get home, she'd had enough for one day and remembered little of it.

She phoned Phil in the evening, asking for his support and attendance at the funeral directors. She'd made the appointment for Friday morning, giving her time to get hold of Matt.

- -

Matt switched on his phone and read the message from Suzy. He'd fallen apart, all he could think about were those last precious hours he'd spent alone with his mother. The thought of if he hadn't driven up to see her haunted him. All those times he'd sent flowers and given her a quick phone call instead of making time to visit came back, too late now and it hurt, unbearably it hurt.

Gina called round to see him. She'd given him a while to grieve, now she was checking to see how he was coping.

He wasn't coping at all, nor was he going to answer the door.

"You know I'm not going to go away," she shouted through his letterbox.

Slovenly, he dragged himself to the door.

Not waiting to be invited, Gina almost barged inside. She was shocked to see him in such an unkempt state. "Look at you," she said enfolding him in her arms "why didn't you call me?"

He'd wanted to be alone.

"I'll make coffee, while you're in the shower."

He padded towards the bathroom without resistance. The reflexion in the mirror was Neanderthal. He was unsure when he'd last washed, shaved or had eaten. He felt numb.

Gina flew round his flat tidying, scooping up clothes from the floor, dirty glasses and mugs, opening every blind and window she came across.

Matt emerged from his bedroom dressed, and feeling better prepared to start picking up the pieces of his life.

"How are you doing?" she sympathised.

"Better for seeing you," he said, meaning every heartfelt word.

She cooked him a full breakfast which Matt knew he'd have to eat, she had the same capabilities of organisation in the business world as himself.

He did feel better and agreed to a short walk along the river for some fresh air. In a few short hours Gina had transformed the pitiful tramp in dire fug, back to the man she loved, coaxing him gently back into facing the world. "Would you like me to drive you to Kirston tomorrow?" she offered. "I could wait outside for you in the car, or come back to pick you up."

"No, I need to overcome this," he insisted. "I'll be OK."

Gina had spent most of the day with him. "I'll come back tomorrow after work, unless you need me before."

Matt held her tight and kissed her before letting her go, "thank you for coming, sorry I . . "

"Matt, you're grieving, don't fight it, you'll be fine, see you tomorrow." She kissed him again before closing his front door.

- -

Phil sat quietly in the lounge, reflecting the last months of his mother's life. The highs and lows, the worries and celebrations had taken their toll, and all for what? He couldn't believe she'd gone. Every night he'd relive that weekend they'd shared together, from finding the bonds to watching her smiling as she fed the ducks. He would be forever grateful for those precious moments together. His eyes filled with tears every time he thought of her smiling.

Julia came and sat beside him, taking his hand.

"I'll be alright, I'm just a bit . . "

"Lost," Julia added." She missed his smile, his antics and Alice had lost her playmate. The pup tugged at his slipper with her sharp teeth, making little playful growls as she tried to shake it. "Ouch!" Phil shouted when one of her teeth caught a toe. Alice retreated looking worried and

frightened. Phil picked her up "sorry," he said, not meaning to shout, and kissed her small soft furry head.
"Who can resist those eyes?" Julia said stroking her. Alice waved her paws in the air, she wanted to play. Phil put her down on the floor and clapped his hands. It was their little game. Every time he clapped, Alice would take off like a rocket, flying round the lounge. Sometimes she'd loose her grip and slide over. Each time she would stop and wait for Phil to clap his hands before racing off again.
Alice crouched down in front of him, frantically wagging her tail, ready to spring and give her loudest bark. With her cheeks puffed out, the pitiful yap made Phil chuckle. He rolled her over and rubbed her furry tummy.
"That's better," Julia said, welcoming back Phil's smile.

Phil phoned Suzy Thursday evening. "If Richard can drop you off at Jarratt's Funeral Director's in Kirston, tell him I'll run you back when we've finished. See you tomorrow," they didn't talk, neither of them felt like chatting.

- -

Matt's fuel gauge flashed and blinked as he turned off to Kirston, he'd forgotten to check it before setting off. It wasn't like him to forget, clearly he wasn't back to his usual organised self. He pulled into a garage coming up on his left. This lack of concentration jarred, he'd be more on the ball from now. He walked into the shop to pay for the fuel, picking up a packet of mints on route and joined the queue to be served.

The chap in front spun the newspaper rack around looking for the local paper, "has the Westdale News come in yet?"

"They're here, I haven't had a chance to load the rack yet," the assistant called back.
When Matt reached the counter, he saw the pile of papers. The main headline plastered across the front page was 'Penns Takeover' above a photo of their office. He picked one up to read later.

It was ideal all three of them meeting at the Funeral Directors. They could each give opinions, choose and make the arrangements together. Mr Jarratt lead, negotiating a date and time for Ellen's funeral service. "I'll just get these arrangements printed out," he said handing the notes to a colleague in the next office. Minutes later he emerged and gave each of them one of the company's blue embossed folders with the details enclosed.

They walked out into the street in silence, relieved and thankful they'd got that part over with.
"I still can't believe she's gone," Phil said, his eyes filling up.
Matt and Suzy drew closer, with heads lowered, Suzy slipped her arm around Phil's waist and Matt gently rubbed Phil's back to comfort.
"Sorry," Phil said trying to regain aplomb.
"Let's go and have a coffee somewhere," Matt suggested as they walked back to their cars. Suzy got into Phil's car, with Matt following behind, all heading for The Black Rabbit pub. They chose a table out of the way in a corner.
Suzy urged while altogether, they should try to finish organising the rest of their 'Mum's day'. The brothers nodded in unison.
Matt agreed to arrange notifications in the local newspapers. Suzy would take care of the flowers. One

huge oval spray to adorn the coffin from them all, stipulating the most colourful flowers the florist could find.
“Where shall we hold the ‘Wake’?” Phil asked.
“Not at Squirrel’s Chase,” Suzy petitioned “I’m not ready to go back.”
“What about here, it’s near the church?” Matt proposed, and went off to speak to the landlord. He returned with favourable news, they were willing to do it, just needed the details. With nobody in the mood to look at other places, it was settled.

Phil suggested staying there for lunch, they’d done enough for the time being. It seemed a good idea and a welcome change of subject. Matt went to fetch some menus from the bar.
Phil’s phone rang, “we shouldn’t be much longer,” he answered.
“Trouble?” Suzy inquired.
“Julia isn’t feeling well, so hasn’t gone shopping. She wants me to pick up some groceries on the way home.” Suzy asked Matt to give her a lift back, so Phil could leave.

Suzy and Matt ate together, talking in general, but conscious of their fragile equanimity.
Back at Matt’s car, she opened the passenger door, seizing the papers and mints before she could sit down. “Been shopping?” she said, wondering where to put them. “Why did you buy two identical newspapers?”
“Did I? I really am losing it at the moment,” explaining his visit to the garage. “I was curious about the takeover at Penns,” pointing to the front page of the papers she held. “Why don’t you keep one to read later.”
Suzy folded one in half and put it into her bag.

"How's he been? . . Richard," Matt asked.
"Thoughtful, kind, really looked after me, I couldn't of got through this without him," she admitted.
"Has he spoken about his job?"
"No, and I've stopped thinking about it. I need to get through Mum's day first."
Matt understood, he couldn't think about looking at property for the same reason. He stopped his car outside her house. "I won't come in Suze, I just want to get home, it's been a tough day."
Suzy said goodbye before getting out of his car. "Take care," she called, giving a wave as he drove off.

Richard was home, watching a football match on the TV. "Want a drink?" he offered, about to get up.
Suzy put her arms around him "thank you," she said "for being 'there' for me," giving him a hug. "I'll make the tea, stay and watch your football," she insisted, walking towards the kitchen.
"Did you get everything done?" Richard called out.
"Nearly, it's been quite a day."
"How long has Phil had that car?" Richard asked.
"That's Matt's car, Phil needed to go home earlier," hearing a touch of envy in his voice. She drank her tea, kicked her shoes off, lifted her feet up onto the settee and closed her eyes.

- -

On Suzy's third attempt, Kate answered her phone.
"How are you feeling Mum?" she asked, recognising her mother's number.
"I'm OK, . . getting there," Suzy sighed, trying to put on a brave face.
"Where's Dad?" Kate paused, . . . "how's he been?"

"Why?" Suzy asked. "Your Dad has been absolutely wonderful, I couldn't have got through this terrible time without him."
"Has he stayed with you?" sounding concerned.
"Yes, he's only just gone back to work."
Kate seemed relieved. "I was worried he . . " She corrected herself "I know what a workaholic he is," and went on to apologise for not returning home immediately after receiving the very sad news.
She'd been attending a set of lectures given by an eminent German professor. With only a few sessions left to complete the course, her father had persuaded her to stay on, insisting there was nothing she needed to do back home. Knowing how close her mother and grandmother had always been, it had been a difficult decision to make. Suzy gave Kate the details of the forthcoming funeral, and agreed to meet her off the train at Westdale. Having Kate home for a few days would be an immense comfort.

- -

Two weeks after his mother's funeral Phil made the decision to return to work, he'd already taken almost a month off.
"Are you sure?" Julia asked.
"If I can't handle it, I'll come home," he promised.

Mrs Finnis greeted him with one of her rare smiles when he walked into his office, expressing her sympathy for his loss.
"How's the new photocopier?" he asked when she carried in his morning coffee.
"Marvellous. Mr Western has some of your client's files, he took them over while you were away."

Phil went off to retrieve them. “Is he free?” he asked Neal’s secretary, before knocking on the door and going in.

Neal Western’s desk was piled high. “Am I glad to see you,” he said, handing over Phil’s files. “They’re all up to date and signed.”

“Thanks Mate, I really appreciate this.”

“I only checked and signed them, your secretary did all the figures and work, she might be an old c . .”

“Curmudgeon!” Phil said swiftly, not wishing Neal to relate to cattle.

“Well, she’s a clever woman,” Neal complimented.

Phil took a closer look at his colleague. “Are you alright?

“Tired, bloody tired, that’s all.”

Phil remembered someone mentioned twins ages ago. He hadn’t taken much notice being bogged down with his mother’s problems. “How old are your babies now?”

“Four months, I don’t know how Zoe copes. If one’s asleep, the other one isn’t. I’m glad to come to work, apart from being knackered,” he confessed.

Phil walked back to his office deep in thought. He summoned Mrs Finnis into his office.

She stood in front of his desk.

“I’ve just been told you did the work on these files,” indicating the pile on his desk.

Mrs Finnis stiffened, “I was trying to assist,” she defended.

“Mr Western is very impressed.”

She blushed. “I don’t think Mr Western is getting enough sleep due to his young family.”

“Mrs Finnis, it’s time I revised your office capabilities and position, and I sincerely apologised for not having done so before.”

She thanked him, but saw no necessity for any change at present.
Phil knew she was canny enough to leave the option open, remaining free to enjoy her comfortable 'Queen Bee' secretarial position.
"Work beyond the call of duty does not go unrewarded in this firm," he announced.
"Will that be all?"
"Is there a chance we could take on some of Neal's work, reduce his workload for a while? Only temporary of course, . . with your help Mrs Finnis? . . It's just a thought," he added as she began to walk back to her desk.
Phil lent back in his chair, having a little pre satisfactory smile. He knew she wouldn't resist, now she'd been given the opportunity to flex her skills.

Julia phoned Phil's office, "how's he doing Mrs Finnis?"
"Absolutely fine," she replied, putting her through.
Julia asked how his day was faring.
"OK really, I haven't completed much work, but I've achieved something."
"What?" she asked, totally confused.
"Tell to you later," he said ending the call.

On the dot of three o'clock, Mrs Finnis carried in a small tray loaded with Phil's afternoon tea and biscuits. As usual she placed it on the left side of his desk.
"Thank you Mrs Finnis," he acknowledged, as he continued to write.
"Perhaps Mr Western could sort out a couple of files for next week," she avouched before leaving his room.

Phil smiled, he knew underneath that icy cold surface there was a warm heart.

- -

With Gina working away, Matt wandered about his flat aimlessly. There didn't seem much point in staying home any longer. The more he slept and rested the more tired he felt.
He arranged to go back to work, deciding to complete two days first, returning to full time the week after.

Everyone was pleased to see him back, especially his secretary Caroline. She'd been consigned to help Jack Finch in the adjacent office while Matt had been away. Unequivocally preferring her prestigious position of being Matt's P A.

On his second day Matt attempted to catch up on the endless paperwork on his desk, flicking through proposals, assessments and figures, absorbing none of it. In his large modern office, sat at his impressive desk, he stopped and looked around. The company hadn't folded due to his month's absence, it was thriving, successfully riding the global markets. He felt no inclination to chase and complete the next ultimate deal, or execute the next financial killing. The great fire to achieve no longer burned within his soul, his eyes had lost their hunter's gleam. His outer appearance may not have altered, but deep inside he felt hollow and numb.

He'd briefly raised 'grieving' and 'depression' on his computer screen, but couldn't concentrate or be bothered to read about either subject. Now he'd had enough and was thinking about going home.

Caroline was at her desk sifting through Matt's post and messages, siphoning the important ones for his

attention, when Sofia from front-entrance buzzed her. "Just to let you know Harvey Granzman's in the building," she whispered, "apparently he flew in yesterday."
Caroline knocked on Matt's door to warn him.

Harvey Granzman was Matt's boss, a powerful man, and Vortorx International's American main executive. He never announced his arrivals, preferring to suddenly appear, keeping everyone focussed and on their toes.
Matt began to gather his things, glad to be going home. At least he had the next two days off.

Harvey Granzman opened Matt's door and stood filling the doorway. "Good to see you back Mathew," he broadcast in his loud American voice "how are you?" Before Matt could answer, Granzman had picked up on Matt's aura, which wasn't raring-to-go. "See James Straks, he's the best. I want you back on the team Mathew." Harvey Granzman raised his hand to say goodbye. "Take care," he called out, walking away, leaving Matt's door wide open.

Matt threw several items into his case, put on his jacket and closed his office door. Informing Caroline as he walked passed her desk, 'he'd be back Monday'.
"You have an appointment with Dr Straks tomorrow at ten o'clock."
"What?" he said, "cancel it, I'll go later."
"I'm afraid it's not an option. Mr Granzman personally arranged the appointment," handing him the details.
Matt sighed, he'd have to go.
"If you're not here fighting fit, you can't earn the company it's millions," she quipped with amusement.
Matt wasn't amused, in the twelve years he'd worked for Vortorx International he'd never felt owned or used.

Caroline's words jarred and for the first time he felt uncomfortable. He read the address she'd written down for Dr Straks Practice. Rankinston! That's bloody miles away he cursed.

-

In the morning Matt still had mixed feelings. He should appreciate Granzman personally arranging the appointment, but Caroline's flippant comment still grated. He got into his car and set off, the sooner this appointment was over the better.

The Consultancy was housed in a substantial Victorian property on the edge of town. The large garden area at the back had become a car park.

Matt stood at the reception desk admiring the grand interior. An elegant wooden staircase swept down with a carved lion on top of the newel posts each side. He expected to be directed to a waiting area, but as soon as he gave his name, the receptionist escorted him through. Dr James Straks was sat, concentrating on a laptop screen on his desk when Matt entered. His consultancy room bore similarities to Matt's own office, bar the wide recliner chair and several framed certificates along a wall. James sprang up from his black leather office chair and shook Matt's hand. "Hi Mathew, I'm James, take a seat," he said in his strong American accent, pointing to the other office chair.

Matt was surprised by James's age, comparable to himself, if not younger.

"Are you a personal friend of Harvey Granzman?"

"He's my boss," Matt answered.

"Then Mathew, you must be an important guy," James flattered.

Matt's body language indicated he was irritated by having to attend this appointment, and realizing James had reorganized his schedule to fit him in made him feel worse.

"Let's see how I can help, then you can get out of here," James accommodated. He'd observed Matt had no physical pain by the way he'd walked in and sat down.
"Are you having a problem sleeping?"
"I lost my mother recently," Matt volunteered.
"And were you close?" Seeing Matt trying to conceal his pain, told James why Mathew Chapman was sitting in front of him.

"If the voice in your head tells you to move on, get up and sort yourself out, but you can't. Life makes no sense. You're endlessly tired, no appetite, can't sleep or concentrate. Have no interest or inclination to do anything, . . that's a form of depression," James's explained. "I've known patients who can't physically get out of bed on their dark days."

"Losing a parent or someone much loved is devastating. That part of you has gone, you can never be the same again, but you will adapt . . . given time. This period of transition is bereavement."
"Regret, . anger, . guilt, . crying, unpredictable mood swings are normal symptoms of grief. Grief and depression often overlap. You have to give yourself time, . . time to heal. Listen to 'this and this," pointing in turn to his own head and heart.

Now he'd had his emotions explained, Matt began to relax. James was easy to talk to.

"You'll have a full check-up here, my colleague Sian Zhan will do that. She's a homeopathic medical doctor. I propose a short course of medication for depression. It won't be an instant cure, but it'll calm and alleviate your symptoms. Take some time out Mathew . . get outside, walk, . . stop and look around you, take in your surroundings, . . absorb, deep breathe, . . embrace your senses."

"Smell the roses?" Matt jested, beginning to lighten up.

"You got it Mathew," James laughed shaking Matt's hand before he left.

Wearing a traditional white coat, Dr. Sian Zhan stood at her open door ready to invite Matt inside. Her short, small frame and straight black hair defined her oriental origin. She smiled, her dark eyes softening as she asked him to take a seat.

He'd expected a Chinese accent and was surprised by her Americanised diction.

"James lists an antidepressant," she said reading, interpreting his notes. Serotonin - a natural remedy for grief depression. It placates anxiety, you will feel the difference." Explaining, to put Matt at ease.

Forever working, he'd never made time for health checks and medicals. He realized he'd not had such a thorough M O T in years. He got back into his car to drive home, feeling better than he'd felt about himself for weeks. Admitting it had been worth the drive.

Gina phoned in the evening, she could tell he was feeling much better.

"I've been to see a doctor, a James Straks," Matt told her.

"Really?" she said thinking he must be mistaken, or she'd misheard. "I should be finished here sometime tomorrow, so with luck I'll see you Friday morning."
"I can't wait," Matt emphasized.
"Nor can I, and I'll bring back your dark blue jacket. I had it cleaned before I left." She didn't mention it was screwed up on his bedroom floor the day she'd tidied. "Love you, see you Friday."

-

On Friday morning Gina stood at Matt's door, his dry cleaning in one hand and a bag of groceries in the other. She rang his doorbell. It was early and she wondered if he would be up.
He opened the door with the biggest smile on his face she'd seen for a while. Without giving her time to put anything down, he put his arms around her and gave her a long passionate kiss. "I've missed you so much."
"Clearly," she giggled, trying to catch her breath. She'd let go of all she was carrying, unperturbed that it fell to the floor. Several kisses later, she picked them up and headed for his kitchen. "It's good to see you looking better, who was it you saw?"
"Dr. James Straks," Matt answered.
"Not the American one in . ?" Gina couldn't think of the place.
"Rankinston." Matt replied.
"No! how did you manage that? I thought he only dealt with the rich and famous."
Matt told her about Harvey Granzman calling in to see him, and personally arranged the appointment.
"So what was he like?" she asked, putting away groceries into cupboards. "I've heard he's amazing, the top psychologist outside London."

“My age, likeable,” . . . . then Matt realised what she had said. “Psychologist? Harvey Granzman sent me to a shrink!” Not for one minute had he thought James Straks was anything other than an upmarket private GP. Matt began slamming cupboard doors in temper. Having a complete strop, feeling humiliated and embarrassed, muttering “he sent me to a shrink!” repeatedly. Finally he stormed off to the bathroom to put away some shower gel. Gina stayed in the kitchen.

He returned some minutes later looking rather sheepish. “I’m sorry, I don’t normally throw tantrums, I can’t think what’s got into me lately. I’m being very negative aren’t I?” He could tell by the look on her face, that’s exactly what she was thinking . . or worse.

She switched on Matt’s coffee machine and sat down, allowing him to make their drinks while he relayed the gist of his appointment.

“Have you taken any of those pills?” she asked.

It hadn’t occurred to him, and went off to fetch them.

Gina took out her phone to answer a call. “I’ll call you back in an hour.”

“Problems?” Matt enquired.

“Hmmm, . . it’s an estate agent in Somerset, has a couple of properties he wants to show us, but not if you don’t feel like it.”

Matt was non-committal.

Gina had draped his dry-cleaned jacket over a chair. “Here,” she said “you can put this away,” handing him the jacket. “The woman at the dry cleaners said she found something zipped into a pocket and has put it in an envelope”.

Matt took out a small white envelope from a pocket, tearing it open to look inside. The little tarnished black cat

charm lay within. Instantly, the memory of his mother giving it to him returned. Emotion squeezed his heart until tears filled his eyes. He couldn't speak.
"What is it?" Gina asked seeing his reaction.
"Mum gave this to me." He took out a handkerchief to wipe his eyes.
Gina took the little charm out of the envelope and placed it in the palm of his hand. Carefully she folded his fingers over it. "Holding this charm makes you and your mother just a touch away," she said gently, embracing him.
"God, this bereavement lark's a killer," Matt said, blowing his nose trying to restore some dignity. He opened his hand to look at the charm. With a hint of a smile, looked fondly at the little cat, turning it over with his fingers.
"Why don't you give that agent a call? I think we deserve a weekend in the country."
"Really?" Gina questioned.
"Really."
"I'll throw some things into a case and be back in an hour," she beamed, giving him a quick kiss before dashing off.

As Matt put a few things into his overnight bag he thought about his mother giving him the charm, and its purpose. Once again he zipped it safely into his inside jacket pocket. He packed the medication, hoping they'd stop his up-and-down rollercoaster of emotions. Country walks and birdsong was exactly what the doctor ordered . . . or shrink, he accepted with amusement.

- -

Suzy began to think of Squirrels Chase, she should go back to start sorting out her mother's things. Julia had kindly offered to accompany her, not wanting Suzy to face the empty house for the first time alone.

A gracious offer, but Suzy wasn't sure how she'd feel watching someone else going through her mother's possessions. She decided to drive up there at the weekend, maybe Richard would go with her as he'd been so caring of late.

"Hello stranger, how are you doing?" Rachel asked with feeling, when Suzy answered her phone.
"All the better for hearing your voice," Suzy replied, thanking Rachel and Elsie for kindly sending cards and flowers.
"I was wondering if you felt like coming out for a meal one evening."
"I'm still all over the place, up one minute, down the next, and making no sense whatsoever," Suzy warned "but it would be nice."
"How about this Friday? I could pick you up if you don't feel like driving," Rachel coaxed. "If we eat at the Bricknell, I can show you the new classroom for my courses."
Suzy accepted.

When she mentioned Rachel's offer to Richard, he thought it would do her good to start getting out and about, but wasn't so obliging when she asked him to give her a hand at Squirrels Chase.
"I've got too much to sort out at the yard," he excused. "They're completing outstanding delivery contracts," he added when Suzy gave him a puzzled look. Penns takeover was still the elephant-in-the-room. Richard never discussed it and Suzy hadn't bothered to raise the issue either . . . . yet.

The girls arranged to meet at the Bricknell Lodge for seven. Suzy was happy to drive, if she left early, she could pop in to thank Elsie personally on the way. She text Rachel to let her know her plans in case she became late. Elsie could be very persuasive with her offers of tea.

Elsie opened the door before Suzy had time to knock. "Come on in 'Ducks'," Elsie welcomed, embracing Suzy in her arms. "You poor girl, losing your mother so sudden like that, I've got the kettle on," she said, turning round walking slowly towards her kitchen.

"Did you see me from your window?" Suzy questioned, knowing from past experience it usually took Elsie a few minutes to get to her door.

"I was looking out for Gwen, 'Ducks', she's bringing me back a bit o' shopping."

"How is your friend Gwen?" Suzy enquired politely.

Elsie didn't get a chance to answer, Rachel came through the front door in a flurry. "There you are," she said to Suzy.

"I'm going to show Suzy around the new classroom Elsie, so we can't stop for tea this time."

"I came to thank you for the beautiful spray of flowers," Suzy explained, before she turned to go.

"That's alright 'Ducks," Elsie said giving Suzy another hug before she left.

Rachel appeared to be in a rush. "What was she talking about?" guiding Suzy outside.

"She was expecting Gwen to drop in with some shopping."

"Just in time," Rachel muttered under her breath.

Suzy was puzzled.

"Once Elsie starts chatting, we'd be there for hours," Rachel clarified, unlocking her car. She took off swiftly to the Bricknell with Suzy driving behind.

Suzy followed Rachel's car to the back of the hotel, security lights flicked on as they parked their cars. Rachel tapped a code into the lock on a windowless door, and lights blinked on as they walked into the building.

"This used to be storerooms," Rachel informed.

The refurbished room was massive, half being new modern kitchen, the rest, tables with chairs. "What do you think?" she asked, waiting for approval.

Suzy walked around wide eyed and seriously impressed. Admiring the large colourful plaques that formed part of the decor around the walls. "I didn't know there were so many food allergies," she said reading down a list on one of them.

"That's what gave me the idea. I overheard a celiac bemoaning the lack of choice whenever she went out to eat. Some people's intolerance and allergies give them migraines, swellings, rashes, or make them feel unwell, but for others it's life threatening. Not simply lactose, nuts or gluten, there's many allergenic."

"Gosh," Suzy murmured, Rachel certainly knew her stuff.

"I've worked with a hospital allergists. With their specialist information, I've been able to work with our chefs to create diverse menus. They've fully embraced this project, plus it gives them the opportunity to teach and demonstrate for a couple of days."

The one, two and three day courses were proving successful, being fully booked, with pre-bookings weeks ahead. It had taken Rachel a year of research, and planning before she could submit her idea to those 'above'. "We're getting cooks from private schools,

guesthouse owners, Nursing home staff, . . well anyone who needs to cater for a special diet, . and we provide a booklet of recipes with each course," Rachel stated proudly.
"The idea's ingenuous and to personally set it up, you're so clever Rachel, . . what else can I say?" Suzy praised.
"It's nice to be able to share my achievement with someone." Admitting when she tried to tell Elsie, her opinion was I work too hard as it is. "Michael's only comment was 'I should ask for more money'," she said despondent.
"That's the sort of thing Richard would say," Suzy grumbled without thinking.
"What's he doing since the takeover?" Rachel asked, locking up, getting ready to drive back round to the front entrance.
"We haven't spoken about it yet," Suzy confessed, "what with the funeral and everything."

Over dinner Suzy mentioned Matt wishing to move to the West country, and had Rachel cooing over the pictures of Alice, captured on her phone.

"Is that the time? I have to go, I'm planning to leave early tomorrow. I'm going to start sorting out my mother's things at Squirrels Chase."
Rachel apologised, she was filling in for staff holidays, otherwise she would have kept her company. "Are you going to stay overnight?"
"I haven't decided," Suzy admitted, still unsure.
"Phone me, if you want someone to talk to," Rachel offered.
"Thank you for this evening, it's been lovely to catch up, and to see your classroom," she said standing up, getting

ready to go, leaving Rachel at the table to finish her drink.

-

In the morning Suzy woke up late, cursing herself and bemoaning Richard for not waking her or saying goodbye. Then rethought the situation more favourably. He probably let her sleep on out of kindness, he'd been so considerate and almost loving recently. Perhaps, when Penns business takeover ended, she'd get her 'old Richard' back.
She lay there, thinking about her evening with Rachel. No doubt about it, Rachel had thrown her heart and soul into her project, and sent up a silent prayer for success to reward her friend's hard work. Blessing the day they'd met up again. Who'd have thought how their lives would have turned out. They'd certainly had no idea all those years ago when their children were small.
She stopped her daydreaming, if she was going to achieve anything today she'd have to get a move on.

Standing outside the empty house with the key in her hand, Suzy had a wobble of anxiety. Taking a deep breath for courage she entered, walking across mail that lay scattered on the floor. She picked up the letters and placed them on the hall table, then began opening windows in every room to dispel the stale air. Hesitating for a brief second outside of her mother's bedroom. "Love you Mum," she whispered, opening the door wide and striding towards the windows.

The next bedroom along had always been Phil's. It was slightly smaller than hers and Matt's. In their sibling childhood wisdom, they'd deemed Phil should have the smallest room being the youngest. Silly now, but they felt justified at the time. His room at the back of the house had the best view down to the bottom of the garden. She walked in to open the window, peering out as she did so. It couldn't be! Her heart thumped as she rushed downstairs to investigate, swiftly walking down the garden path. In front of the seat lay the large oval spray that had adorned their mother's coffin. Suzy was rooted to the spot, the dead flowers presenting a stark reminder.

George turned into Beeches Road intending to visually check Squirrels Chase as he drove by. When he saw Mrs Martin's car parked outside, suddenly aghast, he remembered something. Almost running down the path he saw her. "I'm sorry Lass," he gasped, seeing the shocked expression on her face. He grabbed the withered spray and rushed off with it.

Suzy was sitting on the seat when he returned.

"I'm sorry," he repeated. "Those beautiful flowers, they chuck 'em away the next day. After the service, when everyone had gone, I brought it back. Your Mum loved to sit here, it just seemed right at the time. I shouldn't have done it, shaking you up like that." He felt guilty and was full of remorse.

"It was a kind thought George," Suzy said, now she'd recovered. "Come into the kitchen, I'll make us both a cup of tea." While walking back to the kitchen, she realised he'd continued to cut the grass and promised payment.

"I didn't do it for that," he said quietly."

"Even so, we'd be grateful if you could continue. I expect I shall be here on and off for a while."

Inside, George sat, head down with eyes fixed to the floor.

"She was so happy that day, I was talking to her one minute, . . . and then she'd slipped away."

Suzy patted his hand "thank goodness you were here George," she said kindly.
"I'd best get on now." He drained his cup and got up ready to go. "I usually drive past most days so I'll keep an eye on the place. Bye lass."
"Bye George," she said, seeing him to the door.
It was time she made a start on the jobs she'd come to do and grabbed some large bags out of the drawer.

Mid-afternoon Suzy's phone rang out making her jump, it was Phil. He was checking to see where she was. "Julia thought you'd be at Mum's," he said without thinking. Squirrels Chase had always been known as 'Mums', are you going to stay?"
"I've tons to do," she answered.
"Then I'll be with you about seven, armed with food," he promised.
"I'm OK, I'll be fine," she insisted loudly, but he'd already gone. She hadn't actually made up her mind to stay overnight, now it seemed she would have to.

At half past seven Phil knocked on the door holding a bag of hot fish and chips. "Take these," he said handing them over, while he went back to get his overnight bag and lock his car.
"You didn't have to come, I'd be alright," she stated, tipping the hot chips onto plates.
"I did have to come, Julia insisted, and no you wouldn't." She had to admit being pleased to see him. They sat in the lounge with trays on their laps, eating their supper before it got cold.
"How have you been?" she asked.
"I still have moments," he confessed.

Suzy was worried about Matt, she hadn't spoken to him since the funeral and it wasn't like him not to phone.
"He has got a girlfriend," Phil reminded. "Our intrepid big brother can usually handle stressful situations, that's how he earns his living."
Never-the-less Suzy wasn't sure Matt was OK.
"What can I do to help tomorrow?" Phil asked.
"A trip to the tip, while I carry on sorting Mm . . ," Suzy couldn't say 'mum's clothes', the words stuck in her throat and she fell silent.
Phil got up to make a hot drink.
"If there's any bags for charity shops, I'll take them back with me. Julia's offered to drop them off," he called out from the kitchen.
Suzy raised her voice to ask "is Julia better now?"
"She's still feeling off colour."
"Oh goodness, that's been going on for a while, should she see a doctor?" she called back concerned."
Phil returned, carrying mugs of tea "here you are," handing Suzy her drink before he sat down, without answering her question.
"Phil, is she alright?" she persisted.
"She's pregnant."
Suzy's mouth fell open, that certainly wasn't the answer she was expecting. "No!" she said almost in disbelief. Soon her face began to light up as the information sank in. "Oh Phil, that's marvellous," her eyes filling with happy tears.
"I'm not allowed to tell anyone, she's seriously not out of the woods yet. I've got fingers, eyes, legs, well everything crossed that she'll be OK. We're not allowed to set our hearts on it," he confirmed.

How could they not set their hearts on it? Suzy got up and gave him a huge hug. "It'll be fine," she beamed "you'll see, it's going to be fine."
"Remember, not a word," Phil commanded.
"Mum's the word!" Suzy promised, wearing a grin from ear to ear.
"Before you ask, Mum knew. Julia told her on the day of her party. Mum noticed Julia didn't drink her champagne, so guessed straight away. Our Mum and my delightful Mrs Finnis have the sharpest intuition on Earth," Phil smiled.
"Delightful?" Suzy gave him a wry look.
"I don't know whether we should thank Mum or Alice for our surprise," Phil pondered.
"Go on," Suzy said intrigued.
"Julia has always had her 'restless days' as she calls them, when she can't settle to anything and gets anxious. That's usually when I'd get home to find she'd moved all the furniture around in the house. She had a couple of her 'days' when Mum stayed, Mum took one look at her and said . . . "
Suzy didn't need to hear Phil say the words, already she could hear them being spoken by her mother in her head, or was it her conscience pricking? Those silly words that caused a misunderstanding.
Phil's conversation continued just as Suzy expected, 'what she needed was a baby to love.'
"Julia and Mum had become quite close during her stay. I think after some womanly discussions, Julia accepted Mum's advice and decided to seek her baby."
"And along came Alice," Suzy added.
"When Alice came into our hearts and lives we didn't expect anything more. Mum wasn't surprised when Julia

told her. Said she'd had an aunt whom doctors had declared barren, but after adopting two children went on to give birth to two of her own.
Julia's gynaecologist said it could of been coincidence, but wasn't unheard of."
"And the Porsche you promised yourself?" Suzy teased.
"We'll see, I'll text you 'Pram or Porsche' when we know."

-

After breakfast they loaded Phil's car with bags for the tip. While he was gone Suzy carried on sorting. When he returned, they reloaded his car with charity-shop bags. She declined his offer of a pub lunch, "I'm only going to stay another hour to tidy up. Thanks for coming here last night Phil, it was a kind thought. Now you can get back to your girls," she insisted.
Phil put his overnight bag in the front of his car ready to leave "are you sure you'll be OK?"
"Go on," she said giving him a hug before waving goodbye as he drove off.

She went back inside the empty house and strangely no longer felt alone. It was as if the house and her mother were keeping her company. She emptied the contents from the small freezer into a cool box to take home, and made herself a milky coffee to use up the milk she'd brought with her.

Needing to write a couple of lists, she rummaged in her large bag for a pen. The folded newspaper Matt had given her was still there. She pulled it out to glance through, although most of it now was old news. Waiting for her coffee to cool, she read about Penns takeover which the paper had covered. Blazed across a page inside

was a photo of Mr Jenkins, the new owner of Penns shaking hands with previous owner Mr Hyatt. Windslow Haulage stated it had no plans to close the van delivery side of the business formally run by Penns. The parcel of land used for the lorry park had been sold. New industrial units would be built on the commercial site. Councillor Eric Fowles announced the new business units would provide more jobs and prosperity for the people of the town. Already several small businesses were showing interest. Mr Hyatt confirmed all staff had been successfully relocated or had accepted redundancy.
Suzy wondered which Richard had chosen. He'd never been ambitious or shown any desire to change jobs. With only the delivery vans to organise, his job should become less taxing which had to be better. If he'd chosen redundancy, their dream holiday could go ahead after all. With that positive thought she put the newspaper back into her bag, drank her coffee and got ready to leave.

- -

According to Gina's car satnav Parch's Estate Agents should only be five minutes away, but they'd passed the same line of shops twice.
"Is this Upton or Somerton?" Matt asked, studying the large Road Atlas in front of him trying to be helpful.
"Upton in Somerton, in Somerset I hope," she said getting frustrated. She'd been driving for hours and now was feeling tetchy. They'd planned to make stops along the way, but Matt had fallen asleep so she'd carried on hoping to make better timing. "Plenty of road signs to say how far to get somewhere, but none saying 'this place is called'," she moaned.
"Let's find a cafe," Matt suggested, seeing the same line of shops again.

"Oh no," she laughed recognising them. On a whim Gina turned left, following a lorry down a narrow street.
Matt pointed to a sign ahead for a municipal car park. At last, she could stop and park the car. While she was searching in her purse for change, Matt saw a woman carrying shopping appear from an alleyway and go to her car. "I think I know where the high street is."
Sure enough, the alleyway led to the shops and a café.
"Perfect," Gina said, looking at her watch "we've got an hour before our appointment."

When the waitress appeared with their order, Gina asked the whereabouts of the estate agents.
"Parch's?" the woman queried, and pointed across to the shop directly opposite. Matt laughed, their day was improving.

Leaving their car in the car park, allowed the agent to take them to view properties. Mr Morgan seemed amiable. He'd booked two farmhouses for them to see. They got into the back of his car. Gina smiled, full of enthusiasm. Matt tried to look interested, but he was tired of sitting in a car, and wondered if his lack of energy coincided with the medication he'd started taking.

The first place was a large working dairy farm. Definitely not what they were after, so didn't bother to get out of the car.

The second property was a farmhouse with stables and a busy riding school, once again unsuitable.
"Mr Morgan what type of property have you got written down that we're interested in?" Gina questioned.
"Farms," he replied.
"We're looking for a large farmhouse with a very small amount of land," she corrected him. "Perhaps we should

return to your shop and look through what you've got on your books."
"Let me show you Penhurst before I take you back," and drove for another thirty minutes.

Matt was beginning to feel queasy in the back. One minute they were travelling up a narrow road, the next they were going down, twisting and turning as the road dictated. Mr Morgan parked outside a huge empty dilapidated country house. In its heyday it must of been magnificent. Now sadly, a sorry sight in overgrown surroundings.

Matt got out of the car for some fresh air. Gina voiced her dismay, the appointment wasn't going well.

Back at his Estate Agency, Mr Morgan collated a pile of papers. A photo of each property and it's details listed on every sheet. He slipped them into a folder and handed it to Gina, arranging for them to return the next morning to discuss any that might be suitable.

To revive their spirits, they returned to the little café for refreshments. Gina was disheartened.

"You look like I feel, do you want one of my pills?" Matt joked. "There's four counties here, we can't expect to find our Shangri-La instantly, we need to look around."

"I know," she sighed.

He asked the waitress if she knew of a good hotel nearby. The only close hotel she'd recommend was small, family run and five minutes away.

"That will do, I don't want to sit in a car a minute longer." Gina was too tired to disagree.

-

In the morning they both rose refreshed and ready to resume their property hunt. Gina had picked out three

from the pile that might be worth a look. Relaxed after a leisurely breakfast, they returned to the Agency. This time, taking photocopies of the three they were interested in.
"We'll go and have a look Mr Morgan, and get back to you if we need to," she assured.

The first one took ages to find and was in the middle of nowhere. "Be like living in the wilderness," Matt remarked, relieved Gina felt the same.

The second one seemed a random design, a haphazard collection of buildings. They hadn't felt the desire to see inside either places. The third one looked more appealing on paper.
"Come on," she said "fingers crossed."
They drove for another hour, the sat-nav loosing it's signal from time to time. Gina confessed to having no idea of where they were. Matt couldn't look at the book of maps any longer, it was making him feel sick.
"I'm going to keep driving, we must come across civilisation eventually."
He hoped it wouldn't be too far away, already he could feel his colour draining.

Ten minutes later they drove into a small village with a pub. As Gina pulled in the pub's car park, Matt prayed it would be open. He stood outside the car giving his stomach a minute to settle. "Now that's what I call a proper country pub." He looked up at the dips in the Kings Arm's timeworn roof, leaning brick chimneys, and the lines of small uneven roof tiles, appreciating the spectacle. Outside facing the road, gnarled long wooden planks formed bench seats either side of the door.

It took a moment to adjust to the subdued light inside. Wooden beams crossed low ceilings with a fireplace in each bar. While Matt stood taking in the ambiance of the place, Gina ordered two coffees. There were several men chatting in groups amongst themselves. Matt noticed not only was Gina the only female present, but they were the only ones not drinking beer.

The landlord was chatty. "Not from round ere then, on holiday?"

Gina told him they'd arrived completely by chance. Becoming lost while looking for a property for sale, and showed him the place featured on the page.

The landlord laughed "that's miles away." He could tell they were city folk. "Looking to buy a holiday or weekend place?" he pried.

Matt got up to use the facilities, leaving Gina chatting, revealing their decision to move this way.

A delicious smell of cooking wafted through the pub. "What's that?" Matt asked, sniffing the air as he walked back to his seat.

"The wife's baking day, she's making meat pies, sausage rolls and pasties."

It was an easy decision to wait around for a hot pasty for lunch.

Gina enquired about somewhere to stay, needing somewhere while they looked around the area.

"I'll ask the wife. We let a couple of rooms during the summer, I'll go and see what she says."

He came back a few minutes later. "She says it's OK, so long as you don't want to get in there before three this afternoon. If you want dinner, she needs to know beforehand.

If you're serious about buying a place round ere, there's one I recon will go on the market any minute. Might be the sort of thing you're looking for. You'd best talk to

Sam Carter, he can tell you about it. He'll be in later," the landlord advised.

A double room and two meat pie dinners, were booked before they left the pub for a mooch around the surrounding countryside.

The next small town was fifteen minutes away. Matt drove, giving Gina the opportunity to look out of the window and enjoy the scenery.

They returned at five, having explored another village and a bigger town. Betty, the landlord's wife took them up to show them their room. "I've given you the biggest, the toilet's outside."

Matt flashed a look of concerned to Gina.

"I mean the bathroom is next door to yours. There's nobody else staying so it shouldn't be a bother. Can't have en-suites here, the rooms are too small. Oh, and mind the stairs, the old treads are a bit twisted."

Matt wasn't sure if the walls were out of line or the floor sloped, probably both but it added to the charm of the place.

"If you need anything, let us know downstairs," Betty smiled kindly. "Right, I'll leave you to it. I start serving dinners at half past six."

Matt looked at the old wooden door to the bathroom, convinced his father had one similar on a woodshed. He lifted the metal latch and peered in, being pleasantly surprised to find a spotlessly clean modern white suite and tiled shower cubical within.

Gina had kicked off her shoes and was lying on the bed. "It was worth getting lost, isn't this quaint? If we can

find a house with half the character and charm I'll be happy," she said in her glory.
Matt's vision of 'desired house in the country' wasn't anything so historic.

After dinner he challenged her to a game of darts. "I haven't played since I was a teenager," admitting she probably couldn't hit the board."
With only themselves in the smaller Saloon Bar, they decided to have a go. Three hundred and one, Matt chalked either side of the score board optimistically. "We're going to be here all night," she laughed. True enough, they were useless, darts was not their forte.

Gina volunteered to fetch more drinks from the main Public Bar. A number of people sat about in groups talking and enjoying their evening.
Jack, the landlord came over to serve her. "Sam!" he called across to one of the men chatting, "come and talk to these people."
Sam tried to ignore the request, he wasn't fond of 'townies'. They bought up the cheaper houses and small farms for their weekends and holiday lets. Leaving them empty most of the year and the land unworked, selling up when they got bored with them. Townies didn't help the local farming community.
Jack shouted louder "Sam!", causing people to look around. Sam ambled over to the bar.
"Pleased to meet you," Gina gushed.
Sam smiled awkwardly. She read his attitude loud and clear, smiled, picked up her drinks and headed back to Matt.
"She's bought you a drink," Jack said, handing Sam a pint. "Wouldn't hurt you to show em the Brewer's place." They

both knew it was only a matter of time before it went up for sale. Sam collected his drink and walked across to the Saloon Bar, intending to just put his head around the doorway to thank her.
During opening hours the door was permanently wedged open, allowing easier access for patrons carrying drinks. He didn't see them sat behind it, so stepped further into the room.
"Hello," Gina beamed.
Sam felt obligated to walk round to thank her.
Matt stood up "let me get you a drink," unaware the drink Sam carried had been bought by Gina. Sam sat with them for most of the evening, happy to let them buy him beer.
"I'll be there t'morra, bout eleven if ya want t' look round."
Margery Brewer wouldn't be back for another couple of days. Sam kept an eye on the place while she was away and fed the feral farm cats that lived in the barn.

-

"Not too much for me," Gina requested, when Betty took their orders for breakfast. She hadn't forgotten the large sized portions Betty served the evening before. Claiming she'd become as fat as a pig if they stayed much longer.

Matt struggle to clear his plate. Whether it was the fresh air or local produce, everything they'd eaten had tasted delicious.
"More tea or coffee?" Betty offered as she cleared away.
"That was wonderful, thank you," Matt praised.

Back in their room Matt laid on top of the bed. "I shouldn't of eaten that huge breakfast, I could do with another sleep now."

Gina snuggled up beside him. The weekend away was doing them both a power of good. Matt had relaxed, laughed and become more like his old self. These couple of blissful days together had made Gina set on ending her busy career. All they needed now was to find their new home.
"Come on," she coaxed wriggling out of his arms to start packing her bag. "We don't want to be late for Sam."
"I doubt if he'll be early, he had quite a skinfull last night," Matt reasoned, sitting up.

He carried their overnight bags down to load into Gina's car. She tidied their room and checked for anything left behind. Matt went into the bar to settle their account with Jack the landlord, and for directions to the farm Sam had agreed to show them. While he waited in the car for Gina, he took the little charm from his jacket pocket. "I hope you're going to help us find a house soon," and carefully put it back inside his pocket. Gina appeared at last.
"I thought you were in a hurry."
She held out a paper bag, showing him two of Betty's Cornish pasties.

~ 5 ~

Ashwood Farm wasn't far away. Following the landlords instructions lead them to a closed four-bar gate. Gina got out to see if she could see Sam.

Sam didn't think they would turn up, believing they hadn't noticed he'd deliberately omitted to give them directions the night before. He'd probably never see them again, besides the place wasn't actually up for sale. Walking back to his van, he recognised the woman peering over the gate. Cursing under his breath, went to open it.

Gina drove through into the farmyard and parked next to his scruffy van. They waited for him to join them. Sam lent against his van, took out a battered tobacco tin and began making a cigarette, rolling it up skilfully between grubby fingers. "There's nobody ere, if ya want t' look round." It wasn't his job to sell the place, nor was he going to give them a guided tour.

Matt stood in the yard looking about. The farmhouse was big, tired in appearance but with potential, . . if you were prepared to throw money at it.

Gina had walked around the outside of the farmhouse, and now was heading towards a barn. It could make a huge sized garage, especially with all the rubbish removed. She assumed the other brick outbuildings were to house animals. Matt joined her to wander around. They could see sheep in fields and a wood in the distance. He wanted to ask Sam how much land came with the farmhouse, so they walked back to find him.

“Did y’ see cottages?” Sam asked, and pointed across the yard to the start of a lane. “Two farm labourer’s cottages, Mrs Brewer converted em t’ olliday lets.”
Gina turned round and sprinted off, she wanted to see these.
“Interested in olliday lets?” Sam questioned.
“No, I just want a place to live in,” Matt answered.
“Tell er they’re two bedroomed.”
Matt went to catch her up. She’d found a big wooden box beside one of the front doors, and pushed it over onto its side to stand on.
“Is that safe?” he asked, offering his hand to steady her.
“Yes, it’s solid, full of dry dirt and dead plants,” she said, standing on tiptoe, trying to look through one of the cottage windows. “Hmm, they’re too small and too far from the house.”
“For what?”
“My mother,” Gina replied, quite forgetting she hadn’t actually mentioned her moving with them.
“Your mother?” he asked shocked, this was the first he’d heard of it.
“I can’t move out and leave her behind!” she snapped.
“It’s too far away.”
“When were you going to tell me? When I’d signed the contract and bumped into her in the house! Is there anybody else I don’t know about? ex-husbands? children? You seem to have forgotten the mother you live with!” he sniped angrily.
Gina was fuming, how dare he speak to her like that. She marched back to her car and started the engine. Matt got in with a face like thunder. He’d briefly thanked Sam before Gina zoomed off in temper, her car tyres sending up a shower of stones.

Sam had heard their raised voices, he knew 'a domestic' when he heard one. Judging by their faces, he definitely wouldn't be seeing them again.

Gina drove fast all the way back to Matt's flat in silence. He got out with his bag, slammed her car door shut without speaking. She sped off.

Inside his flat Matt threw his bag to the floor. Yesterday he held all his hopes and dreams in his arms, now it had all blown up in his face. He took the small plastic pot of pills from his pocket and threw it with all the might he could muster. It flew through the air, hit the corner frame of the mirror and ricocheted back, just missing his head. He walked into the lounge and slumped onto the settee consumed with anger and despair. He'd never spoken to anyone so spitefully, let alone the woman he loved more than life itself. What had got into him? These past weeks his moods had become bipolar, yet Gina had patiently stood by him, endlessly supporting him with her love. Now his bitter words had destroyed their relationship.

Calming down, he began to reflect. Appreciating it was natural for any daughter to have a strong bond with her mother, of course she'd want her near. Suzie had always been the closest to their mother. Exhausted by anger, blamed himself for the disastrous mess he'd created.

Gina had driven back on auto pilot in silent temper. Elaine wasn't expecting her daughter home so soon, she assumed the two lovebirds would have dinner together. She heard Gina's car almost screech as it stopped in the drive, the front door slam and her daughter stomp up to her room and slam the door.

‘Oh dear’ Elaine thought, a row, . . and by all accounts it sounded like a humdinger! She’d give Gina a couple of hours to calm down before venturing up with tea.

Gina threw herself onto her bed and thumped her pillows in frustration. Why, why, why? had she pressed the self-destruct button when everything in her life was going so well. Matt hadn’t even met her mother, what had she been thinking? Quite rightly he’d been angry when he felt she had deceived him. She’d never ever loved anyone so much in her entire life. Now it was over, her heart was broken and it was all her own fault. She cried herself to sleep.

Elaine put the kettle on, it was time for tea and sympathy. Her daughter might be gifted in business, but when it came to her own personal life, she was hopeless. Gina was awake, red eyed, laying on her bed staring at the ceiling when her mother came in with her tea.

“It’s over Mum,” Gina tried to explain through tears, sniffs, and snuffles.

“No wonder,” Elaine said, getting the gist of it. “We’ve never met, Gina I might not of liked him either.”

Galloping along in her dream world, Gina hadn’t given Matt or her mother any proper consideration and now she felt wretched.

“What was he like?” Elaine asked, cunningly knowing exactly what she was doing.

“Wonderful,” Gina answered “kind, funny, generous, clever, . . . attractive.”

Elaine pretended to ponder, “then he won’t be lonely for long.” She closed the door leaving Gina to her thoughts.

At three in the morning Gina crept out of the house to her car. Elaine heard the car engine start up and her daughter drive away quietly. She smiled to herself, having a good idea where she was going.

Matt was sprawled across his settee in the dark, asleep and still wearing the clothes he'd travelled home in. He heard the doorbell, it could only be one person. Dishevelled, he went to open the door to let her in. Remaining silent, he'd said more than enough earlier.
"Can we talk?" Gina asked quietly.
He kept her standing by the front door in the hallway.
"I don't live with my mother, she lives with me. She moved in last year when she sold her large guest house in Brighton. I wanted to move to the countryside, she intended to move with me. Not in the same house, just nearby. There have never been any husbands, officially or otherwise. No children, I'm not maternal. If that's a problem," she said sadly "you must say. I'm so sorry about today," she turned to leave. "I love you Matt," she said softly, beginning to reopen the front door.

He pulled her back inside, wrapping his arms around her, pulling her to him. "I've never been so wrong," he said, holding her tight. "I thought I'd lost you forever, can we start again?" Embracing and kissing they inched their way towards his bedroom.
"Matt I can't stay, I've got a plane to catch tomorrow." She checked her watch and corrected herself "today, in eight hours."
"I'm sorry," he said standing still, understanding.
She resumed their kissing "I'm going to be late, . . . very late," she said continuing their journey.

-

When Matt woke up he was alone. He'd intended to get up, at least to make her a drink before she left, but he hadn't heard her go. He swung his legs out of bed and stood up, yesterday's clothes littered the floor. He picked some up on route to the bathroom.
"Ouch!" he winced, treading barefoot on what felt like a stone. Under a shirt, his jacket lay on the floor. He picked it up, shook it vigorously before remembering the charm zipped into a pocket. He examined the little black cat, his foot had rendered no damage. Turning it over in the palm of his hand, he thought again about the farm they'd been looking around with Sam, before everything went pear shaped. Holding the charm inspired an idea.

He found the phone number of The Kings Arms on his receipt. Betty answered, after exchanging pleasantries he asked if she had a phone number for Sam.
"He'll be here later," she said "he's going to cut our hedge at the back."
Leaving his number, Matt asked her to get Sam to give him a call.

At eleven o'clock Matt phoned the pub again. Landlord Jack, recognised Matt's voice "wanting to come back already?" he joked, "what can I do for you Squire?"
"A word with Sam if he's there," Matt asked.
Jack laid the phone down at the side of the till, "someone give Sam a shout, he's out the back!" he called across to a couple of local lads.
Matt could hear general chatter from people in the bar, followed by the sound of Sam's footsteps as he clomped along in his wellies to answer the phone.
"Yes?" Sam answered.

"Sam, is there any chance you could show me around that farm again?"
Sam thought for a moment "You'd 'afft' t' be quick, she's due back t'morra."
"If I set off shortly, I could be there in about four hours. Can I meet you at the pub? I'll pay you for your time."
"I'll be ere," Sam agreed.
Just before Sam went, Matt shouted down the phone "tell Betty I'll want a room tonight."
"What did he want?" Jack asked, being nosey.
"Wants a room ere t'night," Sam said, returning to the hedge cutting outside, keeping his business to himself.

The main roads were unusually quiet, and although Matt knew it was just coincidence, there was something eerie about the way virtually every set of traffic lights he came to, turned green. The light traffic shortened his journey by almost an hour.
He turned into the pub's car park at four o'clock, euphoric at beating rush hour. Then grinned, realising 'rush hour' probably had little effect in this small village. Matt recognised Sam's van parked by the entrance, so he was about somewhere.

The pub was taking delivery of supplies. The driver was busy unloading, stacking boxes onto a porters trolley. Matt parked in the far corner, knowing the lorry would have to swing round to get out of the small car park.

Betty was pleased to see him return. "I've put you in the same room," she said, handing Matt the key. "Your young lady not with you this time?"
"I'm afraid she's away working," and then, thinking of his stomach asked Betty about ordering dinner.

"Cottage Pie with fresh veg, apple crumble with custard or cream?" she offered.
"Sounds perfect," Matt smiled, remembering her cooking was heaven. With his accommodation sorted, he looked around for Sam who was nowhere to be seen. Without a comfort stop on route, Matt headed for the toilets. Sam was in there washing his hands.
"Ya came then," Sam uttered casually, "I'll see ya at farm." He walked out to get into his van. Apart from the lorry, the only other vehicle in the car park was a new dark blue convertible BMW. If that's Matey's car, Sam thought 'ee must av some dosh'.

The farm gate was already wide open when Matt approached. He drove through and parked next to Sam's van, got out of his car and stood looking about. Becoming pleasantly aware of the silence, unless you counted birdsong. He remained still, watching small birds flying about at high speed, twittering as they swooped and dived, zooming around like Spitfires.
"Swallows," Sam said appearing from nowhere. "They comes back every year an' nest in barn, I'll show ya if y' like."
Matt followed.
"Not got y' girlfriend with ya?" Sam acknowledged, as they walked towards the barn.
"No, she's working away."
"Where's that then?"
"To be honest Sam, I forgot to ask, she flew out this morning."
Sam looked bemused, and shook his head, chuckling to himself. "She got on a plane an y' don't know where?"

"It's not unusual Sam, we often spend more time on planes than together," Matt told him.
Sam whistled "won't catch me up there," pointing skywards.
"It's our jobs. Now we've both had enough, that's why we're serious about buying a place in the country."
"Ya not pilots?"
Matt started laughing, "no Sam, we're not pilots."
"Must pay well, I've seen y' cars," Sam said direct.
"I'll happily swop mine for an old Land Rover when the time comes."
"You can av my old van if y' like," Sam grinned.
Matt laughed, beginning to like Sam and his dry humour.
"Don't rush t' sell it, I know just the smarmy git oo'd loved t' av it," Sam remarked.
"Smarmy?" Matt questioned, raising an eyebrow.
They stood in the barn looking up at the swallow's nests along the beams. Chicks peeped out, watching their parents swooping and twittering. Matt felt the urge to duck as one flew past almost skimming his head. "Wow," he said appreciating their aerobatics.
"Look at these little beggars." Sam lead Matt to the back of the barn. He gently lifted an old canvas cloth covering several bales of hay. In a hollow of the bottom bale, four tiny kittens mewed as the light disturbed them. Matt's mouth fell open, seeing two black, and two tortoiseshell coloured, all unbelievably cute.
Sam replaced the cover. "Mum's up there," pointing to a tortoiseshell cat watching them from the top of the bales. He tipped out dry cat food from a box he was carrying.
Matt followed Sam out of the barn. "What will happen to them?"

"They live ere, they's y' eco-friendly vermin control," Sam chuckled.
"How likely is this place to go on the market?" Matt asked.
"I'd put money on it, but y' won't get it cheap. She's started knocking about w' local estate agent. She's not daft, an he'll want money."
"How big is this place?"
Sam lead him to a higher mound of ground past the barn to look down over the landscape. "Those three fields, them three w' sheep in, an that wood," Sam stood pointing them out "an what y'can see around ere, a bit shy o' fourteen acres."
Matt swallowed hard, being taken aback. "Christ!" he said "that's a lot to look after."
"Easy," Sam shrugged, "them sheep aren't er's. Ted Lawson rents fields t' put his ewes on. Ee looks after em, an they keeps grass down."
Walking past the cottages, Sam stopped. "What would ya do w' them?"
Matt looked blank.
Sam pointed to an upstairs window in the end cottage. "I's born in that room, my dad were cowman ere."
Now he understood Sam's fondness for the place. Matt was concerned about the work needed for the farm's upkeep. He didn't want to bite off more than he could chew, financially or otherwise.
"How many men does Mrs Brewer employ?"
Sam laughed "I does most jobs round here, three t' four days a week, keeps this place ticking over."

Matt turned to walk back to his car. "There's a lot here to think about Sam," Matt professed, being realistic. "I do like it, very, very much, but at the end of the day it

will be down to money, . . . and I'd have to bring Gina back to see over it properly."
"She's ad plans drawn up t' convert dairy in t' bungalow if ya's interested," Sam added to the conversation.
Now Matt knew he'd overheard their argument. Before getting into his car, he thanked Sam for showing him round. "If you could speak to Mrs Brewer on my behalf to let her know I'm genuinely interested. I've written my number down for you." Matt handed Sam an envelope containing money, with his number written across it. He started the engine, bid Sam goodbye and drove out of the yard. His mind buzzing with all the new things he'd seen and learnt about the farm.

- -

Elsie looked at her watch "I'd better think about getting back now Ducks," she said to Rachel. "I've got Gwen popping round later."
"Did you get everything on your list?" Rachel asked, finishing her cappuccino. They always stayed for a drink in the supermarket's café after Elsie had done her shopping. It gave her legs a rest from walking around with her trolley.
As far as Rachel was concerned, apart from being Elsie's friend, Gwen was just the nice neighbour a few doors away, who was happy to 'keep an eye' if Rachel went away, fetch odd bits of shopping and stay for the occasional cup of tea.
"I expect she wants to talk about the shop."
"What shop?" Rachel asked making conversation.
"The Golf Club's decided to sell their shop and have given Gwen first option to buy it," Elsie revealed.
Rachel admitted she knew nothing about the local Golf Club, never mind it's shop.

"Gwen and her husband ran it for years, he was one of the Golf Club's instructors. I thought she'd give it up when he died, but she stayed on. Said it kept her busy and the members she knew came in for a chat."
"Why would she want to buy it?" Rachel was wary. If the shop was making a good profit, she doubted the Club would be selling it off.
"I think it's her boyfriend's idea," Elsie continued "he's told her they can put in half each."
"Boyfriend?"
"Oh yes, Duck," Elsie pulled a knowing face. "He's been about for quite a while. You must of seen his car parked outside, the deep bluey-mauve one."
Rachel couldn't explain why, but the hairs on her neck began to rise, something didn't feel right.
"How did she meet him?" Rachel pursued with curiosity.
"I'm not sure, Duck," Elsie stopped for a moment trying to remember. "I think he won some golf lessons in a local raffle and she taught him, . . well it was something like that."

Back home, while Elsie went inside to take her coat off, Rachel carried in her shopping. She'd started to put it away, when they both heard a knock on the door.
"That'll be Gwen, put the kettle on, Duck," Elsie called out.
Rachel went to the door and welcomed Gwen inside.
"She's just changing her shoes, go through."
Gwen was familiar with the house, and made her way to the small sitting room.
"Ah, that's better," Elsie sighed with relief, wearing her slippers and heading for her chair by the window.
"And how are you Duck?" she asked Gwen.

Rachel carried in a tray of tea, she'd added a couple cupcakes on a plate for them to have with it.
"Aren't you staying to have one, Duck?"
Rachel declined, remembering her own shopping was defrosting in the boot of her car. "Nice to see you Gwen," Rachel acknowledged politely, turning to go. "I'll put your cold stuff in the fridge on my way out Elsie," and left them to their tea.
Gwen always raised her voice slightly when she spoke to Elsie, presuming she was hard of hearing. While Rachel loaded Elsie's fridge, she could hear their conversation. Gwen was excited about buying the shop, the Golf Club had accepted their offer. "Dick is going to use his redundancy money, while I sell my house. We can live in the flat above the shop," Gwen chirped.
Rachel closed Elsie's front door and walked to her car.

- -

While Suzy transferred the food she'd bought back home into her freezer, she thought about her time at Squirrels Chase. It hadn't been as difficult as she'd feared, although having Phil's company had made a difference. She couldn't think of Phil or Julia without smiling, a precious new baby to look forward to. "Look after them Mum," she said, sending a prayer skywards.

Just as she was wondering where Richard could be, the phone rang. I bet that's him, she thought picking it up to answer.
"Hi Mum," Kate said brightly. Their tête-à-tête filled a pleasurable hour as they brought each other up to date with their news.
"We've managed to get a cheap last minute holiday," Kate announced.
"We?" Suzy probed.

"Mum, there's somebody I'd like you and Dad to meet." Suzy could hear the joy in her daughter's voice. She'd perceived a while ago, there was a reason for Kate not wanting to come home this summer, . . most likely this 'somebody' could be the cause.

Suzy heard Richard's car come into the drive and got up to switch the oven on. "Hi," she called from the kitchen.

He asked how she had got on.

"Well, we've made a start," mentioning Phil's help.

"It won't take long if you both do it," Richard said. "I expect Phil wants his money."

Richard's words were hurtful. He was wrong, selling Squirrels Chase had been the last thing on Phil's mind this weekend.

"It's got to go on the market one day," reading her expression and attempting to redeem himself. In three sentences he'd deflated her happy mood.

During dinner, Suzy told him about Kate's phone call. "I wonder what her 'somebody' will be like?" she said, with an inquisitive smile. Suggesting, it would probably be best to visit Kate after 'she and her friend' had returned from their holiday. Richard agreed with a grunt, flicking through TV channels trying to find the one he wanted.

"And what have you been doing this weekend?" she asked with cheerful interest.

"Just sorting out a few things," he replied, without volunteering any more information.

By the time she'd unpacked, and sorted out their laundry Suzy was tired. Bathed and in her nightclothes she flopped into bed, leaving Richard downstairs watching yet another football match on the Sports Channel. She hadn't forgotten about the article she'd read in the paper Matt had given her. It was pointless to keep avoiding the subject and decided to tackle Richard the next evening.

-

Before he could switch the television on after dinner, she unfolded the newspaper and placed it in front of him. "So what did you choose, redundancy or relocation?" pointing to the printed words.

He was shocked and totally unprepared for her direct question. "I've taken redundancy."

Now she was shocked, he'd never liked change of any sort. "And?" she challenged.

"I'm going to put the money towards a shop, a sports shop."

She wasn't sure this was a good idea. There were too many small shops going under locally, soon Charity shops would outnumber the retailers. "A shop?" she said, trying not to sound critical.

"I'm buying it with a friend, we're going half each. It will be half golf and half fishing," he stated.

This was a small comfort, at least he wasn't attempting this venture on his own. She wondered which driver had suggested the idea, picturing them sitting round, trying to think of what to do for the best when they heard Penns would be closing. "Where is it?" multiple questions were filling her head.

"Let's see if we get it first," he said calmly.

"So when will you finish at the yard?"

"I'm helping the new manager with existing customers and their routes, but after next week he's on his own, that's it." Richard concluded.

"Gosh," she slowly emitted, trying to take in the end of an era.
Richard looked down uncomfortably, and she wondered if he was having doubts already.

-

Rachel phoned early Thursday evening, checking to see if Suzy was OK, knowing she'd gone back to Squirrels Chase alone. "Can you chat?" she asked, not wanting to interrupt if Suzy was cooking.
Suzy was free. Richard had gone to watch some foreign football match down the pub with his mates. She was catching up with ironing and watching a boring film, so was very happy to stop. The two friends nattered for a while.
"Did you ask Richard about his job?" Rachel inquired innocently.
Suzy repeated the conversation she'd had with Richard earlier. "Why-on-earth does he want a sports shop? I know I'm being horrid, but between you and me, I hope it falls through."
Rachel felt a knot tighten in her stomach, and prayed her suspicions were wrong. "Are you going back again this weekend?" she asked, trying to sound normal.
"Yes, I expect I'll be spending my weekends 'sorting out' for a while.
They said goodbye, Suzy continued with her ironing oblivious to Rachel's anguish.

Rachel tossed and turned, she couldn't sleep with so many inane questions circling around in her head. Intuition and coincidence were no grounds for accusation. For her own peace of mind verifying facts became a priority.

Wide awake at five thirty, there seemed no point in lying in bed any longer. She reached for her phone, somewhere it held Suzy's address. She'd never been to the house but had an idea where to find it. She pulled on a tracksuit, and with trepidation crept out of her house and got into her car.

She recognised Suzy's car. Fortunately she'd arrived home first with Richard's car parked behind. Rachel drove past slowly, craning her neck to read Richard's number plate. She turned her car around, passing their drive once more rechecking. If Suzy planned to be away this weekend, Rachel would be checking number plates on any purpley blue cars parked in Leake Road.

-

At two o'clock Saturday afternoon, Rachel had finished her work for the day. If she drove down Leake Road quickly, she hoped Elsie wouldn't spot her car passing by. The nearer she got to Leake Road, her uneasy feeling increased.

There were no blue or mauve cars of any description parked, and with a sigh of relief she drove home.

At home, Rachel left her bag and keys on the hall table, slipped off her shoes and walked wearily into the lounge. She sat on the settee, leaned back, put her feet up and closed her eyes, promising herself five minutes rest.

"I'm off now," Michael repeated for the second time. Rachel opened her eyes, her son was standing over her.

"What?" she said, trying to grasp reality.

"I've got a gig tonight at The Poachers, so I'll be late in."

She sat up and looked at her watch, she'd slept for nearly two hours.

Michael's 'band friends' were waiting for him outside in their black van. He picked up his leather jacket and guitar from the hall and rushed out to join them.
She stood at the window to watch them drive off. The weather had changed since she'd driven home, now drizzly rain made everywhere look cold and bleak. No matter, a long soak in a warm bath, a girly film on the TV and the leftover fish pie in the fridge to finish off with a glass of wine was the perfect way to spend her peaceful evening tonight. Her intention of repeating the drive along Leake Road began to wane, consoling herself that maybe the car had been just a coincidence. It's colour wasn't unique and she doubted Gwen would get involved with a married man.

-

In the morning Rachel woke early at six. Listening to the falling rain was soothing, knowing she didn't have to get up and leave for work. If Michael had come home, she hadn't heard him. Plans for the day crept into her mind, nothing exciting, Sundays generally involved housework and laundry. She got up to make herself coffee, stepping over Michael's jacket and paraphernalia in a heap at the bottom of the stairs. Her idea of making an early start on the housework evaporated, with Michael sleeping it wouldn't be fair to start making a noise.

Again the idea of some lowlife deceiving Suzy and Gwen gnawed. The rain had stopped. Rachel slipped a coat over her pyjamas, got into her car and headed for Leake Road, planning to drive through as before.
She couldn't fail to miss the purpley blue car parked outside Gwen's house, reading the number plate as she drove by. Painfully, she accepted the truth, . . . it was the

same car! Now she was in an impossible position, 'dammed if she spoke out, dammed if she didn't!' She would return later, Elsie deserved to know the truth. They had never lied to each other.

Despite trying to keep her mind on chores, Rachel couldn't stop thinking about Suzy who was oblivious to her husband's deceit. She left a note for Michael, placing it in the middle of the fridge door, held by magnets, hopefully plain to see 'Gone to Nannas'. Michael had yet to emerge from his bedroom.

The car had gone when Rachel drew up outside Elsie's house. Elsie opened the door, pleased to see her visitor. "Hello Duck, come in. I didn't know you was coming." Then she saw the unease in Rachel's eyes. "what's up? Duck."

"Gwen's boyfriend is married. It's Suzy, and she doesn't know about Gwen."

"Oh my gawd," Elsie sat back into her chair. "We'll have to tell her, Duck," she said, slowly shaking her head. Rachel's eyes flooded with tears, the situation resurrecting painful memories from her own past.

"Come here my Duck, you'll be alright," Elsie hugged her tightly, their 'déjà vu' moment replayed.

There was a knock at the door. Elsie directed Rachel into the kitchen to recover, and went to answer it.

"Hello," Gwen beamed "I've just come to say I'm going into Lanchester tomorrow, so if you need any shopping?" Elsie beckoned her inside.

"We're going to the solicitors to sign the papers for the shop," Gwen relayed, brimming with excitement.

Rachel stepped out of the kitchen to join them. "Gwen, he's married, his wife doesn't know about you," she said, solemnly.
"He's getting a divorce, their marriage has been over for ages!" Gwen bristled, standing her ground. "Anyway, Dick wouldn't lie to me," she spat out angrily.
"You knew?" Rachel was stunned.
Elsie opened the front door for Gwen to leave, shutting it with force behind her.
Rachel's tears fell. Elsie guided her to a chair "you sit there my Duck," kindly rubbing gentle circles on Rachel's back to comfort. "I'll get us a brandy."
Elsie only drank brandy for medicinal purposes, a neat tot with a sprinkle of sugar stirred in. They sat, reflecting in silence.
"That poor girl, first her mum and now this," Elsie said, slowly shaking her head, covering her mouth briefly with her hand.
"I can't tell her," Rachel confessed, feeling destroyed.
"Don't you worry my Duck, she'll find out soon enough. Then she'll need your help," Elsie reassured with compassion.

~ 6 ~

On Monday morning Suzy was having a quick tidy around the kitchen before leaving for work. She could hear Richard moving about upstairs. Normally he would have gone by now, but with only a few days left at the yard she assumed he'd no rigid routine.

He walked into the kitchen to speak to her, sitting himself down at the table and gestured her to join him. She faced him, puzzled, wondering what he wanted.

"Suzy, I want a divorce."

She sat, anchored by shock, unable to take in, or comprehend his words.

"I want a divorce," he repeated. "I should have told you before, but what with losing your mum, I couldn't do that to you. I'll always love you, but I'm in love with somebody else."

She stayed rooted to the chair, paralysed by his statement. Inside she screamed, ranted and raved, questioned and begged, . . . but remained stunned, unable to move, unable to speak.

"I'll take my things and move out Friday," he clarified, and rose from the table. Seeing the result of his words instinctively moved closer to comfort her, but stopped, thinking better of it. "I'm sorry," he said, and walked out.

Dazed, she remained fixed to the spot by his announcement for what seemed an eternity. She had no idea what to do next, her world had just ended. In her heart of hearts, she honestly hadn't seen it coming. Her survival instinct kicked in, she got up and drove to work.

Karen often arrived early, wanting to get on with her urgent assignments before interruptions and the general running of office life distracted her. She was surprised to find Suzy sitting in her office waiting. "Is everything OK Suzy?" she asked concerned.

"Richard's just told me he's leaving and wants a divorce," Suzy announced, numb without feeling.

Karen could see she was deeply shaken. "Suzy, I'm so sorry," she said with genuine sympathy. "Have you had a chance to think about what you want to do? Is there anyone you can stay with for a while?"

"Yes," Suzy lied.

Karen advised more as a friend than her manager. "Suzy, I'll do what I can. Get your doctor to sign you off for a month, I'll temporarily pencil in 'depression' for your absence. Karen put her arm around Suzy to comfort, "phone me if you need anything."

Suzy got up to leave, and with a ghost of a smile, thanked her.

From her office window, Karen watched Suzy leave the building. It wouldn't be long before colleagues started to ask questions, Suzy had always been popular. Soon she'd let slip Suzy's predicament, knowing by experience it was far better for bad news to spread around the offices and burn itself out before Suzy came back, . . . if she came back.

Karen thought about her own sister who'd recently experienced a similar occurrence, when her husband had been distracted by a much younger woman. Sinking her sister to the very bottom of life's swamp, taking her several months before she could start coping again. Her sister wasn't the first, and she knew Suzy wouldn't be the last. "Husbands? the bastards!" Karen muttered angrily under her breath.

Standing in her kitchen, Suzy poured herself a large gin and gulped down half of it. Although she could feel her legs shaking, she didn't want to sit back at the table again. She tipped the rest of the drink down the sink and went upstairs to pack. Without Kate the house felt empty, without Richard their house was no longer a home.
She loaded a few items of food into a box, got in her car and headed for Squirrels Chase. Whatever unsolvable drama or catastrophe occurred, without fail Matt, Phil and herself would be homeward bound. Touching base, whether they stayed minutes, hours or longer, the feeling of safety and the warm welcome from their mother always set them back on life's road able to cope once again.

When she opened the front door of Squirrels Chase the feeling of reassurance and safety embraced her, the empty house felt more like home than the one she'd just left. She switched off her phone. Here in private isolation she could cry, sink into depths her soul had not yet discovered, drink to oblivion and eventually try to face the mess of her disintegrating life. Feeling exhausted and empty she took herself off to bed, accompanied by self-pity.

- -

Several times Rachel phoned Suzy's home number and mobile, leaving her messages. Getting no response, decided to visit Suzy at home.
Roped into an impromptu meeting, Rachel left work much later than usual. Once again she drove passed Suzy's

house. Without cars in the drive and in total darkness, the house appeared empty. She changed direction to Leake Road, half expecting to see Richard's car parked outside Gwen's house. There it was plain to see, now Rachel worried, had Suzy found out?

-

Suzy remained unreachable by phone. If she wasn't in Ashton, Rachel guessed she had probably gone back to her mother's house.

In her office, Rachel rescheduled her hours, giving herself two days holiday to find her best friend. Michael would keep an eye on Elsie while she was away.

Rachel put an overnight bag into her car and set off. She knew her way to Kirston, but to find the house she'd have to rely on a vague memory of when she followed Suzy's car from Rowben Court.

Beginning to recognise the area, Rachel stopped to ask directions at a corner shop. A customer kindly pointed to Beeches Road.

Turning into the drive, Rachel saw Suzy's car parked beside the garage. She was too far from home to fob her off with the excuse of 'just passing', and turning up was rather over dramatic for not answering her phone.

Rachel rang the bell, planning to improvise a reason depending on her reception. There was no answer, she rang again and waited. She was about to walk away when the door opened. Suzy stood before her, eyes red and puffy from crying.

"You know," they both said in unison.

Inside Rachel gave Suzy a comforting hug.

She unpacked a meal and two bottles of red wine from her bag. In the evening the two friends shared food, tears and emotions.

The wine had seemed a good idea at the time, although in the morning they weren't so sure.

"Will you be alright staying here on your own?" Rachel asked, hating to leave Suzy alone again but needing to get back.

"I've got plenty to do here to occupy myself."

"That's not what I meant, . . and switch your phone back on," Rachel pleaded.

Suzy gave a weak smile and raised her hand to wave. She watched Rachel's car leave the drive and closed the door. Alone again, her sadness soon returned. She knew the only way to cope with her blues would be to keep busy, so went back to sorting out her mother's things.

- -

Sam waited for Jeremy Parker to leave Ashwood Farm before talking to Margery Brewer. Why she'd got tied up with him was a mystery. Sam had the cut of him alright, Parker was only out for himself. He might portray a suave full-of-himself character to others, but Sam knew he was full of something less fragrant.

When Parker heard Mrs Brewer had mentioned she was thinking of selling her farm, he was round there like a shot, falling over himself to handle the sale. He'd flattered, wined and dined, and wormed his way into her life.

Sam told her about showing a couple round the farm who were looking to buy a place in the West country. "I think theys genuine, ee come back f' second look. Like t' speak t' yer, if y' be sellin," Sam said, passing on Matt's request.

"What did you think of them Sam?" Margery asked.

"Alright," Sam replied.
'Alright' was praise indeed from Sam.
"Wouldn't urt t' meet em, ee's left his number," Sam suggested, rummaging in his pockets to find it. Margery agreed to think about it, she hadn't officially put the farm up for sale.

- -

"Sam!" Matt said, suddenly recognising his voice and surprised to hear from him.
"She's agreed t' meet ya!" Sam repeated, shouting louder above his van's noisy engine. "But keep yer' edd down, y' don't want that Parker poking his nose in."
"Who?"
"Er estate agent friend," Sam spat out.
Matt felt happy, chuffed to hear Sam's news.
"Thank Mrs Brewer, tell her we'll come up this weekend if that's convenient for her. We'll meet you at The Kings Arms Saturday," Matt said on impulse.

Reality dawned, he hadn't consulted Gina before blundering in making arrangements. His numerical mind sprang into action. Calculations of their combined finances remained unknown and as yet not discussed. He'd need to update his financial profile and assets for an indication towards what money they could lay on the table.
Ashwood Farm wouldn't come cheap.
He thought about Squirrels Chase. Although the idea of selling didn't sit comfortably, he could do with its monetary support. It's sale would have to be discussed with Phil and Suzy, then realised they hadn't spoken since the funeral. He felt a pang of guilt, he'd been so wrapped up with his own troubles, he hadn't checked to see if they were alright.

He phoned Suzy, first her mobile and then her house, but with no answer decided to try again later.

- -

Gina had booked a table for three at Spexhalls for Saturday evening. Her treat for the two special people in her life - Matt and her mother. The meal would also serve the purpose of having them meet each other for the first time. Knowing the importance of first impressions, she'd picked Spexhalls as mutual ground, not at her house or Matt's flat.

When Matt phoned with news of meeting Mrs Brewer, her feelings rankled. To be fair, he hadn't known about the surprise dinner date. Never-the-less her priority remained the same, for Matt and her mother to meet.

At his flat, they sat together watching TV, casually eating a takeaway and talking through their options. Gina agreed to postpone the meal, they couldn't afford to snub Mrs Brewer.

"Couldn't your mother come with us?" Matt suggested, trying to be reasonable. "Another opinion about the farm would be useful."

"Brilliant!" Gina praised "I'll asked her tonight, I'm sure she'd love to."

"Could I meet you both at The Kings Arms Saturday morning? I'd like to talk to Suzy first."

If Suzy was agreeable to sell Squirrels Chase, he assumed Phil would also consent.

Gina had an idea of what was going through Matt's mind. "See you Saturday," she said, giving him a lasting goodbye kiss, before heading home.

-

Matt called Suzy several times without success, and by Friday began to worry. Fearing something was wrong, he phoned his office with an excuse, telling Caroline he planned to work from home. He'd already packed a bag in advance, guessing Gina would push to stay at the pub. Putting it into his car meant one less thing to think about for Saturday.
He wanted to discuss Squirrels Chase. If Suzy wasn't answering her phone, he would have to call in to see her. Matt set off to her house in Ashton.

It looked as if she wasn't home, the curtains were closed and the house seemed empty. Regardless, he rang the bell and banged on the door. Peering through the glass in the front door he saw a collection of mail inside on the floor.
Out of the corner of his eye, he noticed the neighbour's curtains move.
Matt walked round and knocked on their door, introducing himself and explained he was looking for his sister Suzy. He asked the neighbour if they were away on holiday.
"Been no cars in there for a fortnight Mate, we don't know what's going on," the chap said, closing the door.
Matt apologised for the disturbance and returned to his car. The neighbour's remark seemed to imply something odd. Again with no reply from Suzy's phone, he set off to Squirrels Chase, feeling she'd probably be there.

Pulling into the drive, Matt gave a sigh of relief, her car was parked by the garage. He wondered if she'd hear him arrive, expecting her to open the door with her usual exuberant welcome. He stopped the car, turned off the engine and waited.

The place seemed quiet. Maybe she was at the back of the house or in the garden. He stood at the front door fumbling with his bunch of keys, looking for the right one. Finally he opened the door and walked inside calling her name. She'd been sorting out the bureau, judging by the piles of papers around it on the floor.

From the kitchen window, he recognised the figure sitting on the seat halfway down the garden, and strode up to greet her. "Hi," he said expecting a big welcoming smile.

Suzy turned to face him, she didn't need to speak, her face was the epitome of despair. Matt sat down beside her "Suze, what's wrong?"

She couldn't speak, the truth was too painful. Her voice trembled "I'm not having a good day, . . sorry."

"Suze you don't have to be here sorting out Mum's stuff if it upsets you. Phil and I can arrange something," he said putting his arm around her.

"Richard has left me, he's moved out."

"What!" Matt was astonished, completely shocked. "Why? . . . has he got somebody else?" He'd spoken in haste without thinking, knowing too late his questions added pain.

Suzy stood up to walk back to the house. He got up and gave her a hug, "I'm so sorry Suze, I didn't know."

"That makes two of us," she said bitterly.

He followed her back into the kitchen. It wasn't the time to bombard her with questions, or the weekend to mention selling the house.

Suzy began to make them tea, and moving the subject away from herself, asked if he'd found a place to buy?

He didn't answer, awkwardly if anyone could read his mind, it was her. He sat with her at the kitchen table watching her quietly sipping her tea.

His stomach reminded him about food, or the lack of it. "Have you eaten?" he asked.

"There's hardly anything here, I cleared the cupboards earlier," she said softly.

"Come on," he persuaded "I'm hungry, let's find somewhere to eat."

She didn't want to go out or face the world, but had no energy to argue.

Matt picked up on her reluctance, the fragility in her eyes worried him. Waiting for her to lock the door, he glanced across at her car. Judging by the layer of dust, it hadn't moved for days. He couldn't imagine how she was coping with this situation on top of bereavement.

He drove to the corner shop, leaving her in the car. Coming out with a full carrier bag and looking pleased with himself. "Picnic at Gravel Hill?" he suggested.

Twenty minutes later they were sat in his car, looking at the view from Kirston Woods across the valley to the town in the distance. He'd picked the best viewpoint in the car park.

"I'd forgotten about this place," she said, giving him a weak smile. Accepting his spur-of-the-moment picnic idea was to spare her feelings. Apart from a few dog walkers in the distance, they had the place to themselves.

"Tuck in," Matt encouraged, offering Suzy first choice from his pre-packed picnic food.

"Do you want to talk about it?" he asked, giving her the option.

She exhaled heavily, "there's not much to tell. . I didn't know about his affair, . or what triggered it, . . it's not like we argued."
He could hear the hurt in her voice. They sat in silence for a while, watching a dog and its owner in the distance playing with a ball.
"I don't want to go back, . . I feel safe at Squirrels Chase," although wasn't sure if 'safe' was the right word, she wasn't sure of anything anymore.
Matt took her hand, "then stay Suze, it's as much yours as ours," he said, speaking for Phil and himself.
"There's still plenty to sort out, I can be doing that," she reasoned, trying to justify her residence.

Back at the house he checked the time, it was getting late in the day and thought about leaving. He had a long drive to Somerset in the morning.
"What time are you going?" she asked, already reading his mind. "I am OK, you don't have to worry."
Matt heard her words, but wasn't convinced. "I'm just going out to my car," jangling his keys to show her. He sat in the car contemplating what to say, already knowing what he must do. He took out his phone 'staying with Suzy, speak later,' Matt texted Gina, before retrieving his overnight bag from the boot.
"Thought I'd stay and keep you company," he said, walking back inside "and, later I'll cook you to my specialty." If there was one thing bachelor living had taught him, it was how to cook egg on toast with beans and sausages.

Leaving Suzy in the lounge watching TV, Matt got up to cook their tea. He refused all help, "wherever it is, I shall find it," he affirmed.

"There!" he said proudly handing her his creation on a plate.
"Thanks," she said, forcing a smile, appreciating his company rather than his cooking.
"He's a bloody idiot!" Matt expressed with conviction.

Suzy was slowly accepting she'd naively been fed a bucketful of lies, but it didn't stop the hurt of betrayal.
"So tell me about the property you've found," she hadn't missed his earlier avoidance.
From swallows and cottages, to kittens in the barn, she could feel his love forming for the place. "It sounds like heaven," she said pleased for him.
While Suzy poured out her troubles, Matt's listening and concern helped to fill the voids of heartbreak. They talked into the early hours, each getting their woes and uncertainties off their chests.

- -

Gina and Elaine stopped halfway into their journey for breakfast. While Elaine fetched more coffee, Gina phoned Matt. She wanted to know how far he'd got. If the gap wasn't too big, she was tempted to wait for him. Knowing he hated answering his integral car phone while driving, gave him time to pull over to answer.
"Morning," she chirped, bright as the sunshine outside, "where are you?"
Elaine put their drinks on the table and sat down. She could tell by Gina's expression and conversation there was a major problem.
"Trouble?" she asked.

“Matt’s not coming,” Gina answered in disbelief. “But he wants us to carry on without him.”
Elaine didn’t mind, she relished their time away together, something that had fizzled out since Matt had been on the scene. “Just the two of us then,” and waited for the explanation.
Gina told her about Suzy and what had happened. “Worst timing ever!” Gina snapped angrily, her vengeance aimed at Suzy’s husband.
“Is there a convenient time for such matters?” Elaine asked curtly.
“No, sorry,” Gina conceded, accepting her mother’s chastisement. “I’m not great in the mornings am I?”
Elaine gave her the look that only a mother can.
“I don’t know what to say to Mrs Brewer,” Gina worried, walking back to her car.
“Oh we’ll think of something,” Elaine assured.

Gina pulled into The Kings Arms car park at ten o‘clock and recognised Sam’s van parked in the corner. He got out and ambled across to speak to her.
“Hello, have you been waiting for us?”
Sam nodded, “Ee said you was on y’ way.”
Gina introduced him to her mother, Sam nodded a greeting.
“Has Mrs Brewer expressed a time for us to call?”
“T’morra mornin, bout ten. Better then, she be on er own. I’ll tell er y’ be there.” Sam turned round and walked back to his van.
“He’s a character,” Elaine chuckled. “It’s a good job we packed a bag,” referring to the Sunday viewing.
Gina had assumed they would be seeing the farm later on, not Sunday. She’d only suggested taking overnight

things in case they wanted to make the most of the weekend.
"Let's see if Betty has two rooms we can have."
Before they got out of her car, Gina warned her mother not to mention their mission of viewing the farm. "If anyone asks, we'll say I'm showing you the area." She didn't know why Matt had issued that instruction.

Gina introduced her mother to Jack the landlord.
"Can't keep away from us now," he joked.
After they'd successfully booked their rooms and ordered an evening meal, they got ready to leave. "We'll be back around four," Gina said, giving Betty plenty of time to prepare their rooms.
Aware Jack liked to know everything that went on in the village, they didn't hang around for him to start asking questions and drove off to explore.

-

"You've found a gem here," Elaine declared over breakfast. She'd loved everything about the pub, including Betty's cooking.
After breakfast, they gathered their things.
"See you next weekend," Jack called out in jest.

Gina was nervous about meeting Margery Brewer, and hoped Matt's absence wasn't going to cause a problem. They drove through the open gate into the yard of Ashwood Farm. Gina was relieved to see Sam's van already parked. They got out to knock on the door. Elaine glanced around, eager to start viewing the place, wanting to see everything.

A tall slim Margery Brewer answered the door and greeted them. Elegantly dressed with manicured nails, her ash blonde hair swept up into a French pleat. Her image

wasn't the typical farmer's wife, Gina had been expecting to meet.
"I believe Mr Chapman couldn't make it?" anticipating an explanation.
"No," Gina replied nervously "he sends his sincere apologies."
"He's looking after his sister," Elaine interrupted. "Poor woman has heart trouble," patting her chest. "He had to go, . now she's on her own," putting on a concerned expression.
"I'm sorry to hear that, please pass on my regards."
When Margery wasn't looking, Gina gave her mother a glare of disapproval..

They walked around the farm with Sam in tow. Elaine would have preferred a slower pace with so much to see and take in.
Margery took them inside for a brisk tour, finishing downstairs in the large farmhouse lounge for coffee. "Is there anything else you would like to see?"
Gina expressed grateful thanks for her hospitality and showing them around the property. She wanted to know more about the wood and went outside to find Sam.
"Bit of a walk if y' want t' see it," he warned, pointing into the distance.

"Someone mentioned plans to convert a dairy. If they're to hand, would you mind if I could see them?" Elaine requested.
Margery went off to fetch them.
Elaine got up and began to wander across the room, intending to look out at the view from the large windows. A photo on a windowsill caught her attention and she bent down for a closer look.

Margery entered the room.
"I'm so sorry," Elaine apologised being caught in the act. "I didn't mean to be nosey. I had that same trouser suit, I kept it for years."
"That was taken a long time ago," Margery admitted with a smile.
Elaine picked up the photo to inspect more closely. Margery had been stunning. "Didn't you model for Your Space? . . and that knitting pattern company, . what was its name?" she said, trying to remember.
Margery was flattered, there weren't many people who recognised and remembered her earlier life as model. Giving a warm smile, she unrolled the plans, spreading them out across the table with Elaine's assistance.

By the time Gina returned, Elaine and Margery were friends. They'd gone outside to sit on the terrace, chatting about their younger years and drinking glasses of pear cider.
Sam had left Gina and gone back to the barn to finish a job.
Hearing laughter coming from the garden, Gina walked through a side gate looking for her mother.
"Time to go," Elaine announced, seeing Gina appear and stood up ready to leave.
Margery saw them to the gate, bidding them a safe journey home.

"What an interesting woman," Elaine remarked, getting back into Gina's car. "We had such a lot in common, so many memories," she said with a giggle.
"And what were they?" Gina asked.
"The seventies." Elaine felt herself floating.

Are you squiffy?" Gina quizzed with disapproval.
"Don't be ridiculous, I've only had two glasses of cider."
"Hmm," Gina mused. "Somerset cider, probably strong enough to rot your socks." Suggesting a black coffee when they stopped for lunch. "And when did you learn to lie with such conviction?" recalling what she'd said to Margery Brewer.
"A serious heartache wasn't a lie," Elaine reasoned, excusing her behaviour. She smiled to herself, despite her daughter's grumbles, while talking to Margery she'd learned a lot about the farm. Including the knowledge that Gina and Matt would need very deep pockets if they were hoping to buy it.

- -

The aroma of coffee percolating wafted upstairs, enticing Matt to get up and join Suzy in the kitchen. He'd been lying in bed, wondering how Gina and her mother would get on at the farm. He'd yet to meet Margery Brewer and Elaine. This weekend would have been ideal but no matter. All-said-and-done his sister held priority as far as he was concerned.

When he opened the kitchen door, Suzy was busy washing up and greeted him with a smile. "Morning," she said, looking more like her old self.
"How do you feel today?" noting her new strength. Yesterday he feared he'd lost his funny, happy, cope-with-anything sister for good.
Her smile faded. "Thank you for listening last night, talking it through helped a lot. It knocked me sideways Matt and still hurts, but facing my demise has brought me to my senses."

"You've every right to be angry," he said knowing his words trod on emotional eggshells. "Have you thought about your job? . . and house?"
"There's nothing eminent to walk away from," she said, struggling to grasp some pride. "I won't go back and the house can be sold," surprising herself at making decisions. "I'm a glorified secretary at the end of the day, I can work anywhere."
They both knew she was selling herself short.
Matt understood, through twists of fate, both their careers and lives were changing dramatically.
"You can only have toast for breakfast. I need to go shopping, these cupboards are bare."
"Will you be OK with that? Going out on your own?"
"I have to start somewhere," she said, trying to sound positive.
"Then we'll go out for lunch." He wanted to see for himself if she wasn't fooling herself as well as him.

All morning she kept him busy with carrying boxes from the house and restacking them in the garage. When he joined her in the hall, he sat chatting, watching her sorting through the drawers of the bureaux. He showed her the little charm their mother had given him, admitting to her it's personal importance. "Will you be alright here by yourself Suze, . . honestly?"
"I don't feel alone here," she reassured him, aware of his scrutiny, "and I haven't seen any hob goblins either."
He laughed at their private joke.
She asked how he got on with Gina's mother. Matt confessed to not only had they not met, but yesterday he'd stood her up!

He drove to The Forrester, the nearest pub to Squirrels Chase. Consumed with her world falling apart, Suzy had lost her appetite and interest in food. Delicious as the meal was, she struggled.
Matt had no such difficulties, he'd never been able to resist a traditional English roast. Their mother had frequently said 'when it came to food, Matt and Phil had hollow legs'.

Suzy heard her phone pip from inside her handbag. She took it out to read the message, a wide grin forming slowly as she analysed the word.
"Look," she said, showing Matt the screen.
He couldn't make sense of it.
"It's from Phil," she clarified.
He still wore the same puzzled expression. "Pram?"
"Pram," Suzy repeated beaming, and made the large pregnant bump sign over her stomach with her hands.
It took Matt a few moments before the penny dropped.
"No!" he said astonished.
"We're not allowed to tell anyone," she instructed firmly "in case."
"In case of what?" he asked blindly.
She glared at him, "just in case," she repeated.
The young girl serving, brought a dish of treacle sponge with custard to their table. Suzy had only ordered tea. "I don't know where you put it," she said watching him devouring the pudding. "I hope Gina likes cooking."
"So do I," he grinned.
The meal together, and Phil's news had brightened the day for both of them.

"I'm at the end of my phone if you need me," giving her a hug before throwing his overnight bag into the boot

of his car. "I mean it, . . and if you won't answer your phone I'll come back to find out why," he threatened.
"I know," she smiled. "Thanks, I'll be alright now, . . . really."
She waved from the front door until Matt's car left the drive. Today she was a different person, better than yesterday, still unsure of her future, but a whole lot stronger than days before.
She went back to finish sorting out the bureaux, most of the drawers were empty now. She placed the 'might keep' pile into the bottom drawer, and put the items she was keeping to show Matt and Phil in the drawer above. Two envelope type folders remained. She peered into the one labelled 'Short Stories' finding type written pages. The other contained old cards, and goodness knows what else. She left them on top of the bureaux, intending to take them up to bed and check through later.

Carrying a mug of warmed milk to take upstairs to bed, she stopped to collect the folders on her way. Sitting up in bed, she tipped out the miscellaneous one. A mixture of old birthday and anniversary cards, school reports and various childhood certificates of achievement lay before her. She read through Matt and Phil's school reports, laughing to herself at the comments. Their maths teachers hadn't given either of them much hope for the future. If only they could see them now.
Among the cards she saw an envelope bearing her name, her maiden name at that. Tucked inside a twenty-first birthday card from her mother, she found a certificate for twenty-one pounds worth of Premium Bonds. It was so long ago, she'd forgotten about them. Apart from the school reports and contents of her card, she assigned the

rest for the bin. It had been quite a day, and turned over ready to sleep.

-

First thing in the morning Suzy phoned the NS&I office. Her bonds were registered in her maiden name and she needed them changed. John, a man with infinite patience gave her the relevant information. The proof of identification she would need was at her house in Ashton.

With trepidation, she got into her car and started the engine, her thoughts nervously wavering as she sat waiting for the wipers to clear the dusty windscreens. Today, she'd only intended to venture out to Kirston for shopping, going back to their house was a different kettle of fish altogether. Accepting she'd have to face it eventually, she bravely headed for Ashton.

Her heart sank when her house came into view, the closed curtains and overgrown grass made it look neglected. The amount of mail on the doormat told her Richard hadn't been back. She went upstairs to find the items and to pack more of her things. On impulse she phoned Rachel.

"I finish in an hour, stay there, I'm coming round," her friend insisted.

When Suzy opened her front door, Rachel was standing on the step holding a heavy box. "Lunch?" she greeted, and followed Suzy inside to her kitchen. "How are you?" they both said together, and smiled at the coincidence.

"I'm getting there," Suzy replied, trying to convince herself as well as Rachel. "What's in the box?" sniffing an escaping waft of hot food.

"God knows, I asked Leah to put in whatever chef had spare. Have you thought about what you're going to do?" Rachel asked, dishing up the food onto plates.
Resting her elbows on the table, Suzy held her head in her hands. "I don't honestly know, . . I only know what I don't want to do," she sighed.
"Well that's a start," Rachel said rendering support.
"I don't want to live here anymore, but I don't want that woman in my house either. Does that make any sense?"
"Completely," Rachel sympathized.

At six o 'clock Rachel looked at her watch. "I have to go, I usually pop in to see Elsie on my way home, she'll be wondering where I am."
"She didn't need to lose her friend because of me, I'm sorry if it's made things awkward," Suzy apologised.
"Elsie never forgave Adam, so Gwen's got no chance!"

After Rachel had left, Suzy realised she hadn't done half the things she'd meant to. If she drove back, she would have to return in the morning. Uncomfortable as it was, common-sense told her to stay overnight. She took out her list to continue, if she put everything by the front door, she could load her car in the morning.

-

The next day Suzy filled her car to the gunnels, telling herself she could have done with a van. Being back had reminded her of better times, for years the house had been a happy home. Searching for items had created untidiness. She couldn't bear to leave it looking unkempt and unloved. Unintentionally, her tidying evolved into a full blown blitz of housework.

Next, she cast her eyes outside to the long grass, surely that wouldn't take long? Wearing a determined expression and using the last of her energy, she marched up and down with the mower. Dragging it out to the front of the house, resolute to complete the job. Although she ached, achievement felt good. Dishevelled, she began to wind up the lead of the mower, relieved everything was done. Inside and out, the house was prim.

"Afternoon."

Suzy nearly jumped out of her skin. Concentrating on winding the lead, she hadn't heard the postman approach. "Sorry," he said, handing her a postcard and walking on. She stuffed it into her pocket before lugging the mower back to the shed. Washing her hands at the kitchen sink, she checked the time. If she was going shopping in Kirston she'd need to get back. At the front door she flicked through the post from the floor. Three were addressed to Richard. She placed them by the kettle in the kitchen, where they'd always left messages for each other.

She took the postcard from her pocket to read. If it was for both of them she'd leave it for him. The colourful seaside picture depicted Hornsey, she turned it over. 'Dear Mum and Dad'. Suzy's heart almost stopped, any pleasurable feeling of achievement ended. Once again she sat at the kitchen table totally shaken, needing a moment. It had been hard enough coming to terms with Richard's betrayal, how on earth was she going to tell Kate about their split? Kate who'd always been a 'daddy's girl', this would break her heart. Suzy felt wretched, she placed the postcard on top of Richard's mail and walked out of the house, slamming the front door behind her. Any ideas of shopping evaporated when she'd read the card, all she wanted to do now was get back to Squirrels Chase.

Laying submerged in hot soapy bubbles eased Suzy's physical aches, but spending time back at her house had recut painful emotions. She missed her mum, her colleagues, her job and although she hated him for hurting her, stupidly at this moment she missed Richard. Wallowing in a bath of hot water was one thing, wallowing in self-pity was futile. Suzy cursed her soppiness and got out of the bath.

The extra time at her house had provided an opportunity to empty kitchen cupboards. Beneficial for tonight's tea, but tomorrow she really would have to go shopping. She wrote a shopping list and added a couple of things 'to do' at the bottom.

* Send-off identification for bonds.
* Inquire train times for Leeds.

Kate would have to be told, and sadly the sooner the better.

Yet again, after another long exhausting day, Suzy headed upstairs to bed. Tonight she intended to look inside the other folder labelled 'Short Stories by E Chapman'.

She recognised the blue inked small type, written by the old typewriter her father used. The old machine disappeared many years ago, indicating when her mother must have written them. Whether she regarded her stories as unimportant or she'd just forgotten about them, they'd never been mentioned.

Suzy began to read. The first three stories depicting everyday life were cleverly written and enjoyable to read. Just the sort of genre women's magazines featured within their fiction pages.

The fourth and last story appeared longer. Feeling her eyelids beginning to close, wondered whether to start it. One by one, she began to recognise the characters her mother portrayed. They bore different names, but she knew every one of them. People from her childhood, all cleverly woven into her mother's amusing tale.

Dear old Mr Austen, who appeared to be at least a hundred and lived next to the big house at the end of their road. He'd lost weight, judging by the suit that hung off him. Mr Austen always said 'Good morning,' politely doffing his old cream panama hat each time somebody passed by. Unfortunately it wasn't just his clothes that didn't fit, the loose top set of his false teeth had a life of their own. Mr Austen spent hours sweeping the leaves from the pavement outside of his house. He never seemed to notice the wind dispersing the piles, sending leaves dancing passed him.

Mr Morris who ran the paper shop. Their father nicknamed him 'Sorry', not to his face of course. Every time you spoke to Mr Morris, he'd answered "Sorry?" Suzy recalled how their father could mimic him, sending them into fits of laughter.

Nobody could ride a bicycle as slow as Mrs Evans without falling off. She was the very large lady who cleaned for Mrs Daw. Suzy remembered the time when she cycled past, their father - observing her large posterior which completely enveloped the seat, asked their mother if Mrs Evans had a saddle on her bike? Despite trying to tell him off, their mother couldn't keep a straight face.

Mrs Godfrey, whose life revolved around her charitable works. She was always collecting something. Newspapers for the scouts, clothes for church jumble sales, selling raffle tickets, or coming round with her various collecting tins.

"God bless you," she'd say as you parted with your donation. "God help us, here she comes again," their father would mutter under his breath when he saw her coming. So Mrs 'God-help-us', became the name he called her. He would hide if he saw her coming. Suzy remembered the time he'd hidden behind the garage door, but to no avail. Mrs Godfrey had already seen him. When he peeped round the door to see if she'd gone – they met face to face, almost nose to nose! They couldn't stop laughing when he told them.

The baker, their mother never had the heart to cancel, regardless that his bread was stale every time he delivered it.

Gossipy Mrs Randel at the library, Miserable old Mr Cole the greengrocer, and more.

Suzy looked at the bedside clock, disbelieving the time. Smiling to herself, having just walked through her childhood, meeting all those forgotten characters along the way. Gathering up the pages, she dropped them back into the big file envelope. Tomorrow, she'd make copies for her brothers, knowing they'd love it, . . adding another job to her list.

- -

"The wood is full of blue bells every Spring, and the banks along the ditches are covered in violets and primroses. Sam said they hear the cuckoo every year around May and June. Can you imagine that?" Gina said wistfully, sounding like an estate agent selling the place. Matt had been listening patiently for the last twenty minutes. There had been a lot of 'Sam saids' punctuating her account. Analysing her conversation, Matt concluded Sam had picked them to buy the farm. Gina was

beginning to love the place as much as him. "What did your mother think of it?"
"She loved it," and went on to tell him about Margery Brewer and her mother chatting like long lost friends.

Gina reminded him about the dinner she'd rebooked. "Wednesday, eight o'clock at Spexhalls."
Matt became silent again. He'd many things on his mind, paying for the farm was only one of them.
"You'll like my mother, she's much nicer than me," Gina smiled trying to lighten his mood, assuming he was uneasy about meeting her.

- -

Elaine had invested time and money on her appearance, a new dress, a visit to the hairdressers and a professional manicure. As she sprayed on her favourite perfume, she wondered what Matt would be like. If any of Gina's previous beaus were anything to go by, she would need to keep her opinions to herself.

Matt was standing at the bar waiting for them when they arrived. Meeting strangers never fazed him, but tonight he was edgy.

Praying for the evening to be a success, Gina led the introductions. She needn't have worried, Matt and her mother fell into conversation with ease and the farm presented mutual ground.

He liked Elaine, finding her intelligent, attractive and sensed she didn't suffer fools lightly. He listened intently while she spoke about the farm, she'd learned far more from Margery Brewer than either of them knew. Having seen the plans, she thought the converted old dairy could be the perfect place for herself . . . . if Gina and Matt agreed of course.

Given the modest size of the farm, Matt had been surprised it had a dairy and labourer's cottages.
Elaine explained, Margery had sold off most of the land when her husband left.
"I don't suppose she told you how much she wants for it?" He asked casually, never thinking for one moment she'd know.
When Elaine told them, Gina and Matt both fell silent.
"Where did she get that figure from?" he asked gravely.
"Her friend, the estate agent valued it, . . actually I think he could be more than a friend."
"Oh Matt," Gina said concerned "can we afford that?"
"We'll have to see," deciding to change the subject.
Gina's financial mind began to whirr. "Tomorrow, I'll arrange to get my house on the market and I've got savings," she thought aloud. "With the money from your flat and your mother's house we might make it."
Matt looked straight into Gina's eyes, "Squirrel's Chase is not in the equation. My sister can live there for as long as she wishes. It's as much hers as mine and Phil's," he stated firmly.
"But!" she protested, yet could see by his expression he wouldn't listen. She got up, excused herself from the table and headed to the ladies room.

Elaine was impressed by his care and respect for his sister and decided to assess him further. "Mathew, I could help you and Gina," she proposed.
Straight away Matt refused.
"But you could lose the farm."
"Then we'll find another." Thanking her sincerely for her offer and apologised for any offense.

Elaine knew he wouldn't change his mind. She could see why Gina had fallen for him, he was good looking, had a good heart and sound principles. She smiled with approval, her daughter had found someone worthy after all.

Elaine had barely taken her shoes off when Gina appeared at her bedroom door.
"So what do you think?" she asked, wanting her mother's opinion.
"He seems alright," Elaine answered flatly.
Gina pulled a face, she knew when her mother was joking.
"OK, he's great, and quite a dish," Elaine said smiling "you're lucky I'm not ten years younger."
"Only ten?" Gina teased.
"I'm glad my Princess has found her Prince," Elaine said with affection. She said goodnight and closed her bedroom door, feeling relieved, and happy for Gina. At last, goodness knows she'd kissed enough frogs!

- -

At his desk, Matt was going over the figures of Griam Associates, assessing their share market value, credentials and assets from the pages in front of him. It would be his decision whether Vortorx bought out the company and he couldn't miss anything untoward.
Without warning, Matt's office door opened wide. Harvey Granzman strode inside, pushing the door shut with force.
"Good morning Sir," Matt said, looking up from his work.
Granzman started to slowly pace the office, clearly something was on his mind. "Did you see James Straks?"
"I did," Matt answered.
"Top man, great guy, do you feel better Mathew?"
"I do indeed."

Harvey Granzman spun round and leant on Matt's desk facing him. "You didn't attend the Chenoncia Deal in America last week."
Unintimidated, Matt stayed silent watching his powerful boss.
"Why?"
"Because I wasn't the best man for the job," Matt replied calmly.
Harvey Granzman paced the floor again, thinking as he walked. "You sent Hobbs."
"Tom Hobbs covered Chenoncia's history and produced the profile. His pedantic research raised two dark issues, which in turn engineered a sound contract for Vortorx," Matt affirmed, verbally introducing his prodigy. "Tom accompanied me to Dallas and Dubrovnik last year. In January I took him to Cherbourg for the Henburg deal. He's good, deal hungry and ready for action."
Granzman lent over the desk again and looked deep into Matt's eyes with a stare that penetrated his soul. "Where are you going Mathew? Do you want more money? I can't see you rearing sheep!" he questioned slowly, expecting answers. He could taste a lie before it hit the air.

Matt knew there wasn't a place, or company Granzman couldn't intercept at any level. He'd probably had his profile scrutinised, yet Matt had immense respect for him. Granzman was direct, thorough and always fair.
Matt answered with complete honesty. "I have the greatest regard for Vortorx, and I'm proud to of been part of achieving its high position in global markets. I do plan to leave, break free from corporate business and move to the West country."

Harvey Granzman stepped back. Matt knew he'd been checking, wanting to hear for himself Matt's intensions. Granzman walked over to the office window, thinking as he peered out. "Tom Hobbs? Is he really ready Mathew?"
"Give him my position and watch the results," Matt put forth.
"Is that what you want?" Granzman turned, watching Matt, analysing his reaction. He came away from the window and faced him again.
"Give me another year Mathew. Shadow Hobbs, he'll need your support." Harvey Granzman stood in front of Matt, his hand outstretched across the desk ready to shake on the deal. "One year Mathew?"
Matt stood up and shook his hand. "One year Sir," he agreed.
Granzman relaxed, he looked satisfied with the agreement. He turned to leave and walked to the door. Before going out, turned his head and looked back "you have your raise Mathew." Then he was gone.

- -

Tom Hobbs wondered why he'd been asked to drive over to see his executive manager Mathew Chapman at home, he'd never been invited before. The last time he'd spoken to him was during the finalisation of the Griam Associates assessment. He'd heard about Harvey Granzman's sudden appearance and began to feel uneasy. Had he made an error? Tom drove into the private parking area of the apartments, this wasn't your usual block of flats. One day he hoped to aspire to living in such a place. He rang the bell.

Matt opened the door and welcomed Tom inside, leading him through to the spacious lounge. He poured two glasses of scotch and offered seating. Tom stood

admiring the view from the floor to ceiling wall of windows before he sat down. Matt placed a scotch at Tom's side and adjusted the brightness of the room. Slightly lowering the blinds using the remote, knowing full well Tom would be impressed.
"You have a great apartment Mathew."
Matt could hear the unease in Tom's voice. "I'm putting it on the market soon, I'll give you first refusal if you like."
Matt sat down and faced him. "I'm leaving Vortorx," and waited for Tom's reaction.
At first Tom was shocked by the news, then disappointed. He picked up his glass and took a swig. "Does Harvey Granzman know?"
Matt nodded.
Tom sat quiet for a moment, his mind racing. "It's been a huge privilege to work with you Mathew. You've given sublime instruction. When will you go?"
"I've told Harvey Granzman to give you my position," Matt announced.
"Me?" Tom was amazed "but?"
"I'll be at Vortorx for twelve months."
Tom gulped down the rest of the Bourbon, trying to digest Matt's information.
"Granzman will summon you for an interview, so get prepared. Usual procedures apply and not a word until it's official," Matt warned. He got up to show Tom out.
Tom got to his feet, shell shocked and with awkwardness. He held out his hand "thank you Mathew, for putting my name forward."
Matt shook his hand before escorting him towards the door.
"I'll see you later, . . at work," Tom said, beginning to smile as the information started to sink in.

Matt closed the door. He planned to work from home for the rest of the day, needing time to come to terms with his own decisions. The last twelve years had been all about Vortorx, now he'd given away his corporate career, stepping down from the top. It felt strange, yet liberating. On the positive side he'd gained a raise in salary, and knowing Tom was looking for a place nearer work may have possibly found a buyer for his flat.

- -

Gina sat working at her desk, preparing her manager's schedules for the next two months, finalising meeting dates, coordinating hotels and flights. Nothing could be booked until she'd gone through the busy timetable with her boss, manager Laura Dunham-Mace. Laura relied on Gina to consolidate her time away, making it as efficient as possible. As Laura's PA, Gina accompanied her boss throughout her visits abroad, assisting with necessary information and keeping assignments running productively smooth.

It was clear to Gina, over the next month she wouldn't be spending much time at home, or in England come to that.

In the early days of their relationship, if she could slip away to spend a day with Matt, she'd fly back. So in love, she never counted the cost, just their hours apart. However, if they were serious about buying Ashwood Farm, these expensive flights of passion would have to cease. She prayed their love was strong enough to ride these long stretches apart.

Laura listened to Gina's arrangements, agreeing to the punishing timetable with less free time. "No visits home?" she queried, aware of Gina's love life.

"No," Gina answered, keeping her eyes fixed on her paperwork. This was not the time to say she'd happily

leave tomorrow, if she could afford it. “I want to buy a bigger house, now my mother has moved in with me. I could do with an annex,” she explained, slightly bending the truth.
Her manager smiled, “full steam ahead then.” Assuming Gina’s love was cooling, or Matt had bitten the dust completely.
Laura was sharper than a knife, it wouldn’t have taken her long to spot Gina’s house up for sale. Now she wouldn’t have to fend off awkward questions, and if Matt wouldn’t promote the sale of Squirrels Chase, she was determined to find extra cash.

At home Gina sat in the kitchen making a list of items to pack.
“You didn’t drink your tea, would you like me to make you another?” Elaine offered.
“Sorry, I was miles away,” Gina replied, attempting once more to concentrate. “I’ll be flying out to Stockholm on Thursday, then later on to Hamburg. Laura wants to incorporate visits to two manufacturing plants in Germany before we return,” she said with doleful acceptance. “I’ll probably be away three weeks.”
“Not popping back?” Elaine gave her a questioning look.
“No, not this time.”
“He’ll still be here when you get back, and I’ll let you know if we have any viewings,” she reassured her. Elaine was biding her time for the moment. Later on she’d offer to help, . . . besides a few weeks apart would be a good test of their relationship.

-

It would be their last romantic evening together for weeks, Gina admitted as she cooked dinner at Matt’s flat.

Such was her financial commitment towards buying the farm.
Matt also had a new arrangement to explain, telling her about the deal he'd struck with Harvey Granzman. No doubt Granzman would throw every business deal at Tom to test his mettle. Matt was expecting a tough year "but," he vowed "it'll only be for a year, and if it would secure the farm for them, he'd do it."
"Was he angry?" she asked, knowing of Harvey Granzman only by reputation.
"Not when he knew I wasn't jumping ship, he's a good man," Matt disclosed, giving respect.

- -

Suzy had enjoyed their previous trips to see Kate. Richard, having been a long distance lorry driver, drove to Leeds with ease. All she had to do was book a hotel for them to stay overnight and admire the scenery along the way.

This time was very different. She'd had to research public transport to Leeds, trying to find the simplest route and connections.

At Leeds Station Suzy got out of the train, relieved she had made it this far without a hitch. Like the Pope - who'd bent down to kiss the ground once on an arrival, knew exactly how he'd felt. She made her way through to the main part of the station, stopped and looked around trying to get her bearings. Everywhere people were in a hurry, checking their phones, dashing past or both. She took out her phone intending to let Kate know she'd arrived.

"Mum!" "Mum!" Kate shouted and waved, as she wove her way through the crowds to reach her. They hugged tightly, both relived to have found each other. Kate took charge of her mother's case, wheeling it along as they walked outside. Suzy had booked a room at one of the big travel group hotels close to the station. Although only a short walk away, they took a taxi. After she'd booked in, they wandered into the hotel's restaurant for a late lunch. Kate chattered happily, updating her mother with her news.

All too soon the afternoon had slipped by. Kate got up to leave. "I'll see you tomorrow," she said giving her mother a peck on the cheek before departing.
Suzy made her way up to her room. She switched on the TV and laid on the bed, listening to it with eyes closed. Agonising how to tell Kate about parting with Richard.

Tomorrow they'd planned to spend the whole day together, but first and foremost Kate wanted her mother to see her flat, and to meet a very special person in her life. Walking back, she wondered what her mother would make of Jefferson. She hadn't told her about him before, or that they had moved in together six months ago. It had been fortunate she'd come up on her own this time, her dad wasn't keen on 'Yanks' as he called them, . . and Jefferson was American. Kate presumed her father had been too busy at work to visit.

-

Suzy woke up at four in the morning, still in her clothes, lying on top of the bed, wall lights on and the TV talking quietly to itself. She shivered and pulled the duvet over her and went back to sleep.

At seven o'clock footsteps thumped across the ceiling from the room above. She got up and made herself a cup of tea, climbing back onto the bed to drink it. Leaning against the headboard she watched the morning news, taking in none of it. The unenviable task of telling Kate was consuming her thoughts. After her shower she packed away her crumpled clothes, and got ready to face the day.

The taxi drew up outside a terraced house on the outskirts of the city. Suzy checked the address Kate had written down and pressed the bell for 'flat one'.

Kate opened the door and welcomed her inside, leading her through to the main room which served as lounge, diner and kitchen. Kate had never been the tidiest of people, piles of books and coloured scraps of material overflowed from boxes. Scrolls and posters filled a corner of the typical student pad. Suzy sat at the table watching Kate making toast and coffee.

"And this is Jefferson," Kate smiled, introducing the exceptionally tall, dark haired fellow who stood at Suzy's side. He thrust out his hand for Suzy to shake. "Pleased to meet you, Mam," he said in his strong American accent. She hadn't heard him approach and he towered over her. She smiled nervously as he took her hand, "thank you Jefferson, I'm pleased to meet you too."

Kate handed him a mug of black coffee, he sat down opposite Suzy to drink it.

"And where's home?" Suzy asked, hoping not to sound as if she was about to launch into the Spanish Inquisition.

"My parents have a house in Huntington, West Virginia, Mam. Kady is teaching me English," he said smiling across at Kate.

Kate grinned, looking like the cat who had got the cream, . . . all the cream

"I'm improving your English," Kate corrected.

"Not sidewalk - p a v e m e n t, not cookies" he spoke slowly demonstrating her influence.

"Biscuits," Kate added before he could say it.
Jefferson stood up "Pardon me Mam, I have things to do." He topped up his coffee and headed towards what Suzy surmised to be their bedroom.
Jefferson was built like a truck, the material of his tracksuit stretched taught across his athletic muscular body.
"He's very fit." Kate said, giving her mother a wry smile.
Suzy realised the young daughter standing in front of her had become a woman.

Kate brought over more toast and sat down. "What's so important at Penns yard this week?" she asked innocently.
Suzy was refilling the kettle at Kate's sink. Her heart started to thump rapidly when she heard Kate's question.
"I'm going to bring Jefferson down to meet Dad in a couple of weeks, I could do with picking up more of my stuff anyway," Kate continued.
"Dad's not . . . , Dad's not at Penns anymore," Suzy struggled to say as her mouth dried. "Your Dad's not . . ." Suzy couldn't breathe, her chest started to heave. Fighting desperately to fend off tears she turned to face Kate. "Your Dad's . . ," Suzy tried again, unable to speak, hot tears rolling down her cheeks.
Kate sprang up and went to her. "With somebody else?" Kate said quietly, her eyes fixed to the floor.
Suzy looked up and stared at Kate in shock.
Kate pulled off a length of kitchen roll and gave it to her mother to dry her tears. "I came in from college one day and overheard them talking when I picked up the other phone. I thought he was talking to you. Why do you think I've not been home Mum?" Kate said raising her tone.

"College? That was over a year ago, and you didn't tell me?" Betrayed and angry, in the heat of the moment she slapped Kate across the face.

Kate was shaken, her mother had never laid a finger on her before, not even as a naughty child.

Suzy froze, mortified by her actions. "Kate, I'm so sorry," she sobbed.

Kate wrapped her arms around her mother trying to console her, sharing the pain her father had caused. "I love you both," she said sniffing, trying to hold back her own tears.

Hearing their raised voices, Jefferson opened the bedroom door slowly, unsure of what he'd find. Kate stood holding her mother as she wept.

"You guys need some time," he said, grabbing his jacket heading for the front door. He looked back, catching Kate's eye. "I'm going to the corner store," he said leaving.

"Shop," Kate corrected him softly, still holding her weeping mother.

Ashamed and embarrassed, it took Suzy a while before she could regain her composure.

Kate handed her mother a mug of tea "Mum, we'll get over this," she said with forgiveness.

An hour later they were walking around the old part of the city like a pair of tourists. Throughout their sightseeing they chatted, their close bond strengthening as their spirits rose.

Suzy requested a sit down. "I've walked miles," she said putting on a spurt to the next empty park bench.

Sat, absorbing the gentle warmth from the sun, she turned her attention to Kate's future. Her graduation next May would soon come around.

Kate explained her interest in material structure, wanting to work in its future development. She'd covered design and fashion at college, although connected it hadn't held her interest.

Suzy was lost among Kate's scientific explanations.

Kate pointed to a big lorry parked along the road, "someone created that canvas-type covering material. The medical industry want clothes resistant to germs, others want light weight material coupled with extreme strength, or waterproof yet breathable and comfortable to wear. Think of astronaut's space suits," Kate prompted.

Suzy understood Kate's simplified version. "Have you got any companies in mind?"

"My opportunities will be linked to exam results," Kate defined.

Suzy was proud of Kate, she'd always been level headed and known what she wanted. Warmth from the late afternoon sun began to fade, Suzy shivered and suggested heading back.

Kate announced she'd booked a table at her favourite Italian restaurant that evening, giving them all some time together before her mother travelled home in the morning.

Back in her hotel room, Suzy felt tired but happy. After her earlier unforgivable behaviour, she intended to pay for the meal - hoping Kate would accept her appeasement. Checking her appearance in the mirror, all she needed now was a brave smile. Her last few months had been full of brave smiles, . . and tonight she'd need one more.

The evening was a success. Suzy could see why Kate was so happy, Jefferson was her knight in shining armour and he clearly adored her. She'd booked a taxi to collect her from the restaurant at ten, and got up ready to leave. Insisting Kate and Jefferson stayed to enjoy the rest of the evening.

Jefferson stood up, towering above. "It's been a real pleasure to meet you Mam," he said, offering once more to shake her hand.

Suzy ignored his hand and stretched up to give him a brief hug. "Goodbye Jefferson, take good care of my daughter." She moved round to speak to Kate "see you tomorrow," gave her a kiss on the cheek and left them sitting at the table.

Kate relaxed, "she likes you," she said smiling at Jefferson.

Back home in their flat Kate sat quietly, reflecting on the day.

"Your Mom OK now?" Jefferson asked.

Kate explained, reasoning and justifying her mother's behaviour. "I hoped it was just a stupid mindless fling, that's why I didn't want her to know." Running back to Squirrels Chase, leaving everything including her job, Kate realised the impact on her mother's life her father had caused. Kate yawned, too tired to dwell on it anymore.

"Tired girls need their bed," Jefferson said, lovingly scooping her up in his strong arms and carrying her as if she weighed nothing at all.

-

"You don't have to wait, I'll be alright," Suzy told Kate as they walked along on route to the station.

"And go home wondering if you got on the right train?" Kate answered, trying to manipulate her mother's case up a step onto the pavement. They'd eaten breakfast together at Suzy's hotel, making the most of their remaining few hours together. Kate was full of questions, worrying about her mother being able to cope alone. She'd never known her without any future strategy. "I need to fetch more of my things, we'll come and stay over for a few days," she promised.
"I'd like that very much," Suzy replied, trying not to fret. They sat together in the station listening to announcements over the tannoy. Suzy's train pulled into the station, they stood up and said their good byes, both with eyes filling with tears.

Kate got off the bus and began walking back to their flat. When she turned into their road, a familiar figure came into view. Jefferson was jogging towards her. She called to him and waved, her heart thumping beats of love. Sunday mornings he liked to run at least six kilometres, spending hours at the gym during the week. Intense exercise had never been her forte, but that didn't mean she didn't appreciate a fit physique.
"Good timing," she said opening the gate.
"Your Mom get off OK?"
Kate nodded. This weekend had marked a poignant change in their relationship, now her mother was the vulnerable one.
"Did you tell her about 'Thanksgiving?"
"Not yet, she's got enough to deal with at the moment." Jefferson planned to take Kate back home to meet his folks, Thanksgiving would be the perfect forth coming American holiday to do it.

- -

Caroline buzzed through "Mr Hobbs is here to see you."
"Send him in," Matt instructed.
"Would you be requiring refreshments?" she added.
"Not for me," Tom said as he walked in.
Matt shook his head. "No thank you," Tom instructed before closing the door.
He declined the offer to sit, standing purposely in front of Matt's desk before speaking. "I have an interview with Mr. Harvey Granzman on Thursday," pre-warning Matt in case he would be called upon.
"Here?" Matt asked.
Tom nodded.
"He's thorough, but fair. Always be straight with him, and never ever underestimate him," Matt advised "Good luck."
Tom turned and walked to the door. "If I am successful on Thursday, I'd really like a proper look at your flat Mathew," he said before opening the door.
Matt smiled to himself, was a sale really too much to hope for?

With Gina away, Matt could concentrate on selling his flat. He planned to phone two independent estate agents for valuations and express his wish for a swift sale. After two busy evenings getting the place ship shape and ready for viewing, he stood back observing his work, pleased with the result. He hoped it wouldn't stay on the market for long. It was a pain trying to keep the place spotless, . . anyway he'd give Tom first refusal.

Sitting up in bed Matt switched off the TV, it had been 'drivel' all evening. He picked up his phone and scrolled down reading his messages, missing Gina more

than ever. They usually phoned each other at ten, he checked the time, it was quarter to. Gina had texted him earlier in the day, Matt smiled reading her words. 'Give my love to your sister, how is she?' Gina had written.
He didn't know, he'd been so busy, he'd not spoken to her recently. Suddenly an awful thought crossed his mind, did Phil and Julia know Richard had left, or that Suzy had fled back to Squirrels Chase? It was not the sort of thing he'd want to discuss over the phone. Also, he'd intended to visit Margery Brewer while Gina was away. They only had Elaine's version of the farm's sale price. He would need to contact Sam to make the arrangements. It wouldn't be difficult to arrange a few days off prior to Tom's interview, Matt expected a punishing schedule to follow shortly afterwards. Harvey Granzman would want his higher salary earned.
Matt's phone rang out, shaking him from his thoughts and plans "hello Darling," Gina began when he answered.

-

Matt pulled into Wakefield Chartered Accountant's car park. Remembering Suzy's scathing opinion of Phil's secretary, he deliberately hadn't made an appointment to see him. Forewarned, he entered the building and walked through towards Phil's office.
Mrs Finnis was concentrating, tapping away on her laptop at her desk.
Matt smiled, intending to slay this dragon with charm. He approached and placed his impressive business card in front of her. "Good morning Mrs Finnis, it's a pleasure to meet and thank you personally for assisting my brother with our late mother's estate. I need to speak to Phil," he smiled, flashing his hazel brown eyes.

Mrs Finnis was caught unawares, beguiled and clocked his business card portraying his eminent professional stature. She blushed "I'll see if he's free," she said rising from her chair.
Matt took out his phone "or I'll phone him," making his intensions perfectly clear.
Mrs Finnis knocked and entered Phil's office, announcing Matt's arrival. "Your brother Mr Mathew Chapman is here to see you," she said, unfamiliar to blushing.
Phil looked up surprised "Matt? Not being taken over are we?" he joked. "Two coffees please Mrs Finnis."
Matt glanced around Phil's office, compared to his own spacious high end with designer furniture, it seemed he'd stepped back in time. Phil's office held a more relaxed ambience.
Mrs Finnis knocked, and entered carrying a tray. Matt stood up, relieving her of the burden. She smiled at Matt in gratitude, still flushed as she closed the door.
"What have you done to her?" Phil asked, unaccustomed to seeing her smile.
Matt had never been to his office before, Phil picked up his mug of coffee waiting for an explanation.
"Did you know Richard has left Suzy? Gone off with another woman, apparently," Matt announced.
Phil put down his mug, "No!" he was shocked. "Poor Suzy, is she OK?"
"She's back at Squirrels Chase licking her wounds."
"What a rat!" Phil cursed with anger "when did this happen?"
Matt put Phil in the picture.
"Thank goodness you found her, is there anything we can do?"
"Tread carefully," Matt warned.

"How is Julia?" Matt asked with a knowing smile. Phil guessed Suzy had told him. "What with losing Mum, it's been the longest year of my life." Wearing a worried expression, Phil continued "the hospital keep taking her in for observation. Julia's fine, it's me who's in bits." Phil's eyes began to fill, he took out his handkerchief and blew his nose. He'd always been the most emotional one out of the three of them. "So where are you heading?" he asked changing the subject.
"Somerset, to look at a farm."
"For you?" Phil asked.
"Maybe." Matt got up to leave. "Sorry Phil, I have to go. It's good to see you," he said patting Phil on the shoulder.

Mrs Finnis entered Phil's office to retrieve the tray. "I didn't realise you had a brother. He doesn't look anything like you," she said in her normal crisp curt manner.
"I'm the good looking one," Phil quipped, smiling as he opened the door for her.
Carrying the loaded tray, she narrowed her eyes, tutting as she walked past. Phil sat back in his chair, relieved to have her back to normal.

- -

When Suzy woke up, she could hear the rain beating against the windowpanes. She pulled the duvet up to almost cover her head. Awake, snuggled under the covers, she lay there planning her day. She'd told Kate about their split, so that could be ticked off. Next, she needed to sort out her employment. She had already been working on a draft stating her intention to resign, besides, it wasn't fair to expect her manager to hold her position open any longer.

At nine o'clock she summoned the courage to phone Karen's office. Jackie answered, recognising her voice immediately. "How are you?"
"Fine," Suzy replied, avoiding the truth.
"You're sorely missed here I can tell you. When are you coming back?"
"Is Karen free today?" Suzy asked.
"Meetings all morning by the look of things, but I can book you in for two if you want to see her," Jackie offered.
"That would be perfect, thanks," and hung up before Jackie could ask any more questions.

'R you free 4 lunch today?' Suzy
texted Rachel.
'can B, whats up?' Rachel returned.
'going back 2 speak 2 my boss.'
'free aft 12, tex when U arrive' -
Rachel sent back.

Suzy sifted through the pile of papers on the kitchen table where she'd left a rough copy of her resignation. It wouldn't take long to scrutinize and print out the finished item. For a moment she sat back in her chair taking stock of what she was about to do, - leaving the job she loved, a position she'd striven hard to achieve, and her colleagues who'd become friends. With a shimmer of tears, reluctantly she began to type. It was illogical to pretend she would go back. She read it through and signed it, placing it into an envelope and addressing it to her manager Mrs Karen West.

The rain had stopped by the time she had to leave. Raindrops dripped from the trees, their wet leaves glistening in the sun beginning to shine through. She inhaled deeply, there was something magical about the freshness after rain. Clouds cleared uncovering the sun, turning puddles along the road into watery mirrors.

Suzy was escorted to Rachel's office.
"Just give me five minutes to finish this, then we can eat," she said, still staring at her screen.
Suzy started to feel anxious, thinking about her appointment with Karen. "I'll just have a drink, but don't let me stop you Rachel."
"Are you sure about resigning, not burning too many bridges?" Rachel questioned.
"I've been in freefall long enough, I need to grasp some control. I'll get a new job and start again," Suzy answered, attempting to sound positive.
Rachel heard but wasn't convinced. "Have you been looking?"
"No," Suzy confessed, not even knowing where to start. "I'm like a swan gliding serenely across the water, but my feet are frantically paddling underneath, trying not to sink."
Rachel could see Suzy's confidence fading. "I'll wangle Saturday off and stay with you, then we can look for jobs together." She ordered two rounds of sandwiches and a pot of tea for them to eat in her office. "Don't want you keeling over with hunger, if you're planning to present a determined strong willed woman," she smiled.
Suzy checked the time and got up to leave, thanking Rachel for lunch and her offer with job seeking.

Looking for a space to park, she drove passed her usual spot, now taken over by another employee. Getting out of her car, she felt a strange awareness of not belonging anymore.

"Are you really sure about this?" Karen asked kindly.
"I've had plenty of time to think," Suzy replied, surprising herself being able to defend her reasons.
Karen accepted the envelope with reluctance, promising to have Suzy's documents and particulars updated and sent on. It went without saying, she'd provide a glowing reference being genuinely very sorry to see her go. For years, Suzy had been a valued key worker on her team.
Suzy had said all that was necessary, and stood up ready to leave.
Karen gave her a goodbye hug, "look after yourself Suzy."
She closed her manager's door for the last time. Proudly holding her head high and walked out of the building to her car, giving a brief smile to those she passed and speaking to no one. Driving back to Squirrels Chase, a wave of relief swept over her, happy to of got that episode over with, and another thing to tick off her list.

Back home, she picked up the mail from the floor, most being bumf. Not surprising, she hadn't given this address to many. She opened a letter from NS&I, assuming her bonds had been transferred to her married name. A printed cheque for twenty-one pounds was attached at the bottom of the letter. 'Oh dear', that wasn't what she'd intended, perhaps she'd muddled her instructions. It didn't matter, she would re-order more, and maybe round up the value to thirty, wanting to keep them as a memory link from her mother.

"How much?" she asked, surprised to learn the lowest amount she could purchase was a hundred pounds.

“You can cash them in anytime, and have the chance to win each month,” the enthusiastic NS&I lady at the end of the phone explained. Suzy gave her bank details, although she didn’t hold much hope of winning if the last twenty odd years were anything to go by.

~ 7 ~

George had already cut the grass twice while Suzy had been out. He was too polite to ask why she appeared to be there every day, noticing her car frequently in the drive. Today he would knock and ask for payment.

When Suzy heard his van in the drive, she put the kettle on and went out to greet him. “Would you like your tea before or after cutting the grass?” Inviting him into the kitchen, having something to ask. She was hoping he would cut the grass at her own house, although it meant revealing her situation.

“That’s kind Lass,” he said, telling her he’d do the mowing first.

“I’m very sorry to hear that Lass,” he said when she explained her residence.

Suzy got up to fetch her purse. “I’d pay for your fuel George, if you could do it,” she proposed, counting out his money. “I just don’t want to go back there at the moment.”

“He must be a daft begger,” George said kindly. He understood and being soft agreed to oblige.

“George are you OK?” noticing he was fidgety and kept looking towards his van.

“I’ve got Bob in the van.”

“George, why didn’t you say, bring him in. Would he like some tea?”

“He’s a dog.”

“You have a dog?”

"He's not mine, I promised Mrs Kelly I'd look after him while she's in hospital."
"That's very kind of you," giving him a warm smile.
"Not really, she wouldn't get in the ambulance unless I agreed." Explaining he was cutting her neighbour's grass when they heard the dog start barking. The neighbour ran round and found Mrs Kelly on the floor. "Awkward really, I have to keep him shut in the van while I'm working."
"Can I see him?" Suzy asked, opening the back door already on her way.
A chocolate brown Labrador with the saddest eyes, was laying on the floor in the foot well of George's van.
"The poor thing, you can't keep him cramped in there, it's cruel," she scolded.
"He won't eat, I've had him two days and he won't touch anything."
The pitiful sight of the poor creature tugged her heartstrings. "Leave him with me while you're working, he can stay in the kitchen."
"Are you sure Lass?"
She nodded. George pulled a dog bed out from the back of his van and carried it into her kitchen, dragging it into a corner. She watched him bringing the dog, it looked worried, ears down and tail curled down under its body as he followed slowly behind.

George drove off, promising he'd be back later.
Bob curled up in his bed, looking anxious. Suzy filled a bowl with water and put it close by. "You'll be OK here," she said stroking his head.
Remembering the box of paperwork she'd brought back from her house, thought now would be a good time to sit at the table and sort through it. She hoped keeping the

dog company in the kitchen would help him cope with its new surroundings.

At lunchtime, she rummaged through the fridge looking for something suitable, sacrificing the last two slices of ham to feed him. "Enjoy," she said, chopping them up and putting them down. All afternoon Bob ignored the food, remaining curled up in his bed, watching her move around the kitchen with his big sad eyes.

George returned at five, and wanted to know how the dog had been. Bob turned his head away, refusing to acknowledge him.

She realised George wasn't keen on dogs and was clueless about looking after them. "Leave him here with me, I'll look after him until the lady gets better," she insisted, looking forward to its company.

George didn't argue, he was glad to leave the animal behind.

At teatime she added cubes of cheese to the uneaten ham. "Come on Bobby, you must eat something," she said gently stroking his soft brown fur. She left lights on and doors open while she watched TV in the lounge. Bob remained rooted to his bed in the kitchen.

Before retiring for the night, she attached his lead. "Wee wees Bob," she instructed, opening the back door. Every time she stopped, he stopped, they walked halfway down the garden path before she became too cold and turned back. Bob returned to his bed.

She warmed some milk to take upstairs, tipping out enough to fill a saucer for the dog. "Night night Bobby," she said, putting it down for him. Bob stayed in his bed, ignoring her.

A faint noise woke her up at three a.m., she went downstairs to check on the dog. Peeping around the door, he was still curled up in his bed. About to return, when she heard him softly whimpering. His sadness struck a chord. She stayed, talking and gently stroking his soft coat. "We're both missing someone we care for, but yours will come back." She knelt down fondling his silky ears, sniffing, holding back the melancholic tears she could feel forming.
The food she'd provided remained in the dish, as did the milk. Bob's body quivered, was he cold? Suzy took off her dressing gown and covered him with it, tucking it around his head. "Night night Bobby," she said once more, leaving him snuggled and went back to bed.

"Morning Bob," Suzy greeted brightly, entering the kitchen. The dog lifted its head and looked at her. She went over to fuss him, her dressing gown no longer covering his body. She filled the kettle and switched it on, "while that's boiling you are going outside." Attaching his lead, Bob followed, obligingly doing what he was expected to do. Back inside, he returned to the safety of his bed. "Good boy," she praised, giving him a pat on the head before picking up his empty dishes.

George knocked on the back door. Telling her he was going over to her place and asked about the dog.
"He's fine," she smiled, handing George her keys and the address.

- -

Matt walked back to his car, it had been good to see Phil. Now he was free to head for Somerset. Sam had made him an appointment with Margery Brewer for tomorrow, around lunchtime. He started the engine, looking

forward to the scenic drive down. His car phone buzzed, thankfully he hadn't yet moved off. "What is it Caroline?"
"Mr Harvey Granzman has flown into Heathrow. He wants to see you at eight thirty tomorrow."
"Thank you Caroline, I'll be there," Matt replied, ending the call. "Dam and blast!" he cursed. Granzman had always been a loose cannon, but tomorrow of all days! He changed direction to drive home, with Tom's and his own future at stake this was not the time to be awkward with Harvey Granzman.
He thought about the appointment with Mrs Brewer, having already messed her about. It would seem rude to cancel again at short notice. Hoping Granzman wouldn't keep him long, tomorrow he'd need to leave straight after their meeting and drive directly to the farm.

-

Matt barely had time to sit at his desk before Harvey Granzman walked in carrying a folder.
"I hear you were away Mathew." There wasn't much he missed.
"I came back," Matt answered.
The folder was full of forthcoming deals he wanted to go over. Matt sensed Granzman wasn't ready to hand over any reins to Tom. They worked steadily through the folder.
"Tom will be fine, he knows how Vortorx operates. If he makes a mistake, he'll learn from it," Matt said attempting to smooth the way. "I made mistakes at first."
"Yes Mathew, the Culdock and Muick amalgamation, I recall," Granzman added straight-faced.
Matt looked sheepish, Harvey Granzman had the mathematical memory of a computer – he forgot nothing. It had been Matt's second big deal for Vortorx. He had a

gut feeling it wasn't sound, but accepted the figures he'd been given. Vortorx had made a minimal loss on the deal, Matt never doubted his intuition again.

"What do you think of Ophray Systems?" Granzman asked.
"Their financial history is sound. I can't give any negative proof, but " . . Matt stopped, quietly mulling over his thoughts. "I feel something isn't right."
Harvey Granzman listened to Matt's opinion.
"Lowans are interested," Matt added. "I need you to make the final decision on that one, Sir."
Granzman had the same intuit feeling, "let Lowans have it."

Caroline brought in coffee, placing the tray on the desk. Matt thanked her, Granzman remained silent until she'd left the room.
Satisfied with their morning's work, Granzman closed the folder, leaving it for Matt on his desk. He turned his attention to Matt. "You don't have to get back for Thursday."
"I'll be back Wednesday evening Sir, I've plenty here to work on," Matt acknowledged the folder with his eyes.
"I don't want to let you go Mathew, we're alike."
Matt knew he referred to their intuit gut feelings.
"You could set up an office in the West Country."
"Vortorx is global, I'm ready to stay in England."
"Could fund any building renovation, think about it."
Granzman looked straight into Matt's eyes, trying to scrutinise his thoughts.
Matt smiled "no promises Sir, I'll consider it at the end of the year."

“I’ll buy that,” Granzman said satisfied. Never staying still a second longer than necessary, checked his Rolex, rose from his chair and walked to the door. “Bye Mathew,” and was gone.

Matt locked the folder inside his desk, gulped down another cup of coffee and got ready to leave. Working a few days in his own office might be worth thinking about. He wouldn’t want to haunt Tom, but supporting him . . maybe?

The desktop clock revealed he wouldn’t make Somerset before two. He phoned Sam to politely warn Mrs Brewer. “I’m leaving now, I’ll go straight to the farm.”

- -

Suzy needed to go shopping, and added dogfood to her list. “I’m sorry Bob, I’m going out. I won’t be long and I’ll leave the radio on for company,” she said, talking to the dog as if he understood. “When I get back, we’ll go ‘walkies.” Bob pricked up his ears. “Ah, so you know that word.” She cupped her hands around his head, “I won’t be long.”

She’d never walked down the pet-food isle in the supermarket before and couldn’t believe the variety. Having Bob’s company had made a difference. Even if he was only a dog, a borrowed one at that, she was alone at Squirrels Chase but no longer lonely.

In the book and magazine section, she looked for newspapers, and asked the girl loading the shelves if they sold any ‘job seeking’ editions.

“We don’t do anything like that here,” then remembered “this local paper features jobs at the back, if that’s any help.”

Suzy added the paper to her trolley.

Bob remained in his bed, wagging his tail when Suzy staggered into the kitchen carrying heavy bags of shopping. It was a nice feeling, getting her first waggy-tail greeting. She opened one of the tins of dogfood. It didn't smell very inviting, but at least he ate it.

Keys, phone, poo bags and tissues, Suzy checked her pockets before setting off. Bob walked dutifully alongside, stopping to sniff occasionally. She was heading for the patch of waste ground not too far away. The site of an old warehouse, now long gone. Nature had successfully claimed back the area with bushes, tall grass and wild flowers, much to the delight of local wildlife and dog walkers. Suzy perched on one of the big concrete blocks that remained randomly dotted about. She sat for a moment, absorbing the peaceful surroundings with Bob sitting at her feet.

Her phone rang out, disturbing their rest. It was Phil. "Hi Phil," Suzy answered cheerfully. The reception wasn't great, she could hear all sorts of noises in the background, including a loud siren. "Where are you?" she almost shouted. 'Hospital' was the only word she could make out. "Where?" she repeated.

"Hospital, Julia's . ."

After that, all she could hear was Phil crying. "Phil!" she shouted, but the signal faded ending the call. She felt a deep unease. "Oh no, please no," she repeated over and over again. For a lifetime of seconds she sat numb and worried, her phone still in her hand. It wasn't the time to call him back, no matter how desperately she wanted to. Bob stood up watching her. "It's OK," she said, stroking him with one hand, and hunting for tissues with the other.

Her phone pipped. She swallowed hard, hardly daring to look at the screen.
'Say hello to Neville Alexander Chapman, born at 12 noon, 4 lbs.12ozs. Julia and baby fine.' A tiny baby wrapped in a white shawl appeared on her screen.
Suzy wept with relief and happiness. Bob moved closer, watching anxiously, he didn't like her crying. "It's OK," she repeated, stroking him to reassure and snivelling into a tissue now black with mascara. She put her soggy tissue in her pocket. "I must look a mess, I hope you're up to a brisk walk back before anyone sees me." Then smiled to herself. "I'm an Auntie!" she announced euphoric.

- -

Matt was making good time, the mid-week traffic appeared light for the time of day. He was flying down the A30 one minute . . . and stopped the next. A terrible accident had happened ahead, vehicles soon backed up forming a huge jam and nobody could move. Annoying as it was, he wasn't complaining. Sat in his comfortable car, his only hardship was inconvenience of time, his sympathy lay with the people involved in the accident. Some drivers got out of their cars to stretch their legs, others walked forward to help, or to enquire. Outside Matt overheard talk of waiting for the air ambulance to arrive, this was going to be a considerable wait. Reluctantly, he phoned Sam again.

Matt finally arrived in the yard of Ashwood farm at five o'clock. He was embarrassed to knock on the door. Mrs Brewer greeted him politely, invited him inside and began to show him around. He'd had so many questions to ask, but now being very late felt it would be an imposition to take up too much of her time. Caught up with the accident had disconcerted, and now he'd totally lost the moment.

Equally, Margery wasn't sure how the viewing was going, in the disjointed atmosphere she was uncertain whether to offer refreshments.

Matt's phone buzzed.

"Do take it," she insisted.

He was prepared to switch it off, but seeing it was from Phil, thought better of it and apologised yet again.

He couldn't believe what Phil was saying. Elated, Matt declared "I'm an Uncle!" Phil sent through a photo of his tiny new born son. "Look," Matt said to Mrs Brewer, showing her the picture on his phone, quite forgetting where he was and who he was talking to.

"Congratulations," she said smiling.

"Mrs Brewer would you have dinner with me this evening, as an apology for all the inconvenience I've caused you?" Matt invited, still with his head in the clouds.

Margery stared at him, probably longer than was comfortable. She was appreciating the moment. It had been a long time since a handsome man stood before her, smartly dressed in his Saville Row suit asking her out to dinner.

Matt took her pause to be an uncomfortable refusal, and apologised for his forwardness. By now he'd come to his senses, what had he been thinking?

"That's most kind, eight o'clock?" She answered accepting.

Matt beamed "I'll pick you up just before, you'll have to choose where, I'm a stranger here."

Margery closed the door, surprised by the impetuous invitation, and even more so by her acceptance. Her motive had been curiosity. She also had many questions, including wanting to know what would happen to Sam should she decide to sell. His heart and soul was entwined in every inch of the farm.

Matt drove into the car park of the Kings Arms, thankfully he'd booked his room earlier. He acknowledged landlord Jack, collected the key and went straight up to his room to shower and change. It certainly was becoming an eventful day.

He parked outside the front door of the farmhouse. Before he could knock, Margery Brewer opened it, standing in the doorway looking stunning and refined.

He opened the car door for her.

Following her directions, he drove to The Riverside Grill where she had booked a table. The sophisticated restaurant was as he'd expected and perfect for their evening.

Margery was an impeccable dinner guest, and invited any questions he may still have about the farm. Her interest lay in what they intended to do with it. "Keep it as a working farm?" she enquired.

"Apart from some general renovation, we intend to run it as it is, with Sam's help," Matt answered. "Elaine may want a few hens, Gina has mentioned getting a donkey, but they'd all be pets," he insisted, not foreseeing any other changes necessary.

Margery smiled, changing the subject, curious to know of Matt's profession.

At the end of the evening he drove her home, politely escorting her to the door. "Thank you for this evening, it's been a pleasure to meet you. We'll assess our finances and let you know in due course," and finally bid her 'Good Evening'.

Indoors Margery stepped out of her heeled shoes and took off her jacket, feeling glad she'd agreed to the evening. Drawn initially by Mathew Chapman's smile, he'd reminded her of someone long ago, . . who'd had the same hazel eyes, same impeccable manners and charm. Although relishing this sentimental memory, tonight, if she'd been twenty years younger, she would have been smitten.

- -

Jeremy Parker heard that Mr Chapman was back in the village staying at The Kings Arms and shot down to the pub hoping to catch him. Intending to reap maximum money from the transaction, he would tell this 'city oiyk' he was handling the sale of Ashwood Farm. He parked his sports car next to Matt's car and waited.

It was Matt's last free day to spend at leisure. He'd already enjoyed one of Betty's cooked breakfasts, now he was getting ready to drive back. He had hoped to speak to Sam if he'd seen him around. Matt carried his bulky overnight bag down to his car, grateful he'd parked it close to the back of the pub.

Jeremy Parker got out of his car, ready to approach. He watched in jealous awe as the boot of Matt's car opened and rose electronically for him to load.
"Hello, I'm Jeremy Parker. I shall be handling the sale of Ashwood farm for Mrs Brewer. If I can be of service Mr ?" Offering his hand for Matt to shake and presenting him with one of his Estate Agent cards.
Matt shook his hand, slipped the card into a pocket without giving his name.

With hands in his pockets, Parker walked around admiring Matt's car, viewing it as if it were for sale. "I'd like to take this off your hands if you're thinking of selling. I'd give you a good price, . . or I could ease the sale, if you know what I mean," he said with an arrogant smirk on his face.

Sam was changing over barrels for Jack, stacking the empty ones at the back on the other side of the fence, and heard every word Jeremy Parker had said. Sam made his hands into fists, cracking his knuckles one by one, wanting to smack him hard. Jeremy Parker was gut wrenching!
This was Parker's second conversation Sam had overheard. Yesterday, while he was working in the barn, Parker was outside on his phone, bragging about having Margery Brewer in the palm of his hand. "All I have to do is keep her sweet and she listens to my every word."
Sam knew, unfortunately this was more or less true.

Matt looked at Parker with contempt, no wonder Sam disliked this character. "Good day Mr Parker." Matt got into his car ending the conversation.
Jeremy Parker walked back to his car with a cocky swagger, revved the engine and took off.
Matt got back out to take off his jacket. He'd got inside for diplomacy, one more minute and Jeremy Parker would have received his caustic opinion of him.

Sam appeared at Matt's side. "Sellin ya car then?"
Matt gave Sam a withering look. Sam grinned, obviously when it came to Jeremy Parker, he and Mathew Chapman read from the same page.
"I'd rather give it to you."
Sam chuckled "I could do with a new'n."

"In your dreams," Matt laughed, "what are you doing now?"
The sky looked leaden. "By the look o' that, I'm done f' the day," Sam said, looking up at the dark grey clouds filling in the sky.
"Fancy a pint?" Matt offered.
"If yous payin," Sam answered with cheek.
"Come on then."
"Not ere, follow me, we'll go t' Pheasant."
Matt waited for Sam to get into his van, then followed.

They pulled into the car park of the Black Pheasant. The rough-and-ready pub was frequented by the local farmers and stockmen. Men in work clothes, wearing their dirty boots, sat around inside chatting about their jobs and markets.
Matt and Sam approached the bar to be served. Although nobody took any notice, Matt felt conspicuous being smartly dressed. Sam read his mind, "they'll think yer a 'feed rep'," he grinned.

The barman carried in a tray of hot pasties, straight from the oven. He tipped them out onto a plate by the till, covering them with a mesh dome. "I'll be with you in a moment lads," he said, taking back the tray.
The pasties looked inviting, their tasty aroma wafted.
"Want some?" Matt offered.
"I could eat a horse if his arse w' peppered," Sam announced.
Matt ordered the drinks and three pasties, - two for Sam.
"Thanks for telling Mrs Brewer I'd be late, I didn't get there till five."
"Were she OK w' that?" Sam asked, biting into the hot pasty, burning his mouth and swearing.

Matt chuckled, humoured by the scene. "I took her out for dinner to apologise."
"Did ya?" Sam's eyes lit up, Jeremy Parker wouldn't like that.

They talked about the general livelihood grind. Matt doubting whether he and Gina would see much of each other this year, such was their commitment to raising the capital for the farm. Matt outlined the work needed on the property. The farmhouse hadn't had an any remedial work for years, and there was Elaine's conversion to complete.
"What about them cottages?" Sam asked.
"I'd like to get them up together, turn them back into a decent size house at some stage," Matt proposed.
"Fer?" Sam persisted.
"The farm manager," Matt answered. "I wouldn't take on a farm without one."
Sam smiled, they both knew he meant Sam.
"It's a big sum to find," Matt said with honesty. He spoke about his job, relaying the pressure of commerce, giving Sam a glimpse of a different working world.
"When y' likely t' be back?"
"I may have a buyer for my flat, Gina's got her house to sell. I'll need to assess whether it's feasible to make an offer."
They could hear heavy rain falling outside.
"I should start heading back, good to see you Sam." Matt said, standing up ready to go. With the accident still forefront in his mind, he'd be driving home at a sensible speed.

- -

Suzy texted Kate 'would you like to see your new cousin?' Forwarding the picture and message Phil had sent

her earlier. Almost immediately Kate phoned back, chiding her mother for not mentioning her Aunt's pregnancy.
"I wasn't allowed," Suzy confessed "but isn't he gorgeous?"
"We'll be down to stay in ten days. Jefferson is hiring a van so I can take back more of my stuff. Is that OK Mum?"
Suzy was delighted, wanting to know how long they could stay.
"Monday to Friday," Kate answered, almost as excited about the visit as her mother. "I want to show Jefferson where I grew up, and I can meet the new baby."
"You could both stay at home in Ashton if you'd prefer," Suzy offered "the house is empty."
"No," Kate scorned "not without you Mum, we'll stay with you at Squirrels Chase."
"Thank you Kate," Suzy answered, feeling loved and appreciated.

Rachel answered her phone with trepidation, she could see by the screen her caller was Suzy. They hadn't spoken since Suzy had nervously left her office to hand in her notice, Rachel still wasn't sure it had been the right decision.
"Hi," Suzy said brightly. "I just wanted to share some good news, I've become an Auntie!" she declared full of excitement and chatted gaily on about the event. "See you Saturday."
It was a relief to hear Suzy feeling so joyful, obviously resigning had been right for her. Yet, there was something about her distinct change that caused Rachel to wonder if Suzy wasn't telling her something.

Suzy's last phone call of the day was to Phil, they chatted for almost an hour.
"I have to pinch myself every time I see him, I can't believe we have a son," he said, still overwhelmed.

- -

Matt couldn't wait until ten o'clock to phone Gina, he called at nine. "Phil and Julia have a baby, I'm an uncle, a boy, born yesterday," he gushed, getting his words in a muddle.
Gina chuckled, wishing she was back home to share his good news. "Send Julia flowers from both of us, and tell the florist to incorporate the colour blue," she instructed, already planning to buy something blue and cosy to bring back for the new baby.

She also had some good news. Her mother had shown three couple's around her house, and two of them had said it was exactly what they'd been looking for. "Fingers crossed," she told him optimistically.

- -

Rachel needed to plan and sort bookings for the next batch of courses. With menu ideas, memos and charts spread across her desk, she phoned Suzy to warn her she'd probably arrive later than previously arranged.

As Bob got used to his new surroundings, he began to leave his bed and follow Suzy around the house.
She picked up her phone to answer, shushing Bob who wined and scratched at the backdoor to go outside. "Hi Rachel."
"Are you talking to someone?" Rachel asked with suspicion.
"Yes," Suzy teased "my lodger, he wants to go out."
"He?" Taken aback, Rachel forgot about leaving later. "I'm bringing dinner and leaving now, see you soon," swiftly

ending the call. Her imagination ran riot, 'lodger?' A vulnerable woman newly alone cued a possible disaster, what had Suzy got herself into?
Rachel slid her arm across her desk, clearing everything into a box to work on later. She locked her office and walked over to collect the cooked meal she'd ordered to take with her. Nobody could make a Black Forrest gateaux like their head patisserie chef Pierre Jacques. Earlier she'd asked him to save her two portions. Rachel loaded her car and set off, concern for Suzy foremost in her mind.

Bob barked when he heard Rachel arrive.
"Shush," Suzy commanded, "stay," and pointed to his bed. Greeting Rachel at the door, Suzy helped to carry everything she'd brought, although it seemed a little excessive for one night.
"I packed in a rush," she explained "for all weathers."
"Come and meet my lodger," Suzy lead her into the kitchen.
"A dog!" Rachel exclaimed, almost relieved. "Why on earth have you lumbered yourself with a dog? You're supposed to be solving your problems, not adding to them."
"Don't listen to her Bob," Suzy said, switching the kettle on to make drinks. Bob seemed to know he was being spoken about, and wore his worried look. Suzy went over to fuss and reassure him.
Rachel wasn't impressed, she sat at the kitchen table picking off stray dog hairs from her dark suit.
"It's only while his owner recovers," Suzy explained, slightly redeeming herself in Rachel's eyes.

A delicious smell began to seep from the box Rachel had carried in. "Chicken Chasseur, roasted vegetables and Black Forrest gateaux," she confirmed.

Suzy started to unpack the food containers from inside. Often not bothering to cook for one, the meal was a welcome treat. She thanked Rachel, showing her the last item from the box – a carton of double cream.
Rachel smiled, chef Pierre was spoiling her again.

Suzy made sandwiches for their lunch and fed Bob, while Rachel set up her laptop on the kitchen table. They worked together composing a new CV for Suzy to forward, or present at interviews. With that task complete, they turned their attention to job-hunting.
"Is there anything I can do from home?" Suzy asked, casting her eyes towards the dog.
Rachel frowned with disapproval "and sell yourself short on your abilities?" Backing down at Suzy's request, she tapped in a new heading and began reading through the list. "Here's one," she read out "audio typing at home for the medical industry."
"What's that?" Suzy asked with interest.
"I think it's writing up notes for doctors, patient's notes or details of appointments," Rachel guessed. "Shall I request more information?"
Suzy was horrified, "a definite no to that one, what if I spelt a symptom, or medication, or a procedure wrong? I could kill people!"
"I think you'd soon get the gist of it," Rachel continued, concentrating on the screen.
They both looked up at each other, trying to stifle a laugh. "Maybe you're right about that one," Rachel agreed.

Scrolling through several websites and private adverts wasn't particularly fruitful. There was only one other which fitted Suzy's criteria, and her hopes began to fade. She unfolded the newspaper from the supermarket and

turned to the back pages. A similar position to the one she'd just left was advertised locally.
"There you are, it's made for you," Rachel said taking down the details. "Now you've got two to try for."

Suzy thanked Rachel, relieved they'd managed to find something. "All I need now is a suitable outfit to wear. Nothing suits me anymore, I look like a frump, even my dresses just seem to hang.
Rachel grinned "I'm not surprised, you must of dropped at least two dress sizes."
"Never!" Suzy argued.
Rachel stood up and took her jacket from the back of the chair. "Try this on," she instructed, handing it over.
Suzy put it on, her expression spoke volumes. The jacket was a snug fit over her thick jumper but it more-or-less fitted.
"Told you," Rachel affirmed.
The truth began to dawn, she'd hardly eaten anything during those first weeks in shock, only picking at bits and pieces when she remembered. Not cooking daily for Richard had changed her eating habits, missing the odd meal and settling for a bowl of cornflakes in the evening when she couldn't be bothered.
"Don't worry, I'll find you something. It will give me the incentive to sort out what's in my wardrobes," Rachel added kindly.

Considering how long it had taken Bob to accept her and his temporary new home, Suzy was surprised he'd instantly taken a shine to Rachel. He sat close, watching her with his brown soulful eyes, waiting for attention. When Rachel ignored him, he leant against her legs.

She disregarded the dog, assuming he would get fed up and go back to his bed.

The two friends retired to the lounge, they had a lot of family news to catch up on.
Bob had followed, and laid happily at Rachel's feet. She could see the change in Suzy's psyche, a hint of her humorous 'old self' was beginning to show through. Maybe the dog's company had been just what she'd needed. Rachel stretched over to stroke him, by helping Suzy he'd earned her fuss. "I have to admit, he is quite nice . . . for a dog," she confessed gently fondling his soft brown furry ears.

Suzy smiled to herself, from keeping her distance and being irritated by dog hairs on her clothes, to stroking and fussing him, . . Rachel was succumbing.

-

On Sunday after a leisurely breakfast, Rachel was in no rush to return home. Outside, the temperature gradually rose as the sun's warmth gently increased by the hour.
"Shall we take him for a walk?" Rachel suggested, looking out of the kitchen window. "Seems a shame to stay in and waste the day."
When Bob heard 'walk', he pricked up his ears and began to circle her, frantically wagging his tail.
"Now you've done it," Suzy laughed "we'll have to take him."

Handing Rachel his lead and a handful of poo-bags, Suzy put Bob in the back of her car and drove to the viewpoint at Gravel Hill. Looking down across the valley, she pointed out the track from Kirston Woods to the town. "We used to come here for picnics when I was a child. My brothers ran about like lunatics trying to keep their kites in the air." Declining to mention her last visit, after Matt had found her hiding away at Squirrels Chase.

Bob barked with impatience, desperate to get out. "Come on then," Suzy said opening her car door. Rachel happily held on to Bob's lead, but screwed up her nose and swiftly passed the poo bags back to Suzy before they set off. Away from the road Bob was given his freedom to race about. "Look at him," Rachel smiled "he's in his element." They took the widest path towards the woods. "I think you should settle here, if it's where you feel at home. What's the point of going back to Ashton?" Rachel remarked out-of-the-blue.

Suzy admitted she was beginning to think along those lines herself. She would use the time at Squirrels Chase to re-establish her life, to start rebuilding a future, . . her future. "I'll have to face Richard soon, we need to discuss selling our house," forcing herself to talk about him.

Rachel revealed, they hadn't moved. Although she'd heard talk of offers, Gwen's house remained unsold.

Suzy didn't have his address, "if I write him a letter, would you mind delivering it?" she asked.

Rachel volunteered to drop it in, when she next popped over to see Elsie.

Bob raced ahead, crashing through bracken, in and out of sight. He reversed out from a bush, shaking off dried leaves stuck to his coat. Looking pleased with himself, he dropped a ball he'd found at Rachel's feet.

"You've got a friend there, he likes you," Suzy said, stating the obvious. For the next twenty minutes Rachel threw the ball for Bob to chase and fetch, as they strolled along. Realising how far they'd walked, Suzy suggested they turned back. Beginning to flag, it was a relief to see the carpark come into view.

Back at Squirrels Chase, Suzy took off her coat, declaring she was gasping for a cup of tea. Bob sauntered wearily across to his bed, flopped down ready for a long sleep.

While Rachel gathered her things, Suzy wrote a short note for Richard, sealing the envelope with Sellotape and addressing it for his personal attention.

"Thank you for coming. It's been so nice having your company, hasn't it Bob?" Bob remained dead to the world, wagging his tail from time to time in his sleep.

"I feel as though I've been here for days, I'm totally chilled," Rachel professed, finishing her drink.

Suzy walked with Rachel to her car, helping to carry her stuff. Before opening the boot, Rachel stopped and looked around "you should buy this place, you belong here, I can feel it."

"What with?" Suzy laughed.

"I'm serious," Rachel said, getting into her car.

"I'll phone you in the week," Suzy promised, waving as Rachel drove away.

Suzy walked back into the house, lifted her tired legs from the long walk onto the settee in the lounge. Plumped up the cushions, laid back and closed her eyes, giving herself five-minutes to doze and recoup her energy. Later she'd type out two applications for the jobs they'd found, enclosing copies of the glowing reference from her previous manager, in hope it would lead to an interview.

She couldn't logically explain the uncomfortable feeling she got when sealing the envelopes ready to post. Rachel had cancelled her busy weekend to come up and help, it would be ungrateful not to apply. Besides she probably needed a proverbial kick up the rear to make her move on with her life.

-

Awake early and far too soon to get up, Suzy laid in bed allowing her thoughts to meander. Remembering the day before, Rachel's visit had lifted her spirits, . . and Bob's too, those two were definitely soulmates. Her mind wandered on to planning her day. Later, she would pop out to buy a Congratulations card for Julia and Phil.

Bob sensed her moving and scampered upstairs, stood in the bedroom doorway watching to see if she was awake.

Suzy sat up, she'd heard him coming up the stairs "morning Bob." Watching him wag his tail, being pleased to see her was enough to brighten the start of anyone's day. "I expect you want to go out," she said, reaching for her dressing gown.

After her shower Suzy sat on the edge of her bed drying her hair. Switching off the noisy hairdryer, she heard her phone ringing from the pile of clothes on the floor. It rang out for another second and stopped. She'd been trying to do something creative with her hair and was losing the battle. Her straggly locks in need of a colour had begun to skim her shoulder blades, she'd never let it get so long and ratty before. Trying to tame her unruly tresses, she twisted the length around her fingers and pinned it into a make-do pleat, promising herself to find a hair salon. Retrieving her phone from the pocket of her jeans, the screen displayed a missed call. It rang again.

"Hi Rachel," Suzy answered.

Rachel couldn't talk for long, she was manning the reception desk. In almost a whisper, said she'd be working in London later this week and wasn't sure how long for, . . maybe a week, could be longer. "I'll sort out those clothes tonight, can you pick them up before Friday?"
"Will do," Suzy replied.
"What are you doing today?"
"Having a bad hair day!"
Rachel laughed and hung up.
Two minutes later Suzy's phone rang again, "hi Rachel."
"I forgot to say Michael's home this week, so you can call in to pick them up during the day if it's easier. Oops, I have to go, sorry," and ended the call.

Three minutes later her phone rang again. "What have you forgotten this time?" Suzy asked, smiling to herself.
"You wanted to speak to me," Richard said.
Suzy thought her heart had stopped as she struggled to catch her breath, trying to control her emotions. "We need to talk about our house."
"I can do Wednesday afternoon, where do you want to meet?" he asked.
Her mind went blank.
He suggested The Mill.
"Yes, that's fine."
"See you at two," he said and hung up.
Hearing his voice unforeseen had shaken her, she remained sitting on her bed, close to tears.

Bob began barking downstairs breaking the spell, she went down to investigate. George was standing at the backdoor, Suzy beckoned him inside.

"Hello lass, I just called round to see how you were getting on with this ere dog." He'd been feeling guilty about lumbering her with it.
"He's fine George, tea?" Suzy offered filling the kettle with shaking hands.
George sat down at the kitchen table. "Are you alright lass? . . you look as though you've seen a ghost."
"Sorry about this mess," she said ignoring his question, pushing papers scattered across the table to one side. "My friend stayed at the weekend, she was helping me find a job."
"There's a job going at the big school in Kirston if you want it, in the science block," George announced.
"I'm not a teacher George," handing him his mug of tea.
"Miss Blake's class assistant is leaving and she needs a replacement, she were telling me all about it last week."
"I don't know anything about science either," dismissing his information.
"Don't have to, she'd show you what to do, it's getting out the stuff for her lessons."
"Is Miss Blake one of your customers?" Suzy asked, becoming curious.
"Yes lass, and I'll be up there this afternoon. Shall I let her know you're interested?"
Suzy wondered, it would be different, "on reflection, yes please George."
Bob nuzzled her to fuss him. She stroked his head and scratched his favourite itchy spot on his back. "I'll need to come back lunchtimes to let you out," she said talking to Bob, stroking his ears.
George got up ready to leave, "thanks for the tea lass."
Bob followed him almost to the door. "You've fell on

your paws here lad," he said to the dog before closing the door.

"How long has that hairdressers been next door?" Suzy asked the girl behind the counter in the Card Shop, she hadn't noticed it before.
"About a year, it's quite popular. Ladies pop in here after they've had their hair done and I haven't yet seen any disasters," the girl laughed, slipping Suzy's card into a paper bag.
It seemed a good enough reference, Suzy paid for her card and proceeded next door.

Inside Cut Above she stood at the counter looking around, checking the ambiance of the place. According to the suave black and white posters of models staring back from the walls, and the slick modern interior design, this place was cutting edge.
"Can I help?"
Suzy jumped at the woman's sudden appearance.
"Sorry, I was sorting out the shelves down behind this counter." Realising Suzy was a new customer, she lead her over to a seating area. "Tea, coffee or would you prefer a cold drink? . . Fay will be with you in a moment."
Suzy declined the drink, she hadn't been expecting such personal attention. At her usual hairdressers in Ashton, she would have made an appointment and been gone by now.

Fay approached, smiling and introduced herself. Her long tresses began grey at the roots, ending in pale turquoise. She sat beside Suzy making notes from the many questions she asked, then moved Suzy to one of the salon chairs. "May I?" she asked politely, wanting to unclip Suzy's hair to inspect it's condition and thickness. Suzy disclosed her hair appointments usually amounted to a colour, cut, and blow dry, resulting in layers of soft curls. "Would you like to try something different? A change from your 'norm," Fay suggested. "Blended highlights instead of a block colour? We'll do a patch test first, so you've plenty of time to decide." Fay picked the shades and coloured some strands. "You'll look amazing, I promise. See you tomorrow afternoon."

Returning from a short walk around the block with Bob, Suzy spotted a note poking out from the letterbox. She recognised George's spidery handwriting, he must have called while she was out. She read the note.

> 'Miss Blake said to go and see her at the school after lessons. She's in the science block most afternoons till 4.30. The science block is the building far left.'
>
> George.

Suzy waited until after five before she rang Rachel.
"Have you finished?" she asked.
"Yes, I'm just clearing my desk, I've had enough for today."
"Could you ask Michael if I can call on Wednesday, about lunchtime?"
"I'll tell him you're coming, he should be up by then," Rachel laughed.
"I'm meeting Richard afterwards at two, . . he phoned," Suzy revealed.
"How was he?"
"Civil," Suzy answered, wanting to add cold.
"And you?"
"We've got to face each other at some point, I'm fine."

Rachel winced, she recognised a white-lie even though it was said with the best intentions.

-

Suzy felt apprehensive sitting in the chair at the salon, she'd given Fay carte-blanche. With a head full of tinfoil strips, she looked at her image reflected in the mirror unable to picture the finished result.

Fay returned with Suzy's cappuccino and checked some of the foils. "Won't be much longer," she said smiling and went off to wash another client's hair. Suzy continued flicking through glossy magazines glancing at glitz and glamour.

Fay stood behind Suzy's washed and towel dried hair - her scissors poised. Skilfully she snipped, blow dried and straightened. "What do you think?" she said, holding a mirror for Suzy to see the back view.

Suzy stared at the reflection hardly recognising herself.

"Give yourself a couple of days to get used to it. If you really don't like it, I'll restyle it . . free of charge," Fay offered.

Suzy shook her head, swishing her new bobbed cut hair and watched it fall perfectly into place. She smiled "I love it, thank you."

Fay relaxed, pleased with her work, and relieved her new client was happy.

Feeling more confident, Suzy drove to Kirston College. It had been called Kirston Senior School when she had attended many years ago. She parked in the carpark. The school had evolved, trebling in size with a modern impressive façade.

A bell rang from within the building and pupils emerged from every entrance. Like a disturbed ants nest they poured out, calling, laughing and shouting to each other, wending their way home. She stayed in her car giving the place time to empty.

After reporting her presence at the school's office, she walked over to the science block, following the sound of voices inside. Three girls were talking in a classroom. Suzy knocked on the open door and asked the whereabouts of Miss Blake.

The girl with the longest ponytail turned round, "hello," she smiled "I'm Linda Blake." Dismissing her pupils, Linda Blake welcomed Suzy to the school. "You must be Mrs Martin," she said knowingly "you're highly recommended."

"By George?" Suzy said embarrassed. Suzy took to Miss Blake instantly, with her relaxed easy going attitude she would be pleasant to work with.

Linda sat on a desk describing the building, offering to show Suzy around. "Basically the job is preparing the classrooms for each lesson, getting out the equipment etc. Our students range from eleven to sixteen, up to nineteen in sixth form, so there's diversity."

Suzy wondered why the position hadn't been snapped up, was there a catch?

"The money isn't great, it's not full time . . . and it may only be for a year," Linda explained "so I can understand people's reluctance."

"When would the job start? and training?" Suzy enquired.

"You'll need an interview with our Head - Mrs Taylor. She'll have all the relevant info. Once your police check is complete you can come in and help Rosie," Linda replied feeling hopeful. "Rosie has been doing the job these past three years. She'll show you everything, then you can decide. I look forward to working with you," Linda said shaking Suzy's hand.

Suzy drove home, her day had panned out positive after all, . . a new hairstyle and possibly a new job. Bob was waiting for her at the door, whinnying with excitement as she turned the key, glad to have her back home.

- -

Meeting Richard was never going to be easy, a confrontation she'd been dreading as the time loomed closer. Her strategy would be to keep things cordial between them, staying calm and focused. She refused to feed her anxiety with 'what ifs.'

She got into her car and drove to Ashton. Her first port of call would be Rachel's house to pick up the clothes. She was looking forward to meeting Michael, not having seen him since he was a baby, apart from photos on Rachel's phone. She pulled up outside hoping he'd remembered and seen her arrive, rang the bell and waited. After a pause, she heard movement. Michael opened the door, visibly struggling to remember his mother's instructions, eyes customizing to the morning light.

"Hello, I'm Suzy," she smiled, hoping to jog his memory. Standing in his just-got-up unwashed state, the penny dropped. "Case!" he remembered, and looked behind him. "Sorry about that," he said smiling, handing it to her before closing the door.

There was no mistaking his father, Michael had Adam's handsome features. Darker hair like his mother, but with his father's striking sky blue eyes. Suzy loaded the suitcase into her car and set off to her house.

She was losing her bond with the house, it no longer felt like her home. Inside she bent down to pick up the mail, mostly circulars and two letters for Richard. She walked round giving the place a quick check over.

Too early to drive to The Mill, she sat in the kitchen wondering what to do for an hour to kill time. Remembering the case, went out to fetch it. With curiosity and a hint of excitement, Suzy unzipped the lid to peek inside. She took out a dark blue jacket with matching skirt and trousers, underneath lay a similar set in grey. At the bottom, a brand new dress of the finest wool lay folded, complete with labels. Carefully, she lifted it out of the case and held it up against her body. The colour reminded her of the dress she'd bought her mother. Unable to resist, its silky lining rustling as she slipped it on. The green dress was exquisite, goodness knows how much it must of cost. She padded bare foot into the hall to look in the full-length mirror. It could of been made for her. She paraded up and down enjoying the reflection, then shrewdly decided to keep it on.
A collection of uncomfortable dressy shoes still remained at the back of her wardrobe. She ran upstairs to find a pair more suited to the dress.

Daft as it was, she wanted to look her best for Richard. Painfully aware she still had love for him. Not the Richard who'd crushed and abandoned her, but her Richard, the one she'd lived with most of her married life. She refreshed her makeup, gathered up her belongings and drove to The Mill.

She couldn't see his car in the carpark and stupidly hadn't asked exactly where they were going to meet inside. Owned by one of the large brewery chains, The Mill was vast, one continuous huge open plan bar.
She parked by the main door and waited, watching lunchtime customers leaving.

A car stopped in front of hers to let out a passenger. She witnessed a man reach across to kiss the driver before getting out. He wore a navy tracksuit which did his portly shape no favours. When the car drove off, he turned round and tapped on her window. It was Richard. It hadn't occurred to her he wouldn't come in his own car, or not alone.

Suzy silently seethed. They knew her car, had Gwen staged that performance? . . of course she had! As Suzy's heart sank, her hackles rose. With a hesitant smile she walked with Richard to the pub door, this wasn't the time to wear her heart on her sleeve. "I'll just pop in here," she said, excusing herself to the 'Ladies', leaving him to head for the bar. Prevaricating, she combed her hair and washed her hands trying to gain assertion. That act had caught her off guard. 'Don't underestimate me Gwen' Suzy thought, her anger tangled with despair. Her black heeled shoes pinched, but regardless she walked elegantly back.

Richard bought himself a pint and a tonic water with lemon for Suzy. It had been her usual drink, then with afterthought wondered if he should have asked her first. Too late, he carried their drinks to a table and sat down. He watched her walking back, not the wife he'd left, but a woman he hardly recognised. He'd not seen her so slim since her twenties and by the look of her clothes she must have come into some money. He assumed they'd sold her mother's place. It's a wonder she didn't have a new car, he grouched.

Suzy sat down and thanked him for her drink, keeping her voice calm and friendly. "I've brought these," she said handing over his letters.

He seemed uncharacteristically quiet.

"I'd like to sell the house. I think it would be best for both of us," she said biting her lip waiting for his answer.
"Do you want to handle it?" he asked bluntly.
"Yes, I'll organize it after Kate's visit. She's coming back for a few days, I'm sure she'd want to see you," giving him a brief smile. "Is there anything you want to say?"
"I want a divorce," he said, once more trampling her feelings.
A shudder ran through her body. "I married for life Richard. If you want a divorce, you will have to divorce me," starring directly into his eyes. She would have retaliation but on her own terms. It would be easy to rant and rave like a harridan, justifiably angry at the unfairness of her treatment, . . but at what cost? So later he could convince himself he'd done the right thing by getting rid of her. No, a difficult wife would be easy to forget. Suzy wanted to be remembered. Should his relationship with Gwen turn sour, she wanted Richard to think about what he'd lost. He deserved to be haunted by her smile and love.

Richard's phone pipped, he took it out of his pocket and glanced at the screen. "I have to go," speaking with a stony expression.
Suzy noted his new phone, not the old one she'd been trying to persuade him to replace for years. Gwen obviously had more success, another indication of putting her stamp on him.
"If you could phone or text Kate," Suzy reminded.
Richard stood up to go and seemed unsure of what to say next.
"Bye Richard," Suzy said, keeping her tone friendly.
He turned and walked away. She sat for a while, giving them time to drive off. She didn't want them sat in their

car watching and waiting for her to go. She had used up all the thespian skills she could muster to keep her dignity.

Back at home, Suzy kicked off the uncomfortable shoes, ran upstairs to take off the dress and pulled on her jeans and sweatshirt. Needing a walk to clear her head, she clipped on Bob's lead. Striding out at a swift pace, left the house with Bob running obediently at her side. Meeting Richard had roused a tsunami of emotions. Hadn't she looked her best? . been nice to him? . yet she'd sensed annoyance in his voice when he spoke. Their marriage might be over, but she'd hoped to see a little past fondness in his eyes. Walking with determination, she marched on.

The road sign to Kirston came into view. Suzy stopped, realizing how far she'd walked in torment. "What am I doing!" she said aloud. Bob looked up for instruction, panting from the exertion. Power-walking had reduced her tension. "Come on Bobby," she sighed looking down at him "let's go home."

- -

Matt drove into his allotted space in the carpark. It wasn't unusual for him to turn up so early. He preferred the lack of traffic and the quietness of the empty building. Also he achieved more efficiency working first thing, than staying late. He wasn't entirely surprised to see Harvey Granzman's Bentley already parked discretely in the corner. The large glass door automatically slid open for him to enter the building. "Morning Dennis," greeting the security guard standing inside "what time did. . ? "
"Arrived about ten minutes ago," the guard answered, anticipating the question.

Matt headed to his office. He texted a loving message to Gina on his phone while he waited for the hi-tec vending machine to produce it's hot insipid tasting coffee. She may have been away several days, but to him already it felt like weeks. He wondered how long he'd be at his desk before Harvey Granzman paid him a visit. Matt sat down, switched on the computer and began filling his desktop with documents and reports.

Almost on cue, Harvey Granzman entered and stood in front of Matt's desk. "This transition, talk me through your plan Mathew."

Matt looked up from his screen, "Good morning Sir."

He knew the question was said purely to remind him it was his idea and liability. "I'll complete our two current deals, work with Tom on the next two ongoing ones, then step back, . . in support from there on. Tom won't fly until he feels the power of sole responsibility. Wholly at my discretion, Sir," Matt added.

"At my discretion Mathew," Granzman said firmly, adding pressure. Matt knew Granzman still wasn't happy about his withdrawal. He and Tom had a lot to prove, they had to become a crack team before Matt could hand over the reins. He owed it to Tom, Granzman and Vortorx to get it right, this was going to be a tough year!

Harvey Granzman paced around Matt's office digesting his answer. Matt was used to his pacing, he'd never found it intimidating. Granzman made his way to the door. "See you later Mathew," he said walking out leaving it wide open.

"Good bye Sir." Matt took a sip of coffee before getting up to shut his door. This early meeting with Harvey Granzman had been positive, now he could get on with his work.

Matt read through the last paragraph of Atwick's proposed merger, he couldn't find any discrepancies in this revised version. He looked at his watch, no wonder his body ached, he'd been sat at his desk virtually all day. He stood up arching his back, flexing muscles trying to release stiffness. It had been a long, but productive day and he was happy with the volume accomplished. He closed down the computer, stacked folders into piles, and began sifting through papers for Caroline to file in the morning.

Tom knocked on his door and walked in "still at it?"

"No, I'm finished here," Matt said, clearing away the remaining papers and locking his desk drawer. "I'll walk out with you if you hang on. Ready for your interview tomorrow?" Matt asked, putting on his jacket.

"I had it this morning. I came in early to go over the Ipsonne figures and was summoned to his office. I didn't know he was in," Tom said surprised.

Matt smiled, Granzman's unpredictability kept staff on their toes. He wouldn't mention talking to him earlier that morning, "how did you get on?"

"Lots of 'what if?' scenarios, and 'how would you handle?' I told him I do my own research, if I'm not happy with anything I'd consult you. Failing that, I'd back off, I'm not a chancer."

"Good answer," Matt affirmed impressed.

"I thought I'd lost it, when Mr Granzman got up and started walking around," Tom confessed.

Matt grinned "Harvey Granzman thinks on his feet, you'll get used to it, it's how he works. Did you sign a new contract?"

"Yes, but it won't be officially acknowledged until later in the year," Tom submitted.
"This desk is yours as soon as you can prove yourself," Matt stated firmly "you can do it Tom."

"About your flat," Tom looked down, uncomfortably fiddling with his keys. "Even with the twenty K my father's added, this is my mortgage limit." He wrote down a figure and handed it to Matt. "It's an amazing place, worth much more than I can raise, . . one day, maybe," Tom looked gutted.
Matt slipped the note into his pocket without reading it. Tom waited for Matt to lock his office door, before they left together.
In the carpark Matt stopped and pointed. "If Harvey Granzman comes in early, that's where he parks his Bentley. There's a space almost out of view in that corner. Forewarned is forearmed." Matt put his hand in his pocket searching for keys, accidently pulling out Tom's piece of paper with them. "Give me some time to think about this," he said, opening his car door.
Tom bade "goodnight," and walked towards his own car.

Matt was glad to get home, starring at his computer screen for hours on end had given him a headache. After a shower, he made himself a drink and a pile of sandwiches. He carried the loaded tray into the bedroom. Tonight he'd prefer sitting up in bed watching television, rather than being in the lounge alone. His phone rang out. "Hello Gorgeous, you're early tonight," he said, glad to hear her voice.
Gina was excited, bursting to tell him her good news. "Mum's accepted an offer on my house. Not the full asking price, but they're cash buyers and ready to move

as soon as possible. Isn't that great? One down, two to go," She sounded elated.
"Two?" Matt queried.
"Yes, your flat and Squirrels Chase."
Matt went quiet.
"Are you OK?" sensing his silence.
"Sorry, I'm just shattered, a very long day at the office."
"Get some sleep my love, I'll phone you tomorrow."
Matt put his phone on the bedside cabinet, feeling his headache worsen. If he was going to sell Squirrels Chase, he would have to warn Suzy.

-

Still with a shadow of headache when he woke up, Matt had no intention of going into his office. Yesterday's twelve hour day had served him well, getting him far in advance with assignments. Tom's interview being fulfilled meant Harvey Granzman wouldn't be back until next week. He phoned through to Caroline, going over the long list of work on his desk he'd left for her.
His next call was to Suzy, to ask how she was feeling.
"I'm OK," she said, trying to sound cheerful.
He sensed something, knowing each other so well.
"Thought I'd come down to see you, maybe stay over."
"Matt, that would be wonderful." Now she'd no time to dwell on yesterday, and if he arrived around lunchtime as he'd suggested, she didn't have much time to tidy either.

Turning into the drive at Squirrels Chase, Matt felt the unruffled calm of home. For whatever reason, parting with it at this moment didn't feel right.
Suzy opened the front door with a smile, expressing how pleased she was to see him.
"Is that a dog I can hear?"

“Come and meet Bob,” she said leading the way. Bob stayed in his bed, barking. “Shush Bob,” Suzy instructed. After sharing two chocolate biscuits, Bob decided Matt was a friend. She explained his residence while making sandwiches for lunch.

“Are you really OK Suze?” He could see she had lost more weight since his last visit. She’d never been big, but this business with Richard had robbed her of her curves. “I’m OK,” she said, gathering up their empty plates and mugs, putting them into the sink. “Fancy a walk?” The minute she said ‘walk’, Bob gave her his full attention, wagging his tail, thumping it against Matt’s leg.
“Why not,” he agreed.
She insisted they went in her car, not wanting the responsibility of pawmarks on his car’s cream leather seats. She drove to Kirston Woods where Bob could run free, leaving them to walk and chat. She wondered what was bothering Matt, their intuitive gene told her there must be something prompting this spur-of-the-moment visit.

Sucking peppermints and throwing sticks for the dog, wandering along the path beneath Kirston’s majestic ancient trees, Matt began to unwind. The serenity of the countryside was what he was striving for, . . just this one last year at Vortorx he reflected.
He’d volunteered to go walking in hope of whatever was troubling Suzy, might come to light during their conversation. Yet somehow at ease in her company he began talking about himself, unburdening his own anxieties to her. “Eighteen months ago, a long day at my desk was part of the job I loved, now it’s a means to an end.”
He told her about Tom, “he’s more than my prodigy, he’s my ticket out.” Matt chattered on, enlightening her of Tom’s wish to buy his flat. Airing Tom’s financial

situation of what he could afford, and the higher price Matt was hoping for.

She thought for a moment, weighing up the facts. "I'd let him have it. If you've not signed up to an estate agent, you'll save a hefty fee and be spared weeks or months of prospective buyers viewing, price battles and possible failed deals." She thought the answer was obvious, "of course that's only my opinion. If you need a place to stay, you could stay here . It's not so far from your office." She stopped walking. With the bond of perception they shared, she realised he wanted to sell Squirrels Chase. "Unless you need to sell it," she said slowly looking into his eyes.

"Not yet," he said, feeling strangely relieved with his answer. He was glad they came. In a couple of hours of walking in Kirston Woods Suzy had solved his 'flat selling'.

Back home she sent Matt into the lounge while she made tea. Carrying the tray, she stopped outside the door "can you open the door please," she called. With no response she turned round to reverse, nudging the door open with her bottom. No wonder he didn't answer, he was sound asleep on the settee with Bob snoring at his feet. She crept out, leaving them to it.

Suzy was folding towels, when Matt walked into the kitchen.

"Is that clock right?" he said, looking up at the large faced clock on the wall, his hair still tousled by sleep.

"Yes," she grinned "feeling better after your nap?" He'd slept two hours and now was getting hungry.

"Not used to all that fresh air," she teased.

"Not used to all that walking," he admitted. Matt's thoughts turned to food "let's go out for dinner," and preceded upstairs to wash.

She'd already washed her hair and showered while he was sleeping. Now, she stood looking at the green dress still draped over the chair in her bedroom, wondering whether to wear it again. It was the best thing in her wardrobe, although it hadn't worked any magic for Richard, . . nevertheless she put it on.

Matt drove them to The Dolwen restaurant, just outside of Kirston. An up market place, where plates were considerably larger than the portions served, with wisps of sauce garnishing the food centred.

By arriving early, the restaurant wasn't busy, allowing them to pick a secluded table. Matt ordered a large 'well done' steak for himself and the wine. Then sent the waiter round to Suzy to choose the rest of their meal.

His phone laying on the table flashed, illuminating a signal, it was Gina. Suzy watched him taking the call.

"Where am I?" he smiled, repeating her question aloud.

"I'm having dinner with a young very attractive lady, would you like to speak to her?" he jest, holding up his phone to Suzy. Gina waved to Suzy from the screen and said hello.

"When are you coming back? you're being missed," Suzy asked.

"Possibly at the end of next week. My boss is getting homesick, she's missing her babies. Her husband sends her pictures of them each day, she's busy phoning him now."

"Oh dear," Suzy sympathized.

Gina laughed "her babies, Henry and Hero are dachshunds. Oh, she's coming back, 'bye' you two, enjoy your meals."

"Bye Gina," Suzy called.
Matt turned the phone back to his ear "I'll phone later, love you," he said ending the call. "She likes your new hairstyle by-the-way," passing on Gina's message.
"Kate's coming back for a few days," Suzy announced. "With her boyfriend, they're picking up more of her stuff."
"Will she see Richard?" Matt asked.
"I expect so, I met him last week at The Mill," Suzy volunteered. "I needed to tell him about Kate, and said I'd put our house on the market when she's gone back."
"How was he?" Matt asked
Suzy felt the hurt of the meeting return, and struggled to answer. "He seemed irritated with me, he hardly spoke."
"He's probably realized what he's lost. I expect seeing you was a shock, Suze you're looking great, . . really.
Suzy smiled appreciating his compliment, but it didn't stop the hurt the memory revived. "When I got back I took Bob for a power walk to get it out of my system."
"Poor dog!" Matt grinned, topping up her glass with wine.

"That steak was perfect," Matt announced, clearing every morsel. Their meal had been delicious, although walking had initiated good appetites. When he mentioned his legs ached, Suzy giggled. He smiled, glad to hear her giggle again.
"Perhaps Squirrels Chase has a good fairy looking after us," she suggested wistfully, "finding Mum's bonds, you coming to find me, and Bob turning up needing someone to care for him."
Matt raised an eyebrow, convinced the wine was taking hold. The restaurant started to fill. He decided to head back, they could have coffee at home, besides he wanted to phone Gina before she went to bed.

-

After breakfast Suzy began clearing the table. "How are your legs this morning?" she asked, with a cheeky grin.
"They're fine thank you, how's your head?" he replied with equal mischief, remembering the amount of wine she'd drank the evening before.
"I was wondering if you'd like to join me when I take Bob out for his morning walk."
Matt declined her offer. "Shall we visit Phil and Julia today, see our new nephew?"
Suzy beamed with delight.

George pulled into the drive at Squirrels Chase. He didn't recognise the car parked next to Mrs Martin's, perhaps her friend was staying again. He got out of his van and walked around to the back door. Mrs Kelly's neighbour had told him she was due to come out of hospital. He needed to warn Mrs Martin the dog would be going back soon.

Bob pricked up his ears, barked and stood at the back door. Only George came round to the back door, Suzy went to open it. Sure enough, George stood on the step. He hadn't expected to see a man sat at the kitchen table and suddenly felt he didn't want to intrude.
"Hello George," Suzy welcomed, inviting him in. "I'd like you to meet Matt, my eldest brother."
As George stepped inside, Matt rose from the table to shake his hand, pleased to meet him. He hadn't forgotten George's kindness and help to their mother, especially on her last day and said so.

Suzy put a mug of fresh tea on the table for George and topped up Matt's coffee. "Sit down for a moment George, I'll only be one minute." and went off to phone Phil to ask if they could visit.

Matt thanked George for all the work he'd done for Suzy. "That dog of yours has been a Godsend, especially now she's here on her own, loves him to bits," Matt added casually.
George finished his tea and stood up ready to leave "well I'd better get on, nice to meet you," he said making his way to the door. "Tell Mrs Martin I'll catch her later, it wasn't important."

Suzy returned to the kitchen "where's George?"
"Had to go back to work, didn't say what he wanted, just said he'd catch you later."
She passed on Phil's information. Julia and the baby were still in hospital and they'd be most welcome to visit. He'd given her the hospital's details and suggested visiting after two, when he'd be there.

Bob began to circle Suzy, anticipating his walk.
"While you're walking miles with that dog, I'll pop into Kirston to get some flowers, then we needn't stop on route," Matt suggested.
He waited for Suzy to leave with Bob. When she'd gone, he went upstairs to Phil's old room. He'd been considering her idea of staying there during the week. Not necessarily every weekday, but once he'd sold his flat he would need somewhere. It would be more homely and convenient than a guest house. Matt walked around the room using his phone to check sign strength. He could easily turn this smaller room into a temporary office. His expenses would give Suzy a small income and justify her staying at Squirrels Chase. It could work, happy with his decision he left for Kirston.

No matter how quietly they tried to walk, their shoes click clacked noisily along the floors of the hollow sounding hospital corridors. Suzy carried a huge bouquet of pink and white roses. When Matt mentioned the occasion, the florist had wrapped the flowers in blue paper, adding blue ribbons and bows.

They checked in at a Reception Desk and were directed to Julia's room. Matt opened the door carefully, trying not to make any sudden noise.

The new parents greeted them with radiant smiles. Suzy handed Julia the flowers and gave her a kiss on the cheek, congratulating the new 'Mum', Matt followed suit. Phil stepped aside allowing them to peep into the clear sided cot beside Julia's bed. The tiny babe lay sleeping, cocooned in a pale blue blanket.

"He's so beautiful," Suzy whispered, moving closer for a better look. A tiny hand escaped from under the cover, fanning out five tiny fingers before forming a fist.

"Would you like to hold him?" Julia offered.

Matt carried a chair to Julia's bedside for Suzy to sit on. Phil lifted the small bundle and laid their precious baby in her arms.

Looking down with eyes full of love, rocking him gently, Suzy announced she was in heaven. The baby emitted a tiny whimper, opened his eyes for a second and went back to sleep.

"Nice to have a room to yourselves," Matt remarked looking around.

"It's a private room," Julia said, "thanks to Daddy over fussing."

"Daddy," Suzy repeated slowly looking up smiling, catching Phil's eye.

They stayed until Neville Alexander proclaimed with small but strong lungs, he needed feeding.
"Time to go," Matt swiftly instructed.
Julia said 'they should be going home tomorrow and were very welcome to call in to see them anytime next week.'
"I'd love to and I'll bring Kate," Suzy promised. They said their goodbyes, leaving the new parents to get on with feeding their new baby son.

"Wasn't he the cutest baby ever?" Suzy swooned, getting into Matt's car. "He was sooooo scrumptious."
"Certainly something I never expected to see," Matt marvelled.
"It's been an unbelievable year," Suzy reflected. "Who'd of thought of a baby for Phil, you leaving your ultimate job, . . me back at Squirrels Chase and getting divorced. I guess life's full of unexpected changes."
Matt started the engine and headed back. He mentioned thinking about her idea of him lodging midweek. "It could work if Phil agrees. I don't think he's worried about selling the house yet and I could pay you expenses."
She thanked him, appreciating the arrangement would suit her situation considerably and she'd be glad of his company. "I've applied for a job at our old school - Kirston College. It's not full time, or well-paid but it's a start. I'll let you know if it works out."
Matt felt relieved, hearing she was beginning to think about her future. "Are you OK at the moment? . . financially?"
Conscious of his concern, she knew he would ask, and assured him of some savings. She had been saving for many months, squirreling away her overtime payments and bonuses. Accumulating funds towards their grand fantastic holiday, ... or so she'd thought at the time.

Back at Squirrels Chase Matt didn't want to stay long, he'd things to sort out back at his flat. "I'll call you in the week."
She waved, watching him drive away, doubting he'd remember to phone, knowing how busy his life always seemed to be.

-

Matt needed an accurate figure to submit towards the sale of Ashwood Farm. He spent the week trawling through his finances, selling his portfolio of shares, and emptying bank accounts he rarely used, finally transferring the substantial sum into his building society account.
On Gina's return, they'd need to sit down together and decide whether their combined funds were enough to buy the farm. It wasn't just the purchase price, he'd taken into account the significant renovations and dairy conversion for Elaine.

- -

Kate and Jefferson sat at the kitchen table relaying their lengthy journey, while Suzy fussed about, toasting crumpets and making coffee. "Go on," she said spreading butter "I'm listening."
It appeared they'd been making good progress until Jefferson took a wrong turn. According to him 'Kady not knowing her left from her right.'
"Well we're here now safe and sound," Kate laughed.

Suzy suggested, Kate should show Jefferson around, sensing he was itching to explore.
Bob wasn't sure of the visitors. After their initial greeting he stayed in his bed observing them from a distance, . . until they offered him a biscuit.

With the house about to go on the market, Kate wanted her possessions brought back to Squirrels Chase. Compelling full use of their hired van for transporting her things.
Understanding the task, Suzy was content to stay out of the way, enjoying their company as-and-when their busy timetable allowed.

-

Jefferson unloaded the last box, carrying it into the garage. “Where’s this go’n Kady?” he asked in his American drawl.
She pointing to the large stack against the wall.
He threw a large plastic sheet over the pile and watched her anchoring the folds with Sellotape, finally tying a length of rope around it for good measure.
“That should do it,” she said, happy and relieved all of her belongings were safely stored. Two full storage boxes stood inside the garage door, one stacked on top of the other, ready for the return trip back to Leeds. Kate locked the garage door, glad the job was finished. Now time would be their own and walked back together to the house. The aroma of home cooking greeted them as they opened the backdoor.
“All done?” Suzy enquired, taking her steak and Ale pie out from the oven, setting it aside to cool.
Kate looked at the worktop heaving with her mother’s baking. “Are you expecting to feed an army?” she teased, although knowing full well Jefferson could demolish most of it on his own.
Jefferson politely excused himself and went upstairs to shower. He’d done the bulk of the work, lifting stuff down, moving bedroom furniture and loading the van, leaving Kate to vacuum and tidy.

"Mum, come and sit down for a minute," Kate insisted, putting the two cups of tea she'd made on the table. It was the first moment they'd been alone to chat. Kate sat listening, catching up with recent comings and goings of family news. It felt good to regain her close bond with her mother, and a relief not having to keep 'the secret' and stay away. Admittedly not at the house she used to call home.

"We might drive into Kirston later, I want to show Jefferson around, would you like to come with us?" Kate offered.

It was nice to be included, but after spending all morning cooking, Suzy was ready to put her feet up and so declined.

Kate heard Jefferson moving about upstairs. "Sounds like he's out of the shower," and left to go upstairs to have one herself.

Suzy was washing up when Jefferson joined her in the kitchen.

"May I make a coffee Mam?"

She turned to face him, dripping bubbly water from her wet hands. "Jefferson, please feel free to help yourself."

"Thank you, Mam," he said, casting his eyes towards the food.

Suzy dried her hands and put out plates, napkins, cutlery and pickles alongside, "and have as much as you like," she smiled. She'd taken to him the first time they'd met, valuing his manners, and bemused by his accent.

Kate stood watching Jefferson taking pictures of one of Kirston's old timber framed buildings. Her phone

started to ring. Not recognising the number on the screen answered with a puzzled sounding "hello?"
"Kate?"
"Dad?"
"I'd like to see you while you're home, how about tomorrow?" Richard asked.
"Yes, Dad what time?"
"About one? I'd rather not to come to the house, might be awkward for your mother," he said.
"Mum won't be there, I'll be on my own," Kate replied, her heart fluttering from the surprise.
"OK love, see you tomorrow," he answered ending the call.
"Kady, you OK?" Jefferson asked seeing her expression change.
"That was my dad, I'm going to meet him tomorrow at the house."
"Want me to stay?" Jefferson wrapped a strong arm around her shoulder.
"No, just drop me off tomorrow, I'll be fine."

-

After breakfast Kate asked her mother if she wanted anything brought back from the house, as she was going back once more. "I've arranged to meet Dad there," she admitted.
"I'll write a few things down if you're sure you don't mind," Suzy said, trying to sound matter-of-fact and not unduly concerned. On one hand, she was pleased Richard was making the effort, but on the other, she worried what he might say.

"What time back here, Kady?" Jefferson asked before she got out of the van. Kate hadn't thought that far ahead, she'd come early to find the items on her mother's

list. She sat for a minute trying to decide. "What will you do back to Squirrels Chase?"
"Go for a run."
Jefferson's answer jerked her from her own thoughts. He was probably going stir-crazy without his daily run, yet these past few days had said nothing. "I love you Jefferson Slezak," she said, looking into his big blue-grey kind eyes, and moved across to kiss him. "If you turn up after two, that'll give me an hour with my father. If he's still around when you arrive, I'll introduce you."

Kate watched Jefferson reverse out into the road, hold up his hand to wave and drive off.
She picked up the mail from the floor inside and carried it through to the kitchen, leaving the letters on the worktop and unpacked the milk and savoury snacks she'd bought with her.
She thought about her father fondly, having always been his 'little girl'. Although this meeting could feel awkward, she'd have little choice but to accept his new life, besides she didn't want a confrontation. Putting her thoughts aside, she read through the list and headed upstairs.
Instead of looking for the clothes listed, she packed them all, deciding her mother could sort through them later.

She heard a car pull up outside, if it was her father he was early. From the bedroom window she recognised his car, watched him get out, and rushed downstairs to greet him.
"It's good to see you love," Richard said giving her a hug.
"And you too, Dad," she reciprocated.
They sat in the kitchen chatting, drinking cups of tea, catching up with her life at Uni.

"Is this your new look?" she teased pointing to the golf logo'd cashmere sweater stretched across his now wider frame.
"You must come and see the shop. We're not rushed off our feet, but it's ticking over," he said smiling with pride.
Kate refilled their cups and offered the cheese straws she'd bought with her, revealing her mother had made them earlier.
"Have they sold your Nan's house yet?" Richard asked, wanting to know.
His question surprised her. "No, I think Uncle Matt plans to use it for a while," Kate answered, sensing his mood changing. She got up to fetch the letters, slipping her mother's mail into her bag before handing over the rest to her father.
"I saw your mother last week, hardly recognised her, what with her fancy new hair-cut and becoming skinny, . . . suits her though," he added after catching Kate's stare.
Kate felt the atmosphere change, drifting into uneasy silence. "Mum hasn't been on a diet, she's not been well. She didn't know about your affair. When you told her and suddenly left, it was a massive shock," Kate explained.
"Well I didn't know," he said with indifference.
"Dad you destroyed her world. Mum's not living here, she fled back to Nan's house."
"What about her job?" he said beginning to realise what she was insinuating.
"She never went back, she abandoned everything here in Ashton. If Uncle Matt hadn't have gone looking for her . . ."
"How was I supposed to know?" Richard argued.
"Didn't you think of coming back just to see if she was OK?" Kate's eyes began to fill, shocked by his attitude.

"Kate, I didn't know," he stated louder.
"You mean you didn't care!" Kate left the table and stood facing the window, turning her back on him, tears sliding down her cheeks, shoulders shuddering.
Richard's phone pipped. He stood up, switching it off when it started to ring. Making no attempt to comfort Kate or speak, he walked out slamming the front door shut behind him.
Kate sobbed, this was not how she'd imagined their time together.

Richard's phone continued to ring adding to his frustration. He pulled over to answer it.
"Dick, is she coming?" Gwen asked. She'd felt anxious about meeting Kate since Richard had mentioned he might bring her back to show her around the shop.
"No, she can't today, I'm driving back," abruptly ending the call. He was annoyed with himself for walking out on Kate knowing she was upset. He may of chosen to end his marriage, but he never wanted to lose Kate. Her words began to trickle back, the full consequences of his actions finally registering.
He'd planned to end their marriage by causing Suzy the least disruption and pain. She'd always been the organised level-headed one, able to cope with anything. He knew she'd be angry at first, but she'd get over it. If he left, she could stay in their house, keep her job and friends. It seemed best for her and the easiest way to part. When she'd got the money from her mother's house, then she could buy him out. He'd had it all logically worked out, . . . or so he thought.
Kate was right, he should of gone back to check on her. Shamefully it never occurred to him. He wasn't proud of his deceit, burying his guilt deep within.

When Suzy asked to see him, his conscience had uncomfortably prickled. Seeing her again, undeniably attractive, smiling gently, talking as though their parting had hardly bothered her at all angered him.
Knowing the truth now added punishment, but what was done was done. Richard started his car and drove back to Gwen at the shop.

When Suzy opened the door to Jefferson, he politely acknowledged her and ran upstairs. He reappeared minutes later wearing knee length shorts and a t-shirt. "Where's the best place around here to run Mam?" he asked, squatting down to tie his laces.
"Well Jefferson, that's a question I've not been asked before," she said, trying to think. Gravel Hill came to mind, but there were too many complicated directions to explain to a stranger. "Give me five minutes to get Bob ready and I'll take you."
Not wanting to put her out, Jefferson tried to object, but minutes later found himself squashed into her car on route.
Suzy hadn't thought of her car as being small, until she had Jefferson in the front passenger seat. His head bent over touching the roof and his long legs were folded. "Oh dear," she apologised "you don't look very comfortable."
She parked at the view point on the highest point of the hill. From the edge of the car park she indicated various paths and tracks. "Off you go, I'll walk Bob and then wait for you in the car."
"Thanks Mam, I'll see you in an hour."
An hour? Suzy thought bemused, who runs for a whole hour? By the time she'd locked her car and attached Bob's lead, she could just see Jefferson disappearing into

the distance. She couldn't help smiling as the sight of him struggling to emerge from her car came back to her, a memory that would amuse her for some time.

She'd been sitting in the car listening to the radio for about twenty minutes with Bob snoozing on the back seat, when Jefferson came running back into view. He walked across the car park towards them and got in.

"Good?" Suzy asked.

"Awesome, just awesome," Jefferson enthused, not even slightly out of breath.

Suzy handed him a bottled water, and headed back to Squirrels Chase.

"Mam, would you have any objection to me taking Kady back home for Thanksgiving? My folks would sure like to meet her."

"If Kate would like to go, it's fine by me," Suzy answered turning into the drive.

"Thank you Mam," he said, once more hauling himself awkwardly out of her car. He refused further refreshments, wanting to shower quickly and get back for Kate.

They returned late in the afternoon. Jefferson carried in the two heavy suitcases Kate had packed earlier, delivering them just inside Suzy's bedroom. Kate had been quiet and gone up to their room, with Jefferson keeping her company.

Suzy assumed the meeting with her father had not gone well.

Bob began to follow Suzy around the kitchen, almost tripping her up. It was his way of telling her he was hungry, without his reminder she hadn't realised the time. She put down his bowl of food and made herself some sandwiches, intending to eat them in the lounge watching TV. The lovebirds could come down and fend for themselves if they were hungry.

Later in the evening Kate popped her head around the lounge door to ask her mother if she wanted a drink, Jefferson was in the kitchen making coffee. Kate returned with two mugs of tea, leaving Jefferson busy making sandwiches. She sat down, her quietness still evident.
"Thank you for showing Jefferson Gravel Hill, he had a great time."
"I took him," Suzy confessed trying to keep a straight face as the vision of him extricating himself out of her car came to mind.
"In your car?" Kate queried. "Wasn't he a bit squashed?"
"It was . . . a . . . bit . . . tight." Suzy lost control and started to giggle. The more she tried to apologise, the worse she got. Her giggles were infectious and Kate started to laugh at her mum. Soon they couldn't look at each other without setting each other off again. Suzy wiped away her tears of laughter, holding her stomach saying it hurt.
Jefferson came into the lounge carrying a huge plateful of sandwiches with Bob following at his heels. "You OK?" he asked, seeing them wiping their eyes. Kate nodded, she still couldn't speak.
Suzy announced she was going to have an early night, she'd caused enough mischief for one day, and bid them Goodnight

-

The next morning, Kate stood at the backdoor waiting for Bob to come in from the garden. She watched him running around the lawn, tail wagging, nose to the ground

seemingly following a trail. She wrapped the dressing gown she'd borrowed tightly around her, warding off the chill.
The trees were beginning to show their Autumn colours. The long dry summer this year would enable Mother Nature to paint colourful pictures with her leaves. The morning sun was already trying to peek through. "I think it's going to be a beautiful day," Kate announced closing the door after Bob's return.
"Any plans for today?" Suzy asked and suggested seeing the new baby."
"Oh yes," Kate smiled, she'd forgotten about that.
"I could walk the dawg," Jefferson put in quickly "then go for a run."
"We'd only be gone a few hours. Could you find Gravel Hill on your own . . . in the van?" Kate said looking directly at her mother.
"Sure," Jefferson answered, oblivious to their humour.

They'd cooed and cuddled, and heard every detail of baby Neville Alexander's life, thanks to Phil's loving obsession with his son.
"Is he boring you?" Julia chuckled, dispensing more refreshments.
Suzy laughed, telling her to make the most of it. Suggesting he'll probably change his tune when he's had several sleepless nights. Hard to envisage, looking at their little angel sound asleep in his Moses basket. Before they left, Phil handed Suzy three photos, 'just born, mother and baby, and baby with his proud parents'. "I'll send you more as he progresses," Phil promised.
"I insist on it," Suzy said getting ready to leave.
"Oh no, don't encourage him," Julia grinned.

Kate and Suzy said their good byes and headed back. "Wasn't that lovely seeing them so happy?" Kate acknowledged, "even if Uncle Phil was a bit OTT."
"Yes," Suzy agreed, then with a mischievous twinkle in her eye asked "got enough room?"

-

"Gonna have to leave by ten, Kady" Jefferson warned before they went down for breakfast.
"I know," she said, letting out a long sigh.
Suzy knew her morning would be tinged with sadness, as she laid the table for their last breakfast together before they drove back to Leeds. She'd enjoyed every minute of their visit, and getting to know Jefferson - Kate's 'built like a giant, strong as an ox with a heart of gold' boyfriend. Jefferson had the forethought to load the van previously, enabling their last few hours unrushed.

At Suzy's insistence, Kate put together a basket of food to eat on their journey home. Reaching for bananas to add to the basket, she noticed a pile of unopened letters next to the fruit bowl. It reminded her of the mail still in her bag. "Mum, I'm putting these here," she said, adding them to the pile. "Why haven't you opened these?"
"I've been occupied, anyway I didn't think any of them looked important," Suzy said, hunching her shoulders. She picked them up and began flicking through, "these are from insurance companies – my car's due next month, these are adverts, this one's from the Tax Office – probably a new code as I've left work. I'll go through them tomorrow, or this afternoon if I'm bored," she said unconcerned.

With the van loaded and their 'fare wells' said, Kate and Jefferson got into the van to begin their long trip back.
"I'll text you when we arrive," Kate called from the van as they began to move off.
"Make sure you do, 'safe Journeys'," Suzy called out, waving and watching them leave the drive.

Back inside, the house felt terribly empty. "Well, it's just us again," Suzy said, addressing the dog. Bob sat in his bed watching her face intently as she spoke, turning his head back and forth like a corkscrew listening to her every word.
"What shall we do? . . put the kettle on? . . strip the beds and start the washing, . . . or go for a walk?" Their little game always made her smile. Once he'd heard the word 'walk' Bob began to circle, wagging his tail frantically, and not letting her out of his sight. She was just putting her shoes on when her phone started to ring.
"Mrs Martin? Hello, it's Linda Blake from Kirston College, did you get our letter? We have your security clearance. If you're still interested in the job, would you like to come in Monday morning . . . about ten?"
"I'd love to," Suzy answered.
"Great, we'll see you then."
That's good, a step in the right direction, she thought with lifted spirits. "I suppose now you want to go for a walk." Bob barked with excitement and raced to the door, tail wagging, ready to go.

- -

Tom knocked on Matt's office door and entered, "you wanted to see me?"
Matt gestured to take a seat.

Tom sat down, waiting for him to speak. Wondering if Matt was going to dash his dreams of the promotion, had Harvey Granzman changed his mind?
"I accept your offer," Matt said straight faced.
Tom heard the words, but they didn't register.
"On my flat, I accept your offer," Matt repeated.
"Are you serious?" Tom looked mystified. "But you could get more for it on the open market," he said almost talking himself out of the deal.
"I want the transaction cut-and-dried as soon as possible, not officialism going back and forth for months, can you arrange that?" Matt said forthright.
"I'll get onto it ASAP." Tom stood up ready to leave, the status quo not fully sinking in. Seconds later he realised, and smiled with gratitude. "Thank you Matt, Mathew," he corrected, feeling the situation caused for professionalism and shook Matt's hand. "I'll get back to you," he said, leaving Matt's office.

Matt tossed the sheet of proposals he'd just read onto his desk and leaned back in his chair. It was almost five o'clock and he'd had enough for the day, . . no, being Friday he'd had enough for the week. His thoughts turned to Gina, wondering if she'd be coming home Monday.
Tom knocked on his office door and walked in "sorry, are you still working?"
"Nope," Matt said, stretching his arms "I've finished here."
"I just wanted to say I'd understand if you want to reconsider, or if you get a better offer. I don't want you to have regrets," Tom stated.
Matt understood and appreciated Tom's concern, as they'd soon to be working closer together. "It's OK Tom, I've made my decision."

Tom gave a sigh of relief, gratefully followed by a happy grin.
"Oh wow! Now I can phone my parents," he said trying to contain his excitement. "Would it be a terrible imposition to ask, if I could bring them round to see the flat?"
"Whenever you like," Matt said generously.
"How about tomorrow?" Tom appealed on impulse.
Matt wasn't expecting quite so sudden, yet didn't want to revoke. "OK," he agreed, "but not before midday."
"I'll text you tomorrow," Tom grinned, hurrying out of the office.

Matt began clearing his desk, packing up for the weekend when he heard his phone pip.
'Arriving – Heathrow, Fri, 19.00 hrs, any chance you can meet me?'
He read the text and smiled, of course he'd be there. Immediately texting her back 'on my way.' There wasn't time to dash home to shower, so he rushed to the cloak room to freshen up. Back in his office he changed his shirt, making the spare one he kept there suffice. He locked his office and fled the building.

While crawling along in endless lanes of rush-hour traffic, several thoughts crossed his mind, 'why hadn't he told Gina to take a taxi' being one of them. He should of realised half of England's population would be heading to Heathrow, or so it seemed. Finally dead on seven o'clock he joined the long queue to enter the airport carpark. Thirty minutes later he inched into a space, . . what a nightmare! He texted again, letting her know he'd arrived.

When he spotted her, she was sat on a bench looking fed up, nursing a paper cup and facing in the wrong direction. With all the loud noises and bustle of the airport it was pointless trying to shout, and ended up almost in front of her by the time he could be heard. "Hello gorgeous."

Her eyes widened with happy surprise. She sprang up into his arms, hugging him tight. "I've missed you so much," she said kissing him.

Holding her in his arms brought back an immense feeling of the love he'd missed. He took charge of her suitcase, wheeling it passed the outlets and cafés on route to the exit. Wafts of hot food triggered pangs of hunger, "shall we stop to eat?" he asked hopefully.

"I just want to get home," she sighed.

In the car Gina began to relax "I could sleep for a week," she said wearily.

"That's a shame," he said with a cheeky grin.

"Well, maybe not all week," she said, squeezing his leg.

She began to tell him about her flight, but the car's warmth and movement soon had her sleeping.

Arriving back at Gina's house Matt parked behind her car. She roused when he opened the door, filling the car with chilly evening air.

Elaine stood at the front door smiling, ready to greet them, pleased to see her daughter safely home. "Thank you Mathew for picking her up, come in for a moment, the kettle's on," Elaine persuaded.

Matt carried in Gina's suitcase and bags, then followed on into the kitchen to sit down.

Elaine continued making them tea, "have you eaten?"

"I ate before I got on the plane," Gina replied joining Matt at the table.

Elaine looked across to Matt.

"I drove straight from work, I'll pick up something later." Already anticipating his answer, Elaine handed him a round of ham sandwiches she'd made seconds earlier. "They'll keep you going for a while," she said, returning to pour out their tea.
"Sorry Matt, I just wanted to get home," Gina said softly. Elaine sat with them at the table "so how was it?
"Long, far too long, I'll be glad when I can pack it in," Gina answered, and reached for Matt's hand.
"I hear you've sold this place," Matt said, congratulating Elaine "and, I have a buyer for my flat."
"No way!" Gina was amazed. "Ashwood Farm, here we come," she beamed. "Just your Mother's place to sell now, and that won't take long."
"I'm going to hang on to it for a while," he expressed.
"Why? when you need the money!" Gina said, more sharply than she intended.
"I can use it as a base, and my sister . . "
Before Matt could finish his sentence, Gina interrupted "your sister would be better off with the money. For God's sake Matt, you need that money!" she snapped infuriated.
Matt glared at her, tiredness feeding his angst. He stood up ready to leave, thanked Elaine for the sandwiches and walked out.
Elaine remained seated, waiting for Gina to go after him, not wanting to be drawn into the situation. Gina sat stubbornly at the table, fuming with Matt and annoyed with herself.
Elaine left the kitchen, and dashed to the front door hoping to catch him. He was just about to get into his car when she called him.

Not interested in hearing of her daughter's excuses, he ignored her.
"Mathew! "Mathew," she called out, rushing up to the car. Cornered, he stopped and politely waited for her to catch her breath.
"I want to speak to you about Ashwood Farm."
Matt leant against his car, forced to listen.
"I sold a large guest house in Brighton two years ago. A thriving business, employing six staff, and needless to say I got a good price for it. The money is sitting in the bank doing nothing."
Before he could refuse her charity, she raised her hand signalling him not to interrupt. "Gina and I planned to sell our properties and buy a small holding together."
"And I came on the scene," he said getting the picture.
"Yes, and I couldn't be more happy for you both," Elaine said warmly. "Gina is my only child. Mathew if Ashwood Farm is to be my home too, don't you think I'd like to contribute?" Again she raised her hand "how can I design my place knowing you two can't afford it? How do you think that makes me feel?"
He appreciated she had a point.
"Let me pay for the conversion work on the old dairy, or to cut your costs I'll buy myself a place in the village."
Matt realised he'd not given her any proper consideration, or thought about her wanting to help financially.
"If you were in my shoes?" she added finally, waiting for an answer.
"That's very kind Elaine," he said humbled by her offer "and your help would make a significant difference. We'll discuss it one evening, all three of us."
Elaine stepped aside, allowing him to open the car door.
"Goodnight Mathew," noticing the cold air, she shivered.

"I've got people viewing my flat tomorrow, I'll phone Gina in the evening," he said getting into his car. "Goodnight Elaine." He reversed out into the road and headed home.

-

Matt woke up and peered at the time displayed on his phone screen, hoping he'd time to sleep on. Going to bed overtired and with his thoughts whirring meant he hadn't sleep well. He lay there, turning things over in his mind. Gina was right about needing the money from Squirrels Chase, but there was a strong feeling he couldn't explain that forbade him its sale.
Suzy's slimmer frame displayed her brake-up with Richard had taken its toll. Soon she'd have the selling of her own place to deal with, not to mention her impending divorce. Aside from needing a base for his remaining time at Vortorx, it wasn't practical to drive back and forth from Somerset, . . and the conversation with Elaine had raised valid points.
He looked again at the time and groaned, he couldn't turn over for more sleep, he had a flat to clean. Suzy's words came back to him, getting the place shipshape for one viewing was bad enough. Reluctantly he got up, promising himself a lay-in tomorrow.

Tom arrived with his parents at two o'clock as arranged. Matt gave them a swift guided tour around the apartment, then retreated to the kitchen, giving them time to inspect the place on their own. Tom's father joined him, having seen enough first time round and been significantly impressed. Matt apologised for not having all the particulars of the property to hand, his sudden decision and this impromptu visit had caught him unprepared. He'd compile a package of the documents and any necessary information for Tom shortly.

Mr Hobbs senior stood straight-backed looking out of the window. Almost to attention, his stance had Matt wondering if he'd had a military background somewhere along the line.

They could hear Tom and his mother wandering around discussing window sizes and fixtures.

"I'd like to thank you for the support you've given Thomas in his career Mr Chapman, and for this generous opportunity," Mr Hobbs acknowledged. "I bid to reciprocate."

"That won't be necessary," Matt said appreciating his gratitude.

"Prerequisite," Mr Hobbs insisted.

Matt was about to change the subject, when Tom and his mother entered the kitchen. Matt offered them seating, then passed round refreshments and volunteered to answer questions.

"Do you intend to leave any furniture?" Tom's mother asked.

Matt hadn't yet decided, but he'd leave the bespoke items built for the flat. Not his office suite and agreed to make a list to discuss later.

"Thank you for your time and hospitality today," Mr Hobbs senior announced in his direct polite manner. Ready to shake Matt's hand, preparing to leave and usher his family out. "I will personally see this conveyance for Thomas is completed, post- haste."

Matt escorted them to the door. Tom's mother took Matt's hand, smiled kindly and added her gratitude. Tom was last in line "thanks Matt, I really appreciate this today," he said leaving.

Matt sank down into his comfortable leather chair, grateful to have the rest of the weekend free. Suzy was right, as always. Letting Tom buy his flat would cut out no end of bother and agitation.

The doorbell rang twice. Matt rose slowly and walked to the door, wondering if one of Tom's party had left something behind.

Gina stood outside the door. Normally she'd use her key, but after her mini-tantrum the night before didn't feel comfortable just walking in. He opened the door, bemused and saying nothing.

She gave him a weak smile, picked up a shopping bag in each hand and waited to be invited in. "I've brought dinner," she said looking penitent.

He closed the door after her entry, smiled and opened his arms.

Grateful for being forgiven, she returned his kisses, letting the bags slip to the floor.

"Hey, careful!" he teased "that's my dinner." After their long passionate embrace he looked into her eyes "I'm so glad you're home."

-

"I suppose we ought to get up," she said switching off the TV in Matt's bedroom "have you seen the time?"

"It's Sunday," he protested. "I'm flying up to Scotland next week," he warned, sitting up, throwing back the duvet.

"And?"

"If we're going to discuss our finances for Ashwood Farm, we ought to do it sooner rather than later. Harvey Granzman will soon start cracking the whip. He'll have Tom and I attending every Vortorx deal he can arrange," Matt cautioned.

“Is he going to become difficult?” she asked concerned. “He’s making sure Tom’s capable to take over. If results aren’t up to his expectations, he knows I’ll be aware.” “No pressure then,” she sympathised. “Tuesday? . . . Tuesday evening at my place?” Gina suggested “that will give us tomorrow to prepare figures in readiness.” “Tuesday it is then,” Matt replied walking towards the bathroom.

- -

Bob laid in his bed watching Suzy, sensing she was going out. “I won’t be long,” she said stroking his head and putting two dog biscuits down in front of him. “I’ll take you out when I get back.” Trying to ignore the butterflies in her stomach, she drove to Kirston College. Today she needed a boost of courage, considering everything about the job was out of her comfort zone. She parked and headed to the school’s main office to report her arrival. Signed in and wearing a ‘visitors’ badge, she walked across to the science block. Creeping apprehensively along the corridor, listening out for Linda Blake’s voice in the classrooms.

“Hi, are you looking for me?” a woman said peering out from behind a door. “I’m Rosie, . . Rosie Morgan, you must be Mrs Martin,” she said coming out to say hello. The minute Suzy saw her, it became obvious why Rosie wanted a year off. Her white coat only buttoning down to her pregnancy bump. Suzy followed, insisting to be called by her Christian name. Rosie lead her into a large brightly lit store room where she’d been working sitting on a high stool at a workbench. Suzy perched on the adjacent stool taking in the surroundings. “Have you worked in a school before, or done this sort of work?”

"No to both," Suzy answered, beginning to feel inadequate. "It's a good school, the 'Head' Mrs Taylor is hot on behaviour, especially manners. She doesn't take any humbug! Our students, 'not kids' are great. We've got them all here," Rosie laughed "the cheeky ones, the prima donnas and the 'do I have to?' You'll soon get to know them. We'll see Linda –Miss Blake at break time, in about half an hour. I can show you our classrooms – lab one and two, where everything's kept, and go through lab folders and ledgers, timetables and the computer screens. Basically, we lay out the equipment for each lesson and afterwards clear it away, cleaning and storing. Note breakages and monitor stock levels. Simple once you're familiar with it, and not every lesson involves chemistry," she smiled.

"So what do you think," Rosie asked two hours later, "would you like to take it on?"
"There's a lot to remember," Suzy admitted nervously.
"It'll take a little while but if you get stuck, all the information's in these folders. Linda's always willing to help, she's lovely," Rosie said allaying Suzy's fears. "I'll be here for a few more weeks, so come in as often as you like. Same time tomorrow?"
"Yes," Suzy agreed, happy to return "I'll see you tomorrow."

Back home eating her lunch, Suzy thought about her morning. The whole job scenario hadn't been as difficult as she'd first imagined. Utilising her positive mode, she phoned the Ashton branch of Baldwins Estate Agents. An uncomfortable task but a necessity never-the-less, and arranged to meet agent Mr Peter Shaw at the house on Thursday at two o'clock.

Happy with her day's achievements she turned her regard to Bob, who'd begun to follow her from room to room wondering if she'd forgotten something. "Come on then," she said, putting on her coat "let's find your lead."

~ 8 ~

“Hello Mathew,” Elaine said, welcoming him inside “Gina’s upstairs, she won’t be long.”
He’d arrived earlier than expected, according to the sound of the hairdryer being used upstairs.
“She’s put her things on the table in here.” Elaine lead him through to the lounge where a dining table stood in the corner.
Matt’s nose began to twitch, he could smell something, ... something wonderful, . . . something cooking.
“My cake,” Elaine smiled, reading his expression. She returned to the kitchen, leaving him sat at the table switching on his laptop.

“Here you are,” she said some minutes later, depositing a generous slice of chocolate cake in front of him. “Sorry it’s a bit on the big side, it’s still a bit warm and difficult to cut smaller.”
Matt accepted the plate with pleasure, he wasn’t sorry at all.

Gina came in carrying her laptop, with her hands full she bent over to kiss him on the cheek. “I can see you’ve already spoken to my mother,” amused by the cake crumbs stuck around his lips.
“That was the best chocolate cake I’ve tasted in ages,” he praised, wiping chocolatey fingers and his mouth with a paper napkin.
“I’ll pass your compliments on to the chef,” and asked if he’d like a hot drink to wash it down.

She returned from the kitchen with two mugs of tea. "We'll make a start when I've drank this," she said sitting beside him.
"We should invite your mother to join us, she ought to hear our plans if she's thinking of moving with us," Matt advised.
"Mum, come and sit with us," Gina called out.
While Matt wrote the farm's asking-price at the top of the pad, Gina checked the sum she could contribute.
"We need to assess we've sufficient money to purchase, complete the work on the buildings and have enough funds for our immediate future," Matt stated.

Elaine joined them at the table and sat quietly, watching them writing down and analysing figures. "If you buy Ashwood farm, I propose paying the full cost to convert the dairy," she announced.
Matt and Gina exchanged glances.
Surmising their thoughts, Elaine continued "I have no wish to own the property, or to have any written agreements tied into my offer."
Both sat open mouthed, astonished.
"That's incredibly generous Elaine," Matt said humbly, but I could never accept such a benevolence."
"Well I could," Gina said wilfully, addressing her mother. "Pay me and I'll settle the conversion invoices. Thank you Mum," she smiled, reaching across to squeeze her hand.
"Only if you're really certain," Matt agreed in submission "thank you Elaine."
"I'll leave you both to your sums, whatever you decide to do," she said standing up ready to leave the table. "I'm going to order tonight's dinner, Chinese, Cantonese or Indian?"
"Your choice," Gina replied.

"It's Indian then," Elaine resolved leaving the room.

They returned to their figures. Despite Elaine's generous offer Matt wasn't totally comfortable with the financial evidence in front of him. "Don't forget I only have one year's salary guaranteed," he reminded. "After that, technically we'll be in financial freefall with no income."

"I'd happily live in one of those tatty holiday cottages and eat grass just to stay there," Gina admitted playfully, declaring her commitment.

"I know," he said putting his arm across, caressing her shoulders, but we have to be realistic."

"We don't have to convert the cottages, and we might generate some sort of income from the farm," she said with a hint of persuasion.

"Let me digest these figures," he reasoned, concentrating on the sheet in front of him.

Gina sat patiently, praying he wouldn't find any prohibitive reasons.

"Right," he exhaled, looking up, seriously straight faced, . . . then with a wink of an eye "let's buy Ashwood Farm!"

She flung her arms around his neck, elated.

"I can't stay late tonight," he warned. "I've got masses to get through before Friday's meeting. Tom and I are flying to Stirling first thing Thursday."

Nothing could reduce her happiness, hearing Matt's decision was the beginning of her dreams coming true.

"I'll make some coffee before you have to go," she said still euphoric, heading to the kitchen.

Elaine joined him sitting in the lounge and perched briefly on the arm of the settee. She'd sensed earlier he wasn't totally at ease with the figures. "You could always negotiate the sale-price Mathew," she suggested with a knowing smile. She rose to her feet, excusing herself to load the dishwasher, tactfully enabling them to enjoy the rest of their evening alone. "Goodnight Mathew, I hope you have a successful trip in Scotland."

"Goodnight Elaine, and thank you," he replied as she left the room.

Gina put their mugs down onto the coffee table. "I'm so happy," she beamed, snuggling up and kissing him passionately.

"There's nothing's signed and sealed yet," he apprised.

"I don't care, we'll make it work, . . all three of us," she assured.

- -

Wednesday's afternoon lessons were coming to an end. From her stool in the large laboratory storeroom, Suzy could hear the children leaving their classrooms to go home. Her afternoon had been successful, gradually methods and procedures were falling into place. Rosie's kind and cheerful disposition made her instructions easy to follow and absorb.

"I won't be a minute," Rosie said vacating, intending to speak to Linda about Suzy's progress.

Suzy continued to tidy the area.

"I hear you've cracked it," Linda Blake said smiling, standing in the doorway.

"Well, I'm beginning to get the gist of it," Suzy replied, still a little unsure.

Rosie fired several questions, which Suzy answered correctly.

"Disposal?" Linda asked.

"Ah, I haven't covered that," Rosie laughed, "remind me on Monday Suzy."

"You've done really well," Linda praised "I look forward to working with you Suzy, . . . if you take the job.
"Want a cuppa?" Rosie offered, plugging in the kettle "I'm going to unload the sterilizer before I leave."
"Go on then," Linda accepted. "I've got a DVD to check before I go home, the last one kept stopping. I don't want a repeat of that first lesson tomorrow."
"Suzy?"
"No thanks, I'd better get back to Bob. I expect he'll need to go out," she said picking up her bag ready to go.
"Are you still looking after Mrs Kelly's dog?" Linda asked, puzzled "I thought she was home."
"George hasn't said anything," Suzy answered, slightly concerned.
"Then I'm mistaken," Linda accepted.
Before saying goodbye and leaving them to their tea, Suzy agreed to return on Monday. Walking back to her car she thought about George, if Mrs Kelly was home, why hadn't he been round to tell her? He could have phoned if he was busy.

-

Suzy wasn't surprised to see George standing at her backdoor early in the morning. "I got your phone message," he said as she opened the door.
"Is Mrs Kelly home?" Suzy asked sharply.
George looked downcast.
"Why didn't you tell me?" she said, suspecting the truth.
"You'd got s'fond of the blessed thing," he excused.
"I am, very fond, but I can't steal him George!" she admonished.
"I've not had a chance to speak to her yet, I'll go and see her today," he vouched. "I'll come back after work," he turned, walking away.

“I’ll have his things ready,” Suzy called, regretting her gruffness.

After Bob’s walk, she settled him down with a couple of biscuits in his bed, leaving the radio on for company. She’d got used the ritual, telling him to ‘be good,’ before she left the house. Driving to Ashton, she tried not to think of Squirrels Chase without him.

A red car was already parked outside her house when she arrived. The occupant appeared to be eating a sandwich, oblivious of making her steer awkwardly around his car to get into the drive. If this was her estate agent, he was definitely starting off on the wrong foot! The minute she got out of her car, he appeared at her side brushing crumbs from his suit and apologising profusely.
“I do apologise,” he repeated, thrusting out his hand to be shaken. “Peter Shaw at your service, . . Mrs Martin?”
“Aren’t you early?” Suzy questioned, slightly rattled.
“I had a cancelation,” he explained, following her inside to the kitchen.
Suzy took off her coat and draped it over a chair. “Would you like a drink Mr Shaw?” she offered, filling the kettle.
“That’s very kind,” he said, fumbling in his pockets for a pen. He sat down and began removing forms and booklets from a bulging folder he’d put on the table. “I’ll just take down a few details if I may,” still hunting for a pen.
Suzy handed him a mug of tea and a pen from her kitchen drawer. By the end of the interview she’d adjusted her opinion of him. From initial irritation to tolerable, having asked his questions with patience and tact.
“I’ll just take some measurements.” He got up, fumbling once more in his pockets for something, retrieving a small black handheld gadget.

She watched him directing a small red light beam from wall to wall, and note down numbers.

Leaving him to get on with the measuring, she wandered into the lounge to wait. Running her hands along the back of the settee, recalling the months she'd saved to buy it and being overjoyed when she'd found the perfect curtains to co-ordinate, . . all seemingly pointless now. She'd been happy in this house, they'd all been happy there once, . . but that time had passed.
"If you could call into the office to finalise your instructions Mrs Martin," he startled, ending her reminiscing. "I'll come back to video the interior when you're ready. It'll be snapped up once we get it on our website. A pleasure to meet you Mrs Martin," offering to shake her hand again.

Suzy escorted him to the door and watched him drive away. Now she needed to inform Richard about Mr Shaw's visit, but recalling their last meeting at the pub decided a text was preferable. She began to compose, sending Richard the estate agency details and inviting him to remove anything he wished to keep from the house. She read through her words, checking the tone was friendly, not wanting to cause any friction. It was done, she'd started the ball rolling.

Checking the time, realised she should get back in case George arrived early. Driving home, a storm began to brew. The sky grew darker as rainclouds gathered.
She arrived home just in time. A flash of lightening floodlit the kitchen, followed by a crash of thunder. Bob sat quivering in his bed. Suzy sat down beside him trying to comfort the shivering dog, her words lost in the roar of hailstones that followed.

The storm passed quickly, fluffy white clouds replacing grey. "It was only a clearing up shower," she told him, stroking his soft fur. "I shall miss you." She put his lead on top of the box she'd filled with his things and placed it by the backdoor ready for George to collect.

Trying to think of something to fill the time, she remembered the pile of letters. It was about time they were sorted out. She sat at the kitchen table, discarding the obvious adverts and sale offers, keeping the insurance quote for her car's renewal at the end of the month. She hadn't noticed the next letter arrive, perhaps it had been among the ones Kate added. It looked official. She slit it open and took out the contents, flattening out the folded pages. The headed letter from solicitors Bradshaw, Moss & Partners informed her their client Mr Richard Antony Martin was filing for divorce. Yes, he'd asked for a divorce, but in her heart of hearts this wasn't how she had wanted her marriage to end. She read through the pages, struggling to comprehend and deeply shaken. The letter left her feeling discarded and numb. Three more letters lay on the table waiting for attention, but she'd lost the desire to open them.

The house phone began to ring in the background. Debilitated by the solicitor's letter she ignored it, but it's continuous ringing summoned response. It was probably George, so she got up to answer it.

- -

Waking up Thursday morning, Matt reached across for his phone to check the time, then scrolled through checking messages. Caroline had sent his schedule and a reminder of his changed flight time. Now with an afternoon flight, he had the morning free and plenty of time. He read a text from Tom, instead of sharing the booked taxi to the airport, Tom would meet him there.

Without diverting to pick up Tom, Matt arrived extra early at the airport. Sitting in the lounge with a drink and time on his hands, he phoned Suzy. Wanting to tell her he'd agreed to sell his flat to Tom, it being her clever suggestion. He let the phone continuously ring, then wondered if she was out walking the dog. He was about to hang up when she picked up the phone.

The minute she answered, he knew something was wrong.

"You've just caught me at a bad time," she explained quietly."

"Tell me," he insisted, concerned.

She didn't want to, but gradually her words tumbled out, . . . the contents of the letter, meeting the estate agent and Bob going home. It had all been too much, she wept.

Matt tensed, feeling helpless, knowing he had to get on the plane. "Suze, I have to go. I'll come over the minute I get back," he promised.

She could hear the noise of the busy airport in the background. "I just got a bit overwhelmed, that's all, sorry" she sniffed. "I'll be OK, don't worry, I'll see you when you get back."

Matt bristled with tension, he had to do something. He phoned Phil, relaying the situation.

"No worries, I'll phone Suzy tomorrow. We'll take little Nev over to see her at the weekend," Phil assured.

Matt felt better, it was the best he could do under the circumstances. He looked around for Tom, but couldn't see him anywhere. This next meeting was important, he knew Harvey Granzman would be closely watching their performance. They'd soon be boarding, where was Tom?

Matt sat in his seat on the plane, already stressed by Suzy's phone call and angered by Tom's absence.
"Which side do you prefer to sit?," Tom asked, suddenly at Matt's side.
"You're late, I thought you weren't coming," Matt seethed. Tom could see he was annoyed. "I've been at the airport for over an hour, I texted you. I was with a friend, she works for the American airline," he tried to explain.
Matt began to unwind, all the better for knowing Tom wouldn't let him down.

- -

"I told him we'd go and see her at the weekend," Phil said, explaining Matt's phone call to Julia.
"We most certainly won't," Julia frowned with disapproval. "Poor Suzy, we'll go tomorrow, I'm sure you can wangle the day off."
"Probably," Phil agreed, gently squeezing the baby's cheeks making him smile.
"I'll phone Suzy in the morning," Julia announced, already planning the day. "I wouldn't do that if I were you," she warned, watching Phil bounce his son up and down on his knee.
"Why not, he loves it," he answered, making little Nev giggle. The baby laughed, then covered Phil's hand with regurgitated milk. "Ugh."
"That's why," Julia grinned, handing him a wipe.

-

"It's like moving house every time we go out," Phil grumbled, trying to pack all the baby equipment into the boot. "I think you need a bigger car."
"I need a bus," Julia replied, strapping the baby into his seat. "What are you doing?" she asked, watching Phil

squashing Alice's soft bed at the side of the baby seat. "Thought we'd take Alice, might be nice for Suzy if she's missing the dog." He slipped the seatbelt through Alice's harness, hoping it would be OK.
Julia wasn't so sure, Alice hadn't been quite herself lately. She wondered if the dog was slightly jealous of the baby and felt left out, knowing Alice no longer had all their attention.
"Then it will be a good idea to take her with us today," Phil insisted.

When Suzy heard their car arrive, she sprang up to open the door. Julia held flowers, chocolates and a box of cakes, while Phil carried the heavy car seat occupied by baby Nev who was fast asleep. Suzy welcomed them inside, directing them to the lounge where it was warmer.
"These are for you," Julia said, handing the goodies to Suzy. "A little bird mentioned you might need cheering up."
"A little bird with a big beak!" Suzy remarked, thinking of Matt.
Bob started to bark in the kitchen.
"I thought he went back yesterday," Phil said surprised.
"He was supposed to, but Mrs Kelly had an appointment at the hospital today, so George is collecting him later when he finishes after work."
"We've got Alice in the car, do you think they'll be ok together, she doesn't really meet other dogs," Julia voiced concern.
"Bob isn't vicious, I'm sure they'll be alright to have a run around in the garden," Suzy answered, "but he can stay shut in the kitchen if you prefer."
Baby Neville started to squirm and wake up.

"Here you are Auntie Suzy, cuddle time," Julia said lifting the baby out of his seat and handing him to her. "I'll go and give Phil a hand to bring in the bags."
"Bags?" Suzy queried.
"Oh yes," Phil raised his eyebrows "changing bag, spare clothes, spare bottles, spare everything, I never knew one small baby needed so much stuff." Phil carried in two big bags in matching blue teddy patterned print.
Suzy smiled, he had a point.

Phil offered to make tea, leaving the girls to natter in the lounge. He fetched Alice from the car and lead her into the kitchen. She bounded up to Bob and wanted to play, barking and springing at him. Bob stayed in his bed, tolerating her playful nips.
"Leave him alone, he doesn't want to play," Phil commanded. Bob looked worried and unsure as Alice continued to taunt. Phil opened the backdoor and pushed her out into the garden.
While he laid the tray for tea, he saw the solicitors letter laying on the table, picked it up and read it through.
Julia came into the kitchen with Nev's bottle. "I'm going to warm this up before your son starts making his presence known," she said looking for a jug.
"Read this," handing Julia the letter.
"No!" she whispered "It's private."
"Read it," Phil insisted.
He carried the tray of tea into the lounge and put it onto the coffee table. "Watch this," he said to Suzy. He gently squeezed the baby's cheeks and was rewarded by a big smile. "Isn't he marvellous?" Phil beamed with pride.
"I can't believe how much he's grown since I last saw him," she said, enjoying the cuddles. Little Nev started to fidget and fret.

"Shall I go and see where your mummy's got with your bottle?" Phil smiled, talking to him.

"Here we are," Julia said handing Suzy the warmed bottle of milk.

"He doesn't hang about does he?" she mused, watching her nephew drinking his milk without stopping to catch his breath.

"Yes, he's quite a piggy," Julia admitted, looking up from pouring out their tea.

Phil opened the back door to let Alice come in. She bounded in heading straight for Bob. Bob stood up and not wanting to be cornered, flew out of the backdoor and raced down the garden with Alice chasing in hot pursuit. Phil left them to it, taking the box of cakes with him to join the girls.

"Where's Alice?" Julia asked.

"Having a run around the garden," Phil answered, not mentioning she was chasing Bob full pelt, Bob running for his life, just managing to stay ahead.

"And Bob?" Suzy asked.

"He's out there too, they're OK, just having a chase about," Phil said calmly.

"He's not a young dog, I don't want him keeling over with a heart attack," Suzy warned "not on his last day in my custody."

Swiftly Phil offered to refresh the teapot, slipping out to check on the dogs. He couldn't see them from the kitchen window, so opened the backdoor and shouted for Alice. Suddenly Bob raced through a bush towards the house with Alice hot on his heels. Phil grabbed her collar as she chased him inside. "I think you need a rest young lady," Phil professed picking her up, intending to put her back in the car. Bob staggered to the water bowl, drinking

half of it before collapsing into his bed exhausted, rapidly panting like a steam engine. Phil held onto Alice while she drank, then carried her out to their car. He walked back into the kitchen, "sorry about that Bob." Bob was still puffing like a train in his bed. "Anymore tea?" Phil offered carrying in the refreshed pot.
"Are the dogs alright?" Julia asked.
"Yes, they're having a rest," confirming he'd put Alice back in the car," and helped himself to another cake.

All too soon, it was time to think of heading home. With their car loaded, Suzy kissed baby Neville and reluctantly handed him back to his mum. "Thank you so much for coming," she said, feeling much happier than the day before.
"Come and see us, or stay for a few days," Julia offered.
"Maybe, when I've got the hang of this new job at the school."
"Good luck with that, and you know where we are if you change your mind," Julia added with a farewell hug.
"Bye Phil," Suzy said, giving him a 'goodbye' hug. She waved until their car left the drive. Back indoors she checked on Bob who was fast asleep in his bed.

"Are our babies OK?" Phil asked.
Julia looked behind to the backseat and smiled "they're both sound asleep."
"Did you read that letter?"
Julia confessed she had. "I thought it was cruel. Did they need to inform Suzy he'd refused marriage mediation on the grounds of his new stable relationship, surely not." Julia sighed. "She's already been very hurt."

"Matt and I will make sure she's OK," he said with brotherly affection.
"I know," Julia smiled. "She needs someone to look after her, somebody really out-of-this-world special.

- -

Gina sat at her desk airheaded. It had taken her all morning to do a task which normally only took an hour, her concentration shot to pieces by invading ideas for Ashwood Farm.
Her boss often took Friday afternoons off, unless she had a business trip imminent. Gina watched the clock as the time neared one o'clock, hoping Laura would go.
Almost on cue, Laura popped her head around the door. "I'm off now, Max wants to visit a Motorhome and Caravan Exhibition in Birmingham this weekend. God knows why," she said shaking her head and rolling her eyes. "I can't think of anything worse than spending my weekends cooped up and stuck in traffic, the dogs would hate it."
Suzy chuckled in agreement.
"Any plans for this weekend?"
"No, not really," Gina shrugged.
"OK, see you Monday," Laura acknowledged, closing the door.
"Good luck at the exhibition," Gina called out. She thought about the weekend ahead, with Matt away she could catch up with a few things, getting her hair cut being one of them and phoned the salon. "I don't suppose you could fit me in tomorrow?"
"If you come towards the end of the day, . . or I've got a cancellation at two fifteen this afternoon," her stylist offered.

Surprised by her luck, Gina accepted. It was pointless remaining at her desk with her thoughts continually gravitating to Ashwood Farm. Deciding to finish her scheduled work at home, she grabbed her things and dashed out.

Elaine was chatting to Margery on the phone. They'd become friends, calling each other from time to time, although it wasn't something she'd mentioned to Gina. Elaine guessed Sam had discussed Matt's intentions, and it hadn't take a genius to realize Margery's loyalty to Sam. If his family had once lived and worked on the farm for generations, Elaine knew Margery's conscience wouldn't ignore the opportunity to reinstate him.

"Oh yes, they're more than interested, have set their hearts on it. Even if they have to compromise their finances and not renovate the cottages," Elaine stated, knowing exactly what she was implying. Besides, it wouldn't hurt to give the financial situation a little nudge in the right direction, merely paving the way should Mathew heed her suggestion.

Gina rushed into the lounge, dropping her laptop and work bag on the table. "Can't stop, I've managed to get and appointment at the hairdressers," she gasped, running upstairs to change.

Elaine said goodbye to Margery and ended her call.

"I'm going now," Gina shouted, slamming the front door behind her.

Elaine pondered, typical 'sods law' Gina suddenly arriving home early, and wondered how much of her phone call she'd overheard.

- -

Sam was working in the barn, cutting wood into lengths. Yesterday he'd noticed a hole in the hedge up in the far field, and heeled in two Hawthorn saplings to grow into the space. They would fill the gap, but not before Ted Lawson moved his sheep into the field next week. Sheep weren't daft, if there was a hole in a fence you could bet money they'd find it. Sam laid out the pieces on the barn floor, forming a panel to temporarily patch the gap. He stepped back to check the size before fixing together.

Margery heard Sam sawing in the barn. She'd been considering a visit to her sister, so was glad of a chance to catch him. "What are you making?" she asked, walking into the barn carrying the mug of tea she'd made for him.

"Fence," Sam answered, clarifying his current attention to the farm's hedges and gates.

She knew he'd look after the place if she went away, and would go with his agreement. She stayed talking to him, listening as he prioritised jobs on his list.

Jeremy Parker drove into the farmyard. Unnecessarily too fast, sending a cloud of dust into the air with his tyres. He liked to make an entrance.

Sam gave a snarl of disdain, Parker hadn't been at the farm lately which suited him.

Mrs Brewer ended their conversation, walked to the doorway and waved to catch Jeremy's attention. She waited for him to join her. "Hello," she welcomed "not seen you here for a while."

"I'm a busy man, got to keep my customers happy," he smirked with a cocksure grin.

Irritated, Sam began hammering, making as much noise as possible to drive Parker outside.
"Jeremy, I've been thinking, perhaps the sale price is a little high?"
"I've come to take a very special lady client out to lunch," he quick-wittedly flattered, slipping his arm around her shoulders escorting her out of the barn. "Haven't I always done my best to look after you?" he asked, pulling a wounded expression.
Sam stopped banging and tried to listen.
"I've spoken to Mr Chapman, told him any problems and we'd discuss them. I know these people Margery, they can afford it, but just to make you happy, I'll talk to him again," Parker said with a gleam in his eye, ever the salesman. "Now where would your ladyship like to dine?" lowering his head pretending to bow, and steering Margery Brewer back towards the farmhouse, cunningly succumbing her back under his spell.
She gave a coy smile, lapping up his attention.

Sam heard her chuckle. He'd never understood what women saw in toady Parker, the only person he cared about was himself! Sam began to drive nails into the wood with force, there was something about loathsome Parker that ignited his temper. Calming down, he finished the panel and loaded it ready to take up to the field. First, stopping for his dinner. He sat on a straw bale in the barn pouring hot stewed tea from a battered flask and unwrapped two doorstep thick sandwiches, mulling over the morning's events. Mrs Brewer hadn't mentioned her sister before, he smiled to himself reviving hope. So she wasn't entirely alone in the world for the likes of Parker to manipulate and take advantage. He wondered what had prompted her to question the sale price, betting it was the reason for Parker's sudden offer to take her out to lunch.

Sam pushed against the new post holding the wooden panel, testing for movement. Satisfied it was sound, he picked up the sledgehammer and threw it into the back of his van. He drove out of the field, stopping to close the gate before heading back to the barn. If he could catch Mrs Brewer on her own, he'd ask if she'd heard from Mr Chapman.

He hadn't thought of moving back to live at the farm, until Mathew Chapman raised the concept. The idea had stirred a sentimental whim to return.

Not long after the Brewer's bought Ashwood Farm, they moved Sam's family out of the old cottage to complete necessary renovation work. The building was in poor state, warranting his father's agreement to temporary relocate. Leaving the farm broke him, especially when he realised he'd been duped by Steven Brewer. Sam remembered his father's bitterness when the refurbished cottage became two holiday lets. Life was different back then, you had to accept people with money made the rules.

In the barn, Sam returned tools to the big wooden chest and grabbed a broom to sweep the floor. Scooping onto a shovel a mix of sawdust and the bent nails he'd dropped. He heard Parker's car drive into the yard bringing Mrs Brewer back home. Sam peered from behind the barn door, seeing her get out of his car and thank him.

"Now don't forget, leave everything to me," Parker announced.

"Bye Jeremy," she called, waving from her front door.

Parker tooted his car horn and sped off, once again causing a dust cloud. When will that idiot learn to drive properly, Sam griped, banging the barn door shut.

Back inside, Margery picked up the letter from her nephew to read through again. 'Dear Aunt Mim', the letter began. She smiled, it had been a long time since she'd been addressed by that name. Only her sister called her Mim.

During their teenage years, both girls rebelled against their old fashioned names. Joan and Margery became Jo and Mimi, although Jo always called her Mim.

'Please go and see Mum' Carl implored, telling her she wasn't coping since his father died. His letter presented an awkward situation. They'd fallen out, Margery hadn't spoken to Jo for years, . . not since Jo revealed Steven's affair.

Both sisters worked in London's Fashion industry when they were young, only Margery stood in front of the cameras.

Steven Brewer, a talented professional photographer worked for top fashion houses. His brilliant edgy photography earned admiration and yielded constant work. When he discovered Mimi, capturing her radiant spirit through his lens, her success as a model was secured. Deeply in love, she'd set her heart on marrying him.

Steven Brewer lacked moral integrity, succumbing to temptation and shenanigans with the beautiful girls shedding their clothes that surrounded him within the industry.

Tiring of her career, Margery settled at Ashwood Farm to make a home. She chose not to listen to Jo's hints of infidelity, besides Steven always came home. Until Jo disclosed a significant betrayal that ended with a pregnancy. Steven never denied, or discussed the situation when Margery confronted him, he left never to return. Margery hadn't spoken to Jo since.

Twice Margery dialled the number Carl had given in his letter, but hung up before it could be answered. What could she say? Actually, she didn't want to say anything. Margery sat with the phone in her hand, the situation gnawing at her, . . slowly she redialled. After a few awkward bitty sentences, their conversation became easier.
"You will come Mim?" Jo pleaded in desperation.
"Yes," Margery agreed "I will."

- -

Matt and Tom checked into their hotel. The Imperial had been booked in advance by Vortorx, the conference room included for the next day's business meeting. Both agreed to meet later in the restaurant for dinner. Matt went up to his room to freshen up and re-examine the Apex Mercury Systems contract, going over the final set of figures again. Harvey Granzman wanted this significant company added to the corporate conglomerate. The deal was important to Vortorx and probably Matt's last at the helm. His high-ranking boardroom respect came from years of successful deals, target achievements, determination and honesty.

Tom remained in the hotel lounge, relaxing with a newspaper on his lap people-watching, eavesdropping and unnoticed in the background. Catching the odd few words from guest's conversations, and the men who apparently were attending tomorrow's meeting. They drank and chatted freely amongst themselves at the bar, . . . providing him with insight.

Matt and Tom dined early, their discussions consumed entirely by the next day's business. Matt didn't envisage any problems, most issues had been thrashed out ahead so should be straightforward. A rumour of another interested foreign buyer had been circulated, a ruse to raise the odds? This strategy was usual from a trustworthy company.
"I'll do some digging," Tom signalled, pointing to his phone.
Matt bade Tom 'goodnight', arranging to reconvene at breakfast. Happy to forgo an evening in the hotel bar mingling with other guests, and temporarily avoiding the Apex Mercury Systems' team.

-

Tom was eating toast, eyes glued to his phone when Matt joined him for breakfast.
"Did you find anything?" Matt asked casually, referring to the rumour.
"No." Tom answered. Although personally knew there was something amiss judging by the AMS team's body language, but he'd no other proof. The snippets he overheard could be unreliable gossip which he wouldn't repeat. Besides, his presence in the boardroom was to observe and learn.

Charles Pelew was already seated when they entered the conference room, echoing the importance of the deal. Harvey Granzman didn't normally send one of their legal team. Matt acknowledged him and sat down. Charles would remain silent throughout, taking back the completed documents to process, . . unless Matt needed his advice.

At the table Matt welcomed the AMS team, introducing Charles Pelew and his colleague Tom Hobbs. Likewise, Chris Aldwick introduced his trio.

"John Knight?" Matt enquired. For the past six weeks they'd been exchanging figures and proposals, putting this business deal together. Matt was under the impression John Knight would be representing AMS to finalise the transaction.

"He's not here," Aldwick answered.

"Is he unwell?" Matt pursued.

"He'll join us later," one of the cohorts threw in, hardly convincingly.

This was a strange manoeuvre, John Knight and Matt had built trust in one another. A vital diplomatic necessity between companies with a significant forthcoming deal.

Matt listened as Chris Aldwick first addressed the meeting, then to each of his men who read out their department's annual results, future plans and proposals from a printed sheet. Matt asked several key questions, watching them scrabble through unfamiliar notes and waffling answers. He wasn't impressed. AMS was a major company, their representatives knowledge should be fluent and accurate, not being read out from a page. Giving himself a moment to assess, Matt picked up a profit summary paper from the table. "Gentlemen, bear with me while I familiarise my colleague with these current figures."

The recess was accommodated by a break for refreshments. Chris Aldwick's impatience was obvious, clearly the AMS team were under pressure to get the contract swiftly signed. This was not the strategy expected from a company holding the strongest position. Which they were, knowing of Harvey Granzman's keen interest.

Matt assumed AMS would play for time, dragging out details vying for a stronger deal. His instinct of concern kicked in. A lesser man would exploit the advantageous opportunity to strike, but with a strong gut feeling of unease Matt's experience told him to hold-fire . . . something wasn't right. Earlier during the meeting he'd glanced across at Tom, noting him studying the team intensely as they spoke, rather than listening to the details.

The AMS team stood huddled, drinking coffee at the end of the table.

Tom accepted the sheet from Matt, but totally ignored it, his phone holding his full attention. Annoyed, Matt nudged him, glaring as they walked back. Still screen watching, Tom's expression changed to serious concern, he shook his head at Matt before they sat down.

All seated back at the table, Chris Aldwick was eager to continue. Matt sat quietly considering his options. The contract had taken months of planning, if he pulled the deal now he'd either cost, or save Vortorx millions. The atmosphere tensed, Matt looked squarely at Chris Aldwick "My apologies gentlemen, we can't do business with you today." Matt rose from the table and left the room. Tom followed, hearing someone behind thump the table hard in frustration.

"Get me two plane tickets, we're going home!" Matt demanded in full power, striding ahead back to his room. The concierge at the desk called out to Matt as he passed "Mr Chapman, Sir, there's a call for you," offering the phone in his outstretched hand.

Matt knew instinctively it was Granzman, "tell him I've gone to the airport," he barked, walking on.

Tom stopped in the hotel foyer, using his phone to arrange their travel.

Fifteen minutes later, he stood with Matt outside waiting for their taxi. He refrained from speaking, only to convey their flight time, aware of heightened tension. Watching Matt today had been a baptism of fire, they were going to be very big boots to fill.

On the plane Tom's phone held his full attention again, scrolling, looking for the screen to prove Matt was right to pull out. "Look," he said showing Matt his phone. The ANEX US stock market screened AMS shares had suddenly severely plummeted, as had two of their main suppliers. "I knew you were right," Tom said, beginning to appreciate the comfort of the first class seats he'd booked. Matt sat in silence with eyes closed, allowing his adrenalin to subside.

"How did you know?" Matt asked, mulling over his own actions.

"Body language."

"Body language!" Matt snapped, opening his eyes.

"I studied psychology."

"So what?" Matt derided.

Tom wasn't about to retaliate, understandably Matt was in a prickly mood. "It takes ten to twelve years to become a registered psychologist, I did five," Tom said quietly.

Matt looked at him through new eyes, recognising his modesty.

Tom anticipated his next question "one day I realised it wasn't what I wanted to do anymore."

Matt could relate to that, having done the same.

Tom continued "I contacted Carrie's uncle. Brad writes a column in the Daily Wall Street Journal, if there's recalcitrant, he hears." There was talk of AMS trying to suppress investigation results. Accountants working for unhappy shareholders discovered large hidden transfers of capital and dividends. Brad had texted 'the Chinese hate deceit, yesterday they dropped AMS like a brick, losing their biggest market'.

Matt realised he needn't have any more worries about Tom's ability to take over, with his profiling and American journalist contact, Tom was perfectly equipped.

"Carrie?" Matt quizzed.

"Been seeing each other for a couple of years, not planning to settle yet, we both want to pursue our careers."

Matt closed his eyes, slowly winding down "wants to be a high flyer then does she?"

"Something like that." Tom smiled to himself, recalling kissing Carrie goodbye at the airport, resplendent in her American Airline uniform.

After a short doze, Matt roused, accepting coffee from an airhostess. Tom gave him a few moments to focus, "Matt, if I secured AMS information ahead, . . couldn't Harvey Granzman?"

The same thought had occurred to Matt seconds earlier. Had Granzman played his hand through Matt, or was he testing him and Tom, reminding them to never ever underestimate Harvey Granzman. Matt switched off all thoughts of Vortorx, the sooner he could leave this corporate circus, the better.

In the taxi they shared, Matt remained quiet, just wanting to get home.

"Have a good weekend," Tom called, raising his hand as Matt took his case from the driver outside the main entrance to his flat.

Inside Matt closed the door, glad to shut the world out. He left his case in the hall, took off his shoes and walked into his lounge to pour himself a large stiff drink. Gulped it down and poured another, carrying it into the bedroom. He took off his Saville Row suit and draped it over a chair, then sprawled out on top of his bed, happy to stay in all weekend without seeing anyone . . . . except Gina, he'd give her a call after he'd rested.

Ooshing himself up to lean against the headboard, he reached for his phone. Turned off prior to the meeting to exclude disturbance, then left off, knowing Granzman would hound him for a report. Consigning Charles, no doubt to supply the full account. Matt turned his phone back on, smiling to himself noting the copious missed calls. Gina had left him a long text, explaining her spur-of-the-moment decision to take her mother away for the weekend to thank her for the generous offer, knowing he would be away anyway. He gave a deep sigh, all hope of being fussed over and loved this weekend evaporated. In a petulant sulk, Matt finished his Bourbon, turned over and went to sleep.

- -

Early Friday evening, Margery stepped out of the taxi at Jo's address. Not having been to this house before, she stood back, eyes wide, taking in the façade of her impressive home. She had no idea Jo and Frank had amassed such wealth. Margery picked up her overnight bag and started to walk up the broad stone steps to the substantial front door.
Jo opened the door, welcoming Margery with a nervous smile. "Mim! Oh Mim, it's good to see you," she said opening her thin arms to embrace.

Margery was shocked by her attenuate frame, no longer the fit vibrant person her sister had been. She followed Jo inside, stopping now and then to marvel at the lavish interior.

It was getting dark by the time Jo had shown Margery her room, and some of the house. They sat together in the lounge, casually eating sandwiches from a tray while Jo coloured in their missed years, no longer strangers. Frank's garage business had been very successful, gaining more premises, and then moving on to prestige cars. Workaholic Frank sold exquisite cars to the rich and famous until his health suddenly declined. Jo had watched him painfully fade during those last years.

Jo picked at her food, hardly eating anything. "What's it all for Mim?" she asked, her eyes deep pools of sadness. "What's the point of it?" she said looking around her lounge implying affluence.

Margery reached for her sister's hand "you'll get through this Jo, we'll sort it."

"Stay with me Mim, . . please," Jo's voice trembled.

Lying in bed, in one of the sumptuous spare bedrooms Margery contemplated her sister's situation. She may be a wealthy woman living in a sumptuous house, but in reality Jo was lonely, desperately unhappy in her gilded cage, and without help probably not far away from sinking into deep depression.

- -

Under close scrutiny from a tortoiseshell and three tabbies, Sam was putting food down for the farm cats in the barn. He heard a car drive into the yard. At that speed it could only be one person. He watched Jeremy Parker walk up to the farmhouse and knock on the door.

"She's gone to er sister's, won't be back f ' weeks," he shouted across to Parker, hoping to keep him away as long as possible.
Parker got back into his car and sped off.
"An don't come back, you vermin," Sam muttered under his breath.

- -

Initially Margery had only intended to stay overnight, and with matters to organise at the farm, she needed to get back. "I have to sort a few things at home," she explained to Jo during breakfast, assuring her she would return in a couple days.

Margery's taxi arrived. Jo hugged her, saying an emotional good bye. Again, Margery promised to return. Stepping into the taxi, she checked her watch. "I've plenty of time driver, you can drop me off outside the railway station if you prefer."
"Mrs Buckley has requested I drive you home."
"To Somerset?"
"Should take about four hours, depending on the traffic. Are you happy with that arrangement Mrs Brewer?"
Margery accepted the offer, gratefully appreciating Jo's generosity.
The driver introduced himself as Ted, letting her know he regularly worked for Mrs Buckley.

The long journey back in the taxi gave her plenty of time to reflect and make plans. Now, with Jo's health to consider she had new priorities. Jeremy had been trying to persuade her to let him take full charge of selling Ashwood Farm. 'To alleviate her from all the worries and stress of the business' he'd cajoled.

Margery Brewer hadn't appointed Jeremy Parker. One day, chancing his luck, he knocked on her door. Apologised for his forwardness and handed her his business card, explaining he'd heard she was thinking of selling the farm.
Impressed by his polite manner, she'd thanked him for the card, closed the door and didn't expected to see him again.
He called back from time to time, checking to see if she'd had anymore thoughts about selling. Always implying he just happened to be in the area and turning on the charm.

When he heard of a couple interested in the farm his visits increased, as did his attention to Margery. Worming his way into her affections, planning to make a financial killing for himself.

Margery was getting fidgety, she'd been sat in the taxi long enough. Soon they would be passing through Yeovil, Ilminster would follow that. She leant forward to speak to Ted through the driver's open panel, requesting to be dropped off in the High Street at Ilminster. If she got out in Green Street, she could visit Jeremy's shop. "I'm calling in to meet a friend," insisting she could make her own way home from there.
Ted was happy to oblige, knocking forty minutes off her original destination meant he could be home earlier.

Throughout the journey, she had been reconsidering her situation. Realising she'd be spending more time with Jo, perhaps it would make sense to let Jeremy take over the sale. She wanted to tell him herself, knowing her decision would please him, also needing to ask if he'd been in touch with Mr Chapman.

She had never been to his Estate Agency before and only spoken to Mavis, Jeremy's secretary by phone. Margery stood outside, peering in the window. The premises wasn't as big as Jeremy had led her to believe, or situated in the busy main part of town. The sign on the door definitely said 'open' although she couldn't see anyone inside. She walked in and stood by the wooden desk, waiting for attention. Hearing muffled sounds coming from the backroom, she cleared her throat loudly to announce her presence and waited for someone to appear. If Jeremy was out seeing clients, she would tell Mavis she'd speak to him later.

Margery had waited ample time, it seemed pointless to stand there any longer. The door to the backroom was ajar, so she pushed it open a bit more, quietly, not wanting to startle the girl.

Although the light in the small room at the back was subdued, she could make out the figure of Jeremy standing with his back to her, oblivious to her presence. Leaning over his secretary, clearly they were busy! Years of Steven's adultery had left Margery with no tolerance of alley tomcat behaviour. She turned round, picked up her bag and left, slamming the shop door behind her.

- -

~ 9 ~

Matt woke up bright and early. The extra hours he'd slept had improved his temperament and wellbeing. He got up to shower and shave.
Relaxed, drinking freshly made coffee, he stood gazing out through the wall of glass windows across his lounge. The early morning light picking up seasonal changing colours of trees in the distance. Staying at home alone had lost its appeal. He hadn't forgotten his promise to call on Suzy and wanted to check again the size of Phil's old bedroom. In case there was a chance some of his own office furniture would fit inside. Today would be a good opportunity to kill those two birds, so-to-speak. He threw a few overnight items into a bag, grabbed a jacket and left for Squirrels Chase, looking forward to surprising Suzy by turning up early on her doorstep.

He turned into the drive, parked, and rushed up to the front door, hammering loudly to wake her up. When she didn't appear, he looked around for her car and realised it was missing. That would teach him not to forewarn, he grouched. He got back into his car to phone her. "Hi Suze, where are you?"
"Walking to the baby shop in Westdale, I left early to park, why?"
"Thought I'd come and see you," he said, not revealing he was already there.
"I'll be a couple of hours, I've just arrived."
"No worries, I'll call you later," he said ending the call.
He sat for a moment contemplating what to do next, or

rather how to get in. He remembered their mother had kept a spare front-door key wrapped in polythene hidden in the stone wall. Surely it wouldn't still be there, but it was worth a look. Standing in the drive, looking at the low drystone wall that enclosed the raised garden, he tried to remember the spot. He'd a vague memory of it being in a gap between two of the biggest stones, somewhere along the middle row facing the front door. He knelt down, peering into the crevices, most of which were covered over by webs. He looked up, hoping to find a twig or something he could use to poke, he'd never been fond of spiders.

A small weathered wrinkled face with piercing greyblue eyes looked down at him, making him shudder. Suzy must of bought one of those hideous garden gnomes and put it on the raised garden. He chuckled to himself for being foolish and carried on looking for the key. Weirdly he could feel himself being watched, so stopped to look around.

A diminutive, perfectly formed figure of an old man sat on a higher rock watching him. The small man-creature uncrossed his legs, rested tiny gnarled hands on his knees and stared.

Matt froze, this thing was flesh and blood real, he could feel it looking deep into his soul. Matt's heart pounded and he struggled to stand up. The figure remained seated, silently watching Matt grapple with the vision.

On impulse Matt stretched his hand out to touch it, almost on impact . . . . it vanished!

Shaken, Matt went back to his car to sit down. He took a large swig of water from the bottle he kept in the car and wondered what was happening to him. He glanced back, scanning the area. The garden looked the same as always, no elves, goblins or whatever else he'd just imagined. Doubting his sanity, Matt felt deep unease and was anxious to leave.

He drove away without direction, only concentrating on the mechanics of driving. Finally calming down, he stopped driving on autopilot. Despite his unplanned destination, the roads began to look familiar, he'd passed this way before. A large sign appeared ahead signalling a busy roundabout. Whether by fate or coincidence he was heading towards the West country. Having come this far, he chose to continue onwards to Somerset. He could call in to see Mrs Brewer and inform her of their decision to buy. Maybe, ask if she was open to negotiating the price.

He drove carefully through the gate and into the farmyard, parking in front of the house. Then sat for a minute debating what to say, hoping Margery Brewer wouldn't consider his unannounced arrival an imposition. He got out, stretched and reached across for his jacket.
"She's not ere," Sam called out, making his way towards him "gone t' stay at er sister's."
Matt's spirits sank. "I should of phoned," he sighed despondent, accepting the situation.
"Av you spoke t' Parker?" Sam asked, curious to know.
"No? The only time I met him was in the Kings Arms carpark, the day I followed you to the Black Pheasant."
"We could go f ' a pint when I finish ere," Sam suggested, hoping to ask more questions. "Be about n' hour."
"Mind if I walk?" Matt uttered. Doleful, slowly walking away consumed in thought.
Sam watched him cross the yard and head down the lane, telling himself Mathew Chapman was a troubled man.

Matt stopped, having traipsed much further than he'd intended. He leant against a wooden gate. Not especially to watch the sheep in the field, but to reflect how he'd come to be wandering aimlessly around Ashwood Farm. It was time he pulled himself together and headed back. Turning round to walk back, he realised he'd put his hand on a splatter of bird mess. The foul dark green muck coating his palm must of come from the gate. He grimaced, that just about summed up his day so far. Searching inside his jacket pockets for something to wipe his hand, pulled out a white folded handkerchief. It's appearance suddenly tugged a heartstring. He bent down, wiping his hand on the grass to remove the offensive ordure. Unfolding the hanky carefully revealed its treasure, the little black-cat charm sat safely in the centre. He turned the charm over between his fingers, swallowing hard to remove the lump in his throat and replaying the memory. 'Take it with you, it will help you find the right place' his mother had said giving it to him, believing in it's magic. Blinking away tears starting to form, he walked solemnly back to his car and left Ashwood Farm.

Sam glimpsed Mathew Chapman's car momentarily as it drove out through the gate. He got into his van ready to go home, annoyed with himself for missing him.

A taxi pulled into the yard bringing Mrs Brewer home, Sam hadn't expected her back so soon. He watched her march straight indoors, banging the door shut. she was obviously cross about something.

She and Mathew Chapman had missed each other by minutes.

Giving her a bit of time, Sam sauntered over to the farmhouse to tell her. He stood at the backdoor waiting

for her to answer, wondering what had gone wrong at her sister's. Margery opened the door, still flustered and annoyed.
"You alright Mrs Brewer?"
"Yes! I'm fine," she snapped. "I'm fine Sam," she repeated calming down, regaining her composure.
He told her about Mr Chapman driving up to see her, "I think it were import'nt," Sam pushed.
Margery heaved a sigh, "then I suppose I'd better see him."
"I'll phone im, ee can't be far away," Sam volunteered, fishing in his jeans pockets for his phone.
Before closing the door, she announced "Mr Parker is not to be given admittance, he is no longer welcome here. Please shut the gate Sam."
Puzzled, Sam turned and walked towards the farm's entrance. A broad grin slowly appearing across his face, knowing somehow she'd discovered Parker was a shyster at last! Sam stood inside the closed gate, trying to get hold of Mathew Chapman, willing him to answer his phone.

Parked at Yarcombe's large pit-stop garage with shop and café facilities, Matt was sitting in his car eating his way through a pack of ham sandwiches. He'd called in for fuel, and assumed the weird jittery feeling in the pit of his stomach was hunger.
Recognising the number, he ignored his ringing phone. He wasn't in the mood to meet Sam at the pub. He'd a long drive ahead and if he didn't start soon, it would be getting dark before he reached Suzy's.
The ringing persisted. Matt knew Sam wouldn't give up, he'd have to answer.

“She’s back!” Sam shouted down the phone. “I told er, now she’s wait’n f ’ ya.”
“OK,” Matt replied, resigning himself to the inevitable. “I’ll turn round, be there in about thirty minutes.” Lamenting the day was proving to be longer and more tiring than the day before.

Sam was standing by the closed gate when Matt returned. “She wants this kep shut from now on. Think she’s ad a row w’ Parker, ees not welcome ere no more,” Sam said with satisfaction.
“Were they?” Matt wondered.
“No!” Sam frowned, “but I think she thought ee were sweet on er.” Sam opened the gate to let Matt drive through, closing it behind him.

Margery didn’t really mind meeting Mathew Chapman, recalling how he’d been utterly enchanting the evening he’d taken her out to dinner.
She welcomed him into her lounge, offered him a seat and waited to hear what he had to say. He looked drained, his eyes had lost their confident sparkle. She got up to pour two large drinks. “It’s been quite a day,” she sympathised for both of them, handing him the glass.
Matt swallowed a mouthful, feeling the dark liquid begin it’s warm medicinal work. He didn’t usually drink brandy, but at this moment it was comforting.
“You wanted to see me,” she prompted. Then gradually lead the conversation with her articulate questioning, covering every aspect of the farm’s continuation. . . .
“and Mr Carter?” she asked, knowing Matt would hold employment derestriction.
“We couldn’t contemplate buying Ashwood Farm without Sam’s agreement to run it,” Matt pledged. I’m not a

farmer, first and foremost we want the farm to become our home.
"Will you utilize the cottages?"
"Only to house the farm manager, . . finances allowing," Matt rendered. While Margery digested his words, he had the distinct feeling his answers were conformation to prior knowledge. "Will Mr Parker be handling the sale?" Matt asked, keeping Sam's information discrete.
Margery cringed, the mere mention of his name instantly brought back the vision she'd encountered earlier, ... of trousers around his ankles!
"No, I'll appoint my solicitor." Swiftly moving on, she handed Matt the rough draft of details Parker had produced earlier for her to approve.
Matt ran his eyes over the two sheets, construing the valuation.
"It would give me huge satisfaction to know Mr Carter's employment here will continue, and the possibility of his residence reinstated on the farm. Do you understand my meaning Mr Chapman?" She spoke firmly, looking directly into his eyes.
For the second time that day, Matt felt the power of penetrating eyes. He met her gaze "Mrs Brewer, Margery, I give you my word."
She softened, accepting his promise and proceeded with her terms of the sale. "I appreciate the financial investment this farm requires," she said taking back the provisional sheets Matt held, placing them on the low table in front of them.
He watched as she drew a line through the printed sale price of Ashwood Farm and replaced it with her own figure.

Astonished, he wanted to ask if she was serious, but being stunned was rendered speechless.
She stiffened "I'll not take a penny less!"
Momentarily paralysed, he read her figure again.
Margery stood up, offering her hand to shake on the deal. Matt got to his feet and accepted, clasping her hand firmly. His amazed 'thankyou' didn't seem adequate for such massive generosity. Overwhelmed with gratitude he kissed her on the cheek, accompanied by a hug. Releasing her quickly, embarrassed by his spontaneous behaviour. Trying to curtail his elation, he thanked her again for her kind altruistic gesture. With the gleam back in his eyes, he gave her a broad smile, finished his drink and turned to leave.
Margery accompanied him to the door.
"We'll be in touch," he beamed and bade her goodbye. He drove out of the opened gate, giving Sam a 'thumbs up' as he passed through.

Judging by the smile on Mathew Chapman's face, Sam deduced their meeting had gone well, and with no more visits from slippery Jeremy Parker, life at Ashwood Farm could only get better.

Margery topped up her drink and sat contemplating her actions. If anyone had told her at the beginning of the year, 'she would patch things up with her sister and sell Ashwood Farm'. Well, she would never have believed them and no doubt argue that she wouldn't want to do either. Yet somehow, this weekend had managed to do both, . . and even more surprising, she was glad. She could have pushed for the top sale price, but as Jo had come to realize 'what was the point?' It would have been different had life blessed her with an heir. She hadn't

failed to notice over recent years how much the whole place needed modernizing. There was only so much she could do on a shoestring. This way her precious farm would be restored and maintained. Sam's years of hard work and dedication rewarded, and she could return to visit her new friend Elaine.
She thought about Mathew Chapman, being quite taken by his manner, good looks and charm on their first encounter. Deliberating how he exuded natural power and respect. Sam liked him and he was no fool, Elaine favoured him, describing him as descent and genuine. Margery concluded she'd made the right decision to sell the farm to Mathew Chapman and his family.

"Are you still coming?" Suzy asked.
"Yes, be with you in less than an hour," Matt answered, ending the call to concentrate on his driving.

He pulled into the drive for the second time. Elation of sealing the deal with Margery Brewer blotting out the morning's eerie episode.
"You look happy," Suzy observed, letting him in with a hug.
"Oooh, can I smell chicken?"
"Roast chicken," she laughed. "Matt you're such a gannet.

After dinner they sat together in the lounge, catching up with each other's news. "Look at these," she said, showing him the two blue baby outfits she'd bought in Westdale. He thought they were rather small, "will they fit?"
"They're for Rosie's baby, the lady whose job I'm taking over on Monday. I bought this for little Neville," she held up a larger woollen jacket. "I couldn't resist it, there were so many gorgeous things I wanted to buy.

It's Rose's 'baby shower' tomorrow afternoon, but I don't have to go."
"I'm leaving around one o'clock tomorrow, I came to see if you were OK," Matt said kindly "and to tell you I've sold my flat to Tom."
"I wondered why you looked so happy," she smiled.
It was hard not to mention Somerset, but he had to tell Gina and Elaine first.

The sound from the television and Suzy's voice began to fade away. Suddenly Matt nodded forward and woke himself up.
"Am I boring you?" she teased, not mentioning he'd been asleep for a while.
"I'm sorry Suze, I'm not much company tonight. I've been up since six and now I'm shattered, I think I'll take a drink up to bed."
She started to get up.
"No, finish what you're doing," he said, getting up to make his drink."
Suzy carried on wrapping her present.

"What's all this?" he asked, noticing a pile of stuff on top of the bureaux in the hall.
"I've been emptying the bureaux. Can you look through it, see if there's anything we should keep."
"I'll look tomorrow," he shouted from the kitchen.
"There's some short stories Mum wrote inside that brown folder, the last one's really good. Take it up to read in bed, see how many characters you recognise," she called back, trying to persuade him.

"See you in the morning, goodnight," pausing to collect the folder before heading up the stairs.

Sitting up in bed, he opened it, turning the pages to the last story, and to appease Suzy began to read. She was right, by the second page he'd already recognised three people. His eyes began to close, the folder slipped from his hands to the floor, and he turned over to sleep.

-

Peep, peep, p-e-e-p! Matt's phone beeped its usual morning alarm call at quarter to seven. He opened one bleary eye, realised it was Sunday and went back to sleep. At nine o'clock he could hear Suzy moving about downstairs. Half-awake, he remembered the folder and got up to retrieve it from the floor. Getting back into bed to resume reading, and unable to remember how far he'd got previously, began again from the start. The story enveloped people he hadn't thought of since childhood, easily recognisable by their mother's description. Chuckling to himself as each odd and quirky character appeared, reading to the end before he got up.

Suzy sat with him while he ate. "Brunch," she mocked, too late to call it breakfast. They laughed, sharing opinions, reminiscing about the familiar characters their mother had used.

"Would you like the bureaux?" She asked, thinking ahead about making room in case her house sold. Attempting to find space for what might come back.

"Ask Phil," reminding her he'd soon be storing items from his own flat. "Has he read the story?"

Suzy said she'd take him a copy when she delivered the little coat.

As she intended to visit, Matt asked her to buy something for Neville from him, leaving her to choose.

"I'd better get ready," she began, checking the time "are you sure you don't mind me deserting you, it seems a bit rude."
"I'll be going soon," he said, topping up his coffee.
She remembered the pile on top of the bureaux "if you could have a quick look through these before you go," placing them on the table in front of him. "Oh, and I had this cut for you while I was in Westdale," and put a new front door key on top.

"I'm off now," she announced, picking up Rose's present and heading for the door.
"Bye Suze," he called, glancing through, picking out a few items to retain, leaving them on top of the brown folder of stories. At the bottom of the pile lay a sealed white envelope bearing their mother's writing. She'd written across the front 'Merlin – the old'. He assumed it was another story and opened it to look inside. Seeing a sketch he tipped out the contents, curious to see the drawing. His mother didn't have the skill of an artist, but he recognised the subject instantly. She'd captured the little man-creature exactly. Matt tensed, apprehensive to read the preternatural account handwritten in her neat script. She'd recorded each appearance the creature made, her thoughts and fears, her words, it's words, though they were few. Matt read the extraordinary unerring chronical. It would of made a good tale if that's all it had been, but he'd seen it, felt the eyes penetrate deeply into his soul as she'd meticulously described. Finally portraying the strange 'being' as transcendent and eon wise. Matt thought of Suzy, undeniably she'd no idea of this apparition he and their mother had experienced. Without time to fathom, he slid the fanciful pages back into the envelope.

Re-using one of the discarded envelopes from the rubbish, Matt tucked some cash inside to pay for his nephew's new clothes. Writing 'Good luck tomorrow' across the front, he stood it against the kettle for Suzy to find. He looked across at the white envelope he'd left on the table. Whether lured by curiosity or enchantment, slipped it into his overnight bag, unable to explain its magnetism.

He walked out to load his car, lingering for a moment to wonder and stare at the circular raised garden. What had he expected, . . it was merely a flowerbed. His thoughts turned to work and the report he needed to complete. Anticipating Harvey Granzman's Bentley in the carpark first thing tomorrow. Then he thought of Gina and telling her about the sale. He smiled to himself, eager to get back and started the engine.

At six o'clock he answered his phone, recognising Gina's number. "Hello gorgeous, how did your weekend go?"
"Great, we've been to the theatre, shopped, walked and now I'm just glad to be home. When did you get back?"
"I'll come over to see you when I've finished writing this report," ignoring her question.
"I'd like that very much," she cooed, feeling a warm inner glow of being loved, and missed.

Unable to concentrate knowing she was home, Matt abandoned his work and drove to her house.
"That was quick," she said opening the door "did you finish . . ?"
He planted a kiss, stopping her words. "I've got something amazing to tell you," he crowed, looking very pleased with himself, and followed her into the lounge where Elaine

was already sitting. Standing tall, Matt announced "Mrs Brewer's agreed to sell Ashwood Farm to us and she lowered the price!"
Gina was speechless, opening and closing her mouth like a fish, trying to discern.
"She was marvellous, astute, knew exactly what she wanted," Matt praised "and we shook hands on it."
Gina's expression changed "I thought you were in Scotland?"
"I came back early," not mentioning the quashed deal's significance.
"I thought Margery was staying at her sister's," Elaine puzzled, inadvertently revealing their friendship.
Gina didn't notice, her mind was racing ahead, a million thoughts jumbling together. "Oh Matt, that's . . just wonderful," overwhelmed, her eyes filling with happy tears.
"Come here silly," he said, burying her head into his chest, to comfort. He looked up at Elaine, catching her eye "thank you," he mouthed silently.
Elaine acknowledged with a knowing smile.
"What made you go to Somerset?" Gina asked, still snuffling from tears.
"I went to see Suzy, but she was out. Got back in the car and just sort of kept driving," He wasn't totally sure how it transpired, not connecting the strange apparition. He'd already blanked that unexplainable incident from his memory.
"So, it was 'meant to be'," Elaine stated.

Back home, Matt finished the AMS report and closed down his laptop, knowing tomorrow would be a long arduous day.

At two a.m. he was still awake. Lying in bed, his mind whirring, going over the weekend's events. It wasn't any wonder he couldn't sleep, buying the farm would change his life entirely.
Elaine's words kept popping into his head, like an earworm 'meant to be, . meant to be.' He'd never been one to question the metaphors of life, karma or any other strange realms of fancy, but he had to admit this weekend's episode had been surreal. Also, if he was completely honest, he'd felt swept along, rather than the driving force making it happen, . . quite bizarre. Too tired to make any sense of it, or contemplate any longer, he slipped into deep sleep.

-

Turning into the carpark, Matt spotted Tom ahead, parking his car. They'd both come in early, expecting to find Harvey Granzman in residence.
"Do you think he'll turn up later?" Tom asked, seeing Granzman's empty car space.
If he wasn't there already, Matt had his doubts, sensing Granzman was planning something.

At ten o'clock Matt stretched and decided to take a break, buzzing Caroline to order coffee.
Tom knocked and entered Matt's office. "I've bought you these," handing over a large A4 envelope. "My proposal documents, all complete, . . to buy your flat. If you could pass them onto your solicitor."
"That's quick," Matt appreciated.
"My father's firm is very efficient, and of course I had priority."
"Your father's a solicitor?" Matt realised.
"The senior partner," Tom said proudly "which can be useful sometimes."

"Have you got one of his cards?" Matt was considering using his service to buy the farm, his own solicitor being known to drag his heels.
"In here somewhere," Tom said, searching through his wallet, handing over the illusive card at last.
Caroline came into the office carrying Matt's coffee. "Mr Granzman wants to see you tomorrow morning in his office at nine. Is Mr Hobbs staying for coffee?"
"No thanks," Tom answered "I'd best get on."
"Better make that before eight, you know what he's like," Matt warned.
"I'll be ready," Tom said, leaving.

-

Early next morning, Matt walked through the main entrance door. He'd already clocked the Granzman Bentley in its space in the carpark.
"Good morning Mr Chapman," Dennis called from the reception desk.
"Morning Dennis," Matt replied, making his way to his office. Idly peering out of the window at seven thirty while waiting for the coffee machine, Matt saw Tom enter the carpark. He knew Granzman would watch their arrival and wondered why he'd been summoned.

At eight o'clock Harvey Granzman slowly paced his office, updating Matt and Tom to the latest Vortorx prospective. In his positive manner, injecting successful share-price figures here and there throughout his speech, . . as yet ignoring the Apex Mercury System report which lay on his desk, obviously read.
Matt recognised his own wording, the papers lying inches away from where he sat.

Granzman's tone changed, he pointed with annoyance to the report. "Dumb ass incompetence! Lax directorship, managerial stupidity," Granzman growled sitting down, addressing AMS. He focussed eye to eye with Matt, a hint of a smile creeping across his face and nodded. "A good result."

"I worked with John Knight, a knowledgeable AMS man with immense experience and sound principles. Be a shame to lose him Sir," Matt advised, not wanting Knight culled when the Vortorx team took over.

Harvey Granzman sat back in his chair with an sagacious smile, acknowledging Matt's astute perception, appreciating his adroit gift. "I'm arranging a meeting in Guangzhou, China. Huang's company supplied AMS, let's see what they propose. I'll get the details sent through. A good experience for Thomas," Granzman gratified.

Tom looked up, "I look forward to it Sir," embracing the challenge with enthusiasm.

Harvey Granzman's phone gave a single 'remind' beep. Matt and Tom stood up to leave, sensing he was needed elsewhere.

"Good work, you make a strong team," Granzman complimented, planning to exit.

Tom walked back with Matt to his office. "Has he acquired AMS?"

"That's why he didn't turn up yesterday," Matt smiled, perceiving the good mood was the result of a successful lucrative deal. "Harvey Granzman wouldn't miss the opportunity to make a killing."

"He's good isn't he?" Tom confirmed.

"Infinite," Matt agreed with respect.

"China!" Tom relished.

"New territory." Matt accepted. Usually Vortorx's American contingent covered East Asia. Despite Tom's enthusiasm, Matt hoped this would be a solitary occasion. Fearing his time away on future business trips could lengthen.
"Catch you later," Tom acknowledged, reaching Matt's door, walking on to his own office.
Matt took Tom's card from his pocket, sat down at his desk and picked up the phone. "Could you put me through to Mr Alistair Hobbs."

- -

Suzy sat nursing a cup of tea, wondering how best to fill the day. Yesterday had been her first officially employed day at school, and not half as difficult as she'd anticipated. She wasn't required back in the science block until Thursday. Outside was gloomy, the sky overcast with grey clouds. A good day she reasoned to give their house in Ashton its final clean through.

By late afternoon the kitchen and bathroom shone, everywhere was uncluttered, immaculate and smelling of furniture polish. She was upstairs double checking wardrobes when she heard a noise outside. She looked out of the window, Richard's car was parked next to hers. She prayed he was alone, it would be difficult enough to face him.
"I've been getting the place ready for potential viewings," she said nervously, reaching the bottom of the stairs where he stood. "I've asked Mr Shaw the agent to keep you informed. Was there anything you wanted to take?"
He could tell his presence was making her uneasy, noticing the tremble in her voice. He recalled Kate's words, before guilt made him angry and he'd stormed out. "No, there's nothing I need from here." He hesitated for a

minute, watching her. . . Kate was right, she was vulnerable. "If you agree, and sign the divorce papers, I'll pay all the Estate Agents fees. Suzy, I won't take anything else, just my half of the house," he said, trying to redeem himself.
"I'd like that in writing," she whispered, looking down at the floor.
He could see she was near to tears, "I'd better go." He felt bad leaving, yet again convincing himself it was for the best.

Not expecting that confrontation, she took a deep breath, blinking away unshed tears and blew her nose. She gathered up the last of the items she was taking with her and locked the front door. "Good bye house," she said quietly, and drove away. Earlier she'd thought about calling in to see Rachel after dropping off the keys to Baldwins Estate Agents, but now all she wanted to do was go home to Squirrels Chase.

"Hello stranger," Rachel said, surprising Suzy with an evening phone call.
"Rachel!" Suzy answered, her mood instantly lifting. She could hear people chatting in the background and checked her watch. "Are you still working?"
"Yes, for my sins," Rachel explained, "covering Reception for a colleague who wanted a few nights off. It's been manic here," apologising for losing touch, "so how are you?"
Suzy laughed, she'd so much to tell "how long have you got?"
"I'm working at Rowben Court this weekend. I could pop in to see you on the way, if you're free."

"Stay overnight," Suzy suggested. "So we can have a proper catch up."
"Friday?"
"Friday's perfect, looking forward to it already," Suzy confirmed. How strange was that? she mused, only this morning she'd been thinking about her.

-

Opening her bedroom curtains first thing in the morning, Suzy looked out to greet the day. She could see from the window the garden was starting to look scruffy. Coming into October, majority of the summer flowering plants had finished. Without a cloud in the sky, today tidying the garden would be her mission. She was no gardener, their garden in Ashton had always been Richard's domain.
'What a difference a day makes, twenty-four little hours' the song played cheerfully. "You're right there," Suzy answered, talking to the radio in the kitchen, happy and looking forward to Rachel's impending visit. She finished her coffee and went out to the shed to see what gardening tools she could find.

Any plant that appeared straggly or dead was chopped off or pulled out, and lay strewn along the path in the back garden. Including weeds, well, she hoped they were weeds. Struggling to stand with stiffened muscles, she hobbled over to the bench and eased herself down. Now she understood why her mother had positioned the seat there, a suntrap and the best place to absorb the peace of the garden. She closed her eyes, appreciating the gentle warmth from the Autumn sun on her face.
"Someone's been busy."

"Hello George," she said opening her eyes, squinting, before shading them with her hand from the watery sunshine.
"I'm just having five minutes."
"So I see. I was going to cut your grass but as you're busy, I'll come back tomorrow."
"George!" Suzy called, remembering she had something to ask him.
He stopped and waited for her to catch him up, "what is it Lass?"
"I need your advice on something in the garage." She walked along with him to open the door. "I don't know what to do with this?" Her mother's car stood under a thick blanket of dust. "Do you think anyone would want it? I could do with the space."
"How old is it?" George asked.
She didn't know, or when it was last driven.
"I'll ask Jack, he'll have an idea. I'll let you know what he says."
Suzy watched him get into his van, raising his hand to wave as he left the drive.

-

On Thursday, after finishing her work at school, Suzy dashed to Westdale. Back to the Baby Shop where she'd admired their children's clothing. Shopping for little Neville on behalf of Matt, and hopeful Julia would approve.
Arriving home, she noticed George had been round to cut the grass. He'd also written her a note and poked it through the letterbox.

> 'Jack wants to see the car. His
> mate might be interested. He'll
> bring him round Sunday morning.'
> George.

Suzy smiled, grateful for George's help. Removing the car from the garage would create a fair amount of space. If her house sold, she'd have to put the contents somewhere. She couldn't afford to pay for storage.

'This is what I bought for little Neville from you', Suzy texted, adding her message to the photo she sent Matt, before putting away the rest of her shopping.

"Do you want to speak to Julia?" Phil offered when he answered the phone.
"Not if she's busy," Suzy replied with consideration.
"She's upstairs bathing Nev. I usually do it but, I was late home tonight." Phil clarified, and not missing a chance to update her fully on their young son's progress. "I don't think we've got anything planned for this Saturday," answering her question.
"OK, I'll come over in the morning. She could hear Nev crying in the background, "Sounds like you're needed Phil."
"I expect he wants his bottle."
She ended her call, leaving him to happily assist with nursery duties.

-

On Friday afternoon, like most of the children, Suzy was waiting for the bell to ring announcing the end of the school day. Finally it rang out loudly.
She closed the stockroom door and walked across the corridor to Linda Blake's classroom, popping her head around the door. "See you Monday morning."
"Have a nice weekend," Linda called back from her desk in the corner.

Just as Suzy arrived home, Rachel's car came into the drive almost following behind.
Rachel wound down her window, "I left early."
Suzy opened the front door, dropping her belongings inside. "Do you want a hand?" she offered, seeing Rachel opening the boot of her car.
Rachel passed over a stout box, warning her it could be heavy." Once again, she'd brought their dinner.
Hearing dishes inside clonk together, Suzy was thankful to put it down on the kitchen worktop. Looking forward to the meal, her day was improving by the minute.
"This bag contains dog treats," Rachel said, looking around the kitchen for Bob.
"He's not here anymore, he went home. His owner got better."
Rachel looked crestfallen. "I loved that dog, he was a sweetie," she whined. "You'll have to get another one."
"I can't, I'll have to get a fulltime job if I'm going to start paying a new mortgage." Suzy remembered Bob with affection, "he was special, wasn't he? I'll pass these on to Alice tomorrow," she said, peering into the bag.

"Give my compliments to your chef," Suzy praised, full to the brim, forcing down the last spoonful of raspberry mousse.
"I make a point of it, that's probably why I get such generous portions." Rachel exhaled deeply, also feeling full. Her tone turned soulful. "Michael moved out two weeks ago. He and Tansy are renting a place together, . madly in love, apparently. It's very quiet at home," confessing she missed him.
"You'll get used to it," Suzy sympathized.

"Well, there's no dirty clothes left about on the floor, no smelly trainers in the hall, no thumping loud music, and food in the fridge," Rachel admitted, beginning to smile.

Suzy described her new job at the school. "Almost three days a week, not much but it's a start, . . . and I saw Richard on Tuesday. He called into the house at Ashton," she enlightened, mentioning his divorce offer.

"What will you do?"

"He wants to move on. Gwen's welcome to him, he can have his divorce!"

"You've come a long way," Rachel acknowledged.

Suzy realised, come to think of it - yes, she had.

At eleven o'clock Rachel stood up to retire. "I'll leave here before nine and try not to wake you."

"I'll be up anyway. I'm going over to see my little nephew and to deliver these." Suzy slid the outfits out of the bags to show her. They both gave a motherly "ahhh."

-

In her dressing gown, Suzy waved goodbye, watching Rachel drive off to Rowben Court. Not having met up for a while, it had been good to see each other again. Like all true friends, once they got together time vanished. They'd gossiped, laughed, commiserated and both had gone to their beds feeling happier.

Suzy could only see Julia's car in the drive when she parked outside. She gathered up her bags and tapped gently on the front door, just in case little Neville was sleeping.

Julia answered, struggling to hold her lively infant. Welcomed, Suzy followed inside, negotiating a baby-gate along the way. "Does this mean somebody's mobile?"

Julia nodded "I'm afraid it does. He began by rolling over, then squirming onto his tummy. It's not crawling, but he seems to be moving along just the same."
Suzy put her things on the kitchen table. Seeing how much their baby had grown, perceived the clothes would soon fit him.
Julia handed Suzy her wriggling bundle of joy, freeing herself to make them a drink. 'Peek-a-Boo Babywear' splashed across the bags had already caught her attention.
"A few things for our special nephew," Suzy announced. "There's dog treats in the other bag. Where is Alice?" realizing she hadn't seen her.
"Phil's taken her to the vet for her annual injections. I expect they'll check her over while she's there."
"Is she unwell?" Suzy asked.
" Just doesn't seem herself lately."
"Maybe Alice is coming into season?" Suzy suggested.
"That's probably it," Julia agreed.

Little Neville sat on Suzy's lap, listening and smiling while she sang nursey rhymes. Happily chuckling as she played with him. "He's so gorgeous, I could eat him up!" tickling and making him giggle.
In the lounge Julia laid her son on his play-mat, allowing them to chat and drink their tea, watching his antics.

Alice came bounding in ahead of Phil, nuzzled Neville on the floor making him gurgle and laugh.
"So how did you get on?" Julia enquired.
The minute Phil sat down, Alice sprang onto his lap vying for fuss. "Alice is as fit as a fiddle, and . . . . . she's pregnant," Phil said quietly, waiting for Julia to explode.
He didn't have to wait long.

"That's nonsense! She's always kept on a lead when we take her out, or she stays here with us in the garden. She doesn't meet other dogs! She's never escaped or been loose." Julia was adamant.

Suzy sat quietly on the settee, guessing what was coming next.

"Have you let her loose?" Julia accused, looking at Phil.

"I did let her out for a quick run when we went over to visit Suzy, but it was only for a minute. Alice chased Bob so relentless, I put her back in the car. I thought she'd give him a heart attack."

Julia began to sniff the air, picked up little Neville and located the cause. "Excuse us," she said, going off to change him. "Floozy!" Julia growled, scolding Alice as she walked passed.

"Puppies," Phil whispered and nuzzled Alice's soft ears.

"I heard that Mr Philip Chapman!" Julia said, firmly closing the door.

"Oh dear Alice, I think I'm in trouble," he grinned mischievously. "I only get called by my full name when I've done something wrong." Also recollecting it was the only time their mother called him Phillip. Alice turned her head from side to side listening to his voice.

Suzy grinned, recalling the 'naughty' occasions. "What did the vet say?"

Alice rolled over for Phil to rub her tummy. "Probably a small litter as she's very young and it's her first. Pups could be due around the beginning of December. Puppies for Christmas," Phil smiled. "Suzy, you can have first pick."

"I think I'd better be going, I've got car documents to find," she said, feeling awkward and somewhat partly

responsible. "Say good bye to Julia for me, I'll phone in the week."
Phil walked with her to the door.
"Sorry," she said, giving him a quick goodbye peck on the cheek, grateful to be leaving. Halfway home she remembered the copy of their mother's story in her bag, and she'd forgotten to ask about the bureaux. My memory! she cursed. Never mind, it had been wonderful playing with her little nephew. She couldn't believe how much he'd grown, and wondered how long it would be before Phil and Alice were forgiven. Puppies at Christmas!

-

At ten o'clock Sunday morning, George knocked on the back door. "Thought they'd be here by now," he said, standing on the step.
"Thanks for coming today George, I really appreciate it."
"Well, you being here on your own," he smiled kindly.
She was about to offer him tea, when they heard the crunch of gravel announcing someone coming along the drive.
"That'll be them," he said, starting to walk round to the front.

Jack was showing George his new pick-up, standing beside it discussing the wheels when Suzy approached.
"Morning Mrs Martin, we've come to look at your car," Jack greeted. "Well, Micky has," correcting himself. Micky was already standing by the garage door waiting to go in.
"He's keen," George observed.
"He's looking for a little gem to do up for his wife," Jack volunteered.
"It might be quite a project," Suzy warned, looking across at the young lad thinking he didn't look old enough to be married.

"He's a bit of an enthusiast," Jack added. "His dad owns that body shop outside Westdale, - that's car bodies, not women's stuff. Got the keys?"
Suzy bit her lip, praying they were in the car, they weren't in the envelope she carried.

Inside the garage they all stood back, watching young Mickey inspecting the car. He couldn't hide his glee the minute he saw it, giving a long whistle of appreciation, "a Mark-One bread van!"
Suzy knew very little about cars, but it certainly didn't look like a van to her. She handed the envelope of particulars to Jack to examine.
"Volkswagen Polo, 1988, red, no powered steering," Jack dictated, going through the car's documents. "She's an early one, only had two owners," he added for Mickey's benefit.
Mickey emerged from laying underneath, having come prepared with a torch. "How much do you want?"
Suzy stared at him, he was covered in muck and dust.
"You're the first person to see it," George quickly piped up, "Mrs Martin hasn't advertised it yet."
Mickey walked around it once more, pondering. "Two hundred quid?"
George drew in breath sharply, assuming the role of seller.
Mickey lifted the boot, checking the spare wheel.
"Got the original checked picnic blanket to match the seats," George spouted, getting carried away. Jack chuckled at his nonsense.
Mickey lifted the bonnet again, rubbing his chin with a dirty hand, weighing up his decision. "Two hundred and fifty . . . done?" turning to Suzy to shake on the deal.
"Yes, done," she agreed, gladly clasping his grimy hand.

"I'll come round tomorrow lunchtime to pick it up," the young man vouched.
Mickey walked back to Jack's pick-up, getting in and mulling over his purchase.
"Good bye Mrs Martin, nice to see you again. See you, you old so-and-so," Jack chuckled, affectionately saying good bye to his old friend.

Standing alongside George, Suzy watched them leave the drive. "I can't believe that, what if it doesn't work?" She was still grappling with the idea of being paid for something she thought she'd have to pay to get rid of.
"Don't you worry Lass, he knew what he was buying, that lad's been raised on cars. I can see to him tomorrow if you leave me a key," George offered, knowing she worked Mondays.
"Thanks George," she handed him fifty pounds and the garage key held in her hand.
"No Lass," he smiled, giving her back thirty.
Suzy watched George leave, turned and walked back to the house. The money would almost cover her car insurance. "Thank you Mum," she whispered skywards.

- -

Twice Matt noticed Tom running in from the carpark, almost late. At the end of the day he poked his head around Tom's office door, wondering why he hadn't gone home. Tom sat with elbows on his desk, head in hands and appeared to be asleep. Matt gave him a moment in case he was mistaken and Tom was deep in thought.
"You OK?" Matt asked.
Tom opened his eyes, blinking, remembering where he was.
"I'm fine thanks, just tired."
"So why don't you go home?"
"No point leaving yet, I just sit in traffic," Tom yawned.

"Where are you going?"
"Back to my parents place, an hour away, add another half hour to that in rush-hour. I either get here extremely early or I'm late," Tom admitted wearily.
"How long has this been going on?" Matt asked concerned.
"A couple of weeks." He'd been in lodgings nearby since selling his flat, but when the landlord asked him to sign for another six months, he'd moved back home. "I'm buying your place, so it wasn't worth it."
"Why didn't you say?" Matt realised although the sale was going through, there wasn't much Tom could do except wait. "I'll move out."
"That's too much, you don't have to."
Matt looked at the state of him, realising actually he did. He closed Tom's door, planning to chase up his solicitor first thing in the morning and he'd start packing.

"What's going on in here?" Gina asked, peering through the open door of Matt's bedroom, seeing clothes piled high on his bed.
"I'm packing," and explained Tom's predicament. "I'll take most of it to Squirrels Chase. I need to move out anyway, it'll be one less thing to do while I'm around." Predicting Harvey Granzman was planning a very heavy schedule, making full use of his time left with Vortorx.
"You can move in with us," Gina invited, playfully squeezing the top of his leg. "It's nearer to your office than Suzy's place."
"We'll see, . . . how long till dinner? I'm famished," he diplomatically changed the subject.
Gina went off to check the oven.

His next move wouldn't be ideal whichever way he went. He regularly spent hours silently working alone from home, in addition to the time at his office. Gina's house might be closer, but he wasn't sure of the practicalities.

Gina excused, to answer a phone call from her mother. It wasn't like Elaine to disturb her evenings with Matt. He watched her smiling face take on a worried frown.
"Mum's been chatting to Margery. She's planning to accompany her sister to America, they're going to stay with Jo's son. Matt, they'll be out there weeks! Margery's suggested we try to get the sale completed before she goes."
"I'll speak to Mr Hobbs tomorrow. If we all have to go up to Henley, so be it." Anxious to keep Margery happy and not have the sale drag on. He wouldn't relax until the deal had been legally signed and sealed anyway.

-

The next day Matt phoned Gina at work, "preliminary meeting with Mr Hobbs senior, Thursday morning at ten. We've both got to be present. Can you manage that?"
Gina stared at her timetable, there wasn't a gap for weeks.
"I'll be there," she promised, knowing she'd spend the next hour rescheduling and shunting her work along.

In the evening Gina was helping Matt pack more of his clothes. "Can't we eat?" he grumbled, his stomach rumbling and wanting to fetch a take-away. She shook her head, demanding he filled three more boxes.
"Two!"
"Two big ones, you wanted me to help," she bossed.
Matt had to admit, since she'd taken over, more had been achieved. "Tomorrow I'll look into mortgages for the farm,

are your personal accounts ready?" he asked, casually tossing sweaters into a box."

"I'll do that," she said, tipping the woollens out, folding them neatly before laying them back inside the box. "The mortgage, I'd like to organise it. You got the sale, I'll do the mortgage."

He stopped, giving her a serious look of disapproval. He'd always made the important decisions, that was his work, that was his life.

Gina met his gaze with equal stubbornness. "I haven't always worked for Laura's company. I've eight years at Hickson and West building society, Southern division, mortgage department! Matt, I know a sound deal!" she snapped tartly.

He backed down, "sorry, I'm so used to making all the decisions."

"Me too," she relented, closing the lid of the box. "I'll look into it, give me a few days and I'll let you know what I find."

He put his arms around her waist "love you," he whispered, turning her round, pulling her close to kiss.

"I thought you were hungry?"

He stopped, releasing her instantly. "Chinese or Indian?"

"Charming!" she laughed, pelting him with a handful of socks.

-

Matt earmarked the next evening for clearing his office at home. Packing clothes was relatively easy, but sorting, going through, discarding work paraphernalia and rubbish he'd accumulated was taking forever. He'd sat feeding the shredder with old reports and 'minutes' from meetings. The bin liner beside him was crammed full with shredded paper from the mind numbing chore.

Bored with shredding, he turned his attention to the white envelope he'd brought back from Squirrels Chase. It had been inside the first drawer he'd opened, its presence irked. He decided to read through it once more and shred it, 'out of sight - out of mind'. Once again he took out the pages, the sketch on top. Matt studied it closely, intrigued by the pixie-size man's appearance, not that he expected to see it again. She'd captured the little figure exactly as he'd seen it 'sat on a rock, gnarled hands on knees with piercing eyes'. Matt shuddered recalling the day, so shaken up he'd virtually fled Squirrels Chase. The only detail that had remained with him was the creature's soul searching eyes. Matt picked up the rest of the pages, his mother's neat handwriting covering each side. This time as his eyes encountered the words, he could picture her reading them to him, hearing her voice as clear as day. He sat digesting her contentious words - 'from her initial shock, denial, to her acceptance of this ethereal being'. The man creature hadn't reasoned his presence or visibility to her. Her conclusion had been simple and honest, she couldn't explain it but she legitimately acknowledged.

Matt slid the pages back inside the envelope, undecided whether to shred or not. The old cliché truth-is-stranger-than-fiction came to mind, yet he wasn't prepared to accept this illogical concept.

Tired of sorting, he left his office. He'd done enough for one evening and he was ready for bed.

-

By Thursday, several filled boxes lined his hallway, and Matt knew the pile would only grow. If he got a move on, he could drop some off at Squirrels Chase before their ten o'clock appointment. He began to load his car, pleased

to see how many he could squeeze in. Leaving only two boxes behind, Matt set off for Squirrels Chase.
Suzy wasn't at home and assumed she was already on her way to school. He parked close to the front door to unload his boxes, piling them up inside the hall. He intended to leave them there with a note, but on reflection carted them one at a time upstairs to his room. Mission accomplished and satisfied, he walked back to his car. Goodness knows what made him do it, a stupid idea considering he should have already left. Not accepting what he'd read the night before, Matt stood in front of the raised garden. "Merlin," he called and waited. Just as he'd expected, not so much as a leaf stirred. "Merlin," he repeated louder. He smiled, confident that was the end of that chapter of nonsense. Walking back to his car, he gave one last backward glance. The tiny figure of an old man stood watching him. Matt turned round expecting it to vanish as before. The creature sat down, waiting for him to approach. They eyed each other silently, both without blinking.
"Why are you here!" Matt demanded, regretting the question immediately, knowing it didn't have to communicate. He looked again into those penetrating eyes, sensing timeless wisdom. "Would you watch over my sister, . . here." It was a heartfelt request rather than a question.
"Will she stay?" the creature answered slowly, "it will depend on you."
"Me?" Matt couldn't comprehend. Once again the small figure vanished. Matt checked his watch, what on Earth was he doing? He sped down the drive, if he was going to make the appointment with Mr Hobbs, it would be by the skin of his teeth.

- -

It didn't take Gina long to find a good mortgage package. A couple of banks were happy to give a provisional verbal agreement the minute she revealed the equity of the farm, their deposit and Matt's salary. Only one bright spark on the ball, asked about her own employment plans after they'd moved. Gina proposed her new occupation would be letting the holiday cottages. She knew the ropes, deliberately omitting Matt planned to leave Vortorx.

-

Elaine said good bye, ending the call. There'd be no point in beating about the bush, she'd have to tell Gina the minute she came home.

Hearing her car arrive, Elaine stood ready, hovering in the hall, hoping it didn't appear too obvious.

Gina marched through the door in a foul mood, dumping her bag and coat down on a chair.

Whether about to erupt in temper or cry, Elaine knew she'd soon find out. "Had a good day?" she ventured gingerly.

"I told Laura I'd be leaving in the near future. She'd noticed I'd booked a few mornings off for personal reasons and challenged me."

"Well she had to be told, only right to give her fair warning," Elaine commiserated.

"She offered me a raise!" Gina snapped with indignance. "Ten bloody years I've worked for that woman, the first time she offers me a raise is when I mentioned leaving! And! . . when I offered to help, training my replacement. She said no need, they'd soon pick it up!" Snatching her things from the chair, Gina announced she was going in the bath and stomped upstairs.

Elaine made herself a drink and took it into the lounge. She switched on the TV and hoped a soak in the bath would work miracles.

Submerged in warm soapy bubbles, Gina had time to think and mull over her career. With little else going on in her life she'd thrown herself completely into her work. Taken on every extra task and becoming indispensable, accompanying her boss whenever and wherever. Then along came Matt, . . and along came love, proper love. Not the flash in a pan, here one minute and gone the next. Now blissfully happy she'd give up her job in a heartbeat. She stepped out of the bath totally relaxed, her grievances sliding down the plughole with the bathwater.

She made herself some sandwiches and carried them into the lounge, sat nestled against the cushions on the settee with nothing planned other than chilling and watching TV.

"The estate agent rang today," Elaine disclosed. "The Robinsons want to move in on the twenty-third. They did say they were ready when they viewed this place. I said we could accommodate an early move, I thought it would clinch the sale."

Gina stopped eating, "not this month, less than three weeks away?"

Elaine nodded "What shall we do?"

Gina closed her eyes to think. Two facts spun round in her head 'waiting for their mortgage's final acceptance and nothing yet legally signed for Ashwood farm.' She picked up her phone to call Matt for advice. "Can you come round? Now!"

Elaine began to fret. Gina squeezed her mother's hand, "you did the right thing, you sold the house. Now we're free to move. We'll sort it out," she said affectionately, trying to convince herself as well as her mother.

-

"I'm leaving soon," Gina announced, standing by Mary's desk.

"So I heard."

She'd forgotten, yesterday Mary was working in the room next door with the door open.

"She'll miss you."

"Apparently not," Gina said, remembering the conversation.

"Take no notice," Mary smiled, staring at her screen.

"I guess you'll be lumbered until she finds my replacement."

"Won't bother me," Mary tutted, correcting a mistake.

"Unlike you, I work to live, not live to work. I always said you did far too much. When are you going?"

"In a few weeks, if I can get away with it."

Mary stopped typing and turned to face Gina. "So let's see him, lover boy, the one you're giving all this up for," Mary joked, sweeping her eyes around the office depicting their working life.

Gina hesitated, she'd always kept her private life close to her chest.

"Come on," Mary beckoned.

Gina scrolled through photos on her phone to find her favourite one.

Playfully, Mary snatched it to inspect. "Hmmm, he's a looker," she said raising her eyebrows, "I'll give you that."

Mary smiled at Gina, handing back the phone "run out of here and don't look back."

Gina glowed smugly. "I'll bring in cakes," she promised, the usual custom when somebody leaves.

"Make sure you do, . . fresh cream ones," Mary reminded, returning her attention back to the screen.
"I will," Gina called, walking back to her own desk.

- -

"Nearly there," Matt said, lifting the last box out of his car. Suzy held the garage door open for him, he'd almost filled the new space she'd made in the garage. "We've got the farm, by the way," he said grinning from ear to ear, "but I expect you knew that."
She'd known for a while, sensing his deep happiness from within.
"It's going to be sheer chaos for months," he said with equal concern and excitement. "Gina and her mother are going to stay in the house while they clean up the cottages, then move into them while the farmhouse and dairy are renovated. They've got it all worked out. I'll try to get down there when I can."
"Sounds fun." Suzy realised regardless of him staying at Squirrels Chase, she'd probably see more of his laundry.
"We're calling in to see Phil and Julia tomorrow, going to tell them our good news about buying the farm."
"Wait a minute," she said, and ran back into the house.
"Could you ask him about the bureaux and give him this, I forgot," handing over the copy of their mother's story.
"I'd better get back, still tons to do." He said getting into his car. "Bye Suze," and sped off in a hurry down the drive.

- -

"Over there!" Gina pointed, suddenly spotting number ten, Julia and Phil's house. Not having seen them since Ellen's party, she'd bought flowers to break the ice.
"Come in," Phil welcomed "Julia's in the kitchen."
They followed him inside.

Excited to have visitors, Alice frantically wagged her tail and rolled over to have her stomach rubbed.
"Gosh, she's grown," Gina remarked, making a big fuss of the dog that she'd last seen as a cute young puppy.
"Yes, quite a madam," Julia remarked curtly.
Phil got on with making coffee, while Julia hovered by the oven waiting to take out the sausage rolls she'd made. Matt and Gina sat in the comfortable seating area of the huge kitchen. Phil brought over the coffee and joined them, inviting them to help themselves.
Matt already had his eye on the large oval plate of freshly made cheese straws and was ready to pounce.
"The speckled ones contain a sprinkle of paprika," Julia warned.
Gina sat, taking in the surroundings of their fabulous kitchen in wonderment "this is heaven."
Munching through his third cheese straw, amid the aroma of cooking in the warm kitchen, Matt was in total agreement.
Julia put down a plate laden with sausage rolls, warning every one of their 'straight out of the oven' heat.

It wasn't long before a cry from the baby intercom alerted the parents their son was awake. "I'll go," Phil offered, springing up.
"You have an amazing home," Gina acknowledged in awe, helping to tidy after their snack.
Julia smiled accepting the compliment and offered to show Gina around the house.

"Here he is," Phil announced, carrying young Neville in his arms. The youngster's smiles ended when he saw the strangers and became bashful and shy.

"And through here is the conservatory," Julia lead, escorting Gina.
"Let's go into the lounge. If they're going to start talking soft furnishings they'll be ages," Phil suggested, showing the way.
Matt had never seen so many toys in a room. Phil lowered his wriggling son onto the floor. Alice jumped onto Phil's lap the minute he sat down to escape the baby's grasps.

"I thought you might buy a place out in the countryside one day, . . but to leave Vortorx?" Phil was baffled.
"I've had enough of stress. One boardroom looks like the next and there's definitely no pleasure in flying and airports," Matt whinged.
Phil poured drinks "just a snifter," handing Matt a whisky.
"Course, it's not been all work," Matt smirked, a sassy gleam in his eye.
"I'm sure," both sharing a snigger. "But giving up a golden salary?" The accountant in Phil couldn't see the sense. "Matt, it's financial suicide!"
"When Mum fell, my attitude to life changed. Abroad, about to sign another deal worth millions I'd worked hard for, . . suddenly meant nothing. I just wanted to get home. Anyway, there's no point in being the richest man in the church yard."
"Now that wasn't written by an accountant," Phil chuckled.

"What are you two laughing about?" Julia asked, carrying a tray of tea into the room. Gina followed behind with slices of Julia's lemon drizzle cake on a plate.

“To Ashwood farm,” Phil toasted, holding up his mug of tea. They joined him, raising theirs. . . “and to new life,” he added.
Matt and Gina stared at Julia.
“It’s not me,” she protested. “Alice is going to have pups.”
All eyes reverted to Alice.
“Oooh how lovely,” Gina swooned and stretched over to stroke Alice’s soft silky fur. “We’ll have two, One each,” she cooed.
“I don’t want one!” Matt stated.
“Then I’ll have one for my mother. Phil, put us down for two.”
“Looks like you won’t be making quite so many executive decisions,” Phil grinned, glancing at Matt.
Matt smiled happily “now I’d drink to that.”
“OK, I’ll put you down for two,” Phil confirmed light hearted, giving Gina a cheeky wink.

Neville started to get fractious. “He wants his dinner,” Julia said, realizing the time.
Matt stood up, announcing they should think about going. They thanked their hosts and said their farewells, leaving them to feed their son.

“Wasn’t their home stunning, every room straight out of a glossy home magazine. Did you know Julia’s an interior designer? She’s given me lots of magazines to look through and offered her advice with the farmhouse,” Gina continued in praise.
“That sounds expensive,” Matt said, finally getting a word in.
“I’ll see to the house, you run the farm.”

“If that excuses me from involvement with curtains, carpets and such, it’s a deal,” he said trying to negotiate a busy road junction.

Halfway through their journey back, Matt cursed as a thought occurred to him. He’d left something he would need on Monday at Squirrels Chase, so they’d have to call in. “I shall be glad when I’ve finally moved out of my flat. It’s a nightmare trying to live in two places at once. Stay in the car while I run in and fetch it,” he commanded pulling into the drive.

Gina sat quietly in her seat, but her eyes said it all. Normally she wouldn’t accept being dictated to in that tone of voice by anyone, but appreciated he was under pressure. She’d been looking forward to seeing Suzy and hoped she would be at home.

Her car was parked in the drive. When Matt strode up to the house, Gina got out and followed him inside.

Delighted to see them, Suzy insisted they stayed long enough for a drink.

Gina sat down at the kitchen table, making herself at home while he ran upstairs to look for the document.

“Isn’t their place amazing? You can tell she’s an Interior Designer.”

“Is she?” Suzy questioned filling cups with tea, now beginning to understand why Julia constantly changed things indoors.

“I thought you’d know, with your family being so close.”

“Not always as close,” Suzy admitted. “I had a family, Matt worked away, we all met up occasionally, Christmas and birthdays etc., . . just busy people with busy lives. When Mum got into difficulties, it drew us altogether again. She had money, although it took the three of us a while to find it.”

Gina sipped her tea, she'd learned more about Matt's family in five minutes chatting to Suzy, than in all the time she'd known him. "Did you hear about Alice?"
Suzy confessed the story, giving Gina reason to chuckle.
Matt appeared in the doorway.
"Did you find it?"
Showing them, he waved a file "eventually!" he huffed.
Gina got up. "Sorry Suzy, we have to go, a million things to do. We're about to move, extremely bad planning, but there it is."
"Signing the contract for Ashwood Farm tomorrow," Matt divulged.
"Fingers crossed," Gina whispered.
Suzy walked with them to their car, giving each a farewell hug. "Good luck tomorrow," she called, waving as they drove away.
"Your place or mine?" Matt asked.
"I don't mind, it won't really matter," accepting she would end up packing at either one.

- -

On Tuesday morning Suzy got up feeling glum, stumbling over a myriad of Matt's boxes didn't help. She'd never been good at living in chaos. Intending to shift most of them out of her way, she began the task. The only room left with space to accommodate was her mother's bedroom . . . upstairs! By lunchtime, tired of lifting and carrying, she'd had enough.

She walked into the kitchen to check the next job on her 'to do' list. For as long as she could remember, she'd always kept a list stuck on her fridge by magnets. Apart from assisting her memory, it gave her a small sense of achievement crossing them off. 'Car insurance' It had been on her list for a while, but thanks to George's help selling the car, today she would be crossing it off. She retrieved the letters wedged under the fruit bowl, remembering one being her renewal quote and ran upstairs to get the car documents she'd need.

There was a loud knock on the front door. Praying it wasn't another van load of Matt's possessions, went downstairs to answer it.

"Rachel!"

"Just passing, thought I'd pop in to say hello."

"Just passing?" Suzy queried knowing the distance.

"Actually, I'm doing my manager a favour," Rachel explained, following Suzy inside avoiding more of Matt's boxes in the hall. "I volunteered to collect the Christmas Program portfolio from Rowben Court."

Suzy apologised for the clutter. "Matt's moving and is filling this place in transition."

"So, how are things?" Rachel asked, walking behind Suzy, both heading towards the kitchen.

"Much happier for seeing you," Suzy sighed. "I was having a bit of a flat day."

Rachel sat at the kitchen table, bemused "a flat day?"

"Yes," Suzy reiterated "a flat day."

Rachel remained puzzled.

"When you're sad, but you shouldn't be," Suzy tried to explain, switching the kettle on.

"So what's made today flat?" Rachel asked, trying to keep a straight face.

Suzy sighed again. "Apart from this house resembling a tip, Baldwins phoned Sunday and said they've sold our house, . . which is good, but Richard's agreed the sale and he's let it go ridiculously cheap!"

"Ah," now Rachel understood the term. "Elsie would call that 'lost a shilling and found a sixpence."

"Well whatever It's called, I'm so disappointed. I keep thinking about all those years paying that flipping mortgage." Suzy placed two mugs of coffee on the kitchen table and returned to the cupboard for the biscuit tin. "There's no point in dwelling, I'll have to make the best of it. Perhaps I'll find somewhere nice to rent," she said beginning to perk up. "Did you mention Christmas?"

"Yes, we start planning early, months ahead. I could book Christmas dinner for you, me and Elsie at the Bricknell," Rachel offered.

"I can't think about Christmas, it's far too early." Then another thought came to her. "I should offer to give Phil and Julia a hand," she chuckled. "They're going to have their hands full around that time," and relayed the saga of Bob's activities.

"Oh bless him," Rachel beamed. "They'll be gorgeous puppies, Suzy you've got to have one."

"My solicitor's written to Richard. I've agreed to the divorce," Suzy announced, quickly changing the subject. "Richard sent this yesterday," and handed Rachel the letter to read. "While you're reading, I'll quickly phone the insurance people. My mission for the day - renewing my car insurance. I won't be a minute." Suzy gathered up her documents from the table and hurried into the lounge to use the house phone.

Rachel read through the letter. It was clear he'd moved on and wanted his half from the sale of their house.

"Do you need this?" Rachel called out, seeing another envelope she'd left behind.

"No, it's probably an advert, chuck it in the bin."

"It's addressed to you personally and sealed," Rachel protested, about to open it and look inside.

Suzy's attention was taken, answering questions over the phone.
"I don't think it's an advert," Rachel called out, reading the contents. "Suzy, I think you should look at this, . . . now!"
Suzy gave her bankcard details to complete the policy, and waited for conformation. She thanked the agent for his help and re-joined Rachel in the kitchen. "All done," she said pleased, and now able to cross it off from her list on the fridge.
"Forget your list, come and read this!" Rachel insisted, "you've won some money."
Suzy skimmed through the letter declaring it to be a fake and wanted to throw it away.
"Have you got any Premium bonds?"
Suzy nodded, still unconvinced.
"Go and fetch them," Rachel persisted. "Let's see if they tally."
Sure she was on a fool's errand, Suzy tipped out three handbags onto her bed before she found the NS&I envelope.
Rachel checked Suzy's bond holder's number against the one printed in the letter, "Look!"
"I'm sure it's a hoax," remaining obstinate.
Rachel took out her phone "I'm going to ring them. Don't worry, if it's dodgy I'll hang up, then if they trace the call it'll be to my phone."
Suzy watched with nervous concern while Rachel spoke.
"It's genuine, Suzy you really have won this amount. You need to send them your credentials and where you want the money paid, - bank, building society etc."
Suzy sat shell shocked, not knowing whether to laugh or cry, and in all honestly still couldn't believe it.

"Smile, say something," Rachel coaxed.
"I can buy a house," Suzy said slowly in a daze.
"You'd better keep this to yourself, don't want that 'arse' Richard getting wind of it. Your divorce isn't complete yet." She pointed to his letter, "don't rely on that, a rat's a rat!"
"I could come house hunting with you," Rachel offered, getting excited. "I love looking inside people's houses. Do you watch that show on TV, oh, what's it called? Where the poor presenter has to find couples their next home. The husband usually wants a little shed to potter . . . the size of an aircraft hangar, 'she' wants a nice kitchen. The presenter walks them into an enormous dream kitchen and she simpers, wrinkling up her nose 'it's a bit small." Rachel did the impressions of the fictitious woman making Suzy laugh, "you must of seen it, it's a hoot!"

Rachel noticed the time on the clock in Suzy's kitchen, "I have to get back to work. So much for your 'flat day'," she teased.
Suzy stood at her front door, watching Rachel walk to her car.
"I'll phone you next week and not a word," Rachel cautioned, before getting into her car to drive away.
There was no fear of that. Suzy didn't fully believe it anyway and had no desire to look foolish. She waved until Rachel was out of sight. Still disorientated, she closed the door and walked along the hallway, scraping her leg against one of Matt's boxes that stuck out. Rubbing the painful graze on her leg swiftly brought her back down to Earth. "These boxes are going upstairs," she cursed, "starting with this one!"

~ *10* ~

Arriving back home at Gina's house, everyone was in high spirits. Everything had gone smoothly and according to plan. All legal contracts and documents had been signed. Mr Mathew Chapman and Miss Gina Jackman were now the new equal joint owners of Ashwood Farm. Solicitors for each party had enough material to complete their work.

Elaine brought out two bottles of Champagne she'd been saving. Their happiness was profound, celebrating the epic occasion until heads spun from bubbles of the many toasts, and one by one they gave in to fatigue.

-

Matt opened his eyes, blinking to focus, and out of habit checked the time on his watch. He remembered escorting Gina up to her bedroom, . . or did he? She was sound asleep by his side, like himself still fully dressed laying on top of her bed. He sat up and felt the room gently float round, and then remembered the Champagne. Bit by bit his memory returned, . . . they'd done it, they'd actually bought Ashwood Farm! Smiling to himself, he picked up his shoes and jacket and crept downstairs to the kitchen.

Shards of daylight shone through gaps in the blinds. He took a carton of milk from the fridge and filled a large glass, slowly drinking it down. Slipped his shoes on and crept out of the house. Cold air from the early hours of morning braced, filling his lungs. Wide awake and feeling immensely happy, he drove back to his flat.

Gina swallowed two paracetamol, pulling a face as she washed them down. "I shouldn't of drank that bottle of Champagne," she winced feeling her head pound.
"Two magnums," Elaine corrected "we almost drained the second."
Wishing her mother would stop clattering china as she washed up at the sink, Gina checked her phone. Matt had texted a message 'going to look at our farm later, fancy a ride to Somerset?' She phoned him "What time?" trying to sound brighter than she felt.
"Be round at ten, how's your head?"
"I'm fine thank you," she lied "we'll be ready."
"You've only got an hour," Elaine warned, putting a round of toast down in front of her.
"I'm not sure I want that," she groaned, pushing the plate away.
"You'll feel better after you've eaten, . . or I could fry you something?"
Closing her eyes, Gina sipped her strong coffee. "Don't even think about it," she muttered under her breath.

Elaine got into the back of Matt's car, she was as ebullient about the sale as they were. Finally able to see the start of more than she'd ever dare hope for.
"Are you alright?" Matt asked, watching Gina slowly lower herself into her seat."
"Bit of a headache," she confessed, but adamant not to miss the trip.

Sam opened the gate and walked back into the barn. Restacking a few bales of straw which had fallen down, keeping himself occupied while waiting for them to arrive.

He'd been spending extra time clearing out and getting the place shipshape. Although in truth it went against the grain, whoever heard of a working farm being neat and tidy? His efforts were down to Mrs Brewer wanting the farm looking at its best. She hadn't told him officially if the farm was sold, but he guessed the sale was going through. New ownership would bring investment, but the idea of change? He'd got used to doing everything his own way, including the pace. One thing for sure, they'd need him more than he needed to work for them. If it didn't work out, he'd move on.

Matt pulled into the big garage at Yarcombe for a comfort stop. He needed a break from driving and to stretch his legs. Gina had slept most of the journey, waking up when the car had stopped.

In the café Matt recalled his last visit, answering the fateful call from Sam.

"Was meant to be," Elaine wistfully acknowledged, drinking her tea.

Refreshed by sandwiches and hot drinks they rose from the table, eager to get back on their way. Elaine excused herself, heading for the toilets.

"How's the headache?" Matt asked, reaching for Gina's hand.

"Gone, I'm so happy I could burst!" she said beaming with excitement.

"Me too," he slipped his arms around her waist, pulling her closer.

"That's better," Elaine announced, alerting them to her presence.

"Are we ready?" he asked unlocking the car doors

"Ashwood Farm, here we come."

Matt parked in front of the farmhouse. He could see Sam's van alongside the barn. Taking their jackets, the women were glad to get out to stretch their legs and have a walk around.

Matt headed towards the barn, hearing movement inside. "Good to see you again, Sam. The yard's looking good," he said making conversation, sensing a slight awkwardness that wasn't between them before.

"Been av'n a clear up," Sam answered. "Yer got it then?"

An elated expression lit up Matt's face. "Yes, . . with your help, thanks."

"When d'ya plan mov'n in?" wondering when they'd be taking over.

Leaning against the barn door, Matt explained it would depend on Mrs Brewer. He'd no intension of pushing, they'd give her ample time to sort things out, she could leave when she was ready. "Then, the girls will live here, organizing work on the houses. I'll get down when I can, but you won't see much of me, I've got a contract to fulfil. If you see a plane, I'll probably be on it," he joked.

"Busy then?"

Matt nodded "but I'll be counting the days. If you could carry on running the farm as before. Once the houses are done, we'll concentrate more on the farm, . . happy with that?"

"OK Boss," Sam agreed.

Matt smiled as Gina and Elaine walked into the barn. They greeted Sam, before Gina began to relay her plans and itinerary to him.

Sam considered her idea of using the cottages. "Them cottages bin shut two year."

"And?" Gina said, more forceful than she meant to.

"Vermin," Sam warned.
"Mice?" Elaine pertained.
"Them too," a grin slowly creeping across his face.
"Well that will be your first job!" Gina instructed, taking charge.
Sam shuffled his feet uncomfortably and said nothing, he had her card marked.
Matt tapped his watch, hinting it was time to go, "come on you two, it's a long drive. We only came to say hello."
"Goodbye Sam," Elaine smiled warmly.
"Bye," Gina added, her mind elsewhere, buzzing with ideas for the farm.
Sam didn't respond. The women headed back to the car.
"Look after them Sam. Oh, and don't upset Elaine, she's the best cook ever," he grinned. Before finally leaving the barn Matt glanced back, "If I'm not here, I'm at the end of my phone, OK? . . Bye Sam."

- -

With the ink barely dry on the contracts, Margery Brewer arrived back at the farm. It was pointless putting off the inevitable, giving herself a few days to sort out and pack her personal possessions. She'd hired a removals company to deal with the farmhouse contents. They had given her sheets of coloured paper dots to adhere, red for items to pack and yellow for not.

-

The team swept through with impressive speed and efficiency. Loading each packed, labelled box into their huge lorry destined for Henley-on-Thames.
Margery had accepted Jo's offer to move into the annex. A spacious two bedroomed apartment with views of the river, originally constructed within the ground floor for

Frank's carer's who'd lived in. It would suit her present situation and allow her own space.

Hearing Sam arrive in the yard, Margery went outside to catch him, inviting him in for a last drink. They sat in the kitchen on a couple of odd chairs that remained. She gave him a sealed envelope, thick with contents. Thanking him for the years of work and support he'd given. "I think they'll be good for the farm. Mr Chapman seems genuine and sincere, . . you do like him Sam, don't you?"
Sam leaned back on the wooden chair and nodded. "ee seems alright," he said with his wry smile.
"I'll be leaving shortly. If there's anything you'd like from the house, please take it. Otherwise," she handed over a card with two phone numbers and explained their significance. "Mr Hyde's from the Red Cross, he's sending a lorry on Friday to collect everything. The phone number underneath is a house-clearance, in case anything gets left behind."
"av y' got ya' self a place?" Sam asked.
"An apartment, next door to my sister," it was all he needed to know.

Sam carried out her cases, loading them into the boot and back of her car. Attached to the farm most of his life, he'd watched her cope alone with its good and bad years, earning his respect and loyalty.
She opened the driver's door and stopped, standing for a last look around the yard. Becoming choked with emotion, struggled to say "look after it Sam," before getting in.
"Now you take care o' ya' self Mrs Brewer," he said kindly, understanding the heart-wrench. Sam waited, watching her car drive slowly through the gate and away.

He sauntered back to the farmhouse, if she'd left any milk in the fridge he'd treat the farm cats. He took the envelope from his pocket, feeling the thickness, assessing its contents with optimism. Tomorrow, he'd have a look around the house, see if there was anything he fancied or worth flogging. As Mr Chapman said 'there was no rush.'

- -

Elaine sat in a quandary, should she look for a guesthouse, cheap hotel or was it worth renting a furnished place short term? The Robinsons would be moving in at the weekend, she'd have to do something. Her only saving grace had been to organize their own 'removals' to a storage unit Saturday morning.

It would help to know Margery's plans. A delicate situation all round, especially as Mathew had assured her there was no rush.

It was no use, she'd have to bite-the-bullet and ask, all be it in a tactful roundabout way. Elaine planned with care, if she phoned and light-heartedly mentioned Margery's forthcoming trip to America, hopefully their conversation would unveil a clue. Elaine phoned Margery's number, knowing if her idea misfired or 'God forbid' upset her, . . Gina would never forgive! Waiting for Margery to answer, Elaine's nerves began to jangle. With no reply, she dialled the number at Henley and waited.

Once Jo recognised Elaine's number, she picked up the phone and offered to give Margery the message that she'd called. Elaine thanked her kindly, exasperated that her scheme hadn't worked. Now she was in a worse predicament, unable phone again or they'd wonder what was so important. Elaine went back to packing, she would have to think of something else.

"She's gone!" Gina whispered down the phone "Mrs Brewer has moved out of the farm, we're free to move in!"
"How do you know?"
Gina quickly garbled her answer, from which Elaine gleaned 'Margery phoned Mathew and he'd just phoned her.' Suddenly Gina hung up, ending the call. Elaine surmised her boss was close by. She'd become distinctly awkward since Gina had announced she was leaving.
'Thank the lord for that,' Elaine sighed with tremendous relief. Her serenity didn't last as she realised the urgent need to adjust their removals arrangements.

"Can't do Saturday," the chap was adamant, "they've got a job already booked for the afternoon."
She could hear him flipping through pages and talking on another phone.
"Best I can do is . . . . . this Friday, or it'll have to be end of next week. Somerset?" he pondered, calculating mileage and hours, stating a seven thirty start.
"That will be fine, I'll pay you now," Elaine interrupted, desperate not to lose the slot.

With boxes stacked in every room, Gina's house had reached the uncomfortable stage to live in. Also, each room sounded like an empty cave, hollow and echoey.

Elaine started to empty the kitchen, wiping out cupboards as she progressed. On all fours, head in a cupboard, she didn't hear Gina come home.
"What are you doing?" she chuckled, making cheeky remarks about the view of her mother's rear end.
Elaine reversed and stood up, "fitted kitchens may look very smart, but give me a walk-in pantry any day!" She sat on a chair, catching her breath.

Gina filled the kettle, beginning to make tea. “We don’t have to cook tonight, Matt’s booked a table at The Vine for seven.”
Dinner? The day had been such a roller coaster, Elaine hadn’t given food a thought.
He hadn’t given any details about Margery’s sudden decision to move, Gina assumed he’d tell them later that night. “I suppose now we can arrange our moving day,” Gina said stirring her tea.
“It’s all arranged, this Friday, I’ve booked it,” Elaine announced waiting for praise.
“I’ll be working. Laura’s already being difficult because I’m not doing next week!” Gina objected.
“I’ll see to the removals while you go to work,” Elaine offered wearily, wondering if she’d made the right decision.
“I’m going upstairs for a shower,” Gina proclaimed, feeling more positive now things were coming together, . . . well most of them.
Elaine stood at the foot of the stairs and loudly forewarned “if there’s something you can’t find - I’ve packed it!”

“This Friday?” Matt questioned, realising he’d be away. “I won’t be here. I’ve a meeting in London, then Tom and I fly to Guangzhou. You’ll be fine,” he reassured “and you’ll have Sam. I’ll phone him.” He tried without success, assuring them he’d try later. The pub was busy, he got up to fetch more drinks from the bar.
“I’ll give Matt a hand,” Gina said springing up to follow him. “Will I see you tomorrow?” she asked, missing their time together.

"I'll be working late, this trip is important." The stern look on his face reminded her of his position at Vortorx. "I'll phone," he vowed, his expression softening.
Elaine stifled a yawn, closing her eyes for a few seconds.
"Elaine looks tired," Matt observed walking back to the table.
"I'm not surprised, she never stops," Gina revealed.
"Perhaps you should make her," he cautioned thoughtfully.

Outside in the carpark, they stood by their cars ready to go. "See you at the farm," he smiled, giving Elaine a brief goodbye hug.
She wished him Good Luck with his trip to China before getting into Gina's car.
He turned to Gina, promising he'd get down there as soon as he possibly could, before their farewell kisses.

- -

Sam was doing the buying down at the Black Pheasant, treating his mates, round after round. He held up his pint "to Mrs Brewer!" - they all cheered. "The Newcomers!" one of them called out, followed by more cheers.
"What they like?" Bill, the landlord shouted across. Sam walked unsteadily to the bar and sat on a stool. "Good bloke, . but er?" Sam pulled a sour face "draws your backside t' ya elbow!"
"Sam! do you want a lift?" Jake called, offering to drop him off. Sam followed him out, leaving the rest of his mates enjoying themselves in the bar.

- -

"Morning," Matt said, greeting Suzy when she walked into the kitchen still wearing her dressing gown and slippers. "Aren't you running late?"

She poured herself a cup of coffee and joined him at the table, reminding him she wasn't working that day. She'd seen his case by the door and asked about his trip.
He hadn't decided whether to leave for London from his office later that evening or go early tomorrow morning. He'd speak to Tom and let her know. "I could have moved into the farm this weekend," he announced, despondent he'd be far away.
"That's typical Sods Law," she sympathised.
"A removal company is transporting their furniture early tomorrow, the girls will probably follow on," sounding downcast, then suddenly remembered he was supposed to phone Sam.

Sam woke up early as usual. The skinfull of beer he'd downed the night before had little effect, apart from reducing his wodge of money. He planned to check on the sheep in the far field on route to the yard. Ted Lawson's sheep might not officially belong to Ashwood Farm, but he liked to keep an eye on them. Besides, there was little else to do on the farm, it had never been so up together. Later he'd have a mooch around in the farmhouse to see if there was anything that took his fancy.

"Sam!" Matt called out, relieved he'd finally been able to get hold of him. "Could you make yourself available Friday for a removals lorry? Gina and Elaine will be down later."
"What?" Sam could hardly hear. The strong wind was cutting across the top field, noisily tearing the last leaves from the trees.

"I said the girls are moving in at the weekend. Could you be there to see in a removals lorry on Friday?" Matt shouted.
"Yes Boss," Sam shouted back.
"That's tomorrow Sam, Friday tomorrow!"
Sam cursed and stuffed his phone back in his pocket.

- -

Gina stood in the bakery, mindfully doing a headcount while she waited in the queue, adding another four to her total to be on the safe side. It was easier to take the cakes in today. Goodness knows what state she'd be in tomorrow, her head was already buzzing with things she had to remember.

At ten o'clock she bravely knocked on Laura's door, politely offering her first choice from the box. Her boss had drastically changed her tune, bestowing a card and wishing her well in her new adventure. Gina walked through her department dispensing cakes, receiving good wishes from all. Back at her desk, she struggled to concentrate, losing all inclination to work.

The afternoon break was generally around three. Mary walked into Gina's office, followed by several of her colleagues. "Thought we'd spend our tea break with you," Mary announced, looking furtive. Gina guessed they were up to something.
"This is for you, from all of us," Mary chuckled, handing Gina a large cellophane wrapped steel bucket adorned with bows.
"And to go with it," Cathy giggled, presenting a full size gift wrapped shovel. "For your farm. You can think of us while you're shovelling . . !"

“Thank you girls,” Gina laughed, quickly cutting in to end Cathy’s sentence. “Very kind of you all,” she blushed. “I’m sure I’ll be putting them to good use,” and noticed they’d filled the bucket with cards and toiletries.

After their break, one by one the women returned to their desks.

“Laura’s gone, she won’t be back until Monday,” Mary said. “Why don’t you pack up your stuff and go. I expect you’ve still tons to do, . . and don’t come in tomorrow.” They both knew Laura hadn’t worked a full Friday in weeks, if she worked one at all.

“But, what if?”

“Oh, I’ll think of something,” Mary insisted kindly.

Gina flew around clearing her desk and office, making a preliminary trip out to her car. She thanked Mary, wished her luck with Laura, picked up her gifts and left the building. Leaving the company’s carpark, Gina looked back through her mirror. Would she miss her job, Laura and most of the employees? . . . not one iota.

- -

In a sulk, Sam phoned the number Mrs Brewer had given him for the Red Cross, hoping to speak to Mr Hyde. An elderly lady answered, telling him ‘collection day’ in that area was Fridays and she’d be happy to add Ashwood Farm to their waiting-list. Mrs Brewer had misunderstood their terms, Sam’s sulk deepened. She hadn’t left much in the farmhouse, nothing he considered worth taking. Tomorrow he’d tell the ‘removals men’ to unload their lorry into the barn. The two women could sort out their own stuff!

~ *11* ~

On Friday morning armed with her check-list, Gina took over the organizing, leaving her mother to get on with practicalities. Elaine loaded her car with boxes of food, the bedding they'd slept in and put a box labelled 'essentials' in the foot well. After the lorry had left, Gina dropped the keys into the estate agents, leaving her mother to have a final inspection.

It would be a very long drive and not one Elaine was looking forward to. She'd be following Gina, dreading getting parted and lost.

"Ready?" Gina asked, shutting the front door for the last time. She waited for her mother to start her car and then took off. She had said they'd stop each hour, but set on her destination to Somerset . . . somehow forgot. Later, she pulled into a roadside garage with a café, watching her mother follow behind.

Elaine drank her tea slowly, making the most of the interval.

"Not long now," Gina chivvied, being economical with the truth.

The next time they stopped, Gina believed their farm to be less than an hour away.

Elaine felt drained, following was more stressful than she'd realised. Too busy concentrating on where Gina was going to notice scenery, but she could almost swear they'd passed that same church twice.

An eerie Autumn mist had come down, deceiving Gina of her whereabouts. She pulled into a layby, confessing she'd missed a turning somewhere.

Sam went back to the farm to open the gate, and decided to wait for the women to arrive. With nights drawing in, the temperature soon dropped once the sun had gone down. He'd tinkered with the boiler, coaxing it into life to warm the cold house. He couldn't guarantee how long it would run, the blasted thing had always been cantankerous. Mrs Brewer frequently got him to sort it out, plumbers only offered to replace it. He waited in the kitchen, planning to leave the minute they turned up.

Finally they both drove into the yard. Elaine had never driven so far in one day, and had begun to think they'd never find it. She sat recovering, giving herself a moment, watching Gina get out of her car to speak to Sam at the door.

"Made it then?" he said handing over a bunch of keys.

"Where did the removals men put our stuff?"

"All n' barn," leaving her to it.

She walked across to see for herself.

Elaine got out and opened the boot of her car to unload. "Hello Sam," she said, greeting him with a warm smile as he got near. She wasn't sure what happened next, her legs buckled and she began to fall.

"Whoa! y' alright Misses?" Sam caught her before she hit the ground. He carried her in his strong arms and lowered her into the driver's seat of her car. "Ya sit a' while, I'll get this in."

Elaine felt shaky, she watched him lug everything inside.

"I'm OK now," she said embarrassed. "It was a long drive, . . I'm just a bit tired."

Sam escorted, supporting her slowly into the house to the kitchen, moving a chair nearer for her to sit on. He rinsed

out a mug and filled it with water. “ere,” he said in his direct manner, handing it to her.
“Are there any beds?” Elaine inquired.
He saw her looking at the heap of bedding he’d brought in and left on the floor. “I’ll run that up f ’ ya,” and carried it upstairs, returning to the kitchen. “Two beds,” he said, holding two fingers up, indicating.
“Thank you Sam, I’m fine now,” she confirmed starting to feel better.
He could see Gina walking back from the barn, so turned and left by the backdoor.

“Are you OK?” Gina asked, oblivious to what had happened.
“A little tired, I’m going to have a rest upstairs.” Elaine made her way upstairs. She laid her pillow and duvet on one of the bare mattresses, folded it over herself and closed her eyes.

Gina busied herself unpacking the boxes Sam had carried into the kitchen. Putting away food and loading the fridge. Unpacking the last box, she found their kettle, mugs, toilet rolls, washing up liquid, in fact all the necessary essentials you’d need immediately if you moved house. She made tea, carrying it upstairs to her mother and found her sound asleep.
Gina stood by the window, looking out and gave a sigh of relief. Here at last, now nothing could possibly could go wrong.

-

The cold woke Gina early. She’d only chosen the room because it had a bed. Laying there looking around, taking in its faded elegance and whimsically wondering what changes she’d make.

Keeping the duvet wrapped around her body, she made her way over to the window. A thin layer of mist hovered over the fields like a white blanket, almost concealing the wood in the distance. Slowly it dawned on her, they actually owned everything in the view before her. Almost needing to pinch herself to check it wasn't just a dream. She vowed to make living at Ashwood Farm a joy, Matt deserved that. Dragging the duvet along the floor, she walked back to check her phone. There were no messages.

Her thoughts turned to hot drinks. She pulled on a long thick woollen jumper over yesterday's clothes and headed for the kitchen, listening at her mother's door as she passed in case she was stirring.

Gina stood in the big cold kitchen, flicking switches, turning knobs and giving the boiler a hefty thump for luck, but nothing would bring it to life. A big cream coloured Raeburn stood one end of the kitchen, with a conventional gas cooker close by. Gina switched on the cooker, leaving the oven door open to warm the room.

They had brought two enormous electric oil filled radiators with them. Purchased originally for her mother's guest house, part of a backup system which thankfully had never been needed. Their downside was weight, each one weighed a ton. Gina walked over to the barn hoping to locate them.

Against his better judgement Sam drove into the yard, he had been asked to look after the women after all.

"Sam!" Gina shouted from the barn.

By her tone, he realised it had been a mistake. He ambled over to see what she wanted. Despite the cold temperature

a hot, bothered red faced woman struggled to get out from the pile of boxes.
"Mornin," he said with an ironic smile.
"The boiler's died, it's freezing in there! Somewhere here there's two big radiators," she said expecting him to start looking.
Sam waited for her to calm down, "ow's Misses?"
"She's not awake yet," Gina replied.
He took pity, knowing the boiler had never been reliable "plenty o' logs f ' fire."
She hadn't thought about a real fire, and smiled anticipating the adventure.
He showed her where the logs were stored, then watched her gingerly brush off woodlice and pick up two small logs with her soft manicured hands to carry. At this rate, it would take her a month of Sundays! Sam loaded his arms with wood and followed her inside to the lounge, repeating the journey a number of times. He laid the fire, leaving his lighter on the mantelpiece for them to use later, and returned to the barn to hunt for the illusive radiators.
"There!" she said pointing.
He just knew they'd be somewhere at the bottom.
She waited, observing him lift, move and restack hefty boxes to get at them. Too heavy for one man to carry, he went off to find the low-wheel based trolley.
Gina stood by, watching him oil, and wrench the seized wheels back and forth to get them moving.
If he could lever the radiator high enough, she could push the trolley under. He hauled it all into position, lining up the trolley and got a plank ready to lift. "Yer Gonna elp?" he said lifting, almost breathless with the strain.
"Oh sorry," suddenly realising he wanted her assistance.

It had taken the best part of two hours, getting both radiators into the farmhouse, dragging them along inside on a rug. He managed to heave one into the lounge and the other, halfway along the hall. He'd only intended to ask after 'Misses' and to see if they were alright. This wasn't how he'd planned to spend his Saturday, now he was worn out. He took the trolley and ropes back to the barn, and left before she could give any more orders.

Elaine woke with a shiver and looked around, taking a few seconds to register her surroundings. She sat up, peered at her watch disbelieving the time. All she could remember of yesterday was endless driving and a wave of tiredness. She threw off the duvet and stood up. Two steps away from the bed she felt lightheaded and returned back to sit down. Wondering if she should rest a bit longer.

Gina plugged in both radiators, switching them on one at a time hoping the farmhouse's wiring would cope. Her mood lifting as the temperature rose, she'd never been able to handle the cold.

She'd expected her mother to rise early. Always being an early bird, especially with so much to do. It seemed strange and unlike her not to be up. Gina made tea and toast, intending to surprise her mother with breakfast in bed.

Elaine sat up, smiling at the welcome sight. Gina wedged the bedroom door open, allowing the warm air rising from downstairs to take off the chill. Sitting at the bottom of her mother's bed, she asked if she was feeling OK?

"Not really," Elaine answered, still feeling drained.

At the end of the day Gina went to bed shattered. Her mother still looked pale regardless that she'd sat quietly in the lounge all day, Matt hadn't phoned and she suspected Sam was avoiding her. So far things at Ashwood Farm were not going quite according to plan.

-

The next morning while Gina was out shopping, Elaine walked over to the barn. She'd woken up feeling better and planned to make a start sorting out the kitchen. The removals men had stacked their boxes in front of their furniture. Elaine stood contemplating the pile, trying to figure where to start. Hearing a vehicle arrive in the yard, she waited for Gina to appear, assuming she'd come to find her.

"Mornin," Sam blurted, making her jump. "You bettur?"

"Much better, thank you Sam," she answered, sharing her intentions, staring ahead at the heap.

Elaine was unpacking the last box he'd carried into the kitchen when Gina got back.

Sam had earmarked the day for clearing scrub in the far field. He preferred to keep Ted Lawson's sheep there during the winter, where they could shelter behind the old drystone walls. The strong North winds cut across those top fields.

Due to this year's exceptionally wet weather, Spring brambles and saplings had flourished, growing tall taking hold in the meadow. He looked up at the rainclouds coming from the East and cursed, today he'd hardly made any progress. The only way to manage the farm work would be to stay out of sight.

- -

Well?" Rachel asked, waiting patiently for an answer. "Have you got anything to tell?"
Suzy kept her waiting, teasing her with silence "hmmm, . . . possibly." Confessing to a substantial amount, now sitting in her savings account. She could hear Rachel cheering at the other end of the phone.
"So when are we going house hunting?"
Suzy wasn't ready, the status quo still didn't feel real.
"Please, p l e a s e , p – l – e – a – s – e !" Rachel implored.
Suzy gave in, remembering it was only down to Rachel's persistence she was in this privileged financial position.
"I'm booking Wednesday and Thursday off, I'll be with you Tuesday night," Rachel vowed, getting excited.

It felt immensely wrong, not sharing the amazing news of her winnings. She felt guilty keeping it from the family, especially Matt. Although he'd enough going on in his life at present with moving in together and buying the farm. Suzy couldn't encroach on their glorious happiness. Bob's escapade still prickled her conscience and she understood Julia's point of view. It seemed best to let the dust settle there a while longer.
Not telling Kate seemed a betrayal, yet obviated the responsibility to keep it from her father.
Deep down Suzy knew Rachel was right, having her best interest at heart. She would tell them all . . . . eventually. The money was held in her secret personal savings account. The one she'd hidden from Richard, the one she'd used to save for their big special time-together holiday. Oddly, she'd been down to her last two hundred pounds before this magical windfall, less if George hadn't helped her to sell the car. It was almost as if someone was looking after her.

Suzy contacted an estate agency just outside of Kirston. Providing them with a vague description of what she was looking for - two bedrooms, a garden and in the Kirston area. The agent had made arrangements for her to view three properties on Wednesday and two on Thursday.

-

On Wednesday morning Rachel couldn't wait to get started. Being the most enthusiastic, the agent assumed she was the actual buyer and favoured her with his full attention.
Suzy dismissed two ground floor flats they viewed.
They were driven on to the next property, but seeing three rusting cars covered by scruffy tarpaulins filling the neighbouring unkempt front garden. Suzy refused point blank to get out of the car, certain she wouldn't live there.

By Thursday, Rachel admitted house hunting wasn't so easy as portrayed on the television. They sat laughing at the previous house they'd just been to see, recalling the agents description. "Needs a little renovation," Rachel mimicked.
"More like flattening and total rebuilding," Suzy stated.
She was treating Rachel to lunch at The Back Rabbit in Kirston, they were sitting at a table waiting to be served.
"He thought we were a couple, did you hear him?
Probably too much work for two women."
"Dam cheek!" Rachel responded, insisting she was a dab hand at DIY.
"I wonder what the next one will be like?" Suzy pondered.

Back at Squirrels Chase, Suzy thanked Rachel for coming and giving up two of her busy days, knowing she wouldn't of gone to view houses on her own. They'd both disliked the last place the minute they stepped inside, 'just something about it,' they shuddered. Suzy's first attempt at house hunting had been informative if not successful.

"I'll come back next Saturday, in the meantime we'll see what we can find on the internet," Rachel offered trying to inspire.

Suzy waved goodbye as Rachel drove away, grateful to have such a good friend.

At midnight Suzy heard a car crawl slowly along the gravel drive. In the quiet late hour, she listened for familiar sounds of Matt's car. The electric motor that lifted the boot quietly whirred, confirming to her he'd arrived home. She thought about getting up to make him a drink, aware he'd driven from London.

Matt locked his car, carried his case inside and went straight to bed. She'd heard him climb the stairs to his room and quietly close the door. Deducing he was exhausted from the long arduous flight and drive. She turned over and went back to sleep, she would speak to him in the morning.

-

She padded quietly around trying not to wake Matt. If he got up before eight thirty she'd see him before she left for school. A square of paper floated to the floor, disturbed when she grasped the kettle. She bent down to retrieve it 'Back next week, Matt x.' Suzy re-read the note walking to the window alongside the front door, his car was gone. She hadn't heard him leave and smiled to herself, mentally wishing him a safe journey to Somerset.

Matt's eyes began to burn, tiredness wanting them closed. He opened the car windows needing the cold air to wake him. Five minutes on, he pulled into the nearest transport café his Sat Nav had flagged. Parking away from the juggernauts and container lorries that dwarfed his car. He splashed his face with cold water, dabbing himself dry with paper towels, a significant contrast from the luxurious facilities he'd encountered in China. Jetlag confused his usual healthy appetite and ordered a mere black coffee instead.
Back in his car, he rubbed a shaver around his face reducing designer stubble to a five o'clock shadow. Anxious to get back on the road, it would have to do.

Elaine had found a manual for the Raeburn in one of the kitchen drawers. She sat in the lounge with her breakfast reading the pages, trying to make head from tail. She'd used an Aga once before and hoped the gist would be the same. Some simple recipes were printed at the back, just the job for her first trials . . . and errors.

Gina had started a portfolio, making notes of what needed doing room by room, gleaning ideas from Julia's glossy magazines. Once she'd found some reliable tradespeople, estimates could begin. Her first priority would be the cottages, the minute Sam could get them emptied she could make a start. With Sam's continual absence, she'd been reduced to texting him with appeals. His ignoring had riled her and she'd begun to send him curt messages.

'On my way' Gina read, and checked to see when Matt's text was sent. In a flurry of excitement, she flew about tidying and ran upstairs to change.
She was standing at the window waiting, when Matt drove into the yard. Before his car had stopped completely, she raced out of the door ready to greet him. He'd barely time to get out, before she flung her arms around him kissing him passionately. "Welcome home," she said, choking back tears of emotion.
Happiness briefly melted his fatigue, he held her tight relishing the moment. "Will I get this every time I come back?"
"No promises," she beamed, walking with him towards the farmhouse.

In the kitchen Elaine was putting on her coat. "Lovely to see you Mathew," she greeted, giving him a peck on the cheek.
"Going out?" Gina puzzled.
"Yes, off to the village to buy more ingredients," waving her list. "I'm sure you two will have plenty to talk about." Checking her handbag for keys and purse before saying goodbye, she headed for the door.
"Really going shopping or being tactful?"
"Probably both," Gina smiled.
Matt looked seriously tired. "Look at you, you're exhausted." she said concerned, looking into his sore eyes. "You're going to bed!" She led him up to their room and helped him undress.
"I've been warned about women like you," he joked, raising a weary smile.
She pulled the duvet up around his shoulders and kissed his forehead.

"It's so good to be here, . . home," he murmured turning over.
She drew the curtains to darken the room, "is that better?"
She wasn't surprised when he didn't answer, his soft rhythmic breathing told her he was already sleeping.

Matt slept most of the day, emerging briefly to demolish a pile of sandwiches washed down with coffee. Gina retired early in the evening, feigning tiredness to join him.
"Don't stop," she urged passionately between kisses.
Thrusting quicker, he wasn't going to.

-

In the morning he woke refreshed.
She offered to make breakfast while he showered.
"That sounds good," he smiled, getting up and heading to the bathroom.
Downstairs in the kitchen Elaine was getting to grips with the Raeburn. She'd hidden her first calamity, a chocolate cake with a soggy middle. "Is Mathew feeling better?" she enquired.
Gina began cooking their breakfast. "He was ever so tired," she said justifying their lateness in rising.
"Hmmm," Elaine raised an eyebrow. "I'm all for exercise," a curl of a smile on her lips.
Her mother's room being next door had slipped her mind, irritated by embarrassment Gina immediately sent Sam another text. The sooner she and her mother had a cottage each the better!

They sat eating breakfast at one end of the large wooden table, while Elaine mixed pastry in a bowl at the other. In the big farmhouse kitchen, warmed by the

Raeburn wafting delicious smells of baking, Matt couldn't be happier. "Where's Sam?" he asked.
Elaine looked across at Gina, waiting for her to answer. "I don't know, we haven't seen him for a while."
Matt sensed something was wrong. He finished eating, refused another coffee and got ready to go out.
"Where are you going?" Gina asked.
"I need to speak to Sam." Matt picked up his car keys and left.

The two women sat in silence. "I hope he doesn't get into trouble," Elaine said perturbed. "Sam carried me, he's very strong, . . . and he brought in all those boxes full of kitchen stuff, some of them weighed a ton."
"When was this?" Gina asked, alarmed.
"While you were out shopping. I pointed to the boxes and Sam carried them in for me."
"No, when he carried you!"
Elaine assured Gina it was nothing to worry about. 'One minute she had been standing by her car, the next minute Sam was giving her a drink of water in the kitchen'. "I vaguely remember being carried. He's very strong." Elaine repeated.
"Yes," Gina agreed, mentioning he'd lugged the heavy radiators into the house. Elaine was surprised, she thought Margery had left them.
Gina regretted the abrupt text she'd sent Sam earlier.

Matt spotted Sam in the top field and got out of his car to speak to him.
Sam continued to work. Raking up the scrub he'd already cut, and having read Gina's text was too annoyed to talk.

Matt stood behind watching, witnessing the angry force Sam was using. "How is everything working out?" he asked calmly.

Sam didn't answer for some minutes. "I thought I's ere t' look after farm, . . there's only one o' me!" he barked.

"That was the agreement Sam," Matt said, discerning the problem. "I'll be in the Black Pheasant at two. We'll have that drink," he turned and walked back to his car. Sam knew they'd be talking business.

Elaine packed some of her sausage rolls into a box. Adding a beef pasty 'still warm from the oven' on top. She cut off a large slice of chocolate cake, missing out the soft bit in the middle. First laying it on a plate, then into a bag. Stacking it all carefully into a carrier bag and sent Gina to fetch the beer she'd bought the day before as a thank you for Sam.

They heard Matt drive swiftly back into the yard and braced themselves for him coming in. "Did you find him?" He nodded

"How did you get on?" Gina asked with caution.

"He's employed to run the farm and there's only one of him," Matt announced firmly, repeating Sam's words.

"Come on," Elaine instructed, picking up the bag of provisions. Gina followed holding the beer.

"He's up in the top field," Matt directed.

Sam was tying the thicker saplings he'd cut into bundles, ready to drag over to his van parked inside the gate. He heard the women approaching and was in no mood for words.

Gina watched him dragging the bundles along by a rope. Seeing them catch on tussocks of grass across the uneven

field, it looked hard work. “Wouldn’t that be easier using a tractor?” she asked without thinking.
He stared at her “you av n’t got one,” he growled.
“Sam,” Elaine cut in. “We’ve brought you some lunch, . . and we’ve come to apologise for taking up your time.”
Sam stopped and looked at the pair of them, he wasn’t expecting that.
“Sorry,” Gina added.
He shuffled his feet uncomfortably. “I ast t’ finish ere first, a‘for I start summut else.”
Gina gave him her most endearing smile, “yes of course.”
They put their appeasement on the ground by his jacket and turned to walk back.
“Do you think we’re forgiven?” Elaine said, quietly under her breath. Gina nodded, having complete confidence in her mother’s chocolate cake.

In the pub Matt took charge. He bought two pints and walked over to a quiet seat in the corner, expecting Sam to follow. He got straight to the point, wanting Sam to organise the clearing out of the cottages. Instructing Sam, as his ‘farm manager’ to find and oversee men to do the job. If he knew a couple of handymen who’d give the cottages a quick whitewash inside, to get that done as well. Matt handed Sam a sealed envelope, “there’s two grand to get it started.”
Unaccustomed to being called a farm manager and given the authority to hire men, Sam began to appreciate his new position.
Next on Matt’s agenda - he asked Sam to give Gina the names of any trustworthy skilled tradesmen he knew. “I think that’s all,” Matt concluded. Then remembered she’d said they needed a tractor. “I’m not paying for a brand-

new one," he warned, leaving Sam to scout around for a descent sale offer.

With business over, Matt relaxed. He liked Sam's dry humour, listening to his tales, just as Sam was fascinated by Matt's travels. Matt finished his drink and got up to leave, telling Sam he'd be back in two weeks.
Sam zipped the envelope inside his jacket. He wouldn't stay much longer at the Pheasant, not with all that cash in his pocket. It was too soon to decide whether he'd misjudged the boss's girlfriend, but one thing for certain, . . . her mother was a great cook.

-

Gina carefully carried a tray upstairs, she'd quietly slipped down to the kitchen to make fresh coffee and toast. Planning to wake Matt gently with a kiss, repeating the Sunday mornings they'd enjoyed together before moving.
Matt was already awake, sitting up checking messages on his phone. He gave her a loving smile and continued to scroll knowing Vortorx was vying for his attention. He rarely switched off for long from his job.
Gina balanced the tray on a chair beside the bed, waiting for him to finish. He turned off his phone and gently tossed it to land on the clothes he'd left on the floor by the bed.
She handed him his coffee and put the plate of toast on top of the duvet between them to share. Snuggled up beside him, she begrudgingly asked the inevitable 'what time did he plan to leave?'
"Tomorrow morning. I've told Tom I'll be back in my office Tuesday." She beamed, knowing she'd have his company for another precious day, and asked how he'd liked to spend it.

Matt got out of bed and walked over to the window and stood absorbing the view. He wanted to walk around the farm, realise its size and take stock of what they'd bought. Getting some idea of what might need to be done. He pointed to a bank of grey clouds in the distance, hoping they weren't heading their way.
Gina joined him at the window. "We'd better get going, they could mean rain." She pulled on her clothes and went off to find a coat.
He waited for her at the backdoor eager to make a start.
"I'll write Mum a note to let her know where we've gone."
"Tell her we'll all have lunch later at the Kings Arms," he said, holding the door open, hinting impatience.

The fields hadn't looked so vast from the bedroom window, and despite walking for more than an hour, the wood didn't seem to be getting any closer. Gina suggested turning back, the dark clouds looked immanently threatening.
"It won't rain," Matt insisted, walking back along the lane. They were twenty yards from the barn when a streak of lightning lit the sky. Followed by a crack of thunder and hailstones the size of marbles roared to the ground. "Run!" They sheltered inside the barn. Trickles of rain ran from their hair into eyes, down faces and necks. "Won't rain!" she playfully scolded, being soaking wet.

Waiting for the clouds to pass, Gina thought of something she needed to ask. She wanted his opinion on whether to keep the open fire in the lounge. She lead him through to the wood store, loading their arms with logs to carry across to the house.

The rain dwindled to fine drizzle while they filled the hearth and log baskets. Matt looked at the state of his coat and all the mess, totally unimpressed.
Letting him shower first, gave her the opportunity to tidy.

Gina got into Matt's car and sat waiting.
"Oh, I've no need to come," Elaine excused, not wanting to play gooseberry.
"I've booked Sunday roast for the three of us Elaine," he said, refusing to budge until she accompanied him.
Becoming coy, Elaine gratefully accepted.
He stopped to let Gina out, before parking in the Kings Arms carpark. She wanted to nip across to the news agents to pick up Sunday papers and a couple of magazines for her mother.
Meals at the Kings Arms were always delicious, and Betty's Sunday roasts were not to be missed.

Back at the farmhouse Elaine took her magazines up to her room, intending to read them after a nap.
Gina lit the fire. They sprawled out along the big old comfortable settee Margery had left behind. Matt intended to read the papers, but spent more time watching the hypnotic flames as they flickered and danced, changing colours. He hadn't realised how relaxing a real fire could be.
Gina got up to put another log on the fire. "So, what do you think, is it worth all the mess?"
"Totally," he answered, no longer trying to stay awake.

- -

Suzy didn't work Wednesdays. Apart from getting up especially early to make Matt's breakfast, she actually

wanted to see him. She handed him a fresh mug of percolated coffee.
He was sitting opposite her at the kitchen table, clearly in a world of his own.
"Penny for them?" she offered.
"Yes," he answered, not listening to a word she'd said.
He'd arrived back at Squirrels Chase on Monday while she was at school, then spent the evening in his office upstairs, yesterday all day in his office at work, late home, back in his office at home, then went to bed.
"It's like living with a ghost."
"Yes," he said again . . . . . . "what ghost?"
"I know you're there but I hardly see you," she explained with a grin.
He laughed, getting the point. "It's just work."
She asked how they were getting on at the farm?
"Sorry Suze." He hadn't meant to leave her out, everything had snowballed - his job, buying the farm, selling his flat and moving. He perked up and reached for his phone intending to show her photos, but it rang. "I'll be in my office in forty minutes, we'll discuss it then," he instructed the caller before returning his phone to his pocket. "Sorry Suze, I have to go. We'll go out to dinner tonight when I get back. I'll show you the photos and tell you all about it, OK?" He grabbed his keys and left.
Suzy started to clear the table, beginning to look forward to their dinner date.

At five o'clock Matt rang, full of apologies. Confessing he'd be working late, too late to take her out.
"Are you standing me up?" she mocked.

The next morning, while he ate breakfast, Matt gave his phone to Suzy. She scrolled through looking at his photos, occasionally finding one for him to explain. Although she'd never predict he would buy a farm, she could see why he'd fallen in love with the place, the scenery was stunning.

"I'm flying up to Birmingham today, probably be back here next Wednesday." Matt had brought the Denmark trip forward, he and Tom would fly onwards from Birmingham. Another Vortorx counterpart had become unwell in the middle of a deal. Granzman had asked Matt to step in, wanting the deal complete.

She hadn't realised how often he worked away.

"Just part of the job," Matt said unfazed. He wasn't bothered about missing a weekend at the farm. If Denmark proved successful, he planned to take the following week off.

- -

"What did you think of them?" Rachel queried over the phone. She had been sending Suzy details of houses all week from her laptop. Picking two from what seemed the best, they decided to view a bungalow and a semi in a cul-de-sac near the school. "I'll make the appointments for Saturday morning," promising Suzy she wouldn't be late.

-

Rachel dropped a saccharin into her coffee and stirred it round, waiting for Suzy to give her opinion. They had viewed the properties and now were sitting in a café. Both places had been in Kirston, ideally situated for Suzy's job. The bungalow had been perfect, ticking every box Suzy had listed.

"It also had a garage," Rachel was keen to point out. The semi had been redecorated throughout, new carpets, new bathroom and sat back in the corner of the seemingly quiet cul-de-sac. Suzy remained non comital, she still needed time to think.

Back at Squirrels Chase, Suzy was spreading bread for their sandwiches while Rachel got on making the drinks. "Neither of them felt like home," Suzy confessed, not expecting Rachel to understand.
Rachel understood completely, she'd said right from the start Suzy should stay at Squirrels Chase. She thought for a moment. "So why don't you ask about buying this place?"
Suzy looked at her as if she was daft. "I can't afford it, not even with that extra money. Anyway, everyone wants the highest price. When this place is sold no doubt my brothers will be the same."
"Your 'well off' brothers!" Rachel scoffed.
"Matt will retire soon and Phil's got a young family now. I can't ask them to drop the price, it wouldn't be fair."
"Suzy, you own a third of it anyway. I dare say 'the higher the sale price - the higher the fees'. It wouldn't hurt to ask!" Rachel sensed she was sounding bossy and backed down, changing the subject. "Have you heard from Kate lately?"
"She phones occasionally." Suzy answered. Describing Kate as becoming quite her own person since being at Uni and living with Jefferson - no longer the 'little home bird'. She mentioned Kate's impending trip to America to spend Thanksgiving with Jefferson's family.
"Is she nervous?"
"Not a bit, she takes after her father - strong willed."
Rachel had to bite her tongue.

Once again, Suzy suspected there was something Kate wasn't mentioning, but knowing her daughter she'd reveal what it was in her own good time.
Rachel sat listing her busy work schedule for the week ahead, planning Halloween, Firework night and Christmas! Suzy walked with Rachel to the door, thanking her again for her help.
"Don't forget, ask!" Rachel insisted firmly. "If you don't, I will!"
"I will, . . . I will," Suzy called out as she waved goodbye.

In the evening she sat thinking about her day, turning over some of the things Rachel had said. Rachel was a good friend with worthy intentions, even when she spoke her mind. It was easy to live at Squirrels Chase with Matt around, especially with his financial help. The arrangement wouldn't last as Rachel had broached. She'd need to be organized for when he left and started to compose a list. With her finances written down, she had a clearer picture of the situation. It didn't take long to see how tight her circumstances could be, she may have to spend less on a house.

-

Suzy was hanging washing on the line in the back garden when she heard Matt's car arrive. Pegging out the last towel, she picked up the basket and went inside. She'd expected him back the day before. She could hear him clattering about upstairs and called out to ask if he wanted a drink. With no answer she went upstairs to ask, first knocking gently on his open door.

He'd emptied his case out onto the bed and was busy repacking. She stood in the doorway talking to him, "so where are you going this time?"
"Somerset," he said with a broad smile. "For a whole week, . . no," he corrected, "ten days." He took off his suit and threw it over a chair and put on a pair of casual trousers.
"Not jeans, Mr farmer?" She teased.
Amused, Matt opened a drawer, took out a pair of designer labelled jeans, showed them to her before putting them in the case. "Can you get these cleaned Suze," he said, turning round taking out two more suits from his wardrobe, adding them to the one he'd taken off, slung over the chair.
Watching him throw clothes into his case, she could see he was in a hurry. "Matt, can I ask you something?"
"What's that?" he said, pulling a blue cashmere sweater over his head.
"What's the lowest price you and Phil would accept for Squirrels Chase?"
He pulled the jumper down over his body and each sleeve by the cuff, ... and stared at her.
"I've had a bit of luck, a win on those bonds I bought."
He stopped packing, she could almost hear his mind working. "If you're serious, I'll have to talk to Phil."
"I know," she turned away, her emotions beginning to build stifling her words. "I'll leave you to pack, give my regards to Gina." Suzy walked back downstairs, her heart thumping so hard, he must have heard it. No matter, it was done. Somehow she'd found the courage to ask, what would be . . . would be.

She stayed in the kitchen, listening to Matt loading his car. He'd gone up and down the stairs a few times, finally

coming into the kitchen to find her. "I'm off now," he said smiling.
She could feel his happiness. "Safe journeys," she called as he closed the door.

Matt started his car, he knew the journey well. It should take him about four hours, although he'd learned from experience to stop midway for a break. Suzy's question had come as a complete surprise. He'd felt her tension, knotting his stomach, such being the affinity they'd always shared. Squirrels Chase had become her home again, but he couldn't see how she could afford it. Richard would make sure she never got a penny extra out of him. This was a big ask.
His high salary would pay off their mortgage, but buying the farm had stripped his considerable assets. Hypothetically he'd earmarked his share of Squirrels Chase to replenish savings, necessary for his new life after Vortorx.
Bored on the plane, he'd trolled through tractor and farm machinery sales. Naive of such an expenditure, he'd not envisaged spending that much or so soon. The farm was rinsing through his cash.

There'd be no switching off in Somerset with this niggling at the back of his mind. He pulled over into a layby, speaking instructions to the internal phone in his car. "Mrs Finnis, could you tell my brother I'll be with him within the hour. An important matter I need to discuss." He ended the call, not giving her time to reply. A gap appeared in the traffic allowing him to get back on the road. He began to head for Phil's office, feeling his tension begin to ease.

Running Suzy's request past Phil would resolve the issue. He may play the fool, but without exception Phil remained an astute accountant.

Matt approached Mrs Finnis's desk with a smile designed to charm. His sparkling eyes melting her officious countenance. "I apologise for any reschedule, is Phillip free?"

Mrs Finnis sprang up to announce his arrival. Matt opened the door for her. "Thank you Mrs Finnis," treating her to another warm smile.

"Matt!" Phil rose to greet him. "Tea! Mrs Finnis, and sandwiches if there's any going."

"Yes of course," she said in a girlie voice, closing the door.

"What do you do to her?"

"Compared to the businessmen I deal with, she's a pussycat."

"What's up?" Phil looked concerned.

Matt apologised for the drama, explaining his visit. "Your clients?" not wanting to intrude.

Phil pointed to the time on his desk clock, "it's virtually my lunch hour."

Matt rushed over to relieve Mrs Finnis of the heavy laden tray she'd begun to carry into Phil's office. "Thank you Mrs Finnis," flashing his eyes at her with another smile, inflicting a deep blush.

Phil shook his head, smiling with disbelief.

The brothers chatted, discussing recent happenings in their lives, everything apart from their sister's request.

"Still set on leaving Vortorx?" Phil quizzed.

"I'm counting the days."

Phil tutted, still disapproving of Matt's decision.

Their minds turned to Suzy's question. Phil switched on his laptop, tapping in information. They assessed the current value of Squirrels Chase, took off surmised estate agent fees, legal expenses and divided the total by three. Matt looked at the figure.
"Or," Phil began another sum. "The highest price commands the highest fees etc. We could lower the price, use a solicitor to directly handle the payments of our share, she owns a third of it anyway." Phil showed Matt two more lower calculations, depending on which house price they decided to accept.
"So what shall we do?" Matt asked.
"Whoa brother! You're the eldest, this decision is yours," Phil insisted.
Matt looked at the sets of figures. Phil was right, it seemed stupid to pay out high fees, but their own personal settlement could be up to forty grand less. He'd have to think about it - thirty grand was a tractor! He faced Phil "how do you feel about this, . . honestly?"
Phil turned the silver framed photo on his desk around, it was of Julia and Neville laughing. "Matt, look at this pair of tinkers, I feel I'm already the richest man in town. I'll get some accurate figures and send them on to you."

Matt stood up to leave "thanks Phil, I'll be in touch." He got back into his car, texting Gina before leaving the carpark, hoping to be home before evening.

Driving along motorways in darkness was one thing, driving along narrow unlit country roads another! Startled creatures leapt into hedges, others froze, causing brakes to be suddenly applied to allow escape.

He arrived frazzled from concentration, acknowledging the extra time and vigilance required. Now he understood why many countryside dwelling commuters travelled by train.

-

Matt rose late in the morning, the previous week and long drive back had taken its toll. He sat at the kitchen table checking emails on his laptop while Gina fussed around making his coffee.

Elaine was chopping vegetables on a board at the other end. She'd conquered the Raeburn and no longer considered it a foe.

"What are you making?" Gina asked, watching the mound of vegetables grow.

"Beef casserole or beef stew, depending on whether we want dumplings."

Matt heard and looked up from his laptop, "dumplings?"

"Beef stew," Elaine acknowledged with a broad smile, wondering how he managed to eat like a horse without ever gaining any weight. She picked up the cast iron casserole dish with both hands to carry to the Raeburn, and not wanting to put the heavy pot down, asked Gina to open the oven door. A waft of heat escaped, warming the kitchen further. With the main course organised, Elaine started to tidy the kitchen, feeling ready for a cup of tea and a sit down.

While Matt had been away, Gina had begun to think about the changes they could make to improve the farmhouse interior. She'd sketched a few floorplans to illustrate her ideas. Biding her time, she'd wait for the right moment to present her suggestions for his approval.

She was itching to see what progress Sam's men had made inside the cottages, but not wanting to appear interfering had kept her distance.

Elaine had been keeping the workmen happy with regular visits. Supplying them with tea and cake, reporting back snippets of development.

"I'm going to do a couple of hours work. I'll take this up to one of the spare bedrooms," Matt proposed, closing his laptop, resigning himself to the task. Once he'd dispatched his reports, time would be his own.

Gina said she was going to take a bath while Matt was working. She could accompany him to the cottages later, knowing he'd want to see how Sam had got on. She went up to the bathroom, collecting her perfumed bath oil on the way.

Matt was already having a shower, standing under the old fashioned showerhead that protruded over the bath. "Just thought I'd nip in first," he confessed, knowing she'd be hours soaking. Wearing her bathrobe, she sat on the laundry basket chatting, waiting for him to finish. She started to take out her earrings to put in her pocket. They were favourites, the very first present Matt had bought for her.

He switched off the shower and stepped out, grabbing a towel to wrap around.

"Oh no!" she gasped, feeling an earring slip through her fingers and fall to the floor. "Matt don't move, or you'll tread on it!" Unable to see it, she got down on all fours, patting the mat gently with her hands. "Thank goodness," she said, finding it caught in the pile of the bathmat not far from his toes.

He held out a hand to help her up, letting his towel slip to the floor. “Course,” he said, with a mischievous grin “while you’re down there . . ”

In the afternoon, curious to see how Sam was handling the job, Matt mentioned he was going over to the cottages.

“I’ll come with you,” Gina offered, anxious to see inside for herself.

Walking across the yard, Matt stopped to answer his phone. “Thanks Phil, I’ll take a look and let you know what I decide. Give my regards to Mrs Finnis,” he chuckled, ending the call.

“Your brother?” Gina queried, recognising his secretary’s name.

“Yes,” Matt acknowledged, disclosing his recent visit due to Suzy wanting to buy Squirrels Chase.

“Is it down to you?” Gina asked innocently.

Before he could explain Phil’s reluctance, Merlin’s face suddenly came to mind. Matt shuddered, recalling the vision of the small creature looking deep into his eyes. ‘Will she stay? it will depend on you’ he’d said before vanishing. “Oh my God!”

“What is it?”

“Nothing,” Matt said “just something I’d forgotten.”

“Important?”

“No,” he denied, feeling the knot in his stomach return.

It hadn’t taken long to find four strong men when Bill, the Pheasant’s landlord had put out the word, especially as Sam was offering wages in cash.

“Eh up Sam, you got company,” Charlie called across. They peered out of the window. “It’s Boss,” Sam said, going downstairs to meet them at the door.

A large skip stood outside the first cottage almost full. Gina’s eyes wandered across its contents of smashed furniture, wondering if anything had been worth saving. “All damp,” Sam insisted, seeing her look.

While Sam chatted to Matt at the door, Gina slipped inside. She climbed the steep narrow wooden stairs and stepped into the first room off the small landing for a look around.

“Ow do,” the young lad smiled, sweeping rubbish towards the heap in the middle of the bare wooden floor. His sweeping had filled the air with dust. He stopped for a minute to let it settle, “you gonna live ere?”

“Yes, for a while,” Gina replied with a smile and left him shovelling the rubbish into a bucket. The next room had been completely emptied and also the small bathroom.

“Bye,” she called, putting her head around the door before going back downstairs.

Matt and Sam were deep in conversation when she joined them in the small kitchen. “Happy?” Matt asked.

“Oh yes, thank you Sam,” she declared impressed.

“We’ll get out of your way,” Matt said, escorting her out of the cottage. “I’ll speak to you Monday.”

“Right O,” Sam acknowledge.

“Afternoon lads,” Matt greeted, as they passed two young men heaving an old mattress onto the skip.

Elaine assembled four bucket sized mugs onto a tray for the workmen’s tea. “Was Sam with them?” she asked, ready to add another. Gina nodded.

Elaine put five foil wrapped chocolate biscuits on the tray. "They're doing really well aren't they? Charlie said they should start painting next week, after Mick's been in to check the electrics. Mick's his brother - an electrician."
Gina stared at her mother "do you know all their names?"
"I do," Elaine announced smugly, "I've been speaking to them all week."
Declining Matt's offer of help, Elaine carried the tray. A little heavy, but delivering it gave her the opportunity to check their progress. Usually she never got far, one of the men would see her coming and come out to collect the tray.
"Oo was that?" Charlie asked, carrying the bucket of rubbish down the stairs.
"Boss's girlfriend," Sam answered following behind.
"Cor, she's landed on er feet."
Dave had just taken the tray from Elaine at the door, it was too late, she'd overheard.
"Sam," Elaine beckoned from the doorway, "a word!" She waited for him to join her, giving the matter reverence. "Mathew Chapman and my daughter bought Ashwood Farm together!" She turned and walked back to the house, satisfied she'd nipped that concept in the bud.

- -

Robert Dexter stood in the old dairy studying the plans. He turned over the main drawing, reading the architects instructions and notes. The high ceilinged building had remained untouched, left in its original state apart from gaps where equipment had been removed. The whitewashed walls and big white tiles no longer gleamed in the obsolete building.

Elaine couldn't picture the new rooms from the plan. He turned the plan around, matching it to the shape of the structure. Getting Matt and Gina to hold a tape measure, Robert Dexter illustrated the position of new walls on the concrete floor with chalk. "Do you want to make any changes?" he asked.

Finally making some sense of the plan, Elaine wanted her bedroom larger and requested a conservatory built the length of the building at the back. He made a note of her new instructions, adding them underneath the original ones on the back of the plan.

"Presuming we accept to your estimate, when could you start?" Elaine asked with optimism.

Robert Dexter rubbed his chin with a hand, thinking.

"Won't be before Christmas, end of January . . maybe?"

"Goodness!" Elaine wasn't expecting him to say tomorrow, but January?

Gina's hopes were dashed to the floor, she didn't bother to ask about the farmhouse.

"Can I take this?" he said, rolling up the plan.

"I'll get a copy sent to you," Gina sighed, trying to hide her disappointment.

Elaine walked with Mr Dexter to the outer door, bidding him goodbye on their behalf.

Matt put his arm around Gina's shoulder, dismissing her subdued mood. "His isn't the only building company in Somerset."

"You're right," she agreed, cheering up. Matt only had two more days left at the farm and she was determined to make them enjoyable.

-

Noticing a different vehicle outside the cottages, Gina went over to investigate, wondering if it belonged to the electrician. She walked over to the first cottage, entering through the open backdoor.

"Afternoon," a voice said from behind a door under the stairs.

She followed the sound to a man knelt down with his head in a cupboard, checking the meter box inside. "You must be Mick the electrician."

"I am," he mused, head down removing fuses, checking and putting them back.

Gina stood behind watching, curious to see his face. "Is everything in there OK?"

"It all looks good to me," he said, reversing to stand up. "Give me a call when the other one's ready, and I'll come back."

"I don't suppose you know of a reliable builder who could start yesterday?"

Mick laughed, "the lads seem to be getting on OK, they've turned this place round in a few weeks."

Gina clarified, she wasn't talking about the cottages and told him about Robert Dexter's visit. She tried to explain what they wanted, but ended up confusing him and herself.

"Show me," he chuckled, switching off a torch to put back in his toolbox.

She lead him to the dairy, leaving the big doors open for light.

"Did you say you had plans?"

Gina defined their requirements, virtually repeating the same conversation she'd had with Robert Dexter.

Mick looked around "recon you could do this job yourselves, easy, . . . with the right men." She was quick to admit she wouldn't know where to start, but he could tell she was tempted.

"Let me have a word with Pete Bishop, see if he'd be interested in giving you a hand."

While the men stopped for lunch, Sam insisted on giving Gina a guided tour around the finished cottage. The fresh smell of paint superseded its previous one of damp. Sam waited for an opinion, hoping for praise.
"It's wonderful Sam, absolutely wonderful."
"a coupla days t' dry out," he added confidently, now he knew she was pleased.
She'd earmarked this slightly smaller 'two up, two down' for her mother. The galley kitchen wasn't big enough to swing a cat. A big compromise after the large farmhouse kitchen, but at least it wouldn't be forever.

-

On Thursday morning a new dark grey transit pulled up outside the farmhouse. Two men got out, one waited to assist the third. The first chap walked up to the front door and knocked. "Mick said you wanted to speak to m' dad." Over his shoulder, Gina saw an older guy get slowly out of the van and given a walking stick. She went over to welcome, not wanting him to walk further than necessary.
"Pete Bishop," he greeted. "Joe n' Carl, my boys." A single nod given at their names.
"Gina Jackman, pleased to meet you," she smiled, shaking Mr Bishop senior's hand.
"Mick said you've got a barn to convert?"
"A dairy," she corrected, pointing them in its direction, before going back indoors to collect the plans.

Mick had phoned, telling Pete the job was 'going begging', if he was willing to guide Mrs Chapman through the building process. With the winter weather soon to break, months of inside work could not be dismissed lightly. Incapacitated by his knee made this opportunity appealing, however it was a huge commitment.

Inside the building, Gina found Pete leaning on his stick looking up at the beams in the roof. His sons walked about weighing up the strength of outer walls. She handed over the plans for him to study and offered refreshments.
"Three teas, strong with sugar," Joe ordered without looking round, concentrating on an old wooden beam supporting brickwork above a door.
She estimated Peter Bishop to be in his late fifties. Weathered hands and his complexion revealed years of outside manual work. "An accident?" she probed, being nosey.
"Waiting for a new knee operation," Joe answered. "Arthritis, . . . goes with the trade, unfortunately."
Trying to hide her ignorance hadn't worked, "bricklaying, we're bricklayers."
It was freezing cold in the dairy, the open doors making it raw. Gina shivered, and invited them back to the farmhouse for their tea and to get warm.

In the kitchen, Pete unzipped his jacket and sat at the table. Appreciating the warmth and hot beverage. He unravelled the plans to contemplate once more.

"I'll let you know next week," he said rising to go, taking the plans with him.
Having said goodbye, Gina watched them drive out of the yard. She wasn't certain if Peter Bishop was going home to think about taking on the job, or about helping her to do it.

-

"I'm not sure," Elaine said, trying to make up her mind between beige or speckled beige in the carpet shop. Then changed her mind completely and chose the textured patterned one instead.

They moved on to Nolan's Department Store.
Sitting in their café Elaine read through her shopping list, ticking off items. "I ought to name my cottage 'Cheap 'n Cheerful'," she announced, having scooped most of the bargains in Nolan's sale.

Gina sat opposite, staring into her coffee cup, clearly with something on her mind. Matt had left eight days ago, his work superseding but she was used to that.
"Is there something bothering you?" Elaine asked, trying to prompt conversation.
Gina let out a slow sigh, "I'm . . ."
"Bored," Elaine added bluntly.
"No," Gina petitioned. "I miss being academically useful." She'd been an eminent PA, used to tight schedules and paving the way for her boss's successful achievements. She'd had no qualms about leaving her job, but was beginning to need something to get her academic teeth into.
"I expect something will turn up," Elaine smiled, and suggested a last look around Ilminster before they drove home.

- -

Mick put two boxes of fresh eggs on his mother's worktop in the kitchen. He usually called in to see her on Saturdays if he was working in the district.
"What were you doing up at the farm shop?" his younger brother Charlie asked, reading 'Hazlehurst Farm, Fresh Quality Produce,' emblazoned across the bag the eggs were in.
"P. A .T testing," Mick answered. "Where's Mum?"
"She's up the garden, nattering to our neighbour."

Mick looked out of the window. Sure enough, in the back garden Mrs Smith was leaning on the fence between, chatting to their mother. "Has she been out there long?"
"Hours," Charlie mocked, studying the screen on his phone.
"When do you recon that other cottage will be ready?" Mick asked, planning his jobs ahead.
"Sometime next week. On Monday, Sam wants me and Dave to start painting the inside. Been a handy little job."
"What really would be handy," Mick suggested, "would be Pete Bishop running that dairy conversion. I could do with the wiring job."
"And the farmhouse," Charlie added casually. "That's why they're having both cottages done up, to live in while the refurbishing work's being done."
Mick hadn't realised the significance of the cottages, he'd assumed they were for holiday let. That information changed the whole picture, casting an optimistic light on the subject of more work.
They heard their mother coming up the path. "She'll blame Mrs Smith for gasbagging, you watch," Charlie said with a grin.
"That blessed woman can jaw the hind leg off a donkey!" she grumbled, coming through the backdoor.
Mick laughed. "Mum, there's some eggs for you in that bag. I can't stop, got to see a man about a job."

- -

During their last business trip in Denmark, Matt encouraged Tom to take the reins of two important board meetings. Apart from dispensing the occasional verbal nudge, he'd witnessed Tom's confidence building.

Matt resumed his status at Weib-Losugens. His premise, to check Granzman's investment. Vortorx acquired the

Weib-Losugens company eighteen months before, relocating it to bigger premises in Mainz.

Daunted by the prospect of taking over Matt's position, Tom appreciated every opportunity to learn. Observing Matt address fellow board members with polite acumen, listening and skilfully assessing their individual worth around the boardroom table. His prestigious business experience had made him an excellent teacher.

Sitting in a first class compartment travelling back from Mainz to Frankfurt, Tom closed his eyes for a moment listening to the rhythmic click clack, clickety clack of train wheels. With another successful trip almost over, they could begin to relax. Previously Matt kept his personal life and familiarity at a respectful professional distance. Lately, spending more time together, he was becoming a friend and occasionally revealed his humorous side.

Through the train window Matt observed the German countryside passing by. Studying farms and their fields with new interest. Catching Tom watching him, Matt smiled "I'm looking for profitable ideas for our farm." Being told anything connected with slaughter was out of the question, Tom began to make alternative light hearted suggestions. "A theme park, . . music festivals, . . glamping, . . a nudist camping-site for buxom wenches," making Matt laugh. "You could have a couple of phone masts," he suggested with more sense.
Matt stopped chuckling, that was a good idea. Or they could have one of those, seeing a line of wind turbines in the distance.

Tom's thoughts turned homeward, Carrie had texted. She would be back at Heathrow tomorrow morning, and with luck they'd have the whole weekend together.

Matt and Tom boarded a plane at Frankfurt Airport, the flight back to Heathrow being almost the last leg of their journey home. A long day of travelling.
Matt texted Suzy, forewarning her of his arrival. This trip had allowed him to temporary push her request to the back of his mind. The business side of him demanded a sensible price for Squirrels Chase, but in his heart knew such a deal would be impossible. Fairness had nothing to do with it, besides she'd know one way or another it had been his decision alone.

Late afternoon in winter darkness, Matt pulled into Squirrels Chase. He sat in his car phoning Gina, telling her he was back and would be with her tomorrow. She could hear the tiredness in his voice, and was relieved he wasn't going to attempt driving. Tomorrow she'd be like a cat on hot bricks, unable to settle knowing he was on his way.

Aware of his fatigue, Matt picked up his case and made his way inside. Used to travelling he could sleep anywhere, on a plane, hotels, his flat, their farm, but there was something especially comforting about Squirrels Chase. A safe feeling of home, no wonder Suzy didn't want to leave.

Remembering her ghost comparison, he endeavoured to stay awake and converse. He'd eaten and had a hot drink before a wave of tiredness swept over him. He sank back into the soft armchair and closed his eyes.
Suzy smiled, she'd appreciated his effort and understood how exhausted he must of been. Deepening her voice, she teased "is anybody there?" holding out her hands pretending to be a 'medium'. Matt slept on.

“Come on big brother, time for bed,” and shook his arm to wake him.

-

Suzy had left for work when Matt woke up. Drinking his coffee, he sat in the kitchen mulling over his morning’s tasks before he could head for Somerset. Pulling rank, he’d delegated Tom to write and submit the two conclusive reports expected from their trips.
He began loading his car. Across the backseat lay the bouquet of flowers he’d bought at the airport for Gina. He carried them into the kitchen and laid them on the worktop for Suzy. He wasn’t asleep when she played her ‘medium’ joke, just resting his eyes. He chuckled remembering her mischief, writing a note to add to the flowers

from your sleeping ghost
- back next Monday
Matt x

He closed the door, got into his car and headed for Phil’s office. Approaching Kirston, Matt spotted a florist shop and managed to park outside. He went in to buy more flowers for Gina, also picking up a small bunch for Elaine. Back in his car he tried to get hold of Phil, but being unsuccessful had to speak to Mrs Finnis.
“Busy! all day!” she snapped curtly.
Regardless, Matt sent Phil a text warning him he was on his way. Nothing could dampen his good mood, not even the officious Mrs Finnis.

Before locking his car, he took out the small bunch of flowers, bribery for madam Finnis. By sheer luck when he arrived, she was about to enter Phil’s office with his

morning coffee. "Let me take that," Matt smiled taking the small tray. "For you," thrusting the flowers at her, causing fluster. He knocked on Phil's door and marched in before she could stop him.
"Matt?" Phil said surprised.
"I did try to phone you, and texted," he clarified firmly.
"Ah, sorry, my fault." Phil guessed what Matt was being too polite to mention. "I gave strict instructions of 'no disturbances', . . she's good isn't she?" he grinned.
Matt stared, remaining silent.
"So what figure did you decide on?"
Matt confessed confound perplexity. Both brothers hadn't achieved their successful financial position without being astute with money.
"We'll adjudicate," Phil suggested, bringing up the page on his screen. "I still think of Squirrels Chase as Mum's house."
The minute Phil mentioned their mother, Matt pictured her, memorising her soft smile. What would she think of his decision? The solution became instantly clear. "Would you be agreeable to that?" Matt leant forward, pointing to the lowest sum . . . "honestly?"
Phil thought for a moment, then rounded up the figure to form an even number. "Recon I'd be happy with that. . . and she is our sister," he said, looking at Matt, waiting for his reaction.
Matt wrote the new figure down. "That's what I'll tell her, . . . if you're completely certain."
"I'm positive," Phil reiterated.
"Thanks Phil." Matt gave a sigh of relief, grateful they'd agreed a figure. Now he could relax and drive on to Somerset.

- -

Walking back from the bathroom, Matt could hear Gina talking in their bedroom and presumed she was using her phone.
"And don't think you'll be staying there," she dictated firmly, as he opened the door.
"Who are you talking to?"
"Him, Incey Wincey," she said, pointing to a huge black spider on the wall above their bed.
Impressed, he watched her encase its long legs under a glass tumbler, slipping a card beneath trapping it inside.
"Mum and I never had a man around happy to deal with these eight legged beasties," she said, making her way to the window, ready to release it to free fall to the ground outside.
Matt shuddered, he wasn't sure they had 'that man' now.
"How do you deal with them?"
"Don't ask," he said, "let's just say they don't like deodorant spray."
"Matt! Poor spiders!"
"Any other undisclosed skills you'd like to tell me about," he teased.
"Ah, well there is something I'd like us to discuss." She repeated Mick's suggestion about the dairy conversion.
"I'll know more when Mr Bishop gets back to me. I might phone him later, he's still got our plans."

"Tea, anyone?" Elaine offered, filling the kettle. "I'm taking one over to Mick, he's fitting new wall heaters in my cottage. Elaine thought aloud "carpets fitted Tuesday, . .hmm, I could be in there by the end of next week."

Matt waited for her to return before he walked over to speak to Mick, wanting to hear Peter Bishop's credentials for himself.

Gina guessed where he was going. She wondered what Mick would say and what Matt would make of it.
Sitting with Gina in the lounge, Elaine was a step ahead of both of them. "He'll say Pete Bishop is the finest bricklayer he knows, can read plans to the point of . . . 'if an architect has made a cock up, he'll spot it and tell him.' Whether you want a garden wall, extension or a house built, he's the best man to do it. I asked him earlier, when I took over his tea."
Bemused, Gina stared at her mother.

Matt returned, "the electrician's going to phone him. If Mr Bishop can get here early Monday morning, I'll stay to see him."

-

On Monday morning at eight o'clock, Peter Bishop and his son Joe joined Matt and Gina at their kitchen table. Elaine busied herself in the background making tea.
"I'll be straight. Calculating the cost of any brickwork - no problem, but other tradesman would have to list their own material needs and supply costs. . . and I'm not one to sit at a computer." Peter Bishop sat back having said his piece.

Anticipating this conversation, Gina was prepared. First admitting she knew nothing of the building trade and would need total guidance. "Mr Bishop, if you know the tradespeople we should use and the schedule of work, I'd happily source the materials if you tell me 'what' and 'where from'. I've spent most of my working life in front of a screen." She got up to help with the refreshments, giving him more time to think.

"You could ask Neil to come down and do the drains," Joe prompted his father.

Peter Bishop was well aware of his options and the opportunity to give men work, his own boys included. He'd never taken on the actual running of a whole job before, or worked in conjunction with anyone else, . . especially a stranger, a woman at that. It was a massive responsibility.

Gina put down a steaming hot mug of tea in front of him, she could see he was under pressure. "I'd be happy to give it a try," she said with an encouraging smile "with your help."

Everyone sat in silence, waiting for his response. He sat deadpan faced giving nothing away.

"Have a think about it Mr Bishop. You can always let us know," Elaine said, giving the man a chance to escape. He struggled to get up, leaning on the table to rise. Joe handed him his walking stick realising they were about to go. Gina got up to open the backdoor.

They walked, Joe helping his father slowly negotiate the step down.

"Take care Mr Bishop," Gina said kindly, about to close the door.

Peter Bishop walked a few paces, stopped and turned around. "OK, I'll do it, . . . I'll be in touch."

"Thank you," she said shutting the door. "Oh my goodness," Gina beamed with excitement. "He's going to take on the job!"

- -

Suzy came out of Kirston's dry cleaners holding two of Matt's suits. They were awkward to carry, given the long length of see-through plastic covering and sharp edged wire coat hangers. She stopped to fold them over her arm.

"Miss!" "Miss!" "Mrs Martin!" "Miss!" Four young girls from Kirston College shouted across. Waving frantically from the opposite side of the road, having recognized her. Passers-by looked up to identify the commotion.
"They bovvering you Miss?" Alan White appeared behind her, hands in pockets of his scruffy leather jacket.
"No, they're just saying hello," emitting a smile.
"That's alright then." He looked across at the girls, giving them a menacing stare and went on his way.
Suzy watched him walk off, each shoulder rocking back and forth with his thuggish gate. Alan was well known at school for his troublesome behaviour, no one crossed him and pupils gave him a wide birth. Alan's home life was dire, his violent father had a quick temper. Suzy walked back to her car thinking about Alan, touched by his unexpected thoughtfulness. What chance in life did the likes of Alan have, she conceded sadly. Yet was grateful not to have the job or responsibility of teaching him.

- -

Matt put down the phone and leant back in his chair. He'd spent the last hour going over figures, totals and new company proposals with Harvey Granzman. If there'd been any concerns, he knew Granzman would of been on the premises at dawn. With no immediate deadlines or consignment dates to complete, he was considering leaving his office early. Working closely with Tom and delegating more of his workload Tom's way manifested benefits.

Next on his agenda was a phone call to Suzy. It was about time he amended his promise of dinner. Also, it would be a good opportunity to present the figure he and Phil had agreed.
"Are you sure? Tonight? Really really really sure? Not going to change your mind again?"

"There's no need to rub it in," Matt laughed "shall I book it, or you?"
She left it up to him, wanting a surprise. The ironing had no chance of getting done this afternoon, she went upstairs to wash her hair.

Matt hadn't been to The Olive Grove before. He'd overheard Caroline recommending it to a colleague, and being just outside Kirston wasn't too far to go. It turned out to be more smart Bistro than posh a' la carte restaurant. Matt wasn't bothered, so long as they served a decent steak he was happy.

"We haven't done this for ages," Suzy said, sounding like part of a couple. A lot of water had run under the bridge of life since.

He waited until they were eating their sweet before he produced the figure. Written on the back of one of his business cards he'd happened to have in his pocket at the time. "Suze, what do you think of this, could you manage it?"

She read it twice before it sunk in. "Yes, . . that's so kind, more than kind, it's extremely generous," her eyes began to fill. "Are you and Phil sure, really really really sure?"

"Oh don't start that again," Matt laughed. "Yes, for you our sister, we're both quite sure."

"Oh God, look at me," her nose ran, happy tears rolled down her face tinged black with mascara. "I'm . . so . . grateful," she said in between sniffs, trying to locate a tissue.

Matt handed her his handkerchief, knowing for sure he and Phil had made the right decision. "I'll get Mr Hobbs

to sort out the legal arrangements. It shouldn't take him long, he's very good."
Extremely late in the evening, but nevertheless she had to tell someone. Suzy texted Rachel 'I'm going to buy Squirrels Chase.'

- -

Tom knocked on Matt's office door, walked in and placed two folders on his desk. "I've finished those," he said smiling happily.
Not warranting personal delivery, Matt waited for an explanation.
"Actually, I've come to remind you about my holiday. Carrie and I are going to spend Thanksgiving with her family at their other house in America. Ten whole days away," Tom added cheerfully.
"Thanks for the reminder, enjoy," Matt acknowledged with a smile as Tom left his office. Inside he groaned, he'd got used to having Tom at hand. Ten days away . . his competency would be sorely missed.

- -

Rachel phoned the minute she had a free moment. Thrilled for Suzy and pleased with herself for persuading her to ask. "Didn't I say that's where you should stay?" She'd known from the very first moment of walking into Squirrels Chase, feeling its atmospheric warmth, comfort and safety. "Come and stay with me this weekend, we'll celebrate. It will give me an excuse to get out of this place."
Suzy agreed, sensing an underlining in her tone.

-

Arriving home Friday evening, Rachel got out of her car at the same time as Suzy turned up. Every night she'd been coming home late. At present, staffing levels at work were in shambles. The manager was away attending a conference in London, the undermanager, a chef, two waitresses and two of the hotel's cleaners were all off sick with heavy colds or flu. As well as her own work Rachel had been helping Lesley, the poor woman suddenly thrust into the deputy manager's job.

Later, eating their supper from trays balanced on laps, Rachel opened a bottle of red wine.
"Is this the same one you bought up to my place?" Suzy inquired, remembering its rich bodied taste and recalling waking up late with a thick head the next morning.
Rachel nodded, "I haven't had a day off for ages," airing her grievances of working nonstop. The wine helping her grumbles to flow, getting them off her chest and forgotten by morning.

Relaxed, enjoying a late breakfast together, Suzy rejected Rachel's suggestion to browse around the shops. Not a difficult decision to make with the rain pelting against the windows. She asked how Rachel normally spent her Saturdays.
If she wasn't working or catching up with chores, generally she popped in to see Elsie. Spending the afternoon with her, passing the time chatting and drinking tea.
They planned a stress-free day. Proposing the afternoon with Elsie, and stopping off to get fish and chips on the way back. Then watching a 'chick flick' film on the TV in the evening. Sorted!

Elsie's blue eyes sparkled with delight, having an extra visitor to talk to. A little more frail since Suzy's last visit, but her wit remained as sharp as ever.
Talking about her job at the school, sparked everyone's school time memories, filling the afternoon with laughter.
Rachel washed up the tea things, leaving Suzy to say goodbye.
"He wasn't worth the heartache, my duck," Elsie said softly, giving Suzy a hug before saying good bye.
"Bye, ducks," Elsie called as Rachel closed her front door.
"She's such a sweetie," Suzy complemented, getting back into Rachel's car.

Rachel's phone beeped. "I'm going to ignore that," she said about to start the engine, but then it started to ring.
"Might be important," Suzy coaxed.
"I've no idea where it is!" Rachel answered exasperated.
"Oh, wait a minute." She tipped out her handbag into her lap and groaned. "Sorry Lesley, I've got it. I'll drop it in to you now." Rachel picked out a key labelled 'storeroom 4' from the contents in her lap. Yesterday evening she'd been in such a rush knowing she was late, while hanging up the keys had missed one.
"I'm sorry Suzy, I'll have to drop this key off. It shouldn't take long. I swear the Bricknell Lodge has taken over my life!" She parked outside the main entrance and ran inside, telling Suzy to follow rather than freeze to death outside in her car.

Once the engine stopped, the temperature soon plummeted. Suzy got out and walked into Reception, catching sight of Rachel disappearing down a corridor with a member of staff. Keeping out of the way, she

meandered over to a noticeboard on a wall, idly reading the posters.
"Hello Suzy."
She spun round, recognising the voice "Richard!"
"I saw you come in. I'm with that birthday party down there." He pointed down a corridor towards the distant sound of disco music.
She could feel his eyes taking in her appearance and smiled nervously. He stood relaxed, wearing a jacket over casual clothes.
"Have you heard from the estate agents?" she asked.
"I phoned them a while back. They fobbed me off with a cock-an-bull story about a property chain. I only accepted that price because they assured me there wasn't one. I'll phone them again and sort it out."
"Yes please. I'd like to be able to buy a house," she said, giving nothing away.
"You OK?" he seemed genuinely interested.
Suzy looked down nervously, unsure what to say.
"I'd better get back." He turned and walked away.
Rachel returned, out of breath from hurrying back. "Who was that?"
"Richard."
"No! Suzy, I'm so sorry. Let's get out of here."
"It's fine, I'm OK," Suzy insisted. "Fish and chips?"
"Definitely, on our way now." Rachel started her car, switching the heater full on.

- -

Wrapped up in her warmest coat, Gina watched Joe and Carl bang in wooden pegs, marking out positions for walls and drains. Meticulously double checking their measurements against the plan, under their father's scrutiny. Pete Bishop explained the co-ordination. Fascinated, Gina absorbed every word. They left the boys with the plan to finish marking levels.

In the farmhouse kitchen, Pete sat at the table giving Gina the information she'd need to submit to the council. He was surprised how quickly she picked things up, needing only to have things explained once.

"Homework?" Elaine asked, having observed Gina writing in a notebook. Gina smiled, this building project was just what she needed. Learning something completely new and quite possibly, she'd found her niche.

- -

"It could be your Christmas present," Suzy justified, trying to persuade Kate to accept money towards their air fare.

"Mum, we don't need it, truthfully. Jefferson's parents paid for our tickets months ago. Dad's already sent us spending money," slipping in casually he phoned her most weekends.

"Oh," Suzy said wounded, she hadn't realised Richard knew they were going. She was pleased they'd resolved their differences. Kate had always been a Daddy's - girl. Shamefully, Suzy felt a little left out and a teensy bit uncomfortable, not wanting Richard knowing her personal business through Kate.

"We'll come and see you when we get back," Kate promised.

Looking forward to that, Suzy wished them a fabulous time before finally saying good bye.

-

Recently her car had been making strange noises and this morning refused to start. There was only one thing for it, . . she phoned George.

No, he didn't know anything about cars, but he knew a man who did. "Are you stuck Lass?" he asked kindly. Already late and starting to panic, Suzy admitted she was. Twenty minutes later George dropped her off at the school gate, promising he'd get Derek from the garage to look at her car.

At her desk in the lab storeroom, Suzy was checking the equipment ledger. She noticed several test-tube breakages recorded.
"The boys in year seven," Linda admitted. "Rather enthusiastic fizzing eruptions," not forgetting that lesson in a hurry.

Almost at the end of the school day, Rosie popped her head around the door. She had just been in to see the headmistress to discuss her return. "Hello".

Suzy and Linda were both surprised to see her, and wanted to hear how she'd been getting on.
Standing in while Rosie was on maternity leave, Suzy felt she knew where the conversation would lead. It had been a long arduous day, starting with her car and now possibly the ending of her job. "When do you plan to come back?" she asked, trying her best to sound nonchalant.
"I'm not, that's what I've come over to say. Suzy, the job is yours for as long as." Rosie had enrolled for teacher-training and was starting in the new year. The career she'd originally wanted before her family came along. "My mother's retiring at Christmas and has bravely volunteered to look after our children."

Leaving Linda to lock up, Suzy walked back with Rosie, listening to the antics of her new baby son.

Completely forgetting about not having her car until almost at the carpark.
Rosie insisted on giving her a lift home. "This year you'll be able to help with the school's Christmas Pantomime."
Shaking her head and pulling a face, Suzy admitted it wasn't the sort of thing she fancied getting involved in.
"Oh you must," Rosie urged "it's tremendous fun."

George phoned in the evening, stopping mid-sentence, trying to repeat what Derek had diagnosed. "A leak into the transmission, . . . or was it a transmission fluid leak, . . and muck in the ?" George's mind went blank.
Suzy laughed, he understood engines about as much as she did.
"Anyway, Derek could do the job, but it would cost more than the car's worth, . . and once old cars start going wrong?" George warned, passing on Derek's advice. "Said he'd listen out, in case he hears of something suitable and I'll ask around."
Suzy thanked him for his help. She was very fond of her little car. Had owned it more years than she cared to remember, and it had never let her down . . . until now. Thankfully, not working the next two days would give her time to think.

-

Early Wednesday morning George phoned again.
"Jack's got a car for sale. He bought his Misses a new car for her birthday, and they've still got her other one in their garage. A bit bigger than yours and he doesn't want too much for it. Says you can have it for a couple of days to try out. If you don't like it, he'll have it back."
"Jack who found a buyer for my mother's car?"

"That's the one. Shall we bring it round Lass? It's . . . a reliable car."
George sounded pleased with himself, if not a little persuasive. She'd picked up on his pause, sensing there could be a catch?
"Go on then," she agreed to keep him happy. If she didn't like it, Jack could take it back.

Suzy was busy at the back of the house when they turned up. George rang the doorbell, stood back and pointed "What do you think?"
She stared, speechless for a minute or two.
Jack beckoned, opening the driver's door for her to see inside, insisting she got in.
It was everything George had described . . . and a vivid bright yellow! "It's . . very yellow," she mumbled, unable to think of anything else.
"Won't have trouble finding this in a carpark," George broadcast.
Of that, Suzy had no doubt.
"It's M.O.T'd, taxed and insured, in perfect running order," Jack announced, handing her the keys. "Give it a go, see what you think. You can give me or George a call later."
They got into George's van, waved and left. Leaving her standing, staring at the yellow peril.

Matt pulled into the drive. He'd decided to come back and work in his office at home for the rest of the day. He parked next to the yellow car, unloaded and carried his things up to his room. "Who's is that car?" he asked making himself a drink to take upstairs.
"My car's died. George's friend has lent it to me," she replied, not quite giving him the full picture.

"Grim," Matt uttered, grabbing a handful of biscuits to go with his coffee and heading back upstairs.

-

On Thursday morning Suzy sat in the car fathoming the dashboard and controls. She wondered whether to drive it around the block or be brave and take it further. Before she realised, the retail park outside Kirston came into view. She parked and collected her bag for a quick wander around the stores.

Walking back to the vast carpark she spotted it. Standing out from the hundreds of cars, luminous, shining like a beacon in the winter sunshine.

Back home in the drive, she stayed sitting in the car weighing up its pros and cons. Very comfortable and easy to drive, bigger and several years younger than her own were major plusses, . . but bright yellow? She'd need more time to think and phoned George.

"Because I'm his friend and he wants the space in his garage, you're getting a good bargain," George pointed out before she could say a word.

Grateful, she promised to let him know soon.

-

It never ceased to amaze Suzy how quickly the school emptied once the bell had rung at the end of the day. Within minutes, from crowds of lively noisy youngsters . . to quietness. Cutting across the empty playground to the carpark, she caught up with a couple of young stragglers in front, dawdling along walking towards the school gate. One of the girls wore a rucksack. Suzy smiled at the big yellow smiley face emoji emblazoned on the bag.

Strangely, all day splashes of yellow had begun to catch her attention wherever she went.

She opened the front door, picking up the mail from the floor on route. There was a letter from Baldwins Estate Agents. The enclosed statement confirmed true to his word, Richard had paid all the expenses their house sale incurred. The cheque was more generous than she'd anticipated.

So, this was the finally – the last necessary connection. She looked at the cheque in her hand, it wasn't much to show for all their years together. Apart from sending Richard a polite message of acknowledgement, their paths need never cross again.

She replaced the contents back inside the envelope. It was time to move on, time to buy herself a house and car, ... quite possibly a bright yellow one.

- -

Matt looked at his schedule for the week ahead. With Tom away and an early morning appointment on Monday, once again he wouldn't be able to get back to Somerset for the weekend. Resigning himself to working most of Saturday, he picked up his phone to call Gina, expecting to hear her moan with disappointment.

Instead, full of enthusiasm, she told him about Mr Bishop coming over on Saturday to advise her how to run the dairy conversion. He'd be going through the order of work and list of tradesmen. Hearing the excitement in her voice, . . clearly this weekend she'd hardly miss him at all.

Eager to learn, Gina had a myriad of questions for Peter Bishop. Her aspirations galloping miles ahead beyond the dairy to the renovation of their farmhouse.

~ 12 ~

“Time to go,” Matt chivvied, tossing his coat over his arm waiting for Suzy at the front door. All through breakfast he’d felt her tension. A salient day for her, if not for them all. “Would you like me to drive?” he offered giving her a reassuring smile.
“No, I’ll follow. Then you can go on to your office,” she said, trying not to put him out further. With a tingle of nervous excitement, she drove behind on route to Matt’s solicitor.

At his desk, Allister Hobbs sifted through papers for his first morning’s appointment. A stickler for meticulous order, arranging the documents in sequence. He was pleased to have the opportunity to meet Mathew Chapman again, and to personally work for his family.

Suzy beamed, greeting Phil at the door, she hadn’t realised he was going to be present.
Mr Hobbs escorted them into his office, seating them comfortably before guiding them in his precise manner through the legal procedures.

The business complete, signed and sealed, they all shook his hand. He would forward the necessary details to land registry and send on their personal copies.

In the carpark Suzy hugged her brothers and repeated her immense gratitude. She watched them return to their cars, waving to each one as they drove onwards to work.

Before driving back to Squirrels Chase, she gave herself a moment to absorb the magnitude of the deed. For the first time since leaving Ashton she could put down proper roots and stay.

Back home, she went straight upstairs to find her diary. She'd always been methodical, noting down annual reminders for insurances, recording significant purchases and payments etc. Sitting at her dressing table, her heart thumped as she turned the pages finding the date. Savouring the moment, she wrote in capital letters TWENTY SECOND of NOVEMBER. THE DAY SQUIRRELS CHASE BECAME MINE. A wave of emotions swept over her as she underlined the date. She'd never forget this day and no doubt her brothers wouldn't either.

- -

Alice had been following Julia around the house all morning, wandering about unable to settle. Her expanding stomach hadn't gone unnoticed. Alice looked up with big sad eyes, barely wagging her tail as Julia stroked her head. According to the calendar, Alice's puppies weren't due for another two weeks. Concerned by the dog's restlessness, Julia flicked through the whelping booklet their vet had provided.

At five in the morning, Neville cried out in his sleep. Julia got up and crept quietly to his room. Her sleeping infant squirmed about kicking off his duvet. She covered him, shushing softly to comfort and send him soundly back to sleep. Awake now, she went downstairs to check on Alice.

Tucked into a corner of the kitchen in her new larger bed, Alice lay panting heavily. Julia dimmed the lights and sat down alongside her, quietly watching and marvelling the moment. Two new born golden coloured pups lay by their mother, twenty anxious minutes later they were joined by a third. In a whisper, Julia phoned Andrew Knight their vet.

Hearing young Neville had woken up, Phil reached across for Julia. Finding her already gone, turned over to go back to sleep having no intension of getting up so early. Neville's cries grew louder. Phil switched on the bedside lamp squinting at the clock and groaned. Half asleep, he pulled on his dressing gown and stumbled along towards the bedroom of his yelling son.
Avoiding toys the tot had thrown out of his cot, picked up his sobbing son. "Let's go and find Mummy," Phil comforted, carrying Neville downstairs having seen the light on. "Didn't you hear him?" Phil grumbled, walking into the kitchen.

Patiently watching and waiting, Andrew Knight knelt by Alice attending the birth. "Morning," he said, startling Phil by his presence.
"Alice!" Phil gasped, offloading Neville into Julia's arms. He rushed over and dropped to his knees on the floor by her bed. Fearful and worried, Phil spoke softly, gently stroking her muzzle.
Pleased to see him, Alice lifted her head, her body shuddered and the last pup began its birth.
Andrew assisted, easing the pup into a towel. Seeing the small lifeless body, began to frantically rub, willing the pup to breathe. Minutes later the young vet unwrapped the towel to look, and welcomed a small new life into the world. "Hold this little hero for me," he smiled, handing

the bundle to Phil while he gave Alice and the other pups a final inspection.

Satisfied mum and pups were OK, Andrew Knight packed his bag ready to leave. Affirming he'd call back after surgery at the end of the day.

"Gorgeous aren't they?" Julia smiled, joining Phil sitting on the floor by Alice's bed. They sat together in wonderment, quietly watching Alice and her four new puppies sleeping.

Seeking attention, Neville launched his cereal bowl from his highchair, splattering the floor.

"Looks like somebody's ready for his bath," Julia sighed.

"I can do that," Phil offered. He'd decided to stay home the instant he saw the vet leaning over Alice.

While Nev had his afternoon nap and Julia was resting upstairs, Phil sat in the kitchen quietly watching Alice mothering her new pups. They were the cutest puppies he'd ever seen and little Hero, the last one born and runt of the litter had already become his favourite.

- -

Each day, when Suzy checked her phone, she'd find a new photo of Alice and her pups sent by Phil. She could picture him blissfully happy, fussing excessively over Alice and her new family.

Two weeks later, with the puppies continual good progress, Phil called, inviting her over.

Elated, she asked if he was amenable to her bringing a friend.

With an ulterior motive Suzy gave Rachel a call, slipping in the suggestion of spending next Saturday together.

"I wish," Rachel sighed, bogged down with corporate parties to arrange, the hotel's festive bookings almost full to capacity.
"I thought we might go over to see the puppies," craftily sending the latest puppy picture to Rachel's phone. . . and waited, tongue-in-cheek.
"What time?" Rachel instantly texted back, changing her mind.

-

"And another thing," Suzy said, adding one more reason of why she couldn't have one of the puppies. "Don't forget, I'm counting on your re-enforcement should I weaken."
Rachel sat in the passenger seat looking out of the window. Suzy's words going unheeded, rolling away like water off a duck's back.
She turned into a wide tree lined road and parked halfway along, outside Phil and Julia's house.
"Do you think we'll be allowed to hold them?" Rachel asked, beginning to get excited and eager to get inside.
Julia welcomed them, leading the way through to the kitchen. Phil had cordoned off an area in the corner for Alice and her family.
Suzy and Rachel stood, cooing and ahh-ing, adoring the puppies from behind a mesh fence until Phil called them away for refreshments. They sat around a table chatting in-between looking across, trying to get another glimpse of the pups.

Nev was sitting in his highchair supposedly eating a biscuit, having much more fun crumbling it up in his chubby hands. Julia got up to clean his encrusted face and fingers, while Phil prepared Alice's food.

Suzy could see Julia had her hands full while Phil was at work, and wanting to make amends volunteered to help out. "Any weekend you need a hand or want to escape for a few of hours," she proffered.

After Alice had eaten, Phil took her out into the garden, giving her a small break from her pups.

"Two each," Julia said, carefully distributing the puppies. "Cuddle these while I change this little monkey upstairs. "Messy monster," she playfully growled, lifting Neville from his chair and leaving a trail of crumbs as she carried him out.

"Oooh look to them," Rachel cooed, lifting up her two puppies to study their little faces, brushing her cheek softly against their gold silken fur.

Julia returned some minutes later carrying Nev on her hip. She lowered him into his baby-walker, warning the girls to watch their toes. Nev wasn't fussy whose feet he ran over. Reluctantly Rachel handed back her puppies, and watched Julia put them into their bed ready for their mother's return.

Phil came back in with Alice. He retrieved the smallest puppy from Suzy. "This little one is Hero," narrating the account of him almost not making it. "I might have to keep this one," he admitted totally smitten.

When Julia heard, her smile faded, she hoped he might not!

"This one reminds me of Bob," Suzy said wistfully, still holding the only brown coloured pup.

"That's the only girl in the litter, I knew you'd fall for that one," Phil acknowledged. He gave Alice her last two pups, tucking them against her stomach to feed.

Not wanting to outstay their welcome they thanked Phil and Julia, leaving them to get on with the rest of their day. Suzy drove homewards, pulling into the first pub they came across for lunch. Seeing the puppies and giving them cuddles had been the absolute highlight of their week.

While they waited for their food, Rachel took out her phone and scrolled through, looking at the photos she'd taken. Once again they 'oo'd and ahh-d' recalling the moments, while Suzy picked out the ones she wanted sent to her phone.

"Look this one," Rachel smiled, showing the photo which captured Suzy gazing lovingly at the little brown pup.

"You have to have her, she's so like Bobby and she'll be company for you when Matt leaves," Rachel insisted, stating the obvious.

"I can't have a puppy with my job," Suzy challenged. She could adjust her hours, but had to work one whole day each week.

"I can help," Rachel volunteered, stepping in with a solution. On the full day Suzy worked, she'd come over to puppy-sit, utilising one of her days off.

Suzy was tempted to accept her generous offer. Conceding the many school holidays throughout the year meant Rachel wouldn't be needed every week, and it would only be necessary while it was a pup.

"It really would be an absolute pleasure for me," Rachel persisted.

- -

"Look at these," Gina said, showing her mother the pictures Matt had sent through to her phone.

They looked again, going through more slowly, allowing time to marvel at the photos of Alice and her gorgeous new puppies.

"I'd struggle to choose one from that litter, they're all so cute," Elaine remarked. Admitting she wouldn't mind getting a dog for company, now they had space and she had the time for walks. "Later on, when all the building work has been done," she added quickly, aware Gina was looking at her strangely.

"Oh –h-h," Gina lamented, as the memory of an offer she'd forgotten about months ago surfaced to mind.

"Two puppies?" Elaine bit her lip, trying to stifle a smile.

- -

Working in the science block, Suzy rarely needed to enter the main school building. An advantage for her at present, while trying to avoid becoming involved in the school's Christmas Pantomime. Posters displayed on every noticeboard throughout the school invited participants, gave details of auditions and appealed for volunteers. Theatricals had never been her thing, and she dreaded the idea of being roped in.

"Good morning Mrs Martin." Mrs Taylor the headmistress greeted Suzy in the school carpark as she got out of her car. "Have you seen our posters for the Christmas Pantomime?"

Suzy gave an innocent smile, having a foreboding feeling she was being cornered.

"The school Pantomime is for everyone. Being newly appointed I wouldn't want you to feel left out, and I know Miss Henshore can always use an extra pair of hands," she trilled brightly, using the tone of authority usually kept for her pupils. Mrs Taylor locked her car and walked away at a brisk pace towards the school.

Forlorn, Suzy groaned, knowing she'd been well and truly nabbed. It would be unwise to disappoint the headmistress, should she need to request an adjustment of her working hours favourably considered.

-

On Tuesday Suzy stayed after school and begrudgingly made her way to the hall. She peered through the glass panel in the door looking for members of staff. A young teacher holding sheets of music stood talking by the piano, walking off as Suzy opened the door. Suzy's footsteps echoed around the large hall as she gingerly approached the piano. "I'm looking for Miss Henshore?"
The chap standing behind the piano smiled. "Here stands another pressganged volunteer," putting his hand forward to shake, "I'm Tim, . Tim Henshore."
Suzy blushed "is it that obvious?" she giggled nervously.
"Sasha, Miss Henshore's gone to the office trying to get more song sheets printed."
Suzy smiled, perhaps she could help with that, preferring to work with paper rather than pupils. She thanked him and headed towards the office.

"Thanks Joyce," Sasha called rushing out of the door, almost colliding with Suzy. "Oops, sorry," she apologised, dashing off.
Joyce Richardson stared at the many pages of scripts and song-sheets Sasha had given her, spacing them out across the table, wondering where to start.
Suzy knocked on the open office door and walked in, announcing she'd come to volunteer.
"Miss Henshore's just gone back to the hall if you want to catch her," Joyce said, separating pages.

Suzy read the coloured labels attached, numbering the amount of copies wanted. "Would you like a hand?"
Joyce looked up, giving Suzy a tentative smile. "Are you familiar with these?" glancing across at two large floor-standing photocopy printers.
Suzy walked over, recognising the same model which had stood in her own office. The office where she'd once held a prestigious position. "Yes," she stumbled, having an unexpected reminder of her previous job.

"That'll do for tonight," Joyce stated, stapling the last lot of pages together.
Suzy hadn't realised the time, or how quickly the last two hours had passed. Between them, they'd got most of the copying done. Joyce thanked Suzy for her help, inviting her back again if she had an evening to spare. Suzy accepted, she'd enjoyed the work and hoped her good deeds would be noted. Chatting as they worked, Joyce the elder of the two school secretaries had been good company.

- -

Caroline entered Matt's office with two coffees, placing them as requested on the desk. Matt paused his computer, thanked her and waited for her to leave the room. "So you had a good time?" he asked, changing the subject from work while they stopped for a break.
"Amazing," Tom answered, appreciating the time he and Carry had spent together, rather than all the American razzmatazz her family had laid on.
All morning, Matt had been bringing Tom up to date. Forewarning he'd be taking a few days off, having no intension of designating another weekend to work.

-

Trying not to wake Suzy, Matt crept downstairs and out to his car. He started the engine, giving it time to warm while he loaded. His car sparkled under a thick layer of white frost. Shivering, he shook a can of de-icer, breaking the silence in the freezing cold air. His breath billowing as he walked around the car spraying windows. The severe frost created the illusion of a covering of snow. Rubbing his hands together to warm, he wondered what their farm would look like in snow, conjuring up genial ideas of a white Christmas. He got into his car and slowly left the drive.

Suzy squinted, trying to focus on her bedside clock. She'd heard Matt moving about. The more he'd tried to be quiet, the more noise he made. She listened in the darkness hearing tyres crunch along the drive, and turned over, going back to sleep.

Joining the motorway Matt began to relax, appreciating the gritted road surface and the appearing dawn light. Away from Somerset his thoughts had constantly gravitated back to Gina and their farm. Ashwood Farm gave him unmitigated contentment and pleasure, achievements for Vortorx had long lost their glory. Hunger gnawed robbing his concentration so he scrabbled in the consul for mints. Later pulling off the motorway to The Greasy Spoon café for breakfast where he usually stopped, glad for a break.

Matt drove through the open gate and parked outside the farmhouse beside the Bishop's brothers van. Relieved and thankful to be home, he hurried inside to escape the cold. Gina wasn't in kitchen, he smiled to himself and rushed upstairs to surprise her, . . but she wasn't there either. Dejected he unloaded the car, carrying his bags upstairs to their bedroom. Dropping them on the floor to sort later. Back in the kitchen, he flicked on the switch of the coffee machine and sat down wondering where she could be.

Five minutes later she walked through the back door. "Matt, you're early!" she said surprised, throwing her arms around him hugging him tight. He kissed her tenderly, feeling the coldness of her face.

"I've come from the dairy," she clarified, unbuttoning her coat. "It's so good to have you home," sliding her arms around him. Her kisses easing away tension from his long drive.

"Where's Elaine?" he asked, realising she wasn't around. Gina reminded him her mother had moved into her cottage a week ago. "She's made you a chocolate cake. It's in that red cake-tin," and pointed across to the worktop.

He grinned, already the day was turning out better than he'd expected.

Lying beside him in the morning, debating whether to get up. She asked "is there anything you need to do, or want to see while you're home?"

"No, . . not really," he said prolonging their lay in, winding her up, knowing she was dying to show him the dairy. "I ought to thank Elaine for the cake," he added casually with eyes still closed. He felt her sit up and knew she was staring at him. "I suppose," he turned over, turning his back on her . . "I could take a look at that dairy."

"Matt!" she dug her fingers into his side to tickle.

"What?" he turned back with a mischievous grin.

"Mind the cables," Gina warned "the Bishops have set up a string of lights in here." She found the plug and switched them on, illuminating the inside of the building where they were standing. "That's better, now you can see the progress they've made."
Matt looked around impressed. Low unfinished breeze block walls divided, revealing the layout. He walked around taking in the size of the rooms while Gina gave commentary. "Carl and Joe bore holes into the concrete floor to test its stability, but dug footings regardless. The man from the council has passed the drains. Once the walls are up, we can get the electrician in and the carpenter for first fixings," exhibiting her newly acquired knowledge. "Mr Bishop is busy contacting the necessary tradesmen." Satisfied Matt had seen enough, she switched off the lights and closed the door.

They crossed the yard and knocked on Elaine's cottage door. She welcomed them inside, delighted to have their company. Gina went off to make drinks, while Elaine gave Matt a tour of her rooms. "What do you think of the dairy Mathew?" Admitting she wasn't surprised Gina worked well with Mr Bishop, knowing her daughter's determination to tackle the job. "She's taking it all on-board," Elaine boasted proudly.
"So I've heard," he acknowledged.

"Elaine seems very pleased with her cottage," Matt said, taking off his coat, back inside the farmhouse.
"At the moment," Gina agreed, knowing her mother's contentment couldn't be guaranteed to last. Recalling her complaints about lack of space when she first moved in with her. Understandable, she explained, quelling Matt's concern. "Mum's guesthouse in Brighton had been rather

substantial. Typically Victorian, huge rooms with high ceilings and fancy cornices."

"What do you think of this?" She unfolded a plan, flattening it out on the kitchen table in front of him. 'Proposed changes to original floor layout' Matt read. He hadn't realised she planned structural changes. He'd only assumed rewiring, a new heating system and replacement windows, apart from the obligatory new kitchen, bathroom and décor.

Gina began to explain her design, pointing as she did so. "This adjoining bedroom, divided, becomes our on-suite and dressing room, wardrobes etc.

This middle bedroom becomes a Jack-and-Jill bathroom to serve these two double bedrooms, still giving us another single spare room," her eyes bright with enthusiasm.

"And the ground floor," moving on to the next diagram. "Keeping the lounge and kitchen sizes the same, adding utilities to the boot room. Making that biggest 'reception' into your office and adding a toilet next door. Peter Bishop cleverly transformed my ideas into this plan," she said, anxiously awaiting Matt's opinion and praise.

Matt scanned the plans, silently absorbing the information. "It's impressive," he said, looking up, straight faced.

"Well?"

He didn't answer.

Her ebullience increased, "I want to turn Ashwood farm into our dream home." She sat down beside him, turning the glossy pages of the interior magazines Julia had given her, "which designs do you favour?"

His eyes glazed over with disinterest. He'd spent the last twelve years staying in the finest hotels. From Dubai to Paris, he'd experienced every design. Palatial, state of the

art edgy, elegant and plush. To him, despite their luxury, they all signified work.
Gina's lips tightened with impatience. "It's important Matt, I need to know what you like?"
"I like coming back here, just as it is, where I can totally relax."
Gina thought about their mismatch of furniture and the tired furnishings Margery had left behind.
"It just feels . . . homely," he said, trying to atone. "Just aim for comfortable and homely, not state of the art."
"I'll remember that when I do your office."
"I'll design my office!" he said riled, cutting her a serious glare.
"So you do know what you want," she grinned.
"You do the house, I'll take care of the farm . . and my office," he affirmed. "Lunch?"
She hadn't given it a thought, "let's have lunch at The Kings Arms, then we can light the fire in the lounge when we get back."
Coming home to relax, snuggled up in front of a cosy fire, watching TV on a cold winter's afternoon sounded perfect. Matt smiled, "I'll get my keys."

- -

Suzy took a tray of pasties out of the hot oven and put them beside two Victoria sponge cake layers cooling on a rack, filling the kitchen worktop with more fresh baked fare. Butterflies of excitement fluttered in her stomach knowing Kate and Jefferson were on their way.

Jefferson parked his black 4x4 next to Suzy's car. She opened the front door to greet them.
In the kitchen Kate put the kettle on, insisting her Mother sat down. "I can see we're expected," seeing the armada of

food. "That's new," she said spotting her uncle's up-market coffee machine on the side. "I'm sure Jefferson will make full use of it."
While they chatted, Jefferson listened patiently and ate, barely lessening the pile. "Thank you Mam," he said politely, before leaving the table to fetch their bags from the car.

By evening Suzy had seen the many photos of their trip, heard all about Jefferson's family and admired his parents spacious home in the suburbs. They had really taken to Kate, adoring her Englishness and made her feel most welcome.
Suzy suspected Jefferson's sudden offer to make their last hot drinks of the evening was a pre-engineered excuse to leave the room. She'd felt earlier, Kate had been holding something back and presumed it was related to their plans for Christmas.
"Mum," Kate started, taking the plunge. "I've been applying for jobs. My last course at Uni finishes in February. I've been offered a two year contract from Tensk, one of the biggest innovative industrial textile companies, . . in Glastonbury."
"That's marvellous, . . isn't it?" Suzy had a feeling there was more.
"Glastonbury in Connecticut. I'll come back for my graduation in July, and we won't stay out there if I don't like it." Kate gave a nervous smile looking for approval.
Suzy's stomach churned. "If this is your chosen career and what you've been studying for, you must follow your dreams Kate," she stated bravely.

"Thanks Mum." Kate got up to see how far Jefferson had got making their drinks, relieved to have got that revelation over.

-

While they commandeered the bathroom, Suzy went downstairs to start cooking breakfast. She knew they intended to leave before lunchtime, having promised to call in to see Phil and Julia before they went back - the puppies being the main incentive no doubt.

"Budge up," Kate said, playfully trying to move her solid tower of a man along the kitchen worktop with a couple of sassy swings from her hip. He looked down at her and gave a deep chuckle, before stepping aside. It was heart-warming watching them together, Kate was his world. Suzy would never have to worry about her with Jefferson around.

"Kady," Jefferson reminded her of the time, their weekend visit about to end.

"I'm sorry Mum, we have to leave," she said gathering their things, getting ready to say goodbye.

"Look after her Jefferson," Suzy whispered, again having to reach up to give him a goodbye hug.

"I sure will Mam."

"We'll stay longer next time," Kate promised, kissing her mother goodbye on the cheek.

With his impeccable manners, Suzy watched Jefferson walk round to open the passenger door for Kate, and patiently wait until she was comfortable before driving away. Kate had certainly found herself a star.

Suzy stopped waving and closed the front door.

It seemed one minute they were altogether enjoying each other's company and then they were gone. Squirrels

Chase suddenly felt empty. For the first in a very long time, Suzy felt lonely. She wasn't expecting to see Matt before Tuesday and was almost glad to be going to work the next day. Rachel was right, she did need company. It was pointless to mope. She wrapped a scarf around her neck and put on her old coat. Opened the backdoor and walked out into the garden looking for a job. There it stood in the wintery sunshine desperate for attention. Sorting out the garden shed had just become her priority.

- -

"Oh no, they've escaped again!" Julia groaned, reaching for the disinfectant spray and kitchen roll. "Phil, those barriers need to be stronger," she complained, mopping puddles on the floor.

"Little tinkers," Phil chuckled, recapturing two of the puppies from under the coffee table. He was incapable of being cross, one look at their cute little faces just made him smile. "I'll do it now," he said to appease.

The puppies were growing, becoming more adventurous and mischievous by the day. He wasn't sure which one was the main escapologist. He lowered the four of them into a large sturdy high-sided cardboard box he'd found in the garage, dragging his cargo into the conservatory. "Now stay in there while I make you a new pen," he instructed, as if they'd understand what he was saying. Alice curled up alongside the box on the floor. He closed the door to get on with his task.

Using stronger mesh and thicker pieces of wood he rebuilt their pen. Increasing the area, giving them more space to move around. He stood back to admire his work, inviting Julia's approval.

"That's better," she said, testing the new fence for security. "I'll give you a hand to put them back."

Opening the conservatory door, she cursed "Oh no, little blighters!"
The puppies had managed to turn the box over and escape again. They'd shredded her tower of bespoke ornamental baskets and destroyed a tall silk flower arrangement that had stood in the corner. "I'll be glad when they've all gone to their new homes!" she snapped exasperated. Five dogs and a toddler were taking their toll.

Fearless of danger, Neville had developed a penchant for climbing. Clearly bright, he'd already sussed how to get out of the straps in his pushchair. She knew it wouldn't be long before he'd be walking, having watched him pull himself up and go along their settee.
Yesterday in his walker, he'd reached up, banged the panel on the washing machine and changed the program! Their young son was a fulltime handful, never mind the trials the puppies created.

"It'll be much easier when we've only got Alice and Hero," Phil soothed, cuddling the little pup in his arms. They'd bonded, no one could love Hero more.
"No Phillip, I don't think so!" Julia stated firmly, standing her ground.
"Hero stays, we're keeping him!" Phil argued. Infuriated, he strode over to return the puppy back to Alice.

Julia flounced out of the kitchen. She stood in their bedroom giving herself five minutes to calm down, she'd never known Phil show his anger with her before.
Accepting she'd been tetchy, made her way back down to the kitchen.
"I'm taking Neville to the park!" Phil manoeuvred the pushchair out through the door, slamming it deliberately behind him.

Julia took a bin bag from the drawer to clear up the mess in the conservatory, her heart sinking.
She was sweeping up the last bits from the floor when the phone rang. She smiled with relief, she knew Phil couldn't stay cross with her for long. "I'm sorry love," she answered.
"Mrs Chapman?"
Surprised, she struggled to recognise the voice.
Mrs Finnis gave an abrupt apology for the weekend intrusion, but needed to forewarn Mr Chapman she wouldn't be in the office Monday morning. An appointment opportunity had arisen due to a sudden cancelation. "How are the puppies?"
"Growing, full of mischief, you must come and see them sometime," Julia replied, completely thrown by the call.
"That's most kind, we'd love to. We could come today if it's convenient, . . in about an hour?"
"Er . ," feeling awkward, but now unable to refuse, Julia agreed.

Phil didn't recognise the car parked outside when he returned. Nev was fast asleep in his pushchair. Phil carefully lifted it into the conservatory trying not to wake him.

Mr Finnis rose to shake Phil's hand, introducing himself as Gerald and thanking him for the invitation to see the puppies.
"Hello," Phil greeted, very surprised to find Mr and Mrs Finnis sitting in the kitchen each holding a puppy. He'd never met Mr Finnis before or heard Mrs Finnis mentioned him. He looked like a kindly professor, an older

man with a neat short goatee beard, wearing a dogtooth jacket and tie.

Mrs Finnis remained seated cuddling Hero, totally engrossed and besotted.

"Tea or coffee?" Julia offered, glad to escape Phil's questioning eyes.

Forewarning them of sharp claws and needle sharp teeth, Phil chatted, answering Mr Finnis's canine questions.

In all the years Mrs Finnis had worked for him, Phil had never seen that look of intense pure love on her face. Gazing down at the pup with deep tenderness in her eyes.

Julia handed Gerald Finnis a mug of tea, relieving him of the puppy he'd been holding. He sat beside his wife, watching her gently stroking the sleeping puppy cradled in her arms. "Millicent, do you think we could give one of these little fellows a home?"

"Gerald, I believe all Mr Chapman's puppies are taken," she said softly. Smiling at Hero, watching him snuggle to get more comfortable.

Julia looked straight at Phil, holding her breath. Wondering if he might say something, but even after a long pause he remained silent.

"Come along Millicent, we shouldn't hinder these good people any longer. I expect they'll want to get on," Gerald coaxed, trying to get her to surrender the pup.

Trying to clear the lump in his throat, Phil coughed and struggled to speak. "That one needs a very good home."

Julia swallowed hard, his generosity tugging her heartstrings.

Gerald looked at the pup still sleeping soundly in his wife's arms, "do you think he looks like a 'Trevor'?"

"Absolutely like a Trevor," Julia agreed, instantly renaming the pup.

“Mr Chapman are you certain?” Millicent Finnis’s eyes pleaded with hope, . . “he’ll receive the greatest care.”
Phil had no doubts on that aspect. “He’s used to lots of cuddles, he was my favourite.”
The Finnis’s left to resume their shopping, with Julia escorting them to the door. “I know that must of been extremely hard,” she said giving Phil a loving hug.

Awake, Neville got out of his pushchair, crawled to the conservatory door, crying and banging the door wanting to come in.
“Can he get out of that pushchair?” Phil asked, alarmed.
“I’m afraid he can,” Julia sighed, going to fetch him.

- -

Elaine covered the tray of hot bacon rolls she’d just finished making with a tea towel. Ready to take across to the men working in the dairy. A delivery she managed most days, believing them well-deserved for working in such cold temperatures. Also it gave her an excuse to monitor how the job was coming along.

She’d seen Mathew’s car leave the day before and guessed without his company, Gina might need cheering up. “Coo ee,” she called, knocking on the backdoor of the farmhouse and letting herself in.
Gina was chatting on the phone in the kitchen, she waved and signalled to put the kettle on.
Elaine made them both tea, putting the mugs down on the only clear space on the kitchen table. Plans for the farmhouse, papers and lists covered it, along with Julia’s magazines left open at strategic pages.
Gina finished her call.
“Anything wrong?” Elaine asked reading her daughter’s concerned expression.

"Maybe." Gina wrinkled her nose, she'd been speaking to Peter Bishop. He'd just informed her about his hospital appointment, now booked-in straight after Christmas for his knee replacement operation. Insisting he'd be available at home, should she need to consult him regarding the job. "I don't think his wife would take kindly to my pestering phone calls if he's supposed to be convalescing."

Elaine could see her point. "What's all this?" she asked, looking at all the gubbins spread across the table.
"Mr Bishop sourced the best tradespeople for the dairy. It seems stupid to let them go as they finish, when most of them could start working here on the farmhouse. So, I've started to plan the work."
"Could you run the job?" Elaine enquired.
Gina bit her lip, unsure.
Seeing the sense of it and having strong faith in Gina's capabilities, Elaine encouraged her to go ahead. "I'm sure the tradesmen could answer your questions, and if Mr Bishop hired them, they'd be reliable." She started to look through the magazines, flipping over pages to look at kitchens and bathrooms, "can I borrow these?"

Gina took the lid off the biscuit tin and peered inside at the dregs. "I need to go shopping."
"That's what I came to ask you about," Elaine remembered. "Christmas shopping. It'll soon be upon us."
Gina's head swam with questions about refurbishing the farmhouse, but her mother was right. The solution became obvious. If they stayed in a hotel near Phil and Julia for a couple of days, she could show Julia the new plans and seek her advice. Spending the rest of the time shopping with her mother.

"We could see the puppies," Elaine said getting excited. "You are still having them aren't you?"
Gina squirmed. "I'd liked to, but working on two building projects?"
"Then I'll have them. They'd be company for me at my cottage."
"Really?" Gina looked at her mother, bewildered. "They'd be a lot of work."
"But, I'd love it," Elaine declared.

- -

Suzy crossed the playground on route to the office. She'd received a message earlier from Joyce to say 'if she was free after school, a hand would be much appreciated'. Stepping inside the main building, Suzy could hear Tim Henshore playing the piano in the hall. She slowed down to listen, he was running through the entire music repertoire of the pantomime. He'd jazzed up a few familiar songs, making them sound more modern and fun. She cut across the hall on tiptoe trying not to disturb his concentration.

Joyce was getting flustered. The programs were proving fiddly to produce and Sasha had asked for more song sheets.
When Suzy arrived at the office, Joyce gave a sigh of relief. Glad of the opportunity to hand over Sasha's printing job.
"The children are lucky to have such a gifted teacher," Suzy said, mentioning Mr Henshore's piano playing.
"He's not a teacher," Joyce corrected. "Last year's music teacher Mrs Forbes, broke her wrist two days before the first performance in front of the parents. In desperation

Sasha talked him into stepping in. Without Tim Henshore their Christmas Panto would of been cancelled."
Suzy was impressed, "and Mrs Forbes?"
"Left at Easter, moved on to a another school." Joyce lowered her voice, "somehow Mrs Taylor has roped him in again for this year. She can be quite persuasive."
Suzy could vouch for that.

Throughout the evening while they worked, Joyce chatted about her plans for Christmas. Her husband had been talking about getting a dog, but now they'd decided to wait until after. Predicting the pet rescue centres would become busier after Christmas. "Be nice to have a dog in the house again," Joyce said wistfully.
"I'm getting a puppy," Suzy revealed, telling Joyce the saga of Bob. "I don't suppose it will be till the end of January, knowing my brother."
"Have you got a photo?"
Suzy took out her phone. Joyce smiled, oohing and ahh-ing as she scrolled.
Tim Henshore appeared in the office doorway, "song sheets?"
"Mrs Martin is getting a puppy," Joyce said, turning Suzy's phone screen round to show him.
Suzy gathered up the finished song sheets to give him.
"She's adorable. If you need a dog-sitter anytime, I'm your man. I'd better go, Sasha's waiting for these," and rushed off.
Suzy had been surprised by his kind offer, if not a little puzzled he'd not included his wife.
"Christmas carol sheets or outer covers for the programs?" Joyce offered, giving Suzy a choice of job.

"I've had enough," Joyce said, arching her back as she stood waiting for the machine to finish. The pair of them had done well, producing most of the pages for the programs. "All we need now is our pantomime fairy to magic them into book form," Joyce sighed feeling weary. The next day, Suzy wasn't due to start work in the lab until after lunch so volunteered to come in early to help. She left Joyce to lock up.

In the carpark Suzy opened her car door just as Tim stepped out of the darkness making her suddenly flinch. "Oh God! sorry, I didn't mean to startle you," he apologised. "My offer was genuine, . . with the pup. I usually work from home so it would be no trouble. Your photos reminded me of our Flossy, the dog we had. Sorry for making you jump," he repeated. "Goodnight," and got into his car parked beside hers.

-

Working on a table at the back of the school office, Suzy was busy stapling covers onto programs.

Mrs Taylor put her head around the door to ask Joyce how things were progressing.

"Bit of a rush as always," Joyce admitted and gave her a finished program to inspect.

She studied it and smiled, obviously approving. "I believe Mr James has two free periods this afternoon. I'll send him along to help." She closed the door, walking off with a determined look on her face.

Joyce glanced across to Suzy "Oh dear, I hope he didn't have anything else planned."

Suzy began to pack away, tidying up before walking over to the Lab.

Sasha came into the office to look at the programs, focussing her attention on the covers. "Can I take one of these?" proudly announcing one of her pupils had designed the front.

"I heard Mr Henshore playing the piano yesterday. He's extremely good," Suzy praised, loading more finished programs into a box.

"Yes, he has a natural gift. Only needs to hear a tune once, then he can play it, . . . repeating it perfectly," Sasha acknowledged while examining the pages. "As children, I'd spend hours practicing my scales, annoyingly he never had to!"

The penny dropped, they were siblings!

"These are great. It'll give Alan a well-deserved boost," she smiled, slipping the program into her bag.

When she'd gone, Suzy picked one up to scrutinize. Inside, printed at the back, she read the acknowledgements 'front cover designed by Alan White,' and with understanding knew exactly what Sasha had meant.

In the evening, Suzy turned down the volume on the TV to answer the phone.

"Hi, what are you up to?" It wasn't unusual for Rachel to phone from work in the evening. Especially if she was working late, manning reception and bored. Often it was the only time they both had time to chat.

"Nothing really," Suzy replied, mentioning Matt was away and she'd been helping out at the school. "And you?"

As she'd guessed, Rachel was working late. Bemoaning continual busy nights of festive meals and parties were draining. The Bricknell Lodge glittered and sparkled with impressive decorations, large festooned Christmas trees

abound. “Any new puppy pics?” Rachel asked, changing the subject.
Her generous offer to give up free days still bothered Suzy. “It’s such a commitment.”
“And one I’m looking forward to,” Rachel insisted, trying to convince her yet again.
Without realising, Tim Henshore had given Suzy an idea, the name Flossy had stuck in her mind. “I’m thinking of calling the puppy Flossy.”
“Oh, I like that. It’s unusual.” Rachel approved and asked where she’d heard it.
“From a pianist with a disarming smile.”
“Oh yes?” Rachel said intrigued. All of a sudden she heard a loud smash in the main dining lounge, followed by rowdy cheers. “Sorry, I have to go,” she whispered and dashed off to find out what had happened.

- -

Harvey Granzman had gone home for Thanksgiving. It wouldn’t make sense for him to fly back this close to Christmas, but Matt had an instinctive niggling feeling he would appear, knowing his boss’s quirk for the unexpected.
In early morning darkness Matt drove into the Vortorx carpark, and looked across to see if Granzman’s Bentley was parked in its usual spot. The space was empty. Maybe his suspicions were unfounded this time.
Two headlight beams flashed into his eyes as a car turned and parked alongside. “You too?” Matt asked, watching Tom get out.
“I just had a hunch,” Tom said, looking across to Gransman’s empty parking space.
“We’ll leave earlier tonight,” Matt commiserated. They walked together, turning the corner towards the main entrance.

"Look!" Tom pointed, being first to spot the Bentley parked outside the main door.

"Morning gentlemen," the security guard greeted from the reception desk as they entered. Matt reciprocated, and waited for an answer.
"About ten minutes ago, just before you arrived Mr Chapman."
"Thank you Dennis," Matt's tension eased. Another thing he'd learned from experience, the bigger the problem, the earlier Harvey Granzman tended to arrive.
Tom walked ahead to his office, planning to revise recent figures in case Granzman asked for some obscure fact.

Matt switched on the coffee machine in his office and sat leaning back in his chair. He couldn't think of any burning issues to warrant this visit, no big company deals or take-overs were immanent. Granzman should have no financial concerns, these past fifteen months Vortorx had amassed record profits. In fact this year Matt's touch for business had been golden, he'd be leaving Vortorx with a high accolade. He expected his achievements to be respectfully rewarded in this end-of-year's bonus, . . his final one, planning to be gone before Spring. If he had any regrets, it was not having enough opportunities to allow Tom to handle Vortorx's business at his level. He'd amend that issue in new year.

They were summoned, and joined Harvey Granzman in his office. Polite acknowledgements over, Granzman handed them each a printed summary of Rasant, the German company Vortorx acquired four years ago. "Your opinions gentlemen?"

Matt turned directly to the financial figures, usually his final decisions depended on them.
Tom skimmed through all the sheets stapled together.

Granzman paced, coming to a stop by the window and stood staring, watching the office staff begin to arrive. He sat back in his chair ready for answers, homing in first on Tom. "Mr Hobbs?"
Unflustered, Tom turned pages back and forth before answering. From the summary he'd observed Rasant had been successful before purchase, also the 'supply company' Vortorx acquired to incorporate. Two very successful years, before disappointing ones followed. Granzman knew the history, he wanted answers, "and?"
"Split the company back to two. If they continue to fail, sell," Tom advised.
Granzman turned his attention to Matt, who virtually agreed with Tom, but would sell it all immediately. Granzman appeared satisfied. Although he'd already made his own decision, pre-arranging an appointment with Noud Visser. "The Visser's are interested, let's see how much," handing Matt the details. The meeting was over, Matt and Tom rose to leave.
"You've had a good year Mathew."
"Yes sir." Matt smiled, appreciating the recognition.

"I didn't see that trip coming," Matt admitted, catching up with Tom. "Ten o'clock, Wednesday morning, Amsterdam," he read out, realising they'd both have to fly out there tomorrow.
"I'd better make a start on those figures," Tom said reaching his office.

-

They arrived late afternoon at their hotel in Amsterdam. The Rembrandtz was situated in the picturesque oldest part of the city. From the outside a historic aged building, but deceptively it possessed a luxurious modern interior.

In the evening they sat at the rear of the dining room for conversational discretion. Matt scanned the menu, the cuisine favoured Italian more than Dutch. Having a meat preference, he chose Carpaccio. Tom was more adventurous, embracing Spiced Langoustine Tagine.
During their meal Tom revealed the Visser family owned The Rembrandtz hotel. Just one of the facts he'd discovered while researching, adding the Visser's descend from an old Dutch banking dynasty.

Granzman had personally arranged the meeting, pre-booked the hotel and scheduled use of their conference room. Matt felt dubious, beginning to wonder what else he'd planned. Whether or not they were to sell Rasant, intact or otherwise, Matt intended to be on a plane back home tomorrow.

After breakfast, the receptionist escorted Matt and Tom to the conference room. Matt stopped at the door, "this one's yours Mr Hobbs, take over." He stepped aside, following behind Tom when they entered the room.
Noud Visser politely introduced himself, welcomed and invited them to sit at the table.

Matt sat at Tom's side, resolute to stay in the background. He was surprised to find Noud was a similar age to Tom, immaculately attired - Matt recognising Armani. Watching Noud set up his laptop and sift through papers, caught a glimpse of his Omega watch. This young man emanated from an affluent family.

He appeared adept and confident, hosting the meeting in abrupt manner, a usual trait associated to the Dutch.
Matt silently observed, Noud asking questions and Tom giving articulate answers. Impressing both Noud and Matt by his comprehensive knowledge of Rasant.
They broke for refreshments. Matt watched Noud leave the room and guessed, not being given full authority, to make a call.
"I wonder what car he drives," Tom mused, drinking his coffee.
"Probably not one I'd care to leave in a public carpark," Matt smiled.

The young Dutchman returned and their business continued. After a short period of contemplation, Noud Visser made an offer to buy Rasant.
Matt waited for Tom's response, the figure given worth consideration.
Entrusted to attain the best deal for Vortorx, Tom rejected it.
The two men stood their ground.
In uncompromising stance, Tom proposed a significantly higher sum.
Again silence prevailed.
Noud texted a message on the phone laid in front of him, ... the reply transmitted almost immediately. Noud Visser rose to shake Tom's hand, his figure accepted. He signed and dated a short affidavit and passed the document to Tom, announcing "Aart Visser would contact Mr Harvey Granzman." Noud gathered up his paperwork and leant across the table to shake hands with Tom and Matt. He wished them a pleasant stay in Amsterdam, said goodbye, turned and left the room.

"Well done!" Matt congratulated, packing Rasant paperwork and his laptop back into his case. For a brief moment he'd not been sure which way it would go. Pushing Tom into the forefront and watching him achieve the deal had been gratifying. Relieved their work was over, Matt could relax and start thinking about going home.

Tom stood, stowing financial reports and notes into his briefcase, quietly absorbing the success of the deal. They walked out into the foyer.

"You've earned a drink. I'll meet you back here shortly," Matt proposed and went up to pack.

Tom was waiting when Matt returned. "Shall we go out and have a look around, our flight's hours away," Tom cajoled.

Matt accepted, happy to get out of the hotel for a while. They could find a bar, Tom deserved to celebrate.

Outside, Tom began to walk, examining the street map screened on his phone. "There's a Christmas market in the main square," he suggested. The glare he received told him Matt didn't browse around stalls.

Matt followed, bemused by Tom spouting historical facts like a tourist guide, drawing his attention to tablet gable stones on lop-sided houses. Apart from dodging out of the path of bell ringing cyclists, strolling along the narrow cobbled streets observing the architecture was more pleasant than Matt had expected.

They were about to walk passed an A-board, when Tom stopped to read it. The board welcomed visitors with the opportunity to view jewellers working inside. His curiosity aroused, Tom walked through the open door, stepping down into a large bright florescent lit room. With reluctance, Matt felt compelled to follow. Jewellery sparkled inside a long glass counter and from shelves behind.

Warmly welcomed, they were guided towards a workbench in the corner where a bespectacled old man sat hunched over his lathe, hand polishing a gem.

From uncut to finished stones, their friendly host described each stage, pointing to relevant pictures on the wall. He returned behind his counter, leaving his visitors to peruse.

Tom admired the glittering jewellery with coloured stones, mentioning his girlfriend liked sapphires and rubies.

"Sir, these are diamonds. White, black and some of the rarest colours," their host smiled, avidly demonstrating what constitutes to a diamond's value.

Forewarning a limit of €100, Tom asked to see some ladies earrings. "For a Christmas present," he clarified, optimistic their host would achieve a sale. After considerable searching, finally from the lowest drawer, a board of earrings at that meagre price materialised.

Prompted by Tom's mention of Christmas, Matt also bought two pairs. He moved slowly along the counter, peering through the glass looking for a present for Gina. He stopped, gazing down at the sparkling gems. Their host, anxious to oblige, took out an ivory satin padded tray of exquisite diamond rings for Matt's inspection.

From the other end of the counter, Tom watched with apprehension, wondering if Matt was preparing to surrender his single status.

Matt stood deep in thought, mesmerized by the rings. . . eventually asking to see something else. He chose a necklace, a white solitaire diamond suspended from a gold chain. With their purchases elegantly packaged, Matt was eager to leave the premises, all that spending had raised a thirst.

Emerging back onto the street, Tom consulted his map, leading the way across a canal to the nearest café ahead. Matt ordered plates of Bitterballan to accompany their beer. Raising his glass to Tom, he congratulated. "To many more successful deals. Cheers!"
Glossing over their morning's work, Tom harked back to the jewellers. "I never knew you could get black diamonds?"
All be it in a roundabout way, Matt guessed where his conversation was heading. "So how much were those rings?"
"Think of a showroom of refine luxury cars," Matt replied, trusting his answer would close the subject. He'd come extremely close to buying Gina a ring, but with his new monumental unfamiliar future ahead, cautiously thought . . . one thing at a time. He'd a lot to learn about running a farm and settling down. "What time's our flight?" he asked, deliberately changing the subject.
Tom lead the way back to the Rembrandtz.

- -

"I'm going up now," Phil said, peering round the door of his study. Julia was sitting at his desk with a fine bristled paintbrush in her hand, debating whether to use a darker shade. Deep in thought, she didn't hear him come in.
Phil stood at her side looking down at her work, each design a work of art in itself. He'd almost forgotten about her immense talent and pre-baby career, appreciating now why she'd been spending every evening this week in his study.

"A few suggestions in various modes and colours for Matt and Gina's farmhouse," she explained, rinsing her brush. She picked up another sketch to add a wash of colour, "if I can finish this last one tonight."
"It's rather late," he reasoned.
"I've really enjoyed getting back into this," she said, with heartfelt honesty and changing to a thicker brush. "I hadn't realised how much I missed being creative."
"Are you thinking of going back to work?"
"No."
Her answer decreased the concern on his face. "But once those puppies have gone, I'm starting a redecorating regimen throughout this house."
"Oh no, no!" Phil began feigning, "my poor wallet!"
"Idiot!" she simpered, unmoved and used to his accountant's 'dying swan'. "When I completed the décor here, I didn't envisage a baby or puppies, . . . they've all absolutely ruined it."
Phil conceded, he'd wrecked the far end of their kitchen building pens for the puppies, and you didn't have to look far for evidence of tiny teeth and chewed edges. "I'll never regret Alice having her pups."
"Nor will I," Julia confessed softly.
"Come to bed, it's late," he said kissing her forehead.
"Give me five minutes to clear this lot away."
"Five minutes? I'll be waiting," raising his eyebrows with an impish grin.
Julia chuckled, "you'll be asleep the minute your head hits that pillow."
Phil left the study, calling "five minutes, I'll be waiting," as he climbed the stairs.
'In your dreams', she smiled, . . . in your dreams. She packed away her paints and brushes. Tomorrow she'd

laminate her work, attach fabric samples and post them off to Gina. It would be of no consequence if Gina didn't use her ideas. Producing them had given so much pleasure, not to mention rekindling her passion for design. She had a few ideas already, but this time practicality would be foremost, especially with Nev's 'murals' stage to come. Climbing the stairs she heard a sound she recognised, . . gentle snores coming from their bedroom.

- -

Driving up to the house, Suzy saw a light on in her lounge. She either had burglars or Matt was home. His case stood inside the hall with his coat thrown over it. Carrying her shopping through to the kitchen, she heaved the bags onto the table with a groan. A paper bag lay torn open on the worktop with greasy pastry crumbs scattered all around, . . . yes, he was back. She could hear the television and went to say hello. He was fast asleep in the armchair, a cold mug of coffee at his side. She reached across for the remote-control to lower the sound, accidently knocking it into his lap.
"Oops," she giggled and waited to see if he'd wake.
He began to stir and opened his eyes. "Hello," he said blinking, half asleep and surprised to see her standing in front of him. He stretched and sat up, faculties slowly returning.
"Tea?" she offered, walking away to close the curtains. She gave him a new box of biscuits to open, and went back to the kitchen to make their drinks.
"There's sausage rolls on the side," he called out.

While Matt picked out his favourite biscuits, she sat opening the Christmas cards she'd brought back from

school. "Look," she smiled "they're from some of the children," and got up to add them to others on the shelf. He looked around, the cards were the only festive items in the room. "Are you going to put up a tree?"
She got up again and returned to the kitchen.
"I've bought one of these instead," she justified cheerfully, carrying in a big red poinsettia. "They're bright and Christmassy," placing the colourful plant on the table in front of him. Avoiding his question, she diverted the conversation. "So where did you go?"
"Amsterdam, and I'm back in my office tomorrow," he said, eating another chocolate biscuit from the box. "What are you doing for Christmas?"
She had her speech ready. "Staying with Rachel Christmas day, . I'll shall phone Kate, . and later I'll probably call in to see Phil and the family, have a bit of bonding time with Flossy".
Matt became serious, looking straight into her eyes. "Suze, why don't you come back with me?"
"I'll stay next Christmas, when you two have had a chance to settle and the work's all done at your beautiful farmhouse."
"Christ! It should be ready before then!"
She giggled, and promised to stay with them during the school summer holidays.
"Have another think about it, text me tomorrow," he said getting up from the chair. He left the lounge to work in his office upstairs, endeavouring to lessen the next day's workload. Set on finishing early and aiming to get back to Somerset as soon as possible.

Suzy curled up on the settee and swapped TV channels. She was thinking about her own day tomorrow, the school's last day of term. Going in to help Linda Blake sort out the science block wasn't an issue. It was the afterschool soiree Mrs Taylor was holding in her office for the staff, she wasn't looking forward to.

-

Matt drove in extra early. He gave Dennis a generous tip for Christmas, catching him first thing at the reception desk. He'd already given Caroline a gift and the rest of the week off.

At ten o'clock he closed down the laptop, glad to of written his last report of the year. He cleared his desk, locked the office and went to see Tom. "I'm off now," he said, standing in the doorway, exchanging Christmas wishes. "See you in the new year," Tom called as Matt closed the door.

Anxious to be on his way, Matt hurried towards the carpark, his stress levels ebbing with each step towards the car. Working late into the night should of rendered tiredness, but the thought of going home to Somerset heightened his energy.

He knew Suzy wouldn't change her mind and wasn't surprised to find the drive empty. He began to unload his car, carting his belongings upstairs. She'd left a Christmas present for Gina and himself on his bed, with a note alongside. . .

I'll stay next year

~

Happy Christmas
Suzy xx

In the kitchen he wrote her a note, replicating her seasonal wishes. Leaving it by the kettle, weighed down with an exquisitely wrapped gift from the jewellers in Amsterdam. He got into his car ready to leave. An inner glow of happiness generated an effusive smile, he was driving home for Christmas.

- -

On the first floor in Lab 2, Suzy stood looking out of the window watching the school emptying. Children flowed out from their final assembly in the hall, joyful and noisily making their way home.

She sensed their excitement, did anyone ever forget that deliriously happy feeling of last day of term? She thought back, still unable to decide which she'd loved best. The magical one at Christmas, sometimes with snow, or breaking up for six glorious summer weeks.

She walked over to the office. Joyce was busy emptying a large bag of crisps into a plastic bowl. A plate of canapes covered by cling film sat on her desk.

"Are they for the party?"

Joyce laughed, it wasn't going to be a party. Just a few mince pies and mulled wine. Giving the headmistress an opportunity to thank everyone for their hard work throughout the year. Assuring Suzy it only ever lasted about an hour.

Dreading entering the room on her own Suzy offered to help, being glad of an excuse to accompany Joyce.

"Not everyone likes mince pies," Joyce said, handing Suzy the bowl.

Weaving her way around members of staff, she followed Joyce to a laden table, putting down the crisps alongside the festive fare. To familiarize, Joyce discretely pointed, whispering teacher's names and denoting the subjects they taught. Everyone seemed relaxed and affable, happily chatting within their own groups of friends.

Mrs Taylor began to loudly ting a spoon against her glass to gain attention. A circle opened, giving her room to speak. She gave her short speech, the contents as Joyce predicted. Raising her glass at the end wishing everyone a Very Happy Christmas and a Peaceful New Year. After a round of applause, the space infilled as people moseyed back to join their colleagues.

"Joyce!" a voice called.

"I won't be a minute," she said, going off to chat.

Feeling conspicuous standing alone, Suzy went back to the table, planning to have a drink before quietly slipping away. She ladled warm mulled wine into a punch cup ready to sip.

"What's it like?" Tim Henderson asked, standing alongside eating crisps.

She took a mouthful and was pleasantly surprised.

"Actually, it's not bad, . . sort of hot berry punch with?" She pondered . . "cinnamon?"

Tim ladled some into a glass and took a gulp. "Jeez!" he shuddered, screwing up his face and shutting his eyes, . . grabbing more crisps to take away the taste.

Suzy giggled. "I think your wanted," she said, seeing a group across the room beckoning him. "Look, they're waving, you have to go."

He stayed.

"I'm leaving when I've drank this," she apprised.

A stout rotund woman from the group headed towards him.

"Oh no," he groaned under his breath.

"Timothy, you must come and join us," she boomed, taking his arm, trying to persuade him to join her friends.
He disentangled himself. "Sorry, I've arranged to give Mrs Martin a lift home." Outstretching his arm to clear a path through the crowd, he guided Suzy to the door.
Outside, and slightly puzzled, Suzy began walking towards the main gate.
"Sorry about that," he apologised.
"No worries," she was about to leave anyway.
They walked together towards the carpark.
"Miss Soames has set her cap at me," he said, feeling obliged to explain. "Sasha just sees the funny side. It's been rather awkward. There were times I was reduced to hiding."
"Oh dear," Suzy sympathised, pressing her lips tightly together trying not to laugh. The vision of a keen voluptuous Miss Soames pursuing svelte Tim Henderson was too much.
"When do you get your puppy?"
"January," admitting she hadn't yet discussed a date.
"I'd love to see her," he reminded.
Suzy promised when she had the puppy, she'd pass a message through Miss Henderson. "This is mine," she said stopping at her car.
Tim found a folded Pantomime programme in a pocket and wrote his phone number across, handing it to her with a smile. "See you in January." He walked on towards his car, turning round halfway to call out "Happy Christmas Mrs Martin, . . . Suzy."

- -

Almost home, Matt's eyes began to prickle, the long drive and fatigue kicking in. He opened his window for a blast of cold air.

Slowing down to drive through the gate, he was totally unprepared for the vision ahead. "Oh wow!" he gasped. Briefly stopping the car to take it in, his sore eyes welling with emotion.

A large Christmas tree stood at the side of the farmhouse, brightly lit with coloured lights. Fairy lights twinkled around the front doorframe, with a traditional wreath attached to the door.

Matt parked in front of the house, getting out to look at the tree. He stood before it, staring up in the darkness and smiling in wonderment. Across the yard Elaine's cottage was similarly decorated, adding to the festive splendour.

At their front door, he rang the bell instead of using his key.

Gina opened the door "Welcome home," she beamed.

"That's some homecoming," he replied, kissing her.

She led him into the lounge. "Look, Mum found our box of decorations in the barn," the decretive surprises continuing. Matt looked around the room, he'd never felt so happy to be home.

Pouring drinks, Gina proposed a toast. "To our first Christmas at Ashwood Farm." She topped up his drink and cuddled up beside him.

"How big is that tree?"

"Ten foot," she grinned. She'd asked for twelve, but that was the one Sam had brought back. He'd got everyone working together, striving to get it finished before Matt's return. Mick adding the magic of lights.

"It's marvellous," he said, rubbing his tired eyes. Leaning back on their soft comfortable settee beginning to relax. "If I close my eyes, I'll sleep through Christmas," he warned.

-

All morning, trying not to make too much noise, Gina kept herself busy in the kitchen, allowing Matt to sleep late. Discerning he'd woken up when she heard movement upstairs.

He felt as though he'd slept for days, not that it mattered. He had three glorious weeks away from business and the pressure of work. Hearing the treads of the staircase creak, he sat up, . . someone was coming upstairs.
"Hello gorgeous," he greeted, as Gina came through the bedroom door bringing him a mug of coffee.
She sat on top of the bed beside him, resting her head on his shoulder. Listening and catching up with his news, . . . ending with the inevitable subject of when he planned to leave Vortorx.
"Before Spring," but seeing disappointment in her eyes, added "maybe earlier. I could stay here forever," he said, pulling her closer.
She reminded him, they had to move out so the refurbishing work could start.
He didn't see the need to rush, suggesting it could be done in Spring when the weather improved.
She gave a little smile, . . not according to her plans!
Leaving him to get up and showered, she went downstairs to start cooking his breakfast.

"That smells good," he said, walking into the kitchen and began pouring himself another coffee.
At the table, he picked up the morning's newspaper and sat glancing through features that caught his eye.
She served his breakfast, joining him with a round of toast for herself.
He could feel her eyes watching him. "What?" he smiled, looking up, catching her.

"Nothing," . . then contradicting herself, put forward her idea of overlapping the jobs, utilizing the tradesmen. "It makes sense," she reasoned, omitting to mention she'd already arranged an impending start date.

"So what's next on your agenda?" he teased, tossing the paper he'd finished reading aside.
"A walk to the end of the lane, where Sam assures me the holly bushes are red with berries. We could bring home a big bunch to decorate the hearth."
"Where did that come from?" he asked, suddenly noticing the huge hamper stood on the floor behind him. Harrods emblazed across the basket lid.
"It was delivered yesterday morning. I thought you'd ordered it." It hadn't occurred to her to look for a name of the sender. It was tied with a wide red ribbon, finishing into a big decretive bow on top. She unfastened the ribbon and threw it on the table, lifting the basket lid expecting to find delivery details.
Matt spotted a small business card stapled to the ribbon. He read 'Seasonal Greetings, HG.' "It's from Vortorx."
"Fabulous!" she cheered, diving into the basket, looking through its array of lavish goods.
He watched, amused by her excitement. Matt knew the gift held other connotations. He guarded his privacy, colleagues had his mobile number. That was enough as far as he was concerned. He'd chatted to Tom about the farm and mentioned it to Gransman, but he'd never disclosed its actual whereabouts. Was there anywhere Harvey Gransman couldn't infiltrate – apparently not!
Gathering holly had temporally lost its importance, Gina was enjoying herself working her way to the bottom, reading labels as she unpacked.

Matt collected his keys from the side, telling her he was going to unload his car. Last night's Christmas spectacle of the tree and lights had blown him away, totally forgetting the car.

He took his case and sports bag from the boot. Moving round to reach inside for the gifts he'd stowed in the glove compartment. Carefully consigning them into his case, trying not to damage the jeweller's ornate packaging. He smiled to himself, anticipating Gina and Elaine's surprise on Christmas day.

A Post Office van drove into the yard, stopping alongside him. To save the postman getting out, Matt took the letters. The driver raised his hand in appreciation and drove back out through the gate.

Matt put the mail on top of his bag, carrying it all into the house.

Not wanting to clutter the worktop, Gina had put most of the hamper's contents back into the basket. She'd filled the fridge with cheeses and stacked the bottles on the side. "Phew!" she said, sitting down satisfied.

Matt handed her the letters, each one addressed to Elaine.

Gina hadn't forgotten about the holly, saying she'd drop the letters in to her mother's cottage on the way. She didn't recognise the name or address written on the back of a letter from Australia, it was probably from one of her mother's friends. Gina turned the envelope over, admiring the foreign stamps depicting colourful birds, . . birds? . . birds! Eureka! she'd found her excuse.

They walked together down the lane on route to find holly. "We really need to start work on the farmhouse as

soon as possible," she urged, reminding him about the swallows that come back to build their nests in the barn every Spring. "We can't have them disturbed by all that noisy building work, . . can we?"
It was true, they couldn't risk frightening the birds away.
"No," he agreed giving her a knowing look, recognising a devious plan.

"Ouch, . . ouch! he cursed, trying to grab the prickly branches.
"With long stems," she specified.
"Ouch!" Matt cussed, throwing down the spiteful sprigs and stepped back. He'd had enough of harvesting holly.
Gina took the secateurs from him and reached into the spiky hedge.
"Ow, . ouch! It's not funny!" she snapped, nursing her sore fingers, catching his smile.

Sam pulled up behind them in his van. "What you's do'n?" getting out and walking up to them. "Pitiful," he muttered, looking down at their effort, hardly a berry on any of it. He took a wooden crate from the back of his van to stand on, wedging it against the hedge. "Ow much d' ya want?" he asked, flicking open a knife.
"With long stems Sam," Gina appealed.
In a blink of an eye, several branches were thrown down before them. Long stemmed and covered in red berries.
"Enough?" He stepped down and returned the box to his van. "I'll leave 'em on ya doorstep," he said gathering up the holly in his weathered bare hands.
"Thanks Sam," Gina smiled, very grateful for his help.
"Sam, that Christmas tree's awesome," Matt praised, giving him recognition for the farm's decorations.

Sam got back into his van and drove off towards the yard.
Clouds started to drift across, infilling. Robbing the sky of winter sun, lowering the temperature further. Gina shivered and slid her arm around Matt's waist, ready to walk back. Appreciating how lucky they'd been that Sam happened to come along.

Sam had been on his way to call on Mrs Jackman knowing she'd made him a cake.
Elaine invited Sam into her kitchen. He watched her carefully lowering a Christmas chocolate log into a box. "Here's a few mince pies and sausage rolls," she said, adding two bags on top of the lid ready for him to carry. "And pop this card in your pocket."
He guessed there was money inside and tucked it down in a deep pocket. "Appy Christmas Mrs Jackman, an' thanks," he said, picking up the home cooked Christmas fare.
She held the door open. "You're very welcome Sam and wished him a Merry Christmas."

Sam waved and beeped his horn as he drove passed.
"He looks happy," Matt observed.
"I expect Mum's just given him his Christmas cake and bonus."
"How much did we give him?"
"More than enough," Gina smiled, refusing to divulge the figure.

~ 13 ~

Not wanting any fuss, Matt planned his final exit with cunning precision. He'd been taking home personal items for days. Staying behind wouldn't arouse suspicion, he frequently worked late. He transferred his files to Tom's account before removing passwords and private data from the system. Cleared his desk, loading his paraphernalia into a box and glanced around for anything he'd missed. He paused, briefly reflecting the years he'd worked for Vortorx, his position and what it had represented, anticipating locking his office door for the last time. He placed an expensive gift-wrapped perfume and card on Caroline's desk before heading to the entrance.

Dennis, the security guard bid him Goodnight, expecting him to leave as usual.

Matt approached the reception desk to surrender his keys, Vortorx identification and passes, laying them out in a line. "I'm going now," he announced.

The guard was shocked, although he'd heard the rumour. "Good luck to you Mr Chapman," he said, shaking Matt's hand.

"Goodnight Dennis," Matt replied, putting a folded fifty pound note into the palm of the guard's hand. Matt picked up his box and walked out of the building for the final time.

"Can I help you with that Sir?" Tom appeared at Matt's side, walking the last few steps with him to the carpark.

"I thought you'd left," Matt said, plonking the heavy box down by the side of his car.

"I came back, thought it was odd you working late when we've spent all week getting every account up to date." He knew Matt would pull off something like this. "They all think you're leaving next month."

"I know," Matt smiled. "Granzman hates presentations and so do I. Starting tomorrow, this is my new phone number. If you want to discuss anything, I'm at the end of that line," Matt offered with genuine sincerity, passing over the number. He loaded his box into the boot and turned to shake Tom's hand. "Tom, you'll be magnificent."

"I don't have enough words to thank you." Tom's voice wavered, too choked to continue. . . "We would of made a phenomenal team."

"Goodnight Tom," Matt said getting into his car.

Tom raised his hand to wave, watching Matt drive out of the carpark, unmistakeably for the final time.

- -

Matt woke up feeling cold. He missed the warmth of central heating and the comforts of modern living. No matter how long this temporary arrangement of living in the cottage would last, he was counting the days to its end. Feeling certain if he exhaled, he'd see his warm breath billow like steam into the cold air. Playfully he tried and was surprised when it didn't happen. He could get up and turn on the heater mounted on the far wall, but leaving a warm bed required courage. He looked across at Gina almost buried under the duvet sleeping soundly and smiled to himself. Wasn't this the dream he'd worked so long and hard for? He ran a finger gently down her back to rouse her.

"What's the time?" she asked sleepily, with eyes still closed.

“The time? It’s the beginning of the rest of my life living with you here forever at Ashwood Farm,” he whispered.
Gina turned over still half asleep, unaware of his answer.
“What?” she said beginning to wake up.
“I said it’s bloody freezing in here,” pulling her closer.

-

Between the bad winter weather and Harvey Granzman making the most of his last months at Vortorx, Matt had spent very little time at the farm. He’d become out of touch with any progress the builders had made. Now here at last, his time would be his own. Cogitating no more flights to catch, punishing schedules or deals to achieve and far away from the world of commerce.

A eight o’clock workmen began to arrive. Slamming van doors, whistling and shouting, making their way to the barn for their first cup of tea of the morning. A cement mixer started, rumbling noisily and churning its contents. More tradesmen turned up, armed with tool-bags, . . all gravitating to the barn.
Matt looked out from the small bedroom window, the farmyard resembled a building site.

Gina had slipped into the role of project-manager with a natural flare. In her glory watching plans take shape and become reality. “I’m going over to speak to the plumber,” she announced with a hand full of invoices. He could see she was busy and decided to catch her later. Meanwhile he’d award himself a leisurely coffee before going to find Sam.

“You lookin f ’ me?” Sam called out, coming out of the barn. “I’m keep’n out the way o’ this lot,” pointing to the tradesmen’s vehicles with a nod of his head.

“Me too,” Matt admitted, walking over to accompany him.
“So ya’ ere now, . . f ’ good?”
“Yes Sam, for good,” Matt confirmed, tagging along.
Sam stopped in the small field at the back of the farmhouse. He’d been working on the gate and gone back for more wood.
“Strengthnin this ere gate.” Sam clarified before loading his mouth with nails. Matt winced, imagining the taste of metal.

“That’ll do it,” he said, banging in the last nail. “Got any plans f ’ farm?” turning his attention to Matt. He could tell by his blank expression, he'd not yet given it any serious thought. Sam looked across into the distance. “Use t’ av cows n’ all them fields when I were a nipper, an’ milk parlour, an’ dairy ere then. When cows went, we ploughed fields,” he added.
Matt was beginning to get the picture. In its heyday, when Ashwood Farm had been much bigger, it had been a proper working farm. They both realised the farm would need to provide some sort of income.
“Could buy in calves t’ fatten up f ’ market,” Sam suggested.
As much as he loved a good steak, Matt couldn’t see Gina sending animals off to be slaughtered. They’d end up with a herd of pets.
Sam picked up his tools and they started to walk back.

Reaching the yard, Matt could smell bacon cooking, delicious sizzling hot bacon. “What’s that?”
Sam looked at his watch, “leven o’clock, Misses brings out bacon rolls.”

Every workmen stopped what they were doing, downed tools and proceeded to the barn. Elaine waved to Matt and Sam as she walked by, carrying her loaded tray of freshly made hot bacon rolls.
"Is she feeding every tradesman in Somerset?" Matt remarked testily.
"She got a good ed on er shoulders," Sam defended. "Not one o' them blokes as left this site, . . now er place's almost done."
Matt had never doubted Elaine's sharp brain and abilities.

She came out of the barn with an empty tray. "Hello Mathew, lovely to see you here at last," she greeted. "Now, would you men like a hot bacon roll?" She smiled, and walked back to her cottage with Matt and Sam following close behind.

Matt caught up with Gina at lunchtime. She had some good news to tell him. Steve, the 'technical bod' she'd found was coming at three to make a start on his office. "You'll need to double check your plan and discuss where you want everything to go, so he can begin assembling," she instructed. Shrewdly making sure Matt's office would be one of the first rooms to be finished. It was the only room in the farmhouse he'd been allowed to completely design himself.

The short shopping trip to Tiverton planned for Thursday, had turned into a full-blown excursion to Taunton. Ready to purchase new curtains and bedlinen for her new home, Elaine wanted Gina's company to help her choose, appreciating another opinion.
Gina was toying with the idea of staying overnight, giving them extra time to visit the bigger stores. She was

looking forward to a change of scenery, away from the mess and building work at the farm. "You could come with us," she offered, knowing Matt would adamantly refuse.
"I'll stay here, hold-the-fort and look after the dogs," he volunteered swiftly.

-

Matt's office was fast progressing, thanks to IT engineer Steve's hi-tec skill and wizardry.
"All working?" Matt asked cheerfully, delivering more refreshments."
"I've interfaced your new and existing software, it's all linked and talking to each other." Enlightening Matt on each particular module's installation. "Hmmm, . . the new layout's all functioning, . . but?" Steve wasn't happy with something, finally deciding to come back and install a different program the next day. Explaining it would speed up the whole system.
Matt left him to it. He might be competent using the latest IT equipment, but understanding how it all worked was something else entirely.
Walking back to their cottage, he noticed Elaine talking to Sam. Nothing unusual about that, but this was the third time that day he'd seen them together.

In the evening, Gina stormed into their bedroom spitting flames of temper. "I don't believe it! She's changed her mind!"
Matt was sitting up in bed watching a film on the small television mounted on the wall. "What's up?" he asked trying to listen to her and the film.
"My mother!" she retorted, "says she can't go tomorrow." Gina continued to flounce and strop. "I was really looking

forward to it. I can't understand what's suddenly made her change her mind," she moaned, sliding in beside him.

"You can go next week. It doesn't really matter," he said losing interest in the film, gently stroking her back. "Why don't we go out to dinner tomorrow night, just the two of us?"

Her fury evaporated as quickly as it had ignited, curtain shopping in Taunton no longer forefront in her mind.

In the morning Gina stayed in bed, having no specific reason to rise extra early now she'd be staying at home. Matt got up, volunteering to bring her up a cup of tea.

"I'll get up in a minute," she sighed "I've plenty of things to get on with."

"I'll be in my office familiarising myself with the new software," he said, delivering her tea and planting a kiss on top of her head before leaving.

Walking across to the farmhouse, Matt saw Elaine and Sam deep in conversation outside her cottage. He'd an inkling something was going on and guessed Sam would know about it. He waited for Elaine to go back indoors, before setting off in pursuit. "Anything wrong?" Matt asked, catching Sam up.

"Can't say," Sam mumbled, walking ahead.

"Sam!" Matt called, but he continued on his way. "Sam?" Matt repeated louder. Sam kept walking, but not facing him, Matt wasn't sure what he'd said. It could of been 'summat's comin' or 'someone's comin.' He let him go, whatever it was, no doubt he'd find out later.

On reaching the front door of the farmhouse, Matt heard Steve walking up behind him.

“Susan, I’ll be there, don’t worry,” Steve expressed loudly into his phone. “Sorry about that,” he said, following Matt inside. “My wife’s car wouldn’t start this morning so I took her to work. Now she’s worrying I’ll forget to pick her up.” Steve unpacked his work-case, explaining the job shouldn’t take him long. About an hour by the time he’d tested it.
Deciding to come back later, once again Matt left Steve to get on.

Gina was sitting in their small kitchen with bank statements, invoices and bits of paper covering the table.
“Do you know what you’re doing?” Matt teased.
“I know exactly what I’m doing, thank you.” she bristled. With her reading glasses pushed up onto her head, she was obviously hunting for something she’d lost.
He made her a drink and took his own into the sitting room, giving her and Steve time to get on with their work.
Hearing Steve mention his wife’s name prompted Matt to think of Suzy. He wondered how she was getting on, since becoming alone at Squirrels Chase, . well apart from Flossy. He still felt a pang of responsibility, it bothered him knowing there was nobody nearby to watch over her.

“All done,” Steve announced and ran through the new program with Matt, highlighting it’s extra features. “Any problems, just give me a call. I’ll see myself out,” he said, hurrying off to collect his wife.

Sitting in his new office chair, Matt swivelled round enjoying the moment. He’d missed his own personal space. This office would be his domain, and moving in to it would be a pleasure.

He picked up the first box to start unpacking. Family photos were at the top of the box. He spaced the picture frames along a shelf at eyelevel, standing back to admire the effect. Ellen's smile radiated from her photo. Matt smiled fondly back, wishing with all his heart she could of seen her grandson and the farm. Next out of the box came two bottles of the finest Scottish single malt whisky and his four Waterford crystal glass tumblers. The set used to stand on a silver salver in his lounge, but with the rest of the farmhouse still in an uproar Matt left them on the side.

Hearing a vehicle drive into the farmyard, Matt looked out of the window. Astounded, he could hardly believe his eyes. Granzman's Bentley had arrived in the yard. He watched dumbfounded, as Harvey Granzman got out of the car, his driver Bill holding the door. Granzman straightened up, slowly taking in the expanse of the yard.
"Good morning Sir," Matt called out, starting to walk towards him to shake his hand. "Welcome to Ashwood Farm."
"Morning Mathew," Granzman answered, meeting him halfway. "A nice spot," he paused, again looking around. "What have you got here?"
"Six fields, a wood," Matt pointed across to the barn, out buildings and cottages. "We're living there while the renovation work's being done."
"Are you organising it?" Granzman questioned.
"Hell no, my partner Gina is the project manager. She's doing an amazing job." Matt led the way to his office, thanking his lucky stars the room was finished. Bill followed behind, struggling to carrying a heavy crate of champagne.

“Put it down there,” Granzman indicated, a few feet inside the entrance hall. Bill lowered the box to the floor, grateful to be rid of the weight and returned to his duties back at the car.

In his office, Matt removed the empty cardboard box from his desk and offered Granzman his chair. “As you can see, I’m still unpacking.”

Granzman walked around inspecting the room before taking the seat. Matt poured two drinks and put them down on the desk, wheeled the other chair over to join him and waited for Granzman to speak.

“You’re sorely missed Mathew. Business colleagues and our eminent directors abroad send their best wishes,” handing him several cards in sealed envelopes.

“Thank you Sir,” Matt smiled, appreciating their gesture. He wondered how they knew. Had Harvey Granzman informed them, inviting a reply? It wouldn’t surprise him, although he was somewhat flattered.

Granzman drank his whisky, he’d already surveyed Matt’s advanced software, realising his ability to work. “What do you plan to do here Mathew?”

“I have no plans, that was the point of leaving Vortorx,” Matt answered with honest conviction.

“Support Thomas, . . . give him six months,” Granzman challenged.

“Tom will achieve and I won’t shadow him. I’ve left commerce,” Matt reminded him firmly.

“Your partner doesn’t need your expertise here, you said yourself she’s doing a great job.” Frustration strengthening his words, “think about it Mathew!”

Matt remained ambivalent.

"Thomas will progress and excel, faster with you watching his back." 'You'd make a phenomenal team'? " Granzman said slowly, waiting for Matt's reaction.

Matt looked Harvey Granzman squarely in the eyes, recognising Tom's phrase. He appreciated what Granzman was proposing, building Tom's reputation. Commerce was a cut-throat financial driven business, knowing he'd gone, the sharks would circle.

Matt topped up their drinks and sat digesting Granzman's proposal. If Tom truly wanted him in the background to consult and advise, just while he found his feet, he could agree to that. The opportunity to assist could suit them both, easing himself into life at the farm. It was true, Gina didn't need his help with refurbishing the farmhouse. Granzman didn't do social visits, turning up at the farm revealed its importance.

"I won't come back officially, or leave here," Matt stated, laying out his terms.

"You won't have to," Granzman acknowledged. He stood up ready to leave, satisfied he'd got what he came for. His top team had just become stronger - Tom's abilities and determination to succeed backed by Matt's experience and wisdom. He held out his hand to shake on the deal. Matt obliged. "Thank you Mathew." With business complete, Harvey Granzman relaxed evincing the amity side to his character.

"Come and meet Gina," Matt urged, walking with Granzman to the front door. A large box laden with gift-wrapped presents stood beside the crate which Bill must of carried in.

"Gosh, I didn't expect all this," Matt said surprised and humbled by his colleagues generosity and kindness.

"You're sorely missed," Granzman reiterated.

When Matt opened the door, Gina and Margery Brewer stood together on the step, having come over to find him. "Look who's come to see us!" Gina expounded full of delight.
"Mrs Brewer!" Matt beamed, stepping forward to give one of his impromptu hugs. "Gina and Margery, may I introduce you to . . ." Matt started.
"Harvey Granzman, delighted to meet you ladies," Granzman said, taking over, shaking each of them warmly by the hand.
"Mrs Brewer owned the farm before us," Matt explained.
"Matt, darling, you must come and see what Margery has brought us for the farm." Gina was bursting with excitement, she grabbed his hand to drag him along quicker.
"Sorry about this, I'll be back in a minute," Matt announced with embarrassment as Gina hauled him away.
Margery gave a gentle smile, "shall we?" Inviting Harvey Granzman to walk with her, following along behind in their footsteps.

Gina led Matt to the bottom of the garden where he could see a horsebox being reversed into the field at the back of the house. Sam stood by the open gate, waving and shouting instructions to the driver of a Land Rover. Flurried with excitement and anticipation, Gina couldn't stand still any longer. She took off to join Sam inside the field.
Matt stayed behind the wooden fence, preferring it's safety. He'd no idea what size, or sort of animal would emerge

from the trailer. Sam's furtive conversations with Elaine and gate strengthening now fell into place.

Elaine joined him to watch. He eyed her with a suspicious smile, "I expect you knew all about this. When did Mrs Brewer arrive?"

"About an hour ago, just before your visitor. I'd just made Margery a drink and shown her around my new place when 'it' turned up." She answered carefully, not wanting to spoil the surprise.

"What made her get it?" Matt asked, still wary of what was about to appear.

"You did," Elaine laughed. "It was something you said to her."

Matt couldn't recall anything.

Gina closed the gate, while Sam scattered straw across the slope down from the horsebox, waiting for the animal to be lead out. Slowly-but-surely a grey coloured donkey was coaxed and guided out of the box. Sam had a bucket of water waiting for the beast. The donkey paused, surveying its audience before taking a drink. "Ea'll like these," Sam advised, handing Gina a couple of carrots.

"He's got a good temperament and likes a bit fuss," the chap said unclipping the rope leading-rein from the donkey's halter.

Matt watched Gina feeding carrots to her new pet. He called to her, capturing the on-going event with the camera on his phone. She waved back, her face radiant with happiness.

Sam assisted, packing up the trailer, seeing the Land Rover safely out of the field and back on his way.

Matt remained, leaning on the three bar fence watching the new arrival, relieved their gift didn't have big horns. Gina

re-joined him, sliding her arm around his waist. "Isn't he wonderful?" she said totally smitten. "Where's Margery? We have to thank her."
"She's gone off n' that big car," Sam answered, catching them up.
Matt wasn't convinced.
"I see 'em go, when I elp'd chap w' trailer out o' the yard."
"He's right," Elaine concurred, checking the beep from her phone. "Margery's sent me a message apologising for slipping away. Harvey offered to take her back."

In all the years Matt had known Harvey Granzman, he'd never known him appreciate the company of a woman. Margery must of made quite an impression.
"Is he a friend of yours Mathew?" Elaine asked.
"He used to be Matt's boss," Gina explained. "Did you know he was coming today?"
"No," Matt answered. "He just turned up to deliver some leaving-presents from my colleagues. I'm surprised he found us."
"Ee's been ere b'fore," Sam confirmed "last week."
"I doubt it Sam," sure he was wrong.
"Don't get many o' them through village, ee got stuck b'hind Billy Durrell's tractor," Sam recalled with a chuckle.
Matt accepted the truth. Granzman's Bentley wouldn't of driven through unnoticed, reminding him yet again Granzman was always one step ahead.

"Would you two like to join me for a late lunch? I've prepared rather a large buffet," Elaine offered.
When Margery phoned to say she'd organised the donkey's delivery, Elaine had embarked on a flurry of

baking, expecting to cater for everyone. "I wasn't sure if she was going to bring her sister Jo, but it's turned out nobody has stayed."

First, Elaine insisted on giving them a personal tour of her - now finished converted Dairy. She was elated with her fabulous new home, the builders had done an amazing job transforming the derelict old building.

"When do you plan to move in?" Matt asked.

"As soon as Nolan's deliver my new blinds and curtains," she confirmed with obvious pleasure. Elaine checked her watch, she'd been away long enough and wanted to get back to her cottage to let the dogs out.

Back inside her mother's cottage, Gina lifted the lace tablecloth covering the impressive spread of food on the table. "Gosh, how many were you expecting?" she said, grinning.

"When will our place be finished?" Matt asked. He'd had enough of living cooped up in their tiny cottage, it wasn't cosy, it was cramped.

"I've been told two weeks," Gina replied with optimism. Relieved to hear the end was in sight, Matt loaded his plate and sat down to eat.

"Margery left this for you," Elaine passed an envelope to Gina. "I think it's the donkey's ownership and adoption papers."

Gina began reading through the animal's details.

"So, what are you going to call it?" Matt asked.

"He already has a name, Merlin. " Gina answered, "and he's come from the Harpston Animal Sanctuary in Henley, Surrey."

"It's the rescue sanctuary Jo supports. When Margery heard the donkey needed a good home, they organised his adoption," Elaine relayed.

Matt stopped eating, pausing to wonder if this was just a strange coincidence or something of consequence.
"Merlin was admitted to the sanctuary on" . . . studying the page, looking for a date. "The twenty second of November," Gina finally read out aloud.
Matt's mouth dried. Of all the days in the calendar year, on this significant exact date he'd personally arranged Squirrels Chase to be legally signed over to Suzy. 'Will she stay? It will depend on you' Merlin's words haunted. A surreal intuitive feeling coursed through him. He'd re-assessed his opinions throughout his life, was he now compelled to acknowledge Merlin's existence?
"Mathew, are you alright?" Elaine asked, "you've gone very pale."
Gina looked up from reading "Matt! what's the matter? are you OK?" seeing the colour had drained from his face.
"I'm fine, honestly," bluffing away his moment of epiphany, accepting he'd ignored his gut feeling long enough, . . . coming to terms with the truth.

The end

~

A huge heartfelt thank you to friends and family

for their expertise and generosity of time.

I couldn’t of done it without you all.

~

Printed in Great Britain
by Amazon

20581380R00322